DEADLY INTERSECTIONS

JOSEPH WILSON

One Printers Way
Altona, MB R0G 0B0
Canada

www.friesenpress.com

First Edition — 2022

ISBN
978-103-914303-6 (Hardcover)
978-1-03-914302-9 (Paperback)
978-1-03-914304-3 (eBook)

1. FICTION, MYSTERY & DETECTIVE

Distributed to the trade by The Ingram Book Company

To Les!
Hope it's an eight-ender for you. Enjoy!
Joseph Wilson

Dedicated to Barbara Graham, who made this novel possible, and to Kathi Wilson, who made it all possible.

ACKNOWLEDGMENTS

FIRST, I WOULD LIKE TO THANK MY LONG-DISTANCE FRIEND AND fellow author, David Floody, for his unstinting encouragement and helpful advice. David, you really helped me keep forging on with this surprisingly demanding project.

My first readers, John and Debbie Barnett, provided good initial feedback and, most important, unreserved encouragement.

My daughter, Jessica Wilson-Abra did a thorough edit of my first draft and showed me yet again what a bright and talented woman she is. She clearly has a better command of language than her old man. Humbling! Her suggestions concerning police procedures and organization were most helpful.

Freisen Press was without fail professional, encouraging and superbly organized. Thanks to my publishing specialist, Kate de Oude, who was a wonderful support and guiding presence through the whole publishing process. My Freisen editor was amazing. After thirty-two years of teaching English, and after having done a great deal of non-fiction writing, I was pretty cocky about my composing skills. My editor humbled me with her/his comprehensive, precise, and always accurate corrections, revisions and advice. My hat is off to you. And apologies to all those former students of mine who were taught by someone obviously far from the final voice on matters of writing and composition. I trust you survived intact.

In writing a police procedural I came to appreciate even more the women and men in our police departments who work so hard to protect us and our communities. It's never easy, and of course no profession is ever perfect, but we are so much better off because of the fine, necessary and challenging work that you do for us. Serve and protect indeed.

Finally, to all the family and friends who didn't mock the strange notion of someone becoming a seventy-six-year-old first-time author. I promise to take less time with my next effort.

Table of Contents

"Every two people cause an intersection.
Every person alters the world."
—David Levithan

"Every doorway, every intersection, has a story."
—Katherine Dunn

"Life happens at intersections."
—Jack Dorsey

CHAPTER 1
Friendlies

KIRSTEN LOVED MUSIC, BUT THE CONSTANT THROBBING NOISE MADE her want to throw up, and her tight, skimpy waitress outfit kept binding on her. She'd ask why these places always insisted their female help wear these uncomfortable outfits, but she already knew the answer.

She looked around the dim interior of her new workplace. The bar was at one end of the L-shaped room, and along the adjacent wall was the raised dance floor, where two naked women languidly kept time with the techno music. The dimly lit room was about half full, with almost all males. This was only her third day – night, rather – working here, but she had already noted there seemed to be two distinct types of patrons: the ones who sat quietly, often alone, as if pretending not to be there; then the louder ones, usually in groups, usually sitting close to the dance floor, loudly asserting their presence and their assumed dominance over the girls.

The atmosphere here took some getting used to. The owner, Larry, was proud of the new ventilation system he just had installed, even if it was only done to satisfy the latest health department violation notice. Larry was constantly either angry or amused at the town's attempts to shut down Friendlies, his "entertainment lounge". He was a non-descript-looking middle-aged man who looked more like everyone's favourite uncle than the owner of Harmony's sole adult- entertainment venue.

"The tax money I donate to this hick town, the visitors and business I bring in, you'd think they'd make me president of the Business Association," he'd say. Despite the new ventilation system, the air still smelled faintly of spilled beer, sweat, and even the cigarette smoke absorbed by the walls during the years when smoking was allowed.

Larry was hard to pin down. He managed to get the new adult-entertainment license for his "lounge" after some sort of power play at a township council meeting, seemingly orchestrated by one Alexander McKay, a name with particular significance to Kirsten. Ever since, there had been sporadic attempts by the more conservative elements in Harmony to remove this "abomination." Because, although Larry insisted on the genteel label "lounge," this was 100 percent strip joint. Luckily for him there were also powerful elements in town that helped keep Friendlies a going concern.

Larry actually didn't seem like a bad guy. He treated his staff well and appeared to care about their welfare. The other girls all seemed to like him. It grated on Kirsten that they were all referred to as "girls," even by each other, but she knew she had to fit in. Larry sometimes had what he called "staff meetings" after they shut down for the night, as if this was some sort of ordinary retail business. *Interesting staff meetings*, Kirsten thought, *when most of the attendees are casually naked or near-naked women.*

The guys at table six called her over for a refill. Kirsten briskly went over and said, "More of the same, gents? Hope you're enjoying yourselves. Any of you boys interested in some company with one of the dancers?" This had been drilled into Kirsten: keep urging the clientele to go with one of the dancers to the "L" part of the room, which featured screened-off private areas.

That was another surprise to Kirsten: most of the women here were nice to her, even if she was just one of the waitresses, who got to be clothed, though barely, and who never had to visit the "L." The dancers even joked about that, saying things like, "Be right back. Just going to L." The rules were that none of the Friendlies women were touched, ever. Naked lap dances were fine, but the guy had to just sit there in passive admiration. It was unclear if these rules were always followed, because the screened-off areas were private, and the tips could be tempting. If it were ever proven paid sex was happening back there, Friendlies would be closed down. Discretion was essential.

Cherie, one of the dancers, had suggested Kirsten consider joining them. "Look, I know you get good tips, but nothing like what we get. You get used to being naked, believe me. I don't even think about it. You're really pretty. Lots of guys like slender girls with normal-sized tits. And you're in control, always. Larry is really good about that."

Kirsten had to pretend to be tempted, but declined, saying she was too shy for that. She'd said she would think about it. She and Cherie (real name Lynne) chatted a bit. Lynne was in her late twenties, blonde-haired despite her otherwise dark complexion. She was a small, thin woman with suspiciously large breasts. When she didn't have her professional smile pasted on, her face had a quietly wistful look about it. Lynne was absolutely devoted to her three-year-old son. "Look, I'm not going to do this forever, but there's no other way I could make this kind of money. I'm by myself, and raising kids cost money," she said. Strangely, despite the basic nature of the business, Friendlies was in fact a friendly place to work – other than some of the clientele, that is.

That thought brought Kirsten out of her brief reverie and back to the boys at table six.

"Still taking good care of us, Jade? We need some more tender loving care from you," said the big blonde idiot who seemed to be the lead dog. "We need another round too."

Ignoring the smirks and innuendo, Kirsten made herself smile. Bunch of guys just off the golf course, determined to keep the good times rolling, and she had to pretend to be part of that. And there was the real reason she was here.

"You got it. Same for everyone? Youse want some food with it?'

The weaselly guy with the bad hair transplant said, "Only if you bring it, and keep bringing it. Some nachos with the beer'd be okay too."

Kirsten thought, *why can't they at least be more original and creative, or better yet, respectful* As if that would ever happen in a place like this.

The prematurely greying guy in the loud golf shirt said, "Look, the girls up there are okay, but I bet you could do better. Ever want to give it a try?" His hand caressed the back of her leg.

Kirsten looked over at the raised dance platform. The lights were a bit brighter there, shining on the two naked women gyrating mechanically to the music. Kirsten could tell they were both bored, both tired, and likely both ready to call it a night.

Slipping away from him, Kirsten replied, "Look, sorry, guys, I'm just a waitress here, and you know the rules. No touching. Now let me get those drinks and nachos for you."

She moved over to get their drinks and place the nacho order. She noted a guy sitting in the dim light at the end of the bar, jotting something down in a notebook. He looked vaguely familiar to Kirsten, but she couldn't place him. The last thing she wanted was to meet someone she knew. She gave the guy a brief, mechanical smile ("Always keep smiling at the customers. Remember, Friendlies is a friendly place that guys want to keep coming back to."). She took the drink order back to table six.

As she placed their drinks on the table, grey-hair guy said, "Look, about what you said. We don't come here for 'no touching'. I pay, and I tip. Why not join me over in one of those back rooms?" He looked at her quizzically, as if trying to place her.

Kirsten kept the smile fixed on her face and replied, "One of the other girls will be happy to oblige. I'll send one over if you want. But I'm not allowed to go back there." *And never would in this lifetime*, she thought.

She slipped away, knowing their eyes were following her as she made her way back to the bar. She raised her eyebrows to Dan, who was working behind the bar. "Idiots!" she muttered.

Dan gave her a quick grin. "Our core clientele. They pay the bills. They're goofballs, but harmless goofballs. You're handling them just fine."

Larry slipped up beside her. "Look, if we're going to make this work, you have to make them happy. It's your job. It's what we do. So just relax and go with it. Flirt with them. We'll make sure things don't get out of hand."

Just then there was a loud crash in front of the dance floor. An obviously drunk customer grabbed at Jilly, one of the dancers, and pushed her against the table. As she grabbed the table for balance, a jug of beer tipped off and shattered on the floor, drenching the drunk guy's pants and shoes. Enraged, he lunged at Jilly, who backed away, shouting at him, "Fuck off, you fucking loser. Don't touch me."

A large man with a cast on his left arm stepped in front of the drunk. "Look, you don't want this to happen. How be you just leave, and we'll clean things up here."

The other guy sitting at the table, a tall skinny guy with a scarred face, leapt up and drunkenly shoved the bouncer away. "It's her fault. We were going to pay. Then she spazzes out and starts with the insults. Make her fucking deliver." The bouncer gave him a push back with his good arm.

By this time Larry had come over, and he said to the bouncer, "Let's cool it, Mike. How be you guys sit down and we'll get you a free round."

Scarface said, "No way. We want what we came for, you greasy prick." He shoved Larry out of the way.

With that, Mike drilled Scarface with his good arm and gave a vicious backhand with his cast to the head of the drunk. Both of them fell hard to the floor. Pieces of plaster littered the floor. A second bouncer, Max, came over, and they got the two patrons up and pushed them, staggering, to the door. Mike came back holding his broken cast and gently swearing. "Damn it, but I think I re-broke the damn thing. Got to get this cast fixed, boss. Max has to take me over to Lakeside to the ER."

Larry muttered, "Sure, sure, I guess. But don't be long. We've got no protection now. I should fire you, Mike. We've talked about how to handle guys like these without all the drama. But damn it, that guy shouldn't have laid hands on me. Max, take him but get back here quick."

Over at the bar Kirsten groaned quietly. "Guess we're on our own now, Dan, and I have the happy gang over there. I may need a rescue."

Dan replied, "I just sling beer, I'm no fighter. And you can take care of those guys."

Kirsten picked up the tray of nachos and made her way back to the three golfers. As she was setting the tray down, big blonde guy said, "Welcome back, Jade. We were getting lonely, despite the entertainment over there. Too bad your large friends had to leave." With that, he slipped his hand under her short skirt and squeezed her butt cheek.

Kirsten pushed his hand away and gave a tight grin. "Like I said, all I can do is serve you beer and food. Not going to serve you anything else, so you need to keep your hands off."

Grey hair said, "Unfriendly talk, for a place that calls itself 'Friendlies.' And say, I think I recognize you, and the name isn't Jade. It's something weird, like Swedish or something. My daughter went to school with you. What the hell – you were the school all-star, Ms. Brainy but Beautiful. What are you doing working in this dive?"

Big blonde guy stood up. "Well, so it's old times, and we're all just friends here. Let's go over where we can get really friendly." He started to push Kirsten toward the L. She braced herself, grabbed his arm and, using his momentum, threw him over a table and crashing into the wall. She whirled around as grey-haired guy moved toward her, arms raised threateningly. She kicked him squarely in the balls and pushed him over the table, making beer and nachos cascade over hair-transplant guy.

Hair-transplant guy started to scream at her. "Stay away! Shit! You can't do that. That's assault. I'm a township councillor. I'm calling the cops."

A middle-aged woman who had been sitting alone over at a dimly lit corner table had come over by this time. She put her finger in hair-transplant guy's face. "Shut up, shorty. First, it appears she can do that, and actually pretty damn well. Second, it's self defense, not assault. Third, it's your friends who should be charged with assault. And fourth, the cops are already here. Me. You can leave right now, quietly, or, if you really want to, we can pursue the matter at police headquarters. But if we do that, it'll only get worse, a lot worse, for you. Got it?"

Blonde guy and grey-haired guy both struggled to their feet, the latter bent over holding his crotch and quietly moaning. They grabbed their stuff and, muttering, turned with hair-transplant guy to leave. Blonde guy turned back and said, "Okay, Jade, you win round one. You won't always have a crowd around." Kirsten feinted a punch to his face, making him flinch backwards.

She said, "There's no more rounds, loser. You're just going to crawl off with your idiot friends and bitch about your bad luck. You're done. And, you've just threatened a police officer."

Grey-haired guy smirked at her. "I remember your name now. Kirsten. You were the school ice queen. Miss Perfect. You were going to be Harmony's big success, but then you disappeared after high school. And look at you now. Punch-ups in a cheap strip joint dressed like a whore. You, a cop? People are really going to want to hear about this."

Putting up his hands defensively, he backed away. "See you at the next school reunion." The three of them pushed their way out the door, cursing and sending dirty looks back at the people staring at them. The room quieted down and soon was back in operation.

Kirsten turned to her fellow officer. "Sorry, Jane. I lost it. I fucked up."

Jane grinned ruefully at her. "Well, if you're going to blow your cover, do it in style. Must admit it's been an interesting evening. Let's get you out of those damn clothes and I'll buy you a drink, but not here. And I want to hear all about this school all-star business."

Kirsten walked over to where Larry was standing by the bar and said, "Guess our little operation here is over, not that it ever had any real chance of success. Sorry about the mess, but I guess you're pretty used to this kind of stuff. Thanks for your cooperation. Say bye to the other women for me and tell them thanks."

And to Dan she said, "Guess I didn't need that rescue after all. You two take care now." With that, she followed Jane out the door.

The quiet guy sitting at the end of the bar scribbled a few things in his notebook and, looking thoughtful, soon followed them out.

CHAPTER 2
Arthur

ARTHUR WALKED CAUTIOUSLY UP TO THE DARKENED HOUSE, EVEN though he was sure no-one was at home. His boat was beached beside the pier, with its small motor carefully, but temporarily, disabled. Always had to have a back-up plan, an excuse for being there, even if there was no way he would ever need it. He was too careful to make a mistake but being careful meant being ready for anything.

The house was one of the larger ones, and he had carefully watched it for many days now, being even more observant than usual during his routine surveillances. And who would ever notice him? A nondescript local, floating around the weed-beds in his small, square-prowed punt, and rarely facing the shore. Usually facing out to the lake, seemingly intent on his fishing. The occasional quick glance toward the shore – his shore, if only people realized it – let him check what was going on there. He was sure he was safe tonight, but after what he had witnessed a few nights back, a little further down the lake, he knew there was no such thing as being too careful.

Arthur had been out on a moonlit night drifting around the lake not too far from the shoreline beside the new houses. It was a quiet night, with a few sounds coming from the second house from the entrance to the subdivision. There were some cars parked beside the house, and some sort of gathering seemed to be happening. He could hear the odd muted male laughter and loud shouts. This made Arthur stay closer to the other end of the row of houses. Then he heard some quiet grunts coming from beside one of the houses. In the dim moonlight he saw a man dragging something heavy toward the shore. The man stopped beside a rowboat beached on the shoreline and heaved his load into the boat. In the dim moonlight Arthur could make out that it was a body that had been dumped into the rowboat. The man seemed to smear something onto the rowboat's gunnel.

Arthur quietly poled his boat into some reeds near the shore. He watched as the man pushed the boat out on the water, jumped in and rowed a few hundred yards away from the shore. He struggled to lift the body over the gunnel and then eased it into the lake. It looked like the guy in the water started to struggle, but the other man reached over and held his head under water. Soon the struggle was over.

Arthur was frozen with horror and shock. It seemed sure he was witnessing a murder, but he had no idea what to do. The core principle of his life was to keep strictly to himself, to avoid contact with others whenever possible – except for children; children were safe. But this man moving so efficiently and confidently scared Arthur to his core. This man was danger itself. It was unthinkable for Arthur to directly intervene, and he had no way to communicate with any authorities even if he wanted to. All he could do was watch, silently, immobilized by a fear he had never before felt, and not reveal his presence.

The man rowed back to shore, got out of the boat, turned it around, and gave it a strong push so that it drifted to within a hundred yards or so of the body floating in the water. The man then hurried back to the nearest house, got into a car parked beside it, and quietly, without headlights, drove toward the exit of the subdivision.

Arthur gradually quietened his breathing and tried to decide what to do. He thought of going over to the body to see if he could help, but the man had been floating head down for several minutes now. Hearing loud voices coming from the direction of the party house, Arthur turned to see four or five men making their way along the shore toward him. He hunkered down in his boat and pushed further into the reeds. The men were walking unsteadily, and he could hear their grunts and laughter. They started to head toward the house, but then one of them pointed out toward the rowboat floating not far offshore. The men argued loudly about what they should do.

Arthur knew he had to get out of there. People were now here and would sort things out. What would they make of him being out there by himself, claiming to be a witness, but with no good explanation of why he was even there? Could they protect him from the dangerous man who had committed this crime? He quietly poled his boat through the reeds, staying close to the shore, until finally he reached his house on the shore across from the houses. He sat quietly for a while, in the shadows, watching the activity across the lake: the vehicles with flashing lights, the spotlights put up on the shore, people rushing around shouting instructions. He watched until it finally all quieted down and then he crawled into his bed, hugging himself until he fell asleep.

And now, a few days later, Arthur had decided he could return to his routine surveillance, his need to monitor this area despite the possible dangers it held for him. After all, this was still his land. He continued toward the darkened house.

Arthur had grown up on the shore of this isolated, medium-sized inland lake, fittingly named Silent Lake. Growing up, he was able to explore the lake and the surrounding swamp and woods whenever he wanted. His parents didn't seem to keep track of what he was doing. He preferred it this way. He could avoid the human contact that felt so threatening to him. He could melt into the remote landscape that always felt welcoming to him. He grew up there, felt at peace there, and could be fully alive there.

The rest of his life was only a place he had to inhabit, a place where he could pass as whatever people seemed to want. Son. Student. Acquaintance, because he had no real friends. Later, maintenance worker in the township public utilities work yards. His parents had eventually slipped away to the quiet deaths that seemed somehow appropriate to the quiet, withdrawn lives they had lived. They were backwoods people, with few friends and with small families they could easily keep at a distance. Their main lesson to him – don't trust anyone. Keep to yourself, look after yourself. Our family house on this small, remote lake is all we need.

They thought he was a good son, mostly because he caused them no bother. He was quiet, obedient, and never challenged any restrictions they put on him. They took this as being a form of love, that he fully shared their shut-off world with them and was happy living as they did. They never really knew how he felt about this, and he was fine with that. He co-existed with them, just as they co-existed with the broader world. The place where he really lived was out in his own private, semi-wilderness world, where he could be with himself, the only person he trusted.

Except for school, he rarely left home, and after his parents passed away within weeks of each other, the whole place was his. They had him late in life, and probably by accident; he had no siblings. He was still young, barely into his thirties, and there was no one he had to please. He was a good worker for the township. He knew how to do road maintenance year-round and was handy at fixing equipment. His work duties meant he had little contact with others, and he could easily avoid entanglements with them. He gently rebuffed social invitations, and seemed to everyone like a quietly genial guy, though a painfully shy and withdrawn one. A good guy, always reliable, good at his work, always ready to fill in for others, part of the background.

He let them think he spent time with his extended family and friends who lived near him, an easy fiction since he lived sixty kilometers away from the township offices in Lakeside. His co-workers would sometimes make fun of him when he wasn't around, but he never bothered anyone. He seemed harmless, just a quietly eccentric recluse. Good old reliable and forgettable Arthur.

He knew most men found a woman with whom to share their lives, but he really didn't want to share his. High school had been difficult, with its pressure to fit in, to date, to socialize. It was often agonizing. Luckily his parents didn't interfere in his social life, other than the odd wistful enquiry from his mother about whether or not he was seeing anyone. There had been a few women who tried to become acquainted with him, even a few he thought he liked. But he remained unattached. Some people wondered if he was in the closet, but most realized he was just a shy, awkward loner, content with what to others would be an unbearably lonely life. He always found unthreatening ways to blend into the world and cause it to leave him alone.

Arthur had escaped from high school as early as he could. His one real involvement with his father was learning how to do repairs, how to run equipment and build things. His father was handy and resourceful. He mocked people who went to university and got high-paying jobs, because they had no idea of how to fix anything, to build anything or do anything that was really useful. "If Armageddon comes, people like me will be okay, because we can actually do things to survive. They'll die off in no time at all, and their money and arrogance will be of no use."

Arthur agreed with his dad. He could take care of himself. His father's real legacy to him was a sense of independence, a pride in being almost totally self-sufficient. His summer job with the township had easily transitioned to a full-time position, despite his limited formal education. He was sent on the odd short training course and stayed on top of whatever he had to know to do a good job, something he was quietly proud of. He served a real use in the world, and deserved his quiet, limited place in it.

After getting through two funerals and the well-meaning intrusions of neighbours and acquaintances, Arthur seemed set for life. He owned the house and the twenty acres it sat on. He made enough money to meet his basic needs. Most important, he was able to spend as many hours as he wanted in his private world, the lake and surrounding marsh and woods. He could fish in the lake and motor around it in the punt that he had made, powered by the small trolling motor he had bought. He could pole it through the marshes and enjoy the quiet solitude there. He could wander around his woods, checking things out and keeping track of whatever was happening. He was an amateur bird watcher and keen observer of animal life.

His father had taught him how to hunt, and he did so but it was only things he could eat: rabbits, wild turkeys, the odd deer, and, once, a wild boar. He enjoyed being able to provide much of his own food, including the small garden he kept up, a legacy from his mother.

Occasionally he encountered other people, but it was a remote and fairly wild area. No groomed trails or sandy beaches. Lots of insects, no amenities, nothing to make most people want to come again. He was mostly all by himself.

Until he wasn't, and never would be again. Developers from town had found this remote lake and talked the township into making a road into it, thankfully on the other side. Arthur hadn't believed it when he was assigned to help build the access road. He thought of refusing, but that would be making waves, and he knew he had to witness what was going to happen. The new road was bulldozed through the woods, right through many of Arthur's special places. Small causeways and bridges were built over some of the marshy ground, and some of the swampy areas were drained. Places that had been the world Arthur grew up in were obliterated, so that he started to carry in his mind images of a fallen personal world that only he would ever remember. He often felt gutted, displaced, and discarded. For the weeks and months involved in the job he was a scarred shell. No one seemed to notice this, given his usual remoteness.

He took a few rare sick days when he couldn't face seeing more desecration, but always had to come back to witness the full extent of this attack on his world. No-one would ever believe this land was really his, in a way that it could never belong to anyone else. He suffered wounds no-one could ever understand, much less appreciate. He wondered how he could carry on but was too numb to make any real plans.

Once the road was in, the houses went up. Large lots, fronting on a picturesque small lake, privacy afforded by lot-bordering trees. Exclusive executive homes for the wealthy who would never have visited the area before its transformation. People who would live here, but never feel the bones and roots of the land. The fronts of the houses faced the lake, so that the driveways led up to the backyards and the sides of the houses. The main lawns were on the lake side, where the families spent their leisure time at home. Thankfully the lake was not overly large, so one of the few demands made by the township was to bar power boats. After a few initial canoe forays on the lake by some of the new owners, it soon became mostly deserted, a pretty backdrop for the transplanted urbanites now living there.

The new owners were aware of the ramshackle place across the lake, and soon found out as much as the locals could share about the owner. They regarded Arthur's place mostly as local colour, proof they actually were living in the country. They soon became accustomed to the harmless recluse who would often drift around fishing for whatever the lake yielded. He was just part of the background, and they were never really interested in connecting with whatever was out there in their bedroom community. They worked in town, their friends and families were in town, and this was an exclusive and private place for them to spend the quiet down time in their still town-centred lives.

It took Arthur a long time to decide how he would carry on. Moving elsewhere was not an option. Much of his previous world was still here, and the detailed memory map of the rest would forever live in his mind. He watched the happenings across the lake with a strange combination of detached numbness and quiet anger. He was dimly aware that only he could be the custodian of his remembered special world and of the parts that remained. He would never be able to explain it to anyone else, or even in any clear, precise, objective way to himself. He just knew it was true, and necessary. He had to adapt to this intrusive new reality if he were to carry on.

So, he bought a powerful telescope for his house and placed it in an upstairs window. He had his boat for more close-up surveillance. He could still privately visit what was left of the marshes, and the more remote parts of the forest. But increasingly his interest was in the identity and lives of the people living across the lake.

This interest would develop in ways he never would have predicted. But for now, back to his latest nighttime surveillance.

CHAPTER 3
The Silent Lake Flasher

KIRSTEN AND JANE WERE SITTING IN THE LOUNGE SECTION OF Harmony's only decent restaurant. Kirsten leaned back in her chair, stretching and giving her body a shake, as if to shake off the memory of her brief and unpleasant time at Friendlies. She had stopped at her small apartment to shower and put on some casual clothing. Her light-brown hair was back in a simple ponytail, and she wore no make-up. She was a tall woman, slender and fit. The most attractive feature of her face was her hazel eyes, which constantly looked around the room. She usually had a guarded, even sombre expression on her face, but tonight it was mostly one of relief.

She took a sip of her white wine and looked over at her companion. Kirsten wasn't a fan of beer, and never really had been, despite growing up in Harmony. After her brief stint as a waitress at Friendlies she was all the more sure she never would be – another small way she wasn't really of this place, even though she had grown up here.

Jane Walden was a stocky, strong-looking woman in her early forties. She sat upright in her chair, quiet, but with her fidgeting hands betraying an inner energy. Her auburn hair was cut short, framing a pleasant-looking face with laugh lines around her mouth and her brown eyes. She could have been taken for an office worker or teacher, except for the alert way her eyes, like Kirsten's, regularly glanced around the room.

Jane said, "So glad we're done with that. I was fine being your back-up but hope I never have to spend any more time in that bloody place. We have to talk about what's next. Now that Jasper's latest brainchild has failed, just like we thought it would, though maybe not this spectacularly, we have to steer him toward something that might actually work. Also, I *will* file an incident report about tonight's little fracas in case those idiots try to follow up. My experience, though, most guys try to forget it when a woman gets the better of them. I don't think we have anything to worry about."

Jasper McKnight was the captain of the small provincial police detachment in Harmony. Ever since township council had voted a few years earlier to have the province take over from their local police service, Jasper had been the area's top cop. He was a local, had developed a web of personal connections in Harmony and was the man firmly in charge. Jane, who had served in this detachment from its inception, had quickly come to understand that Jasper McKnight was a woefully inadequate police officer.

However, life was mostly quiet in the little backwater of Harmony, and so Jasper's shortcomings rarely caused many problems. Jane learned how to do damage control when they did. She had come to a rueful understanding of the truth behind the old clichéd question, "Do you want the man in charge or the woman who knows what's going on?" Jasper's superiors showed no interest in taking on the messy task of replacing a man they had promoted to the position of detachment captain. They couldn't allow their judgement to be called into question. Besides, Harmony's community leaders, all cronies of Jasper's by now, seemed quite content with their police captain, and Jane, good old Jane, would help keep things on an even keel.

Good old Jane looked over at her new colleague, now looking much more comfortable out of her ridiculous waitress outfit. "Look, Kirsten, I know you weren't sure about coming back here to your hometown, but Jasper felt we needed someone who could fit in with the locals. When he came up with this Friendlies undercover plan, we pointed out there was the chance someone would recognize you. I mean, Undercover Assignment Rule One is it had to be a total stranger, but he thought that after ten years away no-one would place you. Seems, as usual, he was wrong."

"I'm still puzzled why he thought this whole thing would get us any useful information. Is this sort of thing standard police procedure here?"

"Not really. It's just that Jasper's main approach has always been to work connections, ferret out information, and find out what he invariably calls 'the lay of the land.' By the way, speaking of being a local, do you know you slipped back into the Harmony dialect? Like in, 'Youse want some food with it?'"

Kirsten laughed. "Yeah, guess I was trying too hard to fit in. Spent long enough growing up around here that the old dialect is still lurking inside somewhere."

"I'm curious about what it was like for you growing up around here, but business first. Maybe it was a long shot thinking our suspects would come to their favourite bar, get drunk, and let something slip, but we are literally clutching at straws here."

Kirsten almost grabbed some straws from the glassful at the table to say, "You mean literally like this?" but that was the sort of smart-ass comment that often made people wary of her. Besides, she liked Jane, who in the short time they'd been together had been good to be around and had been good to her.

Jane continued, "So much for Jasper's big hope that you could overhear something from them, or maybe weasel something out of them. Maybe see if they said something to one of the girls. I know that guys like to brag when they're trying to impress women, especially in a dive like Friendlies, but that was still a real longshot. I shudder to think about how our wonderful male boss and his bosses thought you might accomplish all this. I think there was a little too much enjoyment of your undercover outfit – ironic term, given how little cover there actually was. They knew they couldn't use an old broad like me in that place. Boy, I'd like to see the exact wording of Jasper's request for an undercover officer."

Kirsten giggled and said, "I've got this rude image in my mind of one of those idiots sitting with a big-time hard-on, trying to impress a naked woman on his lap with his big-time business schemes. Imagine the re-enactment in court of how she got this vital information that, of course, she immediately reported to me. McKnight's plans always this good?"

After they had finished laughing, Kirsten continued. "So, we – or rather you – make our report to the captain, make him and the senior brass unhappy, and then what? I suppose we did please Larry tonight, because he never wanted us at that dive of his. I think he especially didn't like the leverage McKnight put on him. But will you still need me around here anymore, now that my undercover days are over?"

Kirsten said this with a little regret, because it was sort of fun being back here – "here," not "home" – because growing up it had never really felt that way to her. However, she had needed a change from her posting down south, a chance to create some personal profile, and maybe garner an overdue promotion. All too many people thought she had sold herself short in becoming a cop, but she enjoyed it, and was looking forward to more responsibility. And there were some minor personal entanglements down south she was glad to escape, though she might now have to return to them.

"Well, your posting here was an actual transfer, so I think you may be stuck until the next round of transfers opens up. Besides, it's not so bad, despite our dickhead bosses. Try to find a place without that problem! And I like having a gal pal here. I like you."

Kirsten smiled back. Jane was the sort of person she had avoided at high school, someone who seemed perfectly comfortable being a local. But Kirsten was trying to weed out the tinge of snobbery that she feared had always been part of her makeup. It wasn't totally the fault of everyone else that she often didn't seem to fit in. Maybe she could do some long overdue personal reflection back here in this quiet backwater, make some necessary changes. Maybe after ten years away she could get some perspective on her painful adolescence. She smiled and compulsively reached over to give Jane's wrist a quick squeeze.

Jane continued, "Jasper and our bosses are the big thinkers who will decide on any next steps. McKay is clearly up to something, and we need to find out what it is. But on to the important stuff. What's this high school queen/all-star/Ms. Perfect stuff?"

Kirsten gave a small smile. She liked Jane, the wine was doing its work, and she was just coming down from the adrenaline high of her Friendlies dust-up. Maybe she should share a bit of her personal history of this place, so difficult at the time, a bit of a cliché now.

"Some people may call this vacation country now, but when I was growing up it felt to me more like Ontario's Ozarks. As you know, the high school draws people from the whole surrounding area, so it always seemed to me like a strange mixture of local cliques and country kids. I was smart, and didn't try to hide it, though I also tried to keep a low profile. The teachers mostly loved me. I was a good athlete, and liked physical competition, though I refused to become – God help me – a cheerleader. I worked backstage on the annual school show. I worked on the school newspaper.

"God, I was actually nominated to be the school queen in my graduating year. I guess I didn't mind being thought attractive, but I declined. Well, actually my nomination got cancelled, but that's a story for another day. Bottom line, in some ways I was a real high school success story, but I never really fit in. I was always pissing someone off. I never found a comfortable high school niche. Or maybe it was just me who was strange. I guess I just couldn't find a way to make it all work."

Kirsten paused, thinking back on the turmoil she had felt then, the feeling that she was doing nothing wrong, but was being punished anyway. As an adult she understood how adolescents could secretly enjoy wallowing in their emotions, but she also knew how real the pain had been.

Jane drank some of her beer and said, "Well, in my school time here, just after the last ice age, I was mostly just one of the crowd. So, tell me more about life in the star chamber."

Kirsten smiled at the term, but somehow Jane made it a real question, not a veiled insult. "I know I didn't make it easy for people. I didn't mean to, I just did. I had friends, but few close ones. I dated, but the guys always seemed unsure how to approach me. There were rarely follow-up dates. School just became four years I had to get through, and I did. As graduation approached the teachers had glowing predictions for me. I was going to be the big success they could later all reminisce about.

"My parents supported me, loved me, but I was some of alien to them. A late-in-life only child who I suspect seemed more like a foundling than their real kid. They were immigrants from Sweden. Dad was an electrician and Mom got part-time work in the local township office. They are good people, but they don't read much. They think it's a waste of time to pay attention to politics, the arts, and the big bad outside world. And so what to make of me? They moved down south to be closer when I left home for university and they had both retired. We get along fine, and they have always supported me, but I constantly managed to disappoint them too."

Jane nodded her head and smiled ruefully. "Let me guess. You were going to be doctor or lawyer, and instead you ended up just being a cop. For my parents, that made me a surprise big success. Bet it wasn't that way for you."

"In a word, no. They didn't understand why someone who graduated from university with high marks didn't find a way to cash in. They knew I could have continued on and become some sort of big-salary professional, but instead I learned how to control drunks in a bar. I remember in my first patrol year when they visited me in hospital after some druggie broke my arm. Surely I would come to my senses now! Worse yet, no wonderful husband and beautiful grandkids. The quiet disappointment just continued.

"We get along. It's okay, but still a little bit sad. And yes, I do like guys. Just that I guess I'm still too demanding for them. I know they're not all like those dickwads at Friendlies, or our oh-so-sensitive-and-respectful bosses, but it's just never really worked.

"I got inklings that my old friends and enemies from up here were surprised, and maybe disappointed, or maybe secretly happy at my great fall from grace. You heard Mr. Grey-haired Jerk back there at Friendlies. I can't even remember that guy, but he sure remembered me, and in no positive way. I'm talking too much. Tell me more about you."

"Grew up around here. When they decided it was okay for a woman to be a cop, for reasons I still don't really understand I endured the gauntlet of cop school, and here I am. Always worked somewhere in the region. Got posted here when the detachment was formed. So, career local cop. Finally made detective when the good powers that be decided even this area needed detectives. I get along with the guys at work okay, because I give them no choice. Married. Divorced. No kids."

She paused uncertainly, and Kirsten looked a little closer. "So, I spilled all. Give, girl."

"I found out I get along better with women, and I've found a good one. We don't make a big deal of it. People know, but believe it or not people around here are good at quiet acceptance if you cause no trouble, and we don't. Simple story."

Kirsten ruefully grinned. "I think that those idiots who think sexual orientation is a matter of choice have no inkling that if it were, most women would be joyous lesbians."

They both laughed and took another drink. Kirsten said, "So, Cagney, or are you Lacey, are we going to make our bosses keep us together to break this thing, whatever it is, wide open?"

"Yep. Sounds good. Really good. But back to the important stuff. Tell me why growing up here was so weird, other than high school, which is always weird. Some examples."

Kirsten thought. "There's lots, but here's a really good one. I had a pretty good friend when I was in grade ten. One day her dad and uncle took us out to the woods for berry picking. There was this pretty lake, but it was hard to get to, surrounded by swampland and deep woods. So, we hiked into the woods until we got close to the lake and found some wild raspberries. Her dad told us to stay close, but I could see a really good thicket farther on and we slipped away. My plan was it would be a big surprise for them when we quickly filled our buckets. We're busy picking away, when she gasps and grabs my arm. I turn around, and not too far away there's this naked guy just standing there, watching us, with a raging hard-on.

"We're frozen. He just stands there with a strange little startled grin on his face. After what feels like ten minutes, really maybe three seconds, Mary starts screaming, we both do, and we run back to her dad and uncle. They calm us down and we finally manage to tell them what happened. They go thundering back to catch this creep. He's trapped between the lake and us, nothing but swampland and deep woods all around. Scared to be alone, we go running after them. But there's no sign of the guy. The lake is empty, with only some old house way over on the other side. Everyone goes quiet, but there's no sound. No thrashing through the woods. No splashing from the lake. Empty silence, like someone had beamed him up. Like he was some sort of phantom.

"It takes a while, but we finally contact the local cops. They patrol all the neighbouring roads and check out the woods as best they can. The head cop, you know, Adam Westfield, asks us for details. He's calm, and really nice, and we tell him as best we can what happened. Mary keeps saying how big the guy was, and how scared she was. I was scared too, but when the cop asks me what his face looked like, little Miss Smart Ass tells the truth: 'It wasn't really his face I was looking at.'

"He laughs, but Mary's father gets really angry. 'That the best you can do? I've been told about you. And you make Mary follow you away even though I said stay close? You risk my daughter's life with some sex maniac? And now you're actually enjoying this?'"

"And so what happened? They surely caught the guy."

"Nope. The cop talked to the only family who lived in the area, but they clearly had no idea what was going on. They were a bit strange. Almost hermits. Their kid was a bit older than me and went to our school. Always dressed in shabby clothes and kept to himself. A loner, inarticulate and painfully shy, barely passed every year, but harmless. He was not all that big, so he couldn't be Mary's sex monster. And there's no way he could have gotten away from us and across the lake to his place without being seen. The police searched the area for a few days, and even brought in dogs, which seemed to pick up only animal traces, nothing that led anywhere. They eventually gave up.

"I think people started to doubt our story – two adolescent girls who invent this weird, backwoods sex monster, a phantom who disappears into thin air? No one else sees or finds even a trace of him, though I sure as hell *did* see him. So, I become even more suspect, and her parents decide Mary can no longer be my friend. That's a sample of my life growing up around here."

Jane shook her head and chuckled. She finished her beer and asked for the tab. "Time to go. And if your backwoods phantom sex is still around, he's lost a lot of his home. I assume it was Silent

Lake, and it's all built up with huge homes now, at least on the good side where they built the new road a while back."

Kirsten yawned and nodded. "Well, I have to admit I sort of enjoyed today. Nothing like sorting out a few assholes to perk a girl up. Back to the routine tomorrow."

But they would soon find out nothing would be routine again for quite some time.

CHAPTER 4
An Unexpected Meeting

ARTHUR SHIVERED A BIT AS HE LOOKED AROUND THE DARKENED back yard. The darkness and his trust in his careful preparations redoubled his feeling of safety. Several times he had aborted a nighttime visit because he sensed risk. Usually there was none, but the events he had witnessed a few nights before underlined it was never totally safe and could become quite dangerous. He knew how careful he had to be. No one would ever understand why he had to oversee and protect his territory. He knew that distant surveillance was not enough, so he had to be there in person, look around, monitor what was there, relive and keep alive memories of what he used to experience there.

His visits brought back childhood memories in stark, vivid detail. This present spot, the large jungle-gym house (he now had identifying names for all twelve houses), was near the site of his most vivid memory. When he passed into his teen years, he had trouble identifying with his new adolescent body. His parents never talked to him about personal stuff like that. He had no source of relevant information and could make only partial sense of things he overheard at school. He knew there was dangerous power in his new body because his mother offered oblique warnings.

"Now don't touch yourself down there."

"You have to try not to mess your sheets."

"Talk to your dad." But he never did, and his father avoided any such conversation.

He soon discovered a new pleasure in his private excursions into the woods across the lake. He would remove his clothes and carefully prowl around, free and natural, just like all the wildlife around him. He knew he would never meet anyone there, but he both feared such a possibility and trembled in strange anticipation of what that would be like.

Then there was the day it actually happened. He walked around a bushy spruce tree and stepped into a small clearing that was one of his favourite spots. There were two teenage girls busily harvesting berries. At first, they didn't notice him, and he stood rooted to the spot, trembling with apprehension, yet full of a strange anticipation. His cock stood harder than it ever had before.

Finally, one of them turned and saw him standing there some fifty feet away. She gasped and grabbed the other's sleeve. They both stood there, frozen and clearly afraid. He couldn't move, didn't want to move. He had no desire to harm them in any way, to talk to them or move any closer. He just wanted to stand there before them. Soon one of them screamed, breaking the frozen tableau. The girls dropped their berry pails and ran back on a faint trail leading into the woods, one of them yelling, "Dad! Uncle Fred! There's a naked guy. Help!"

The spell broke, and he bolted back to where his clothes were. He scrambled down to his boat, which was moored in the reeds. He felt panic and fear, yet a calm part of his mind took over. He knew he would be seen if he headed straight back across the lake, so he poled his boat deeper into the swampy area surrounding the lake's west end. He poled the boat because that was silent, with no oars getting caught in the reeds and making splashes.

When he heard the people crashing down to the shore, he stopped and hid in the swampy undergrowth. He could make out glimpses, barely, of at least two men looking around the lake shore and across the open water.

Carefully and slowly, he poled deeper into the swamp, around the rim of the lake and up to the edge of his family's property. He took an inner channel that led around to the back end of a short dock his father had made. He left the boat and crept back to where the winter's wood supply was waiting to be split and stacked. He set to work, moving as fast as he could to make the stack as large as possible.

Some time later his father called out to him. When Arthur answered, his father came back behind the house, where Arthur was working.

"Arthur, come with me. There's a cop showed up with questions."

Arthur's mother was standing in the yard, hugging herself and looking down at the ground. The cop was an older guy, leaning casually against his cruiser. "Arthur, I need to ask you a few things. There was an incident across the lake this afternoon. Did you see anyone over there earlier, running away or acting suspiciously?"

Arthur muttered, "No. Been working around back. Didn't see anyone."

"Been working there all afternoon, have you?"

"Yeah. Got to get the wood ready for the winter."

His father interjected, "It's one of his main chores. He got a good part of it done today. Like I told you, we keep to ourselves here. Didn't see nothing across the lake or anywhere else."

The cop paused and considered. "Well, two young girls report a big dangerous guy threatening them. The two men who were with them are pretty worked up, and who can blame them? But the girls said he was a large guy in his twenties or thirties. Clearly not either of you. Too bad you didn't see anything, because we need to catch this guy."

Turning to Arthur, he said, "Look, son, be careful around here. It may not be safe. You make sure you keep a good watch. I don't want to hear of anything else happening out here." Nodding to the family, he slid into his cruiser and slowly backed out of the rutted driveway.

Arthur and his parents stood quietly, and then his father turned to him. "Arthur, you're going to stay around the house for a few days. We don't want any kind of trouble. That cop told me a bit more about what happened over there, and it wasn't good. You mind what that cop said, and what I'm telling you now."

Arthur's mother looked nervously down at her feet, and then over to him. "I'll start supper. It'll be okay if we just stick to ourselves."

Arthur went back to his wood stacking, working more slowly now. He didn't know what his parents were really thinking, because he rarely did. They didn't want trouble, especially with outsiders, and he was good at making sure he didn't cause any. But he would have to be far more careful. The memory of him standing naked before those two girls was burned into his mind, vivid and alive. But no more naked excursions. No more unnecessary risks. He couldn't risk anything breaking into his real life.

He had learned some valuable things.

The outside world could be dangerous and threatening to him.

But if he stayed cool and in control, he would be okay.

But he had to be very, very careful.

He had to have back-up plans and escape routes.

He had to make sure he fit in okay with the outer world and gave no one in it any reason to probe into his personal world.

His memory of the two girls made it clear how powerful girls were to him, but he knew he would have no closer connection with any of them. He liked girls, he was intrigued by them and felt no threat from them, not like he did from many of the boys at school. But he knew his real life could only survive by itself, alone but never lonely. He was learning how powerful and sustaining his memories could be.

———

Now he was back at the scene of this powerful memory, a place only he could access. He sometimes wondered what happened to the two girls. They had clearly been frightened, and he regretted that. Once he saw them, all he had wanted was for them to see him, but how could they know that? But he was sure they would be okay. They had protections and lived in a world that took care of them. They didn't have to work like he did to protect his life.

He looked around the darkened yard again and picked up a child's pail that was sitting beside the sand box. He needed small souvenirs for each of his children, things they wouldn't miss, unimportant things that helped him feel connected to them. He needed to feel connected to them if he was going to be able to keep protecting them.

As Arthur slowly adapted to the growing community across the lake, he came to realize his prime concern was the safety of the children. He knew from memories of his own growing up that childhood was deceptively difficult and even dangerous. Children needed the opportunity to grow up like they wanted to. They needed support. Some of his support had certainly come from his parents and even from school. But most of it had come from the lake, the woods, the swamp – from his personal world.

He knew that for the children across the lake most of their support would come from their parents and the broader world they lived in. That was how most people grew up. He also knew that he was not like most people, that he could be seen by them as weird and even dangerous.

He fully accepted the personal world he inhabited and also knew how powerful the natural world could be for a child, even a natural world that had been terribly damaged. So, he took it as his responsibility to monitor their growth, to be a distant, invisible part of their lives. He had to be ready to help them if he could, even though he really had no clear idea of what form that help might take.

Arthur was used to living with strong feelings that he would never be able to explain in any typical, normal way. He didn't feel the need to probe his growing feelings of connection to the children. He just recognized the truth and importance of this connection to him. It helped him move past the trauma he had suffered when his world had been so brutally attacked. It gave him a way to remember and honour his growing up here. It gave him a way to connect with a current reality he couldn't change.

Arthur was not a man with any sense of irony, with any appreciation of history, philosophy, or culture. If he were such a person, he would have appreciated the monumental irony of the community across the lake being named "New Eden."

CHAPTER 5
Picture This

WHEN KIRSTEN SHOWED UP AT HEADQUARTERS AT 10:00 A.M. Sunday morning, Jane was waiting for her outside the captain's closed door. The detachment was housed in a section of the municipal office building. Unfortunately, no one had managed to make the place look any less institutional. There was light-green paint, beige carpets, a minimum of decoration, and stark fluorescent lighting. Kirsten wondered, not for the first time, if there was some secret design school out there that aimed at making public offices as bland and bleak as possible, maybe to keep the public away or at least keep people from staying any longer than necessary.

Jane looked over to her. "Jeff tells me we need to wait until the captain is ready for us." Jeff Ripley, the third detective in their detachment, was sitting at his desk, watching them. He was a black man who retained a hint of the Jamaican accent he had developed in his first five years before his parents had immigrated to Canada. He was a tall, medium-built man with a constant look of bemusement hiding behind a friendly face. Part of his bemusement came from the feeling that, despite his having served for almost two years in

Harmony, Jasper McKnight was still uncomfortable with him, and treated him more like the invisible man than like one-third of his detective complement.

Jane said, "He's likely in there deciding on which expression he'll use. From good to bad, they range from 'benign, content granddad' through 'quietly disappointed dad' to 'furious old-time gospel thumper.' I'm hoping for 'quietly disappointed.' And if he starts to bluster, that means he has no idea of what to do and is clutching at straws. Best thing then is just stay quiet until he winds down."

Kirsten thought, *lot of clutching at straws around here*, but managed to keep it to herself. She was seriously working on weeding out her snide comments, though she found that hard to do.

Jeff waved them over to his desk. "I don't know if it will help, but I caught him at his desk yesterday staring at a picture on his phone. I managed to get a glimpse. It was you, Kirsten, when you were trying on your undercover outfit."

Before they could digest this, a stern voice coming from behind the closed door directed Jane and Kirsten to come in. Captain Jasper McKnight was busily shuffling through some papers on his desk, seemingly ignoring them. Jane briefly raised her eyebrows to Kirsten and gave a little warning shake of her head. They stood waiting.

Jasper McKnight was a short, balding man who, when he was around his officers, had a constant look of disapproving exasperation on his face. When hobnobbing with his many friends and acquaintances around town, he tried to look more like a sage, knowledgeable powerbroker deserving of the town's respect. He practiced standing as tall as he could, and as much as possible avoided standing next to tall people, especially women. It didn't help his acceptance of his new detective that Kirsten was at least two inches taller than him. He was a regular churchgoer and belonged to the local Masonic Lodge. Since his wife's death the year before he had spent more time with his lodge brothers and at various public events around town.

Kirsten wondered what it was about this office. It looked like a cop's office – pictures on the wall of McKnight with various people, mostly male, all white and mostly middle-aged or older. Pictures of the queen, the prime minister and the Ontario premier. Framed clippings. Regulation filing cabinets, bulletin board with various alerts and memos. Open closet holding a standard dress uniform. Even a locked gun cabinet holding his holster and sidearm, three rifles, and a pair of shotguns. She thought, *if a production team had Martha Stewart design a cop's office for a CBC crime show, this would be the result.* That was it! McKnight was sitting in the middle of a carefully crafted movie set.

The captain set the papers aside and looked up at them, glaring from one to the other. "I expected more from the two of you. Petersen, I told you to show some finesse and judgment. There might be some questions about Mr. McKay, but he's a big deal in this town. Family always has been. Darn it, I've even been invited to his house. I didn't bring you in here to assault his friends, even if they somehow feel the need to spend time at a place like Friendlies."

A slight pinkness had appeared on McKnight's cheeks. Jane gave Kirsten another warning glance. McKnight carried on, his voice getting louder. "The place has been legal ever since council opened things up around here, but it was supposed to be just for the tourists. I warned them not to do it, but they don't always know who to listen to about what's best for this town."

McKnight paused to compose himself. "So, okay, McKay wasn't there, only those friends of his, but your job was to give them an opening, see where things led to. In short, to do what you were sent in there to do."

Angry at the unfair dressing down, Kirsten burst out, "The only opening they were interested in was my butt crack, and there was no doubt where things were leading to. And I was sent in there as a cop, and a cop doesn't overlook assault."

There was a shocked silence, broken only by Jane's sudden coughing fit.

McKnight gathered himself together, cheeks showing some red now. "That's just what I mean. Being a good cop means obeying orders. You want to be a cop, girl, you learn some respect. This, this … fiasco … was reported, and the uniforms filed a report. I had to intervene with the superintendent to unfile it."

He was shouting now. "We both had to work on the media: 'important police operation.' 'Can't allow you to report it.' And 'it was really just the usual bar brawl, not even the first one there that day.' Kept you two out of it. I had to talk the superintendent into keeping you here, Petersen. And now, what now? I do my job, protect my officers, like I should, and what do I get? You've fu… you've fouled up the only thing we had going. So, what do I do now? I've got pressure to get answers, and now you just add to the pressure." He paused, gasping.

Breaking the brief silence, Kirsten spoke up, ignoring Jane's frantic pull on her sleeve. "Look, it's too bad the undercover operation didn't work. Who could have predicted the bouncers would have had to leave, and that those guys would turn out to be such total idiots? But, Captain, you were smart enough to point out that this thing seems to involve financial stuff. If you approve, we can work on tracking the money. You know, quietly access relevant financial records and find out what's going on there. I know how to do that sort of thing. It was a big part of what I did down south. And I had a colleague who was a wizard with financial scams. He owes me. Let me call him, get him onside."

Patting her pockets, Kirsten said, "Must have left my phone in the car. Let me use yours." She grabbed the phone sitting on McKnight's desk. "So how do you open this thing?"

McKnight reached for the phone, but Kirsten had turned around, seemingly to get more light. "Now, is it this button?" Jane looked on, mouth slightly open, quietly astonished.

McKnight blanched, and said in a strangled voice, "Yes, you're right, you're right. That'd be a good approach. But best we handle it from here. I want you to get right on it. Walden, you help her. Just give me back my phone and I'll clear the way for you to get information at the bank and the township offices."

He managed to snatch back his phone, retreating back behind his desk, and punched a few buttons.

Jane and Kirsten were just getting to the door as he finished with his phone. "Just hold on. Yes, look into the financial stuff, but first some other things. Petersen, there's been thefts out at New Eden. The uniforms were out there, but we've got a full detective complement now. That place is in trouble. We have to reassure people out there. Tomorrow, you get out there and see what's going on. Walden, I want you to look into this problem with the parking meters at the municipal lot. It's costing the town a lot of money, and there's lots of angry complaints coming in. First things first, you two. We've got to make sure things are in good order around here before we go any further. Just be sure to send your reports in to me before you start on this financial stuff."

After they left McKnight's office, Jane pulled Kirsten over to their small conference room and shut the door. "I don't know whether to laugh or just get pissed at the captain yet one more time. I wasn't coughing, I was trying not to laugh, or maybe pee my pants. I've always just tried to manage our wonderful leader. But you, you blew him out of the water. And nice deflection to this financial stuff. I didn't know you were one of those figures-wizards."

Kirsten smiled and said, "I'm not really. I helped out a little with some of that stuff, enough to know where to start. And I do have that colleague, friend, really, down south. He'll help, and I think the financials we'll have to look into here will be a bit easier than the ones we were dealing with down south."

"Maybe, but there's been a lot of interest up here recently from outsiders carrying briefcases, nosing around and not saying much.

It might be interesting seeing what McKay really had going on, and with whom. But too bad Jasper got his phone back so quickly. You had him twisting on the leash. Haven't seen him before with quite that colour. You really had him going."

"I wasn't just randomly punching buttons. I was emailing his whole picture folder to myself. Leverage will be there, if and when we need it. I need to thank Jeff for the heads up. And thanks for telling me about the blustering. We gave him the solution he needed and shut him up. Also, since he has no idea about how to do any of this, we'll be on our own."

Jane said, "Plus he had his small victory at the end. Put us girls back in our place. Not bad, not bad. Let's sort out this New Eden crime wave and the great parking lot mystery, and then get back to being Cagney and Lacey. I'm starting to enjoy this."

Chief Jasper McKnight sat back in his chair, trying to control his breathing and bring his heart rate down. He had to stay in control, had to make it to retirement. It wasn't far off, and in his last performance review, the supervisor had said, "Maybe we can move that along for you." He could imagine the grand dinner the town would organize to thank and honour him. He might be a provincial cop, but he was managing to finish up in his town, a perfect ending to a respectable career.

He thought back to when he was transferred back here, after he finally made captain. Sure, maybe no-one else had really wanted to be posted here, but they didn't appreciate being where a man could do real policing. He remembered that idiot Johnson saying, at the annual meeting's closing dinner, "So, McKnight, you win the consolation prize. Get to disappear back into the boonies." It might have been the boonies to an ambitious lout like him, but here a captain could make a real difference, and Jasper certainly had. He knew how to keep people connected, how to make sure the right thing always got done. His town, his region, was quiet and orderly, other than sometimes when the Natives stirred things up, or more recently after Friendlies opened. However, there was never anything really serious, not while Jasper McKnight was in charge.

This recent business with Alex McKay was troubling. He and Alex always got along. Both of them understood how everyone would benefit when things were kept in order by the people who deserved to be in charge. He remembered Alex's dad, a real pioneer who had helped keep the town and surrounding region prosperous. The *McKay Window and Door Company* had been the town's main manufacturing concern. Jasper had worked there in the summer during his later teen years. Mr. McKay Sr. had taught him a lot about smart management. He had helped him become a strong leader.

It was too bad the manufacturing company went under a few years back, after Alex had switched their production line over to those new synthetic window frames. It wasn't his fault the material tended to break down in bright sunlight and the windows had to be replaced, and sometimes replaced again. But it underlined what Alex's father had always said: "Trust local, stick to what works, give people a solid, reliable product."

Alex was an okay guy, but he trusted unproven ideas way too much. The manufacturing and agricultural support part of *McKay Enterprises* were both gone now, but Alex seemed confident there was lots left. Over drinks at the golf course Alex had once told him, "It's the investment and development stuff that really brings in the money, Jasper. That's what I always wanted to emphasize. The other things were just white elephants."

A while back, when Quinlan at the bank had come in to talk to Jasper about his concerns over Alex's financial dealings, Jasper wasn't sure what to say. "Well look, Mike, Alex is a local guy from a good family. I hear what you're staying, but I'm sure it's okay."

Jasper felt some vulnerability given the fact he occasionally socialized with McKay. He wouldn't call him a friend, but he was part of Jasper's web of important local connections. He thought of that business a few nights previously, when he had accepted, with some prodding, a sudden invitation to play poker with McKay and some of his friends. And then the business about that Handstrom idiot not showing up, and McKay insisting they go down to the house Handstrom had recently been staying in to see what was up. He was shocked by the discovery of Handstrom floating out in the lake, obviously the result of a drunken boating accident. Luckily, he had been there and able to take control, though it eventually meant yet another squabble with their arrogant new know-it-all coroner. Obviously, McKay had nothing to do with this accident, but Jasper had to admit life was never quiet around Alex McKay.

Back at the bank, Quinlan had replied, "Alex has done business with us for a long time, but frankly, his fiscal profile has been getting pretty compromised for quite a few years now. When we got disquieting reports about those offshore securities he wanted to use for collateral to back his new project, we couldn't ignore it. Maybe I've been overlooking the danger signs for too many years, but head office flagged his account, and they want answers. We were able to provide backing for him to establish the options he needed on the land he wishes to purchase, and to do some preliminary assessments, but head office has put a hold on any further financing until they get some clarification on this collateral. "

Jasper tried to advise prudent caution in proceeding with this matter, but Quinlan's superiors had alerted Jasper's superiors. They were the ones who insisted on action, and insisted Jasper bring in extra help. It'd been Jasper's masterstroke finding Petersen. He remembered her from years back. During her teen years she had a reputation in town as being some sort of loner know-it-all troublemaker. And then there had been that last business, just before she left for university. But she was a local, and Jasper thought he'd have better luck controlling her than some aggressive male wannabe trying to make a name for himself. It helped that Petersen's bosses were fine with immediately approving her transfer. It also helped that, when she arrived and he saw what the grown-up Petersen looked like, he had the brainstorm of doing the undercover operation.

However, the undercover thing at Friendlies had turned out to be a failure. Petersen had really screwed it up! He had thought Jane would at least keep things under control, but not so. Jasper knew that good policing centred on making sure you heard about stuff, got information, and then quietly worked with it – none of this obscure financial stuff, or high-profile investigations. And he also knew that with the undercover operation he could then truthfully tell Quinlan and his superiors that he had an investigation going. With any luck things could drag on till his retirement.

He didn't really understand why he had done the picture thing. Petersen had turned out to be an attractive woman, one reason why he thought up the Friendlies idea. When the women were in the office finalizing how things would work, and Petersen had tried on her outfit, he had just surreptitiously pushed the camera button on his phone, and somehow the picture had turned out –an accident really. The outfit was too brief for her to hide a weapon, or even some sort of communication device, so Jane would be there, over in the corner keeping an eye open and ready to step in. The uniforms were set to respond instantly to any call for backup. It was a good plan, darn it, if only Petersen hadn't freaked out. Jasper had never been to Friendlies, but surely a seasoned police officer would understand what she had to do in a place like that to get the job done! He still wasn't convinced women were cut out to do real policework.

Then she had grabbed his phone! He remembered the quick panic he had felt. He had erased the picture as soon as he could after he got his phone back. So why had he taken the picture in the first place? Sure, his social life had been quiet after Gladys had passed. She had appreciated what he gave her. A stable home. High standing in the community. He was a good, God-fearing man. Too bad they had not managed to have a family, but they were fine together. He honoured her, and certainly wasn't someone who would look at revealing pictures of young women, much less take such a picture. He felt a quick flash of shame but knew this wasn't who he really was. He would just have to be more careful now, just stick to being the real Jasper McKnight.

He had to admit Petersen had come up with a sound idea. He could assure his superiors that it was really her special expertise with financial investigations that Jasper had researched so he could really dig into things. This would be more proof Jasper had things under control here. Surely it would take a while for Jane and Petersen to look into whatever this financial stuff was. They might even discover that Alex, in fact, was involved in some bad stuff.

Of course, reliable old Jane was still around to keep things on track. He trusted Jane. She was a local and so really understood things around here. Jasper could talk to her. They worked well together. He wasn't sure why she sometimes talked like she did, like saying, "I'll get right on it, Chief." What was this "Chief" stuff? He was her captain, not her "chief." He sometimes thought about that when he looked at old stuff on TV, like *Get Smart* and those silly *Naked Gun* movies. But those chiefs were idiots. He really wanted her to call him "captain," his proper title.

She sometimes seemed to be manoeuvring him, like Gladys did. However, overall, their relationship was fine. He could trust Jane. Maybe he had been too rough on her with the parking lot thing. But darn it, his detectives did need to know who was in charge.

Captain Jasper McKnight went back to his retirement magazines, the ones with the fishing boats and picturesque golf courses. Retirement would be nice, but somewhere around here, like New Eden, if only it had places smaller than those palaces Alex had insisted on building. Because Jasper's connections were here, and people here respected and appreciated him.

For a fleeting, disquieting moment, while he was looking at a beach picture, he wished he hadn't been so quick erasing that photo of Petersen, but then he quickly turned the page.

CHAPTER 6
Tim and Mr. Hopps

MONDAY MORNING SAW KIRSTEN PREPARING FOR HER VISIT OUT TO New Eden to investigate the Great Missing Toys Mystery. She realized that this was just Jasper's way of putting her in her place, but she could make good use of the opportunity. It gave her a pretext for sizing up McKay in person before he realized she was really looking into his financial and business dealings.

She first checked the report filed by the uniformed officers, not that there was much to report. A few items, mostly kids' toys of various sorts, had seemingly just disappeared. The complaint had been filed by Alexander McKay. She decided to touch base with Keith Sanderson, the uniformed officer who had written the incident report, and called reception to see if he was in. Hearing that he was in the squad room, she headed down there after first checking in with Jane for her assessment of Sanderson.

Jane said, "He's a good guy and a good cop. Been around for a while now. He's respected in the community and by everyone here. He seems quite content to be a uniformed officer. He does none of the bullshit that career-climbers do. He's a competent and dependable cop, the first guy I think of when I need help from the uniforms."

Downstairs, Keith Sanderson was thinking about the new addition to the detective complement, the first expansion of their ranks since the local detachment had been established. Petersen's first few days had been quiet ones as she got settled in and ready for her first assignment. The details about that had been hush hush, not that Captain Crunch ever shared much with those in the lower decks. All they had been told was to be ready to instantly respond to any call for help from Friendlies. They were to keep a close eye on any newcomers to town and, most emphatically, to keep their mouths shut.

Nothing like being kept well informed by the big thinkers upstairs! Nothing new there. There were rumours that Alexander McKay was the target of McKnight's big new investigation, but nothing definite had been shared with them. Petersen certainly had broken in with a bang. He had to respect a fellow cop who could take care of herself. And now she wanted to do a Monday morning check-in with him.

Sanderson looked up as Petersen entered the squad room. He saw a tall, athletic-looking, attractive woman in her late twenties or early thirties. Her light-brown hair framed an oval-shaped face featuring lively hazel eyes. She wore the usual female detective outfit of dark-blue suit and white blouse, and practical low-heeled brown shoes. She seemed to be wearing only light make-up. All-in-all, she maybe looked more like an up-and-coming business executive than a cop, but the overall impression was of a confident woman who definitely should be taken seriously.

He stood and offered his hand. "Good to finally meet you. Welcome to our quiet little town, though not so quiet for you last Saturday. Nice work, by the way. Things can get pretty hairy at our favourite tits and ass joint. I hear you more than held your own."

Once the language would have fazed her, but she had become used to male colleagues seeing if she would react like a cop or like an uptight civilian. It was a small rite of passage, and she had come to understand why they did it. She wanted to be part of – what? – the clan, maybe? The brotherhood, which now included women? Maybe more like a tight-knit family: you didn't have to really like each other, but you had to stick together and be able to trust each other, always, immediately, and without fail.

Kirsten knew she was being quietly checked out. Cops had to know who they could depend on. "I'm glad it's the *only* tits and ass bar in town. Bet they give you guys more work than you really need. I'm afraid I sort of lost it when those creeps came on to me, but luckily they were all talk and bullshit follow-up. Surprising how easily the basic training kicked in. But the captain wasn't too happy about it, which is why I need to talk to you this morning. My punishment is to investigate the thefts out at New Eden. I read your report. Anything else I should know?"

"Not really. It was a real joke. Kids lose things all the time. I think ol' Alex just wanted to get the parents off his back. Seems they have a lot of complaints about life in Paradiso McKay. Calling us in showed them just how responsive Mr. Big Shot is, at no cost to him. We talked to the parents. There was no pattern to the thefts, if that's what they were. No witnesses – zilch. A waste of time. So now Captain Crunch wants to send out a detective? To make sure we did our job properly?"

"More like punish the new kid who doesn't know how to be a good little girl. So what's with the 'Captain Crunch' stuff?"

"Don't you have a name for him up in the executive suite? 'Captain Crunch' works for us. What's yours?"

Kirsten thought of the picture of Captain Crunch on the cereal boxes: an old, ridiculous, uniformed naval officer, a figure of comic ineffectiveness. "Captain Crunch. Not bad. Look, I can't share any nicknames with you. Of course, I always give my commanding officer all the respect he deserves. Bottom line, I'm trying to get out of trouble, not in to more."

"A hint?"

"Think green and think food. All I'm going to say. Look, this is just my slap on the wrist to remind me who's in charge. I'll go out there, I'll ask a few questions, and I'll file a report that will likely be the same as yours. Then I'll get back to my real job. Speaking of which, I think it's no big secret that I was transferred here to look into McKay. Anything you can share about him?"

"Word is he's in real trouble with his New Eden fiasco. There's a lot of pissed-off people out there, and there's some thought he really over-extended himself financially. McKay Enterprises used to be a solid company when his father was alive. Old McKay was not the most congenial guy, but he was a sharp businessman who always seemed to play by the rules. He certainly was important to this town's economy. After he inherited the family business, Alex maybe had some bad luck, but then he has always seemed like the guy who creates his own bad luck. For some time, there's been rumours of shady financial stuff, but nothing solid has come to light. It maybe didn't hurt him that he and CC – the captain – seem to be pals. He always seems to get more help from the township than other local business types do. It seems he's connected there too. That's about all I can tell you, except I just don't like the SOB."

After a bit more conversation, Kirsten thanked Sanderson for his help and left. She was glad they seemed to be on good terms. She got the feeling that the whole detachment got along pretty well, perhaps united by a shared dislike of Jasper. When she got back to the detective offices, she found out McKnight was away for the day at a meeting of regional captains and administrators. She decided to put the trip out to New Eden off till Tuesday, and to first start taking a preliminary look into McKay's finances and business activities. The better the handle she had on that the better the read she could get on him Tuesday.

Kirsten decided to first call Staff Sergeant Tim Yeoung, her former colleague and resident financial expert at her previous posting. She had been assigned to work with Tim to help him run down leads from the various finance-based fraud investigations he was pursuing, as part of a joint police fraud unit. Always keen to learn, she had tried to pick his brain about how to do this type of investigation, one far removed from her training.

Tim was a thirty-six-year-old Asian who looked much younger. He was a wiry and compact man, seemingly driven by constant energy despite the often tedious (to her) nature of his work. He dressed casually and looked more like a college lecturer than a police officer. He was friendly, approachable, and instantly put people at ease. He was also one of the best financial investigators in the province, a dogged and persistent researcher, a killer witness in prosecuting fraud artists, a bit of a legend.

She remembered how, after she kept asking for details about his various investigations, he finally sat down with her and said, "So, you want a crash course in Financial Investigation 101. Be careful what you ask for. I mostly get blank looks by about the third sentence when I try to explain this stuff. Cops aren't naturally cut out for it. It seems that I am suited for it, for some reason – and don't – don't – say it's because Asians are naturally good with numbers!"

Smiling, Kirsten had said, "Well, I've always been a quick learner. I promise to pay attention. And right on about Asians and numbers, as long as you stay away from the usual women and numbers stuff."

Tim extended his hand, grinned, and said, "Deal. Yeoung Financials Investigations 101 it is. You'll be glad to hear the tuition fee is quite reasonable – dinner with me this Saturday."

Kirsten took the extended hand and said, "Dinner so we can get started on the tutorial, I presume? You know what they say about socializing with people at work."

"I do, of course. Yes, a working dinner. We need to establish a good teacher-student rapport. Yeoung Financials Investigations is a very upright and reliable institution."

Kirsten did have doubts about going out with colleagues. In fact, she had long had reservations about any form of dating. She liked men, at least the good ones, like her dad and a few of the guys she had met since high school, though high school had been pretty much of a disaster. The problem was sorting out what she wanted from her life, and therefore what sort of relationship she was looking for. She had asked Tim for some time to think about his invitation.

Kirsten's high school dating challenges had intensified when she slowly came to realize that none of the traditional female roles held out for her were in the least bit attractive. Marriage and family as a primary life goal seemed reductive and somewhat silly. Sure, marriage and family if that happened in some sort of natural way, but what about who she was? Train as a nurse, or teacher, or office worker? She knew she was smart, and knew she needed an active, challenging career of some sort. More important, she had to – what? In some sort of hard-to-understand way she had to sort out what kind of woman she wanted to be, what kind of life she would lead.

Her parents were understanding and supportive, but somehow baffled by her doubts. They were immigrants who had worked hard to establish themselves in this remote part of their new country. They had come to Harmony because her mother had relatives from Sweden who had settled in the area, one an electrician who took on her dad as an apprentice. Eventually he came to own and operate the business. Her mother, drawing on her secretarial training in Sweden, started to work part-time at the local municipal office.

When Kirsten came along, they became doting parents, determined their daughter would find a secure place in Canadian society. Once it became clear Kirsten would be an only child, they became all the more focussed in helping her fit in. They would always be outsiders to some extent in this conservative little town they had chosen as their new home. They would always somehow be the new people, the foreigners, even after many years of residence in Harmony.

Kirsten was a surprise to them, a beautiful baby who grew through a strong, happy, and active childhood until she reached adolescence and started high school. There she did well in her classes, usually near the top, but didn't seem to have many friends. She often seemed withdrawn and quiet. At parent-teachers' nights they received mostly positive responses, but also hints of difficulties: not fitting in well with other students; sometimes moody and withdrawn; sometimes sarcastic and sharp-tongued. There were concerns about her social skills. By the senior grades her guidance counsellor told them there were concerns about some of the conflicts she got into, like her school newspaper interview with the new vice-principal, or that lunchroom thing that had led to her brief suspension. It was hard to get Kirsten focussed on possible career-paths, on what post-secondary directions she might take ("Because she really must go on to university. She's so bright!").

Her parents weren't totally sure about what going to university entailed, only that it was something their high-achieving daughter should do. They encouraged her, set money aside for her tuition, and waited for their mystery of a daughter to become more comfortable with her peers and life in general. They tried out career possibilities on her. "You're doing so well at school. Do you want to be a teacher? A nurse? A secretary?" And, even, "Your school says your marks are good enough to get you into law school, or medical school, or a business program. That would be wonderful, if that's what you want."

Ah, that big question for Kirsten. What did she want? The well-meaning encouragements and suggestions from her parents and her teachers seemed like white noise to her. She wanted to feel comfortable being Kirsten, whatever that meant. Careers and university were secondary to that. It was all too confusing.

Until one incredible day in her grade eleven English class, when something rather amazing happened, something that brought surprising clarity to her.

Her English teacher was Miss Baker, a young, self-possessed and obviously very bright woman new to the school, having moved to Harmony from Toronto. She had made a real impression on the conservative and firmly traditional Wyandot Secondary School. In warm weather she might come to school wearing a sundress. She didn't skip over the juicy bits in Shakespeare. She was obviously attuned to what was going on in the greater world outside of Harmony. She stood in real contrast to the other, more constrained and conservative women teachers at the school.

On that fateful day, Brian Hopps had joined Miss Baker's class. He had been transferred there because he'd simply worn out his former English teacher. Desperate for a solution, the vice-principal decided to see if Miss Baker would have any success with him. Tucked away in the back of his mind was also the thought that this just might show how good this overly confident young woman from Toronto actually was when faced with a real challenge.

On this early winter day, his first day in class, Brian Hopps sat lounging in his desk, front of the class, shoes off, radiating boredom and quiet contempt. After some minutes of putting up with his muttered sighs and contemptuous looks around the classroom, Miss Baker had given him a long look and then gingerly picked up his shoes and put them over on the radiator beside the window ledge. "Perhaps this will help you concentrate better, Mr. Hopps."

Hopps, with a bit of a sneer, said, "Well, you take good care of those shoes for when you bring them back to me."

She paused briefly, seemed to think about it, and then said, "Well, I wouldn't want those really nice expensive shoes to get too dried out over the radiator."

She strolled over to the window, opened it, looked back at Hopps and over the class, and then dropped the shoes one storey down into a snowbank. "There, that should keep them from drying out too much. And you'll be getting them yourself, Mr. Hopps. After class is over. Has your narrow little mind absorbed all that, Mr. Hopps?"

Hopps started to get out of his desk but stopped when he saw the look on her face as she stood there, arms planted firmly on her hips, totally unyielding. He slowly sat back down.

"Those shoes cost a lot," he whined. "My dad will have something to say about this."

"I look forward to a heart-to-heart talk with your daddy, Mr. Hopps. But for now, I strongly, strongly suggest you do your best imitation of a real student for me."

He sat there quietly until the end of class, showing a strange mixture of anger, fear, and confusion. When class was over, Hopps had to walk in his socked feet through the crowded halls and then outside to struggle, through the snow. Word had quickly spread, and soon the air was full of student catcalls and insults coming from the windows on that side of the school. Kirsten looked on as Hopps struggled to put his shoes on, but slipped and fell sideways into the wet snow, drawing a fresh round of cheering. He finally got his shoes on and hurried off for home without going back inside for his coat.

His father did come in after school for a meeting with Miss Baker and the vice-principal. Before long there were sounds of laughter from behind the closed office door. They emerged from the meeting, handshakes all around. Mr. Hopps said, "Welcome to our community, Miss Baker. I like your style." The vice principal wore a look of thoughtful reappraisal.

Next day Brian Hopps returned to class, wearing a pair of winter boots and accompanied by his father. He muttered a brief and obviously rehearsed apology and returned to his desk. Mr. Hopps gave a little wave to the class and left. Brian Hopps would never be called a good student, but afterwards he was never again a real problem. And Miss Baker had almost no discipline issues.

The incident was the centre of gossip and discussion for days afterwards. Kirsten heard her fellow students trying to understand how Miss Baker could be so intimidating. What was it about her? She was friendly, an excellent teacher, and yet was always in total control. What was it about her?

Kirsten knew exactly what it was. Quite simply, Miss Baker was the real thing, a confident woman who knew who she was and required the rest of the world to respect that. Kirsten was still unclear about university and career but had become certain about one key aspect of the woman she would be. And now, some twelve years later, an experienced police officer, she still had warm memories of her wonderful grade eleven English teacher.

Kirsten shook her head, retreating from this powerful reverie. Strange how being back in Harmony had stirred up so many of these memories in her. She continued to think about her spotty high school dating and relationship history. She had often thought that her social life would have been much simpler if she had compliantly accepted the way Harmony subtly and not-so-subtly tried to mould her into its version of acceptable womanhood. However, she had always felt at some level that she could never be that type of woman. She remembered that amazing talk she had had with Miss Baker after her famous lunchroom dust-up.

She liked boys, and later men, but surprisingly few of them ever seemed really comfortable with her. She had never thought of herself in high school as a ball-breaker, or later as some sort of fem-Nazi, but somehow all too many males had seemed to perceive her as being demanding and unyielding, as some sort of threat to their masculinity.

Tim Yeoung was not like that. They hit it off well at their "working dinner." They did talk shop, and Tim was obviously interested in mentoring her, but he also was interested in her, and they shared a few details of their personal lives. After the dinner, they went their separate ways after a friendly handshake. Afterwards they often ended up having a coffee together and the odd working lunch. There were more dinners, ones that quickly became real dates. They shared more about their lives. Tim had also felt like an outsider at high school. For him, there was the convenient high school stereotype where he could safely hide: the brainy, nerdy Asian guy. He, like Kirsten, had found university to be a great freedom, a much more responsive, energetic, and accepting environment. They traced their similar career paths into policing, though Tim had quickly found in policing a positive focus for his ability with numbers and financial systems.

Tim was interested in Kirsten's experience of small-town life, wondering how anyone could survive growing up in Harmony – or at least survive intact. He was patient with her attempts to learn the ins and outs of financial investigations, congratulating her on her progress, being honest about her struggles with it.

"You're doing okay, Petersen, better than most, and I think you understand the basics. But there's an art to seeing how financial scams get woven together by con artists and big-time financial manipulators. It's an esoteric combination of boring numbers stuff and free-flowing imagination. Sure you want to try to go further with this?"

Surprisingly to her, Kirsten didn't. She had not experienced much failure in learning anything, but Tim was clearly not describing failure to her, but rather a realistic limitation. What she had learned would help her be a better cop, but financial crimes could never be her professional focus.

Her personal relationship with Tim had developed quite nicely. The friendly handshakes had moved through hugs to gentle kissing, to not-so-gentle kissing, and then to quite wonderful sex. Tony had been admirably patient, and as a lover somehow managed to be respectful, caring, personal, and passionate all at the same time. They briefly talked about possible futures together, but quickly discovered their present reality was quite fine. They both were career driven, were still exploring the lives they were living, and were enjoying what had become a good and special friendship.

They didn't really drift apart, but rather settled more into their friendship, with, as they both would sometimes joke, a really nice occasional benefits package. Eventually Tim met someone with whom long-term future possibilities did make perfect sense to him. He shared with his close friend Kirsten the development of his growing feelings for Clara, the woman who would become his wife. They subtly altered their friendship, ending the benefits part with a warm, if ironic, handshake. Kirsten was careful to become friends with Clara and was Tim's "best person" at their wedding.

She sometimes marvelled at how positive her relationship with Tim had become, especially given the chaos and shortcomings of all too many of her previous relationships. Tim Yeoung was one of the few people in her life she cared about and could really trust.

Now Kirsten found herself calling her friend and former mentor in hopes that he could bail her out. Because she had not really been forthcoming with Jasper. She was nowhere near ready to conduct a thorough financial investigation into Alexander McKay. She fervently hoped Tim could come through for her. Luckily, Tim was in his office.

"So, Ms. Small Town Girl, how's the visit back to where it all began? Ready to come back to civilization, or have you gone all hillbilly on us?"

"Well, Mr. Urban Sophistication, I actually was able to investigate a possible new career for when I get tired of being an underappreciated and overlooked police officer. Big tips, meet lots of new people, much more casual uniform, even the chance for the odd bit of exercise." She filled Tim in on her episode at Friendlies, and the subsequent events.

"Somehow I can't see you as a career cocktail waitress. It sounds like you made a real impression on the locals, though. This adds a whole new dimension to what you bring to policing. But where are you now with this big investigation into your local con artist?"

"It remains to be seen how much of a con artist he is. Now that we're through with my new captain's big undercover fiasco, I'm hoping to get things on track. He's set me up to meet with the local bank manager, the guy who first came to him with concerns about McKay's finances. I'm not sure why McKnight feels he has to monitor my every step, but he's some protective of what he calls 'his town.' I'm first supposed to be following up on some damn theft bullshit out at McKay's housing development, but the captain is away at some sort of meeting. I've arranged to meet the bank guy this afternoon. Any tips from Mr. Financial Crimes Expert?"

"To start with, just get the basic information. Make sure it's specific. Don't accept something vague like 'We have some doubts about the securities he's provided.' Get it in writing, the original documents, if possible. Find out exactly what the securities are, when the information was provided, precisely what negotiations occurred to establish the loans or line of credit or whatever. Find out exactly how these transactions varied from the bank's previous business with this guy. Why, again *exactly*, are they concerned? Why come to the police? You mentioned before that it was the bank's head office that contacted our financial crimes unit. They initiated the brass getting you transferred up there to get more information about this guy, though I suspect they thought your investigation would be a little quieter than you having bar brawls dressed in your underwear. At any rate, find out what instructions they gave your local bank guy."

"Tim, my alleged good friend and supporter, don't make me sorry I shared details with you about the Friendlies stuff."

"Well, sorry to tell you this, but word's already filtered back here about your introduction to undercover work. Too juicy a story to stay under wraps. People are getting a whole new appreciation for your range of abilities."

"Shit! Just try to squelch it if you can. I was happy just working quietly in the background. It sure wasn't my idea, and it'll never happen again. And thanks for letting me give you all the details when you already knew most of it. Shit!"

Chuckling, Tim said, "It just gives a little more colour to your stellar reputation. It'll die away, don't worry. We all need a little shake-up every now and again."

"Which is why you've buried yourself in the most quiet, esoteric, and hidden part of policing, the financial crimes unit? Got any plans to go undercover, maybe at, say, a gay club, Mr. We All Need a Shake-up?"

"Maybe I'll just stay being boring old Tim Numbers Guy, buried in back rooms with my computer. I will try my best to return your reputation to its previous pristine under-the-radar level. But seriously, do keep in touch with me. If there's more involved than just a local scam of some sort, I can likely look into any broader connections. Remember, the bank's head office is already involved."

"Thanks. Appreciate it. Talk to you soon."

Kirsten appeared promptly at 12:00 noon at the bank and was ushered into the office of Branch President Mike Quinlan. He looked like many other bankers Kirsten had encountered: middle aged, trim moustache, carefully cut grey hair, three-piece suit. A rather bland but authoritative appearance, as if to subtly imply trust and reliability. However, he also looked vaguely uncomfortable, as if Kirsten presented some sort of threat to him and his bank. She settled into the chair across from his desk.

"Mr. Quinlan, thanks for your time. I think Captain McKnight has explained why I'm here."

"Yes, yes, of course. Though I thought when I first approached Jasper that we could keep this matter contained. It doesn't help our town to have rumours about improprieties circulate. I trust I can count on your discretion."

"Yes, of course. But you know that your bank's head office has expressed its concerns to our financial crimes unit. That's what got me sent to Harmony, though of course I'm operating under Captain McKnight's authority and direction. I need to get more information about Mr. McKay's dealings with your branch."

"I just wish our head office would appreciate that our bank plays a significant role in Harmony. I know they want all of us local bank managers to feel like we are just cogs in a big machine, but frankly we used to be able to do our job better when we could focus more on the needs and realities of our town, not the dictates of some MBA sitting in an office in Toronto."

Quinlan had been getting increasingly agitated as he voiced his concerns, but now paused to regain his composure.

"Sorry, sorry. I have great confidence in Captain McKnight, and I'm sure we can sort this out locally. Now, what information do you need?"

Checking her notes, Kirsten said, "Our information is that your bank has played a significant role in the business affairs of Mr. McKay, and of his company, McKay Enterprises. That in fact for some decades this bank and McKay Enterprises have enjoyed a close relationship. However, it seems Mr. McKay has experienced some recent business losses, especially with his development at New Eden. When he approached your bank for further loans, both to satisfy his current creditors and to underwrite a new business venture, namely the purchase of a land package somewhere near here, you expressed your concerns to him, and essentially turned him down unless he could provide solid collateral or reliable financial guarantees. Is that accurate?"

"Yes, yes. That's right. McKay Enterprises has been our most significant commercial client and our relationship had long been most beneficial, to both sides. But when Alex took over the company after his father's death, he quite frankly started to make some questionable business decisions. For a while the company itself was the collateral for our financial support and involvement, but the company has been shrinking for some time. It now has few physical assets and has become more of a speculative development concern. We were able to underwrite much of the New Eden development, but the cash flow has been irregular, and frequently negative. We are hopeful that the development will prove profitable, but all of the houses have been sold, and Mr. McKay has made financial commitments to his buyers, which severely compromise its potential profitability, things like mortgage and insurance guarantees, plus covering some repair costs."

"It sounds like McKay Enterprises is heading more toward bankruptcy than it is to future financial stability. Why would your bank even consider further financial support?"

"Well, Miss Petersen, I hope you can have some appreciation for how a town like Harmony works. I understand you grew up in Harmony and graduated from our high school."

"Word gets around. Yes, I grew up here, but this is my first time back since I left. And it's Detective Petersen, please. So, do explain how a town like Harmony works."

"We have to take care of ourselves. Our province is controlled by the needs of large cities like Toronto and London. Despite what the politicians say, rural Ontario is not very important to them. McKay Enterprises has long been an important part of our town. Say what you want about Alexander McKay, but he does generate economic activity. It is to the greater good of Harmony to support local business to the fullest extent possible. Confidentially, head office might think we are just part of some larger corporate balance sheet, but this is a living town, and our bank has a moral obligation to help keep it alive and prospering. I admit we went out on a limb in supporting McKay Enterprises recently, but if local business dies, the town eventually dies, and with it this bank. Central office may not care, but I do."

Quinlan had again been getting quite agitated. Kirsten found herself accepting the sincerity of his belief in his community, but also could see why the bank's central office was alarmed by recent developments. Alex McKay was likely not the only person whose livelihood, career and reputation were on the line. She paused while Mike Quinlan again sought to compose himself.

"I appreciate your frankness, Mr. Quinlan. And rest assured our goal is simply to get this matter sorted out. It seems you were initially unable to extend further loans and financial backing to Mr. McKay. What changed things?"

"Alex was rather desperate when I gave him our initial response to his application. He confirmed what information we needed to reverse our denial and asked me to hold fire for a few days while he consulted with some business associates. Sure enough, he returned a couple of days later with a man named Mr. Piggot, who said he represented a financial concern wishing to support and financially underwrite McKay's latest enterprise. He said they were really confident about its success. He gave me a portfolio giving some background about this financial concern, 'The Maitland Group.' He expanded on what the portfolio said about the financial guarantees they would provide. Here is a copy for you. The portfolio provides a great deal of information, but look, this was getting way over the head of a local bank manager. I had to turn the whole matter over to head office for verification, and I presume that's when they contacted your superiors."

Kirsten accepted the portfolio, glanced at its contents, and quickly realized it was way over her head also.

"Thank you again for your co-operation, Mr. Quinlan. I will carefully look at this." *Or Tim will,* she thought. "I'm sure my superiors are also checking it out. But a question. If this mystery organization was so confident about Mr. McKay's new project, why involve your bank? Why not support him directly?"

"It's not as simple as that. Alex's financial matters are quite convoluted. We are not his only creditor. The portfolio details how The Maitland Group would pay off his other creditors and accept responsibility for future obligations, like the repairs at New Eden. Further, they would provide secure financial commitments held in trust in a bank in the Bahamas. The Bahamas! What do I know about anything like that?"

"Again, why not underwrite McKay directly? Why involve your bank as a middleman of some sort?"

"Mr. Piggot explained that it was simpler to keep things local, to continue McKay's established local business routines. He explained that his company did not want to be involved in the daily management of this matter, but rather would just provide the necessary financial umbrella so our bank could do the local management, as we have done for so many years. He said he appreciated that my superiors would have to verify and confirm what The Maitland Group offered, and that he had had sent all relevant information directly to them.

"I was deeply perplexed by all this, but it was clearly out of my hands. I was authorized to forward to Mr. McKay the modest amounts he needed to take out options on the land he wishes to purchase, and to take care of what he called necessary assessments and collateral costs. But now I am awaiting the approval of my superiors to provide the much more substantial amount needed to complete the purchase of the land. I must admit I am concerned about the delays taking place with that. Mr. McKay has been most insistent that he be authorized to proceed, given what he calls significant time pressures, and given the financial guarantees Mr. Piggot provided. That's all I can tell you, but I do wonder why you have been sent here, since really the matter seems to rest with whatever your and my superiors are doing."

"Thank you again for your cooperation, Mr. Quinlan. My role is limited to confirming any relevant local information, especially about Mr. McKay. You have really helped with that. We all understand how important confidentiality is in this sensitive matter, so please just wait for more information from me or directly from my superiors."

With that, Kirsten made her exit, in many ways more confused now than ever. If higher levels in the police service were involved, why had she not been told more? Why had she not been given a contact, like Tim, in the financial crimes unit? She headed back to headquarters and immediately called Tim to get some much-needed clarification.

Tim asked for some time to look into things and promised to promptly call her back. She was surprised when "promptly" turned out to be less than an hour later.

"Look, Kirsten. Bit of a clusterfuck here. There is an investigation being done here in the unit. They were triggered by the nature of the information provided by this Maitland Group. They have been under investigation, quietly, for some time because of some shady connections, particularly with this bank in the Bahamas. We've been very discreet, so they likely thought there was no reason for any sort of concern in them backing McKay's little project. Except, with the alarm bells going off here, it seems it may not be such a little project after all. Our lead investigators wanted as much information as possible, quietly collected, about McKay and his various business dealings. Since you had some local background there, you were sent to head that up. All this was explained in precise detail to Captain McKnight. You were to work with him, and he was to forward reports directly back here.

"But is this guy some sort of idiot asshole? The investigation was to be discreet, not involving public bar brawls. He's reported little back here, and we can't seem to reach him. So, our superiors have decided your new contact is me. You are to continue, more carefully this time, and report everything you find promptly to me. When we finally track down McKnight, we'll put as firm a gag on him as we can. Do not contact the bank again. We have people working directly with Quinlan, who appears to be scared shitless, by the way. It may make him easier to control.

"Really important thing, we want to see where McKay is going with his little project, so we have asked the bank's head office today to give approval to Quinlan to give McKay the financial green light to finish his land purchase. They are deeply concerned with this whole business and have been cooperating totally with us. Please do find out all you can about this project of McKay's, but again, discreetly. And, Kirsten, be careful. We don't know what all is involved here, but it is more than just some little con job in Hicksville. Ok?"

Kirsten assured Tim she would be careful and would play it by the book. She wondered where McKnight was and what it would be like dealing with him now. She and Jane had planned to meet that evening for drinks and debriefing. She trusted Jane but would have to decide how fully to confide in her. Deep in thought, she sat at her desk, trying to make sense of it all, and deciding how to proceed.

CHAPTER 7
The Great Parking Lot Mystery

MONDAY MORNING ALSO SAW JANE STARTING OUT ON MCKNIGHT'S punishment assignment. Investigate some parking lot issue? For this she had become a detective? Harmony was never going to give her the splashy, high-level investigations featured on those endless – and totally unrealistic - TV cop shows. But to investigate … what? … defective parking meters? She was a cop, not a mechanic. But then, she was working under Jasper McKnight, the chief of the ridiculous. So, yet again, Jane sucked it up and followed orders.

First, she checked the reports on file. Several citizens reported they had been mistakenly ticketed, and often towed, from the main municipal parking lot. Harmony had evolved before cars had taken over the town, so there were no large, standard parking lots near the downtown. This had increasingly become an issue for local businesses, so town council had bought up some vacant lots behind Main Street, requisitioned a few falling-down buildings, and had created a meandering, irregularly shaped lot wrapped around the back of most of the downtown businesses on the east side of main street.

More recently council had decided to install parking meters to add to the municipal coffers. Initially there were complaints about having to pay for what had for a long time been free, but good sense and fiscal prudence had won the day. However, the problem arose of people refusing to feed the meters, and after the municipal police force had been dissolved in favour of using the provincial force, there was no-one to enforce the metered parking. The provincial force did NOT do municipal parking enforcement! Hiring some form of parking enforcement would defeat the purpose of trying to make money off the parking lot, and the other metered parking on Main Street.

The solution was a masterstroke of creative fiscal thinking. They negotiated a deal with the local tow truck operator. He was officially empowered to do a two-level enforcement: when a meter expired, he was to put a large red warning notice on the offending vehicle's windshield. If the vehicle was still there an hour later, he was free to tow the vehicle to his impound lot. His profit came from the $200 charge for releasing the car. The municipality got $50 of this as their share.

Of course, this also caused protests, but the official response was reasonable and firm. Parking was a privilege you paid for, and there was an hour's grace time before a legitimate towing fee was applied. The vehicle had to be towed so others could legitimately use the parking spot. Towing cost money. The $50 reimbursed the municipality for possible lost meter revenue and for 'processing fees.' Eventually everyone got used to the system, and it generally worked well.

But then, a few months back, the towing company had been taken over by a new owner. The number of towing infractions gradually increased until it reached unheard-of levels. Many towing victims insisted they were towed long before their paid meter time had expired. The towing company owner could always provide the required proof that the meter had indeed expired. Technicians brought in from the parking meter company established that all the meters were in perfect working order. The upsurge in offenses was a genuine conundrum. Some sort of mass forgetfulness? A symptom of previous slack enforcement? The complaints would usually go to the merchants, who then complained to the police. Some angry alleged violators would complain directly to the police. They were not put off by assertions that it was not a police matter. Township council and the towing company stood by the fairness and accuracy of the system and refused to accept any responsibility.

So, it seemed McKnight was doing Harmony a good turn by looking into the matter, but Jane knew it was really because he just didn't want the hassle. Of course, he dumped the odious little matter into someone else's lap: Jane's. She was a fan of detective novels and movies and realized this was a bit like the classic closed-room mystery: seemingly no possible solution to a baffling enigma. She thought of what her favourite fictional detectives might do in the unlikely event they took on such a picayune problem.

Sherlock Holmes would invoke his famous observation, "When you have eliminated the impossible, whatever remains, however improbable, must be the truth." So, that likely meant it just was some sort of sudden mass parking-meter violation. Except Jane also was an amateur student of mathematical probability: why such a sudden and inexplicable upsurge? What had changed? Holmes might just smoke his pipe and claim that it was merely an improbable truth, but then Holmes always had been a somewhat tiresome male egotist. Was his logic always so impeccably unassailable?

Next, Hercule Poirot. He would engage his famous "little grey cells" and figure out what no-one else could see, except he too was a male egotist, even if he had been created by a female author. And the female sleuths? Miss Marple, Kinsey Milhone, and V. I. Warshawski would likely just nose around until they bumped into the solution. So, she decided the latter is what she would do, though, in deference to the aforementioned male sleuths, with little grey cells engaged, and on the lookout for logical answers.

Jane drove to the parking lot to get a look at the potential crime scene, though she couldn't imagine what the crime might be. After carefully feeding her meter, she looked around, but all she saw was a strung-out parking lot, about half full, with no subtle clues lurking there for her to discover. And no Arthur Conan Doyle or Agatha Christie to point the way for her. She walked around the lot and checked every meter, a surprising number of which had expired. She also checked in with several downtown businesses, but no one could offer any insights. She returned to her car, puzzled to see that the meter had expired despite the fact she had paid the morning maximum fee.

As she stood trying to figure this out, she heard a voice call out to her. "Detective Walden. Up here." Looking up, she saw a man sitting on the first-floor balcony of one the units in an adjacent apartment building, one of the few in Harmony. It was Sid Ray, local journalist and frequent pain in the butt. He had worked for the *Harmony Herald* before that local newspaper had finally succumbed to fiscal realities and had closed its doors. Since then, he scraped together a living as a stringer for various southern media outlets that sometimes wanted details on the few local news stories worthy of urban interest. He supplemented his income by doing various custom writing and research tasks and acting as an occasional teacher at Wyandot Secondary School.

"I think I know what you're investigating, and I can be of real help to you. Come on up, apartment ten, and I'll fill you in. Look, I can see you're hesitant, but I promise you won't regret it. Come on, what have you got to lose?'

I've got time and personal frustration to lose, Jane thought. She supposed Ray was just like every other journalist, always probing, questioning, being sceptical and almost always a general pain in the ass. But, dealing with the media was an unavoidable part of modern policing, even in quiet backwaters like Harmony. Stifling a sigh, she entered the building and went up to apartment ten

She was let into the apartment by a short, ferrety-looking man, likely in his early thirties. He was slightly balding, dressed in nondescript casual clothes, and quivering with nervous energy. "So, Mr. Ray, what good citizen service are you prepared to offer me?"

Ray replied, "I assume you are looking into the parking meter stuff that has been pissing so many people off."

"Let's say I am. What can you tell me?"

"Come on out to the balcony. I can explain better out there."

They moved out to the balcony and sat down in some rather rickety lawn chairs. "I know what's going on here, and it's not some minor issue with the meters. I'll tell you what I know, but first I need your promise of exclusive rights to the story when it breaks, and exclusive interview rights. I promise you, there's a real police issue here for you, and a good story for me."

"No promises, but I'll respect your wishes if I'm able to do so. But why are you so eager to help?"

"I understand why the police are leery about reporters, but we've both got jobs to do. Solving this thing will be a feather in your cap, and it might be a big enough public interest story to help me get back to full-time reporting. Nothing against Harmony, but there's not much here for someone who craves doing some real journalism. If you're not sure you can trust me, I was there at Friendlies when you and Kirsten had your little dust-up with the locals. I could have reported that, but it seemed to be part of something bigger, and I didn't want to compromise your investigation. Therefore, I sat on it."

"I'm glad you did, but I'm not yet ready to swallow this 'concerned good citizen' role you are scripting for yourself. And since when are you on a first-name basis with Detective Petersen"?

"Kirsten and I went to high school together. We worked on the school newspaper, helped each other in a couple of difficult situations. I was at Friendlies trying to scope out some sort of story.

Not likely, but it's one of the few places where things sometimes actually happen around here. That little dust up with the bouncers wouldn't cut it. And, just so you're really clear, I *am* trying to act like a good citizen, but as a good citizen who ends up with a good story."

"So you weren't there at Friendlies trailing around after Detective Petersen?"

'No. Look, I didn't even know she was back in town until I recognized her at Friendlies. I just couldn't believe she ended up back here as a cocktail waitress in a strip joint. I mean, I lost track of her after she left for university, but we were buddies in high school. She was clearly destined for big things. I really liked her. I mean, *really* liked her. I was shook when I saw her there, so I just sat back in the corner. I didn't know what I'd say to her. 'Kirsten, good to see you. Interesting new job you got.' It made some sense when she outed herself as a cop, but I was still shook. I mean, the Kirsten I knew in high school becoming a cop? Nothing against being a cop, but it was a real surprise to me. So, good citizen, yes, but good friend too, even after all these years. I didn't want to compromise her.

"Back to matters at hand. I hope you will trust me. I'm being serious here. Can we give this a try?"

"Let's see where it gets us. And thanks for the Friendlies stuff. I can't tell you any more about that, but it would have been tough for the force, and for Kir … Detective Petersen if it got widely reported. So, what have you got?"

"Like I told you, I'm always nosing around for stories, particularly something big. I often sit out here, so I couldn't help but notice the uptick in meter violations. The new tow truck operator, Harold Scrivener – I went to high school with him too. Mention him to Kirsten. They've got some interesting history together. Scrivener was clearly making some big money, and he always has been a pretty shady character. I wondered what was going on.

"Scrivener appeared to be following the rules. He'd check the meters, put the warning notice on violators' cars, wouldn't tow until an hour had expired. But he was towing a lot of cars, from a variety of parking spots. I noticed he always went directly to specific cars at specific meters when he patrolled the lot. And usually different meters. I got out my binoculars and zoom lens. Strange things emerged. He sometimes missed cars with expired meters when he was zeroing in on his target cars. Stranger yet, he would come back after towing cars and would seem to be checking the meters they had been parked at. And really stranger yet, when he patrolled in the evening, he would stop at random meters and check them. The next day any cars he towed would almost always come from those particular meters.

"I started to roam around the lot and check cars out. People would usually opt for either the full morning or full afternoon charge. The meters would be accurate initially, but when I checked about an hour later, hours before the time should be up, they would be expired. A bit later old Harold would show up. I took pictures of these cars and their meters, documenting this sudden expiry of the time. I took shots here from my balcony of Harold harvesting these cars. The cars were clearly legally parked, but Scrivener was also legally towing them. So, what gives?

"Next, some research. I tracked down a technician working for the company that manufactures and services the meters. He agreed to help me out. It seems if you have the right tools, you can get into the meters and make various adjustments. One adjustment is to change when a violation is to be indicated. It can be set to be, say, one hour after the money is put in, whatever that amount is. It can later be reset to accurately reflect the actual time paid for. All this can be done quickly, so it looks like you're just checking the meters.

"Scrivener would prepare some target meters the night before. The next day, he checks those spots, tows the alleged violating vehicle, and then comes back later to reset the meter. The aggrieved citizen makes a big fuss – and who can blame them? But if the meter is later checked, it's working fine. Scrivener is always notified when some mass check of meters is about to occur, so he'll suspend operations until the check is done. This allows him to make sure all the meters pass the test. Ingenious. Works just fine. Unless your intrepid investigative journalist is on the case. And he is, with full documentation, which he is pleased to pass over to you. I was planning to come into the station very soon, so the timing of your investigation is perfect."

"Or," Jane said, "You were planning to break the story, embarrass everyone around here for being so lax, and reap the glory. Except you saw me here, figured you could get some good official information and quotes, and so get a better story. Or maybe you figured we were on to Scrivener and you'd lose your exclusive scoop."

"Detective Walden, I am shocked – shocked! – at your cynical attitude. Let's focus on the positive, how we can help each other."

"Seems you like old movies, like *Casablanca*, as much as I do. Okay, but this is NOT going to be the start of a beautiful friendship. Your evidence, as described, will certainly help, but we need our own direct evidence, free of any potential, um, enhancement."

"Then you really have come at the right time. I'm ready to harvest today's evidence, but gladly will step aside for you. Here's what I suggest."

After further consultation about specific details, Jane contacted the meter company's regional office and arranged for one of their technicians to come and help out. He arrived before noon, and Jane briefed him about what was going to happen. In the early afternoon, with Ray's help, she was able to photograph several cars that had time on their meters until 6:00 p.m. She and the technician took notes for each car, documenting the time and the information. They were able to come back an hour later and she got shots of the same cars with now-expired meters. Some time later, from Ray's balcony, she took video footage of Scrivener's tow truck arriving at the lot and heading directly to one of the target vehicles, which he towed away. He soon returned and headed for another target vehicle, after first going to the previous target meter, opening it with some sort of tool and seemingly making some sort of adjustment. This process was repeated three times, for a total of four towed vehicles.

After each of Scrivener's moves, Jane had the technician check the meter's settings. Detailed notes were taken in each case and initialed by Jane and the technician. As Harold Scrivener arrived to harvest one last vehicle, he was surprised to be accosted by a middle-aged woman who identified herself as a police detective. She had him escorted to police headquarters by two uniformed cops who had pulled in behind his tow truck.

After he was informed by the cop he now knew as Detective Walden of the evidence the police had, he said he would say no more until he could meet with his lawyer. An hour later his attorney, John Armstrong, arrived. He and Scrivener went to an empty office and soon were involved in deep conversation. Armstrong was well known to Jane. He was usually the lawyer appointed to represent indigent clients that no one else wished to take on. His client list was full of small-time thieves, drug offenders, and accused sexual predators. He rarely won, but never seemed to expect that he would. He was adept at working out deals that would reduce his clients' punishment, reduce the burden on the courts, and generally piss off the police who had worked so hard to develop the cases. He seemingly was respected by no one, including his clients, but had become a routine cog in the area's legal system.

After several minutes of close, intense conversation with Scrivener, Armstrong called Jane in for consultation. He told her his client was ready to make a deal, but it had to be a solid one endorsed by the Crown Attorney. Jane arranged for a meeting of all parties for the next morning. At 9:00 a.m. Tuesday morning, the parties met in the department's conference room. The Crown Attorney's office was represented by one of their senior members, Beverley Crowder. Jane had informed them that this case had the potential of uncovering some sort of local conspiracy with elected officials, and so demanded careful handling.

Armstrong began. "My client recognizes that there is significant evidence against him, though we are concerned about possible entrapment issues and are concerned about the central role of a local journalist in this matter. I believe the courts would be very uncomfortable with that."

Crowder, making an impatient gesture, broke in. "Let's get real here. I have had a preliminary look at the evidence the police have gathered and am fully confident the investigation was done by the book. Mr. Ray was working independently on his coverage of the events, but in fact did co-operate fully with the authorities. Detective Walden corroborated and documented all the evidence she gathered, and it is that evidence, not anything offered by Mr. Ray, that we are proceeding with. The case is about as airtight as any I've ever seen. The charges are serious: theft, conspiracy to defraud, breach of the public trust. There may be future charges if any damage was done to the towed vehicles. Also, if any of Mr. Scrivener's victims wish to be involved – and believe me, they most likely will– there may be charges of extortion. There likely will be civil actions, which are not our responsibility, but which will go badly for your client once we obtain the convictions we certainly will get. We are looking at serious jail time given the conspiracy and breach of public trust charges. There will be serious fines and seizure of his property. In short, your client is in a world of trouble, and unless you give me something substantial, right now, I'll go back to my busy schedule and my office will continue to prepare for prosecution of your client. So, what have you got? What do you want?"

Armstrong had been making placatory gestures while Crowder spoke. "Ok, we fully recognize the seriousness of the situation and the likelihood of conviction. My client is willing to divulge the names of others involved in this matter, including elected officials, and provide full details. But he needs some guarantees. Jail time of less than a year, and in a medium-security facility. He will provide full return of all money owing to his, uh, aggrieved customers, and will reimburse the municipality for reasonable claims of lost revenue. However, there must be no other punitive financial penalties. To be perfectly frank, right now you can prosecute him for theft, and in the process severely embarrass all those local officials who somehow let it all happen. The reporter will get his story and will be the hero in all this. But why was it him and not the police or township council that stopped this little enterprise? Sure, my client will suffer serious punishment, but do you really want all the other fall-out from this?

"Make us a serious offer, a solid deal that will mean my client will pay the consequences of his bad decisions but will be able to carry on with his life. In return you will get a much more serious case. There were other people involved in this matter, elected people and an employee of the meter company. You will be on top of all this and will nail the real criminals; you'll do some real good for this community. I'm talking about a win-win."

Crowder thought for short time, and then responded. "Let's proceed like this. We'll go off the record, and you will tell us what you've got to offer us. If it is as good as you say it is, I will go to my superiors and recommend more lenient treatment of your client. If we can establish that sort of general framework, we can then formally offer you specific terms in return for specific sworn testimony. So, should we have a little chat?"

Jane was as sceptical as police officers usually are when deals start to be negotiated. Part of her just wanted this snivelly little creep to get the serious punishment he deserved, and for his greasy shyster lawyer to crawl back into his hole. But, if bigger issues were involved, it made sense to go after them. She swallowed her feelings of resentment and paid close attention to what Scrivener had to say to them.

He told a meandering story about how a few township councillors arranged for him to get exclusive municipal towing rights in exchange for regular kickbacks. To begin with it was a fairly lucrative deal for all concerned, but a rather limited one. But then Councillor Ted Passmore came to him with a bigger plan, one that could mean some real money. He arranged for a three-way meeting with one Grant Sylvester, a technician with the company that manufactured Harmony's new parking meters. Sylvester explained how, with special equipment he could provide, the meters could be accessed and adjusted to allow for the resulting scam. He patiently taught Scrivener how to make the adjustments on the meters. After much practice with a parking meter Sylvester provided, the scam went into operation. Passmore monitored the reaction of township council to the upsurge in towing offences and made sure council and other local authorities accepted that it was just a normal occurrence. The three split the proceeds. Jane and Crowder were sure Scrivener skimmed extra money off the top for himself, but all three were well rewarded for their efforts.

After Scrivener's confession, Jane excused herself to meet up with Kirsten to head out for their New Eden investigation. Crowder went back to consult with her colleagues about the exact details of the proposed deal with Scrivener and how to follow up on the information he had provided. Sid Ray went back to his apartment and wrote the article he would submit as soon as Scrivener was formerly charged.

On the day of the initial investigation, Sid Ray and Jane Walden had some time to kill between the various events Jane had to document. She had become more relaxed with Sid and lowered some of the reserve she always maintained when talking with media people. She appreciated the solid work Sid had done, and also how willingly he had shared with her. She amazed herself by discovering she trusted and actually liked a reporter. They chatted about various things, but Jane couldn't contain her curiosity about Sid's high school experiences with Kirsten and asked him about that time.

"I was in grade eleven when Kirsten started high school. I had firmly carved out my niche as nerd school newspaper guy. When school clubs' day was held, she talked to me about joining the school paper. Frankly, it was hard to get kids to join up. I had some help at various times, but it was mostly a one-man show. She started to write some things, and they were pretty good. By the next year she was my main staff writer. I really, really liked her, and we had become sort of friends.

"It was in her grade-ten year when things got really interesting. The school got a new vice-principal, a really unpleasant little jerk named Mr. Andrews. I mean, who wants to be a vice-principal? They aren't teachers anymore, and mostly are looking for ways to move up the ladder. We had some good ones, but also some real idiots. This guy's name might have been Mr. Andrews, but we all called him by his nickname, Napoleon, hung on him because he was short, ambitious, and caused a lot of damage. This guy was the worst.

"Napoleon acted like he was in charge of everything, ordering the teachers around mercilessly. Word got out that at one staff meeting he made a little speech about professionalism, about how real professionals took care of their assigned duties and played by the rules. He then noted a few teachers were failing to do newly assigned noon hour supervision duties. He capped it off by naming four alleged offenders and saying something like, "I trust you four will henceforth show us you really are professionals. However, if you continue to ignore your responsibilities, we are going to have to have some serious conversations.

"Student discipline is the main thing for vice-principals, but Napoleon always acted like it was beneath him. He was more concerned with punishment than with getting to know something about the students and seeing how he could really help them. Rather than try to put them on the right course, he treated them like chronic offenders. He made them feel resentful, and all the more likely to cause more problems.

"This guy was soon feared, hated, reviled by everyone. It was clear he was trying to make a name for himself at the expense of our school. A few months into the school year Napoleon came to me about the school paper doing an interview with him. Really, he ordered me to do it. I was sure it was just part of his plan for self-promotion. I was so pissed off that I shamefully passed the assignment on to Kirsten. She did the interview and presented the final product to me. It made Napoleon look like a bit of a jerk, but Kirsten insisted this was what he ordered her to write.

"The paper came out, staff and students both liked the way it revealed the true Napoleon, we became unwilling temporary rock stars, and Napoleon was so mad he insisted on a formal hearing into the matter. I can't remember all the details, but Kirsten had taped her interview with him and could prove she did, in fact, write the article exactly as ordered. The part I do remember clearly is that Napoleon ended up accusing her of just trying to make him look like an idiot. She memorably replied, 'You don't need my help in doing that.' I can still remember all the people around the table trying to stifle their laughter. It was all downhill for Napoleon after that. He soon left the school and disappeared somewhere into the system. People were unsure whether to admire Kirsten or be a bit afraid of her. She immediately returned to her desired quiet, withdrawn role in the school."

Jane thought, *Looks like she learned early how to deal with people like Jasper.* Aloud, she said, "But why they didn't fire this Napoleon guy? He sounds like a total turkey."

Sid raised his eyebrows and replied, "I think you know most organizations work like this –protect themselves and never admit to errors. Even, I dare say, the police. I'm thinking, if I may be so bold, of your boss."

Jane said, "Of course the police department is perfect and never makes personnel errors like that. But, fair enough. The thing I can't wrap my head around, though, is that this powerful guy, seemingly terrorizing the whole school, protected by the system, is brought down by a fifteen-year-old girl. Who doesn't really go after the guy – what grade ten student could? – but just defends herself, amazingly well, it seems, and somehow wins total victory. And does not want to relish the spoils of that victory. Is that what you've just told me? Did she do it on purpose? Was it planned?"

Sid replied, "Questions I couldn't answer then, and still can't now, though I sometimes think about it."

Jane said, "So, another mystery. You said earlier that you, quote, 'really, really liked her.' Do I detect a high school crush here? Why weren't you able to ask your buddy/crush/whatever how she did it?"

"Two things. First, she is a very private person. We were buddies, we hung around together as misfits – though misfits for very different reasons . . ."

"Like what?"

"I had no real choice. Look at me. I was an unattractive, non-athletic, scrawny little nerd who was custom made to be a school misfit. I accepted that label because it gave me a semi-safe role in that hell called high school. I would have loved being one of the cool kids, but that just wasn't in the cards. That's why I so enjoyed those few moments of fame I mentioned.

"But Kirsten was brainy, talented, athletic, and attractive. She could have been a school star. Instead, she chose to evade the spotlight. She either couldn't or wouldn't fit into that high school crap. Maybe misfit is the wrong word, because it implies you want to fit in, and can't. Maybe it was more that she just chose to be an outsider."

"The other reason?"

"Look, even in the movies Gollum doesn't get Wonder Woman. To me, Kirsten was amazing. She chose to be pals with a skinny nerd at least two inches shorter than her. I cherished being her pal. I made sure I didn't push it by intruding into her life too much.

There's no way I could ask her really personal stuff. Life is what it is. You'll have to ask her yourself how she managed to pull that thing off, if she'll tell you."

Afterwards Jane thought a lot about what Sid had told her. She didn't want to invade the privacy of a new friend who was obviously still a private person. But she also had sensed a real connection in her quickly developing friendship with Kirsten. And she was very curious about Sid's dramatic little story. She and Kirsten had decided to get together that evening for drinks and debriefing before Tuesday's resumption of investigation into one Alexander McKay. Perfect time to find out more.

She was also eager to get Kirsten's read on a very interesting story Sid had told her involving McKay and the great parking meter mystery.

CHAPTER 8
The Naked Truth

THAT MONDAY EVENING JANE AND KIRSTEN MET AS PLANNED, THIS time in Kirsten's little apartment. They were learning that privacy, sometimes a rare thing in Harmony, was becoming more necessary for them.

Kirsten's apartment, rented on a monthly basis, fully furnished, was on the second floor of a renovated old house on a quiet side street. Growing up here, Harmony had just seemed to her like a boring little backwater, lacking the flash and energy of the exciting places featured in movies and TV. She just took it for granted. Now she was realizing what a pretty little town it was. Most of the residential buildings were older brick structures, built when attention was paid to detail and quality. The back streets featured large lots with many mature trees, well-tended lawns, and carefully trimmed shrubbery. There was no vinyl siding anywhere, no modern monster homes fronted by two-car garages. No cheap little disposable bungalows. It was as quiet and laid back as she remembered but featured a serenity and grace the younger Kirsten had not appreciated.

The downtown also featured substantial and distinguished older buildings. Many had been renovated and repurposed, but they all kept most of their original charm. There were no mini malls, no neon lights, no tacky fast-food places. It was like a little time capsule, a holdover from a quieter and less frenetic time. With minor alterations, Harmony could have provided the location for a movie set a century earlier. Kirsten was surprised to find she quite liked the appearance of her old hometown. However, she had to remind herself this was the more prosperous part of Harmony, an area called "Upper River" for some reason. Because of the small river that skirted the edges of this part of town? Because the residents thought of themselves as "upper" in some vaguely privileged way?

Kirsten's family had lived in what was referred to, disparagingly by the Upper River people, as "Lower Town." It also featured older brick houses, but smaller and more modest ones, without the architectural flourishes of Upper River. When she had taken a nostalgia walk through Lower Town after her return, she found it was still the working-class area. Older cars, more modest landscaping, pleasant and inviting dwellings but not suggesting long-established prosperity and entitlement. She had found her old house, relatively unchanged, her mother's flower borders still there, glimpses of a vegetable garden in the backyard, the maple tree she had liked so much still flourishing beside what had been her bedroom window. It had been a comfortable and secure place to grow up. It was not until the adolescent Kirsten had gone to high school that it was subtly but firmly impressed on her that she was, in fact, a Lower Town girl.

The two women settled down in Kirsten's modest living room with a bottle of red wine and a bowl of potato chips. Both obviously had information to share. Kirsten was still wrestling with how far she could trust Jane with her new information, and so told the older woman to go first.

Jane gave a condensed version of the great parking meter mystery and repeated what Sid had shared with her about his high school time with Kirsten. "So, Jasper may have thought he was punishing me with the parking meter stuff, but it turns out to be the most interesting case I've ever handled. Jasper will of course draw as much praise to himself as he can, how he was on this from the beginning, taking care of his town, protecting the public good, stuff like that. But I also get to be Jane Walden, star detective. Or at least until we go back to the usual round of stolen bikes and domestic disputes. Your old friend Sid Ray was really helpful. He should get the real credit, and likely will once he breaks the story.

"Seems he was a real fan of yours back in the day. Like you were pals. Even seemed to have a bit of an unrequited crush on you."

"We were pals, but just about school newspaper stuff. Really, I found it easier to hang out with a guy two grades ahead of me who just wanted to work with me on the paper, no other motives. And none of the weird competitiveness and judgmental crap I got from a lot of the girls in school. He was okay."

She paused for a moment, struck by a sudden memory. "Oh my God. I'm remembering some conversations we had when I was in grade eleven and he was in his final year. It was near the end of the year, when kids were pairing up for the annual high school monstrosity called the grad prom. One day Sid started to talk about the pairing-up process, how the school stars sought each other out and the rest just tried to sort out whatever they could. He seemed to be mocking it, like he had no interest in being part of what he disparagingly called the 'high school meet market.' He said that if he went to the grad it would be stag, if he went at all. But he also asked me if I was managing to avoid all that stuff. He kept coming back to the topic for the next few days. My God, I was totally oblivious at the time, caught up like always with my own little issues, but I think he was really trying to work himself up to ask me if I would go with him."

"So, would you have accepted? Sid told me that in high school you were Wonder Woman, while he was Gollum. Would Wonder

Woman have gone with Gollum to the, what did you call it, high school monstrosity?"

"I was no Wonder Woman, even if Sid saw me that way. More like a high school Bridget Jones. And he wasn't Gollum. He was a sweet guy. Always treated me well. Really helped me on a few occasions. He was one of the few friends I had in high school. I honestly don't know if I would have gone with him, but I wouldn't have hurt him, not intentionally, at least. And I had an excuse – I was even more skeptical about the grad than he was. I just wish my skepticism had saved me from the big schmozzle I got into in my graduation year."

Seeing Jane's enquiring look, Kirsten put up her hand and said, "That little disaster is for a later time, if at all. God, you'll be thinking my high school time was nothing but a series of various-sized disasters. That was Sid at Friendlies? I'm going to have to seek him out. I'm glad you like him, because I certainly did."

Jane said, "You may want to talk with Sid sooner rather than later, because while we were waiting for things to happen, he shared an interesting little anecdote about McKay. Seems that one day, soon after he started his parking lot surveillance, Sid saw McKay come out of the back door leading into the building where our MPP has his constituency office. The only other occupants are a hair salon, a thrift shop, and the regional office of a cosmetics distribution company. I don't think McKay was buying used clothes, getting his hair styled or looking for opportunities involving cosmetics. Sid said McKay came out and sat in his car, seemingly deep in thought. A few minutes later a stranger came out of the same door, and he too didn't look like he was interested in clothes, cosmetics, or hair styling. Sid said that even at a distance he seemed at the same time nondescript-looking, but also a bit dangerous. Sid's words.

"In the meantime, Scrivener had shown up and was preparing to hook up to a white SUV, which turns out to be dangerous guy's vehicle. Sid looks on through his binoculars. The stranger goes up to Scrivener and holds out some money to him. Scrivener shakes his head, like this isn't enough. He starts to turn back to hook the guy's SUV up, and dangerous guy's arm suddenly shoots out, grabs Scrivener by the throat, bounces him off the SUV, and Scrivener goes down. Dangerous guy gets into the tow truck and backs it into a vacant slot. Scrivener is sitting on the ground, dazed. Dangerous guy throws some bills at Scrivener, points his finger at him, pushes him out of the way, and drives off in his SUV, but not before he looks over to McKay and gestures for him to get out of there, which McKay does. Scrivener eventually gets up, lurches over to his tow truck and drives away, not to be seen again until two days later.

"Sid isn't sure what he's just witnessed, but knows it was nothing routine. Who is this guy? What's his connection to McKay? Were these two actually meeting with our MPP? So maybe this little parking meter thing has given us some new information about McKay. Oh, and Sid got the SUV's license plate. I ran it, and it's registered to some company I've never heard of, and which I could get no real information about. Add it up: dangerous guy, secret meetings, a little violence, mysterious white SUV – on TV they're always black, aren't they? And all this in quiet little Harmony. What do you think?"

Kirsten sat quietly digesting this information. She had to make some key decisions, and right now.

"Jane, you're dead right that there's some big-time stuff happening here, and McKay's right in the middle of it. I've been sworn to secrecy by the financial crimes unit and warned to keep things strictly to myself, but I'm tired of the pressure. They want me to act like some sort of lone wolf up here, where I'm still the new person in the department, and where I can't trust my boss, the guy who sent me out on a crazy undercover fiasco. A boss who lied to me, took private pictures of me, and who now can't be reached. And I'm thrown into the deep end of some big-time conspiracy that's frankly way over my head, and I'm supposed to get some sort of information in some sort of way for some purpose no one will really explain to me."

She stopped, settled her breathing down, hugged herself, and then took a large gulp of red wine. Jane looked on in surprise at a seemingly always composed and in-control woman who was clearly now quite upset.

"Kirsten, I'm not sure what to say." She moved over beside Kirsten and put her arm around her colleague's shoulders. Kirsten initially stiffened, and then seemed to give in and accepted the hug. After a few moments she sat up and gave Jane a tight little smile. Jane returned to her chair.

"You better fill your glass, Jane. I'm going to lay some heavy stuff on you, if you're up to it. I'm starting to realize I've paid a price by not trusting people enough, like with poor old Sid. I've got to ask you a couple of important questions. First, are you ready to take some risks with me? I mean, I don't want to dump you from being star detective one minute into being rogue cop the next. But this isn't routine stuff. Should I continue?"

When Jane nodded yes, Kirsten said, "Question two. Can I really trust you? Can we trust each other? We've not known each other for very long, but I feel, I don't know, simpatico with you. I'm not used to quick friendships, but I feel good about you, and I really do need some help. I've just trashed the boss you've worked with for several years, and I guess I'm the person bringing some dangerous information into your quiet little town. Frankly, my friend's advice to you might be for you to stay safely out of this. So, what do you say?"

Jane thought for a moment. "Jasper's my boss, but he's not a very good cop, since we're being frank. I mean, he really screwed up with the Friendlies stuff, but that's par for the course with him. And I don't like the way he has been treating you, and also Jeff, for that matter." Big sigh. "I think I've gotten too complacent. I've spent too long accommodating Jasper and ignoring too many things. Like, Jasper said he was away today because of a regional meeting at headquarters. I started to wonder why this meeting was news to me. I checked, and there was no such meeting. So, you're not the only one who's feeling left dangling in the wind."

Jane paused, and then said, "What do you know about that drowning in Silent Lake that happened just before you got here?'

"Not much, just a few things people said. Fill me in."

"There was a poker game out at McKay's place. Just a few of McKay's cronies, and believe it or not, Jasper. Our captain was out there hobnobbing with people we are now supposedly investigating. It seems like another of McKay's associates was supposed to be there, name of Will Handstrom. He advertised himself as being a paralegal, and McKay, being as cheap and slapdash as he usually is, used Handstrom for some of his legal work, serving people, looking up information and so on. He often had to get a real lawyer for his business dealings, but Handstrom was one of his go-to guys. So, it seems McKay called several times down to Handstrom, who McKay was letting stay in a vacant house a few places down, because Handstrom's wife had kicked him out.

"Eventually McKay evidently suggested they take a break and go down to see what was up with Handstrom. When they got close, they could see a rowboat out on the water and a little further out something looking like a body floating there. Jasper took charge and they called in Fire and Rescue and some uniforms. The rescue guys retrieved the body and the boat. The uniforms started to take witness statements from the poker players and some of the neighbours. They said Jasper stopped them since it was clearly just an accident. Jasper ordered them to just keep the scene under control.

The coroner showed up and started to investigate, but the uniforms said Jasper loudly informed her it was just an unfortunate accident, that she should just have the body taken away. She was angry about how disturbed the scene was and wanted to investigate further. The upshot – she took samples from what seemed to be a blood smear, the victim's as it turned out, on the boat's gunnel. She insisted on doing an autopsy, which identified a cut on Handstrom's forehead consistent with hitting it on the gunnel. He had drowned and had a significant blood alcohol reading. He had died shortly before the body was discovered. So, in the absence of any contradictory evidence, she had to rule it as death by misadventure. The uniforms had found a half-empty bottle of rye in the house, and no evidence of anyone else being there. The official story: Handstrom got drunk, decided to go out in the boat, slipped, hit his head, fell into the water, and drowned."

Kirsten said, "But you have some problems with the official story?"

"Yep. Why didn't Jasper call me or Jeff out since he was a witness? The man was dressed in a suit and was wearing leather shoes, hardly appropriate for a late-night boat ride. Why not interview everyone there? Why rush to judgement? Why not at least explore other possible explanations? Some neighbours told the uniforms, before Jasper shut them down, that a few days before they had overheard a heated argument between Handstrom and McKay at McKay's place. And how convenient for McKay and his pals to now have Jasper as an alibi, if they needed one. Why not a full forensic investigation of the house, the boat, and the beach? Why rely on a cursory examination of the scene by Jasper and the uniforms?

"In short, I can't be sure that there was no foul play involved, and I couldn't look into the possibility because of Jasper. I'm not happy at all with what's going on with McKay and with Jasper's involvement. So, sure, as long as we are talking about playing by the rules, being good cops, everything above board, include me in, sister. There's too much stuff happening around here that I just can't ignore any longer."

Jane paused and took a big gulp of wine. With a bemused look on her face, she said, 'Life's gotten a lot more interesting since you showed up. Hey, and since I'm the new star detective around here, let's step up the game.

The two women smiled and shook hands.

Kirsten filled Jane in on all the new information that had come her way that day. Jane had some questions, and they talked things through, trying to make sense of it all. Eventually they decided they would both go out to New Eden the next day after Jane was finished with the Scrivener follow-up. They would use the theft investigation as their pretext for trying to find out more about McKay and his tangled dealings. They would quietly try to find out more about McKnight's whereabouts and actions. They were both starting to wonder if the captain was just being his usual incompetent and unreliable self or if he was somehow really mixed up in McKay's schemes. Why did he withhold, from both of them, information about the McKay investigation that HQ had passed on to him? Why did he use such an inept investigative plan as the Friendlies fiasco? To actually deflect any real investigation? There were all the questions about the drowning. Jasper was a friend of McKay's. Was he also part of McKay's support system, or even more deeply involved?

It was starting to get a bit late, but after they had sorted their plans for the next day, Jane said, "All this has been more than interesting, but I need to ask you about what Sid told me about your high school newspaper dust-up with that evil little vice-principal. You do seem to have had your share of interesting high school adventures, so tell me more. Like, did you actually plan your campaign against this Napoleon guy?"

Kirsten chuckled. "So, from these new big-time mysteries back to my high school trivia? Okay. I sometimes think about that episode, because it was a turning point for me. No, I didn't plan to go after him. I mean, I was just an obscure little grade ten student. But from the start I was put off by this guy. Like most adolescents, I was struggling with the gap between what adults said about reality and my own experience of it. Why did things so often seem false and off-kilter? I mean, here's a vice-principal who is supposed to be a trusted educator, a guy dedicating his life to kids and education. So why all the rude treatment of everyone at school? And when Sid gave me that interview job, why did this guy try to control what I wrote? Why did this guy, paid to look after my education and welfare, treat me like a silly little cipher?

"The real reason Napoleon failed was his arrogance and stupidity. I mean, he really set himself up for defeat. So, I'll happily claim having a strong survival instinct, and maybe some ability to do some fast thinking, but nothing beyond that. No fifteen-year-old wunderkind."

Jane was shaking her head. "Well, wunderkind enough. I still think it was pretty damn impressive. I'm starting to think there was some truth to Sid's Wonder Woman stuff. But one more thing. Sid said you have some personal history with our parking lot desperado, Scrivener. What was that all about?"

"Getting close to my bedtime, but I'm still too wired to go to sleep. Maybe a bit of a late start tomorrow, given the week's worth of things that happened today? This will take more wine and your genuine interest in my high school traumas. But maybe we *should* end tonight with a little semi-light nostalgia. You game?"

"Pull the cork, woman. Tell all." And with that, Kirsten went on to narrate what was not semi-light nostalgia, but really a foundational event in her life.

"I remember it was a sultry, warm Saturday afternoon in early September, and I was hanging out with two friends, pals really, Molly Peters and Valerie Montrose. It was so hot we decided to bike out to the stream leading to Silent Lake, to see if we could at least find some cooler air.

"We left our bikes in some trees just off the road and started to trek along a pathway at the edge of the stream. There was swampy ground, which meant we had to take off our shoes and even do a bit of wading. The mosquitos loved the shorts and T-shirts we were wearing. The air was so humid it felt like we had to push through it. Eventually we came to a place where the stream widened out into a quiet pond with a small beach area surrounded by trees and brush. Other than the croaking of frogs and the odd bird call, it was still and quiet. A gentle breeze kept the bugs away.

"We sat down trying to recover a bit. I remember Valerie saying how cool and inviting the water looked, that we should have brought our swimsuits.

"We started to talk about going skinny dipping, how it was something girls really shouldn't do, but how unfair it was that boys could. They remembered about the naked guy I had seen a couple of years before over by the lake, but I reminded them nothing had happened since, and it happened a ways away. We decided it was unfair for boys to have all the fun – why shouldn't we do what we wanted? – and that we should ignore Harmony's stupid unfair little rules and go for it. Before you knew it we were all out of our clothes and into the water.

"It was wonderfully refreshing, and we drifted around, with the odd little water fight, mostly just enjoying being cool. Suddenly we heard the sound of snapping twigs. We were startled and felt kind of vulnerable, being out there naked. Then we saw someone hiding in the bushes on the shore. It was your parking lot master criminal, Harold Scrivener.

"We all hated him. He was one of the country boys who bussed into our high school. He always seemed out of place there, mostly because he was constantly forcing himself on people. He'd butt into conversations, trail around behind other kids, and always seemed to be lurking around. If kids let him stay, there'd soon be silly insults, off-colour comments, and weird non-sequiturs. He seemed to think he had the right to do and say whatever he wanted, despite people's obvious discomfort and disapproval. The kids found him to be someone to avoid, aggressively if need be. It was harder for teachers to escape him. One of the kids once heard a teacher describe him as a strange little misfit, saying that he wished Harold would just go away.

"So, there we were. Scrivener emerged from the bushes and walked over to where our clothes lay on the grass. He said something like 'It seems like I've become part of your private little gathering. Why don't I guard your clothes until you come out? Or if you want to stay unfriendly, maybe I'll just take them with me. Let you go back to town like that. How do you three little snobs like having someone else call the shots for a change?'

"We huddled under the water, covering ourselves as best we could, whispering urgently to each other about what to do. But then Scrivener stood up and started to undo his pants. He said something like 'I'm going to give you a little treat, seeing as you're putting on such a nice show for me.'

"I remember I just snapped. Before I knew what I was doing, I shouted, 'I'm not going to take this shit from that little asshole.' Mad as hell, I surged through the water toward the shore, making no attempt to cover myself." Kirsten paused, took a deep drink of wine, and ruefully shook her head. "There I was, a naked little sixteen-year-old, and I think I said, 'Harold, for the first time in your stunted little life you get to see what a naked girl looks like. Likely the last time until you get enough money to pay for it. I'll give you a guided tour, since you're such an ignorant little prick. This is my left tit, this is my right tit, and this is my bush. Getting all that, are you? And don't you dare pull that ugly little thing out, if you can even find it. Scram! Get the fuck out right now!' I mean, those maybe weren't my exact words, but that's how I remember it.

"God, I think the next thing I said was, 'Harold, get your twisted little self out of here, right now. You're going to leave, we're going to get dressed and head straight to the cops. They'll charge you for being a fucking disgusting little Peeping Tom. Got that, you fucking little prick?'"

Harold shouted that he had the right to be there, that it was public property and I couldn't tell him what to do. Then he made a grab for my boob. I knocked his arm away and then punched him as hard as I could, square on his nose. Harold fell to the ground and lay there, trying to stop the flow of blood, squealing a mixture of insults, cries of pain, and whining. He threatened to report me to the cops, said that they would charge me.

"I was still ranting, something like 'Charge me, a girl, for defending herself against a big brave guy like you? Is this after you're arrested for being a fucking Peeping Tom? Everyone's going to love hearing how your nose got rearranged by a girl. Scram! Get the fuck out of here before I really hurt you.'

"He scrambled to his feet and scurried away, sobbing wildly and hurling insults back at me. I just stood there, suddenly exhausted. The others waded ashore. I remember Molly, who never swore, saying 'Omigod, omigod omigod. What just happened? Omifuckinggod!'

"We stood looking at each other, nervous laughs, trying to calm down. Valerie said I was suddenly some sort of Amazon warrior, and that she was too scared to do anything.

"I remember thinking it couldn't have been me, that I had just snapped. I didn't even think about being naked. I told them the little asshole was enjoying his power too much, sort of using our nakedness against us, that it wasn't bravery or anything, just pure anger that suddenly exploded because I couldn't let him control us.

"I remember we looked at each other. One of us started to giggle, and soon we all were laughing hysterically about the 'guided tour' and his 'miserable little prick' and the whole weird thing.

"We wrapped our arms around each other, a group hug of relief and celebration. I remember feeling something entirely new, a strong jolt of pure joy and friendship.

"I remember proper little Molly finally pulling away. I think she said 'It's not that I don't love you guys, but we're sort of naked here. we don't want people to start ragging us for being lezzies.'

"We decided to go celebrate our great victory and see if the long arm of the law actually did try to hunt me down. We quickly dressed and headed back to our bikes. In town, as we were sitting in the Harmony café drinking cokes, Adam Westfield, you know, the town constable, sauntered in and came over to our booth. I was so uptight, I think I can remember exactly what was said.

"'Room for one more? I need to talk to you. It seems like you three had quite the afternoon. How's the swelling on your right hand, Kirsten?'

"I swallowed and stopped massaging my painfully swollen hand. I blurted, 'It's okay, but look, what really happened was ...'

"Adam said, 'A while ago Harold Scrivener and his mother came to see me after they got his nose looked at. It's not badly broken, but broken all the same. He had a nasty cut behind his ear. I heard some disjointed story about how three naked banshees set on him as he was just minding his own business walking in the woods. He was lucky to escape with his life. I dug into his story a bit, and his mother and I finally got a more complete picture of what happened.

"'I assured them he wouldn't be charged if he just quietly went back home and in future was much more careful about his behaviour. I assured him we don't charge people, even naked banshees, for defending themselves. The last I saw of him, his mother had her thumbnail planted in his ear and was leading him out to her car. She seemed to be lecturing him about respect and being a gentleman.

"'Now, I've got to tell you a few things. First, it appears he *was* assaulted, but it also appears he had it coming to him. I don't think it would do the Scriveners or you three any good if this went any further. It's not officially on the books, and there is such a thing as natural justice.

"'Second, unfortunately, girls do have to be careful, more than boys do. That's not fair, but until we create a better world, there it is. So do be careful. Please.

"'Third, I think you'll be fine now. There's not much real grit or character in that poor little bugger. I think he'll just go away, but if not, there's a reason to come visit me at my office.

"'Fourth and last. Kirsten, if you want, I can teach you how to break a nose without hurting your hand. The lessons are free.'

"I was amazed. Here was an adult who actually took me seriously, who really wanted to help. I mean, I had a reputation around town of being some sort of insulting know-it-all. He didn't treat me that way.

"After he left, we sat quietly for a moment and then talked the whole thing over. We agreed on what our version of the day's events would be, but we were sure it would likely be own little secret.

"After I got home, I told my parents about how I had tripped in the woods and smashed my hand on a rock. It was best just to get past the whole thing. Except the next day proved I was wrong."

Kirsten looked over to Jane to make sure she was still awake.

Jane said, "So in fact you do have a history of personal violence. I think I'm even more happy now that Scrivener is going down. I see what you mean by a strong survival instinct. You mentioned more happening the next day. I need closure here, girl. One more glass of wine, please, and then the final chapter to your great skinny-dipping adventure."

Kirsten poured them each another glass of wine, sighed, and carried on with her story. "It seems the next day Scrivener, always wanting to ingratiate himself with people, talked to one of my school enemies, one of the Upper Town cool kids. In the cafeteria that day she started to razz me about being a lesbian running around naked in the woods with my two friends. I can't remember all the details, but somehow I made her look suspect by listening to the school reject, Scrivener, and being all too interested in his weird stories about naked girls. I think I made it look like *she* was the secret lesbian. We ended up in the principal's office, with my rival and I both getting three-day suspensions. I remember the principal was really a nice guy and protected me from the girl's big-shot father getting more done to me. My favourite teacher had a talk with me, to make sure I was okay, and even though she didn't know, or want to know, the details about Saturday, she congratulated me on standing up for myself. So, it all soon blew over, but I was seen by the kids as being all the more strange and sort of dangerous The parents of my two pals made them stop seeing me because I was a bad influence. Life carried on. I carried on, but I remember feeling more confident in myself."

Kirsten looked over at a clearly drowsy Jane. "So, now you're caught up on latest episode of Kirsten's little high school dramas. Thanks for staying awake, though it looks like you barely are."

"Right about that. Thanks for sharing. Amazing story. I think I'm starting to understand more about you becoming a cop. But it is late. I'm off for some shuteye. Let's hope tomorrow is a little less exciting."

Neither woman realized the excitement was soon going to get much more intense.

CHAPTER 9
McKay in Deep

ALEXANDER MCKAY WAS A DEEPLY TROUBLED MAN ON THIS MONDAY night. He roamed through the dark downstairs of his white elephant of a house thinking about how close he was to success. He was almost there but needed to finish it. Had to, or else …

He deliberately kept the lights off because he needed to think with no distractions. Victoria was still away visiting her sister, or so she said. Likely shacked up somewhere. The kids were mercifully at their summer camp. They never stopped whining. Toys that mysteriously disappeared. No friends. Not allowed to go anywhere because it could be dangerous. The ghost that came out at night. Why did they have to live here, away from all their friends in town? And the terrible scare a few weeks ago ….

Brandi (*Why oh why had he let his wife choose a stripper name for their daughter!*) had slipped away one evening to go swimming even though he had told her over and over that it was still too cold and there were weeds in the lake. She was under strict rules (*Why do I always have to be the bad guy making the rules no one obeys, and then I get angry, and it all goes to horseshit again!*). She could only take her ten-year-old self down to the lake if someone was with her, and he was too busy, always, and Victoria (*When had she stopped being Vicki?*) seemed to have little interest in her two kids anymore. Had she really wanted to have them, or was it just another way to tie him down and keep him trapped?

He had heard the bell on their dock ringing, and after he went outside to check, he heard Brandi wailing and whimpering down by the lake. He ran down to find her on the dock, shivering and distraught. After he got her back to the house and Victoria had managed to quiet her down, Brandi haltingly told her story. She said she knew she would be able to swim out into the lake okay because she was doing so well at her swimming lessons (*More damn money, and someone always had to drive her there – usually me!*). But the water was cold, and as she treaded water before heading back, her legs got tangled in the weeds, and then she couldn't break free, and she kept trying so hard, but she slipped under the water, thrashing and trying to scream and swallowing water and ....

She was unclear about what had happened next. She was struggling and semi-conscious, and then it felt like she was dragged free, then she blacked out, and then she was on the dock, shivering and coughing and alone and afraid. She didn't know how she got back there. She didn't remember ringing the bell on the dock. Clearly, she had managed to find a reserve of strength and had fought hard enough to get back to the dock, lucky to survive. He felt a rush of love for her. She was a tough little kid. She could be a royal pain, but he did love her.

Later, after she had thought more about what had happened, Brandi said she had thought at first her dad had rescued her, had pulled her out of the water and onto the dock, that he had rung the bell. But then her dad had come running, and he was the only person on the dock with her. Alex overheard her later telling her brother that maybe the lake ghost had saved her, but he was not to tell their parents because her dad got mad when she talked about the ghost. Alex remembered that the last time she had mentioned the lake ghost he had flipped out, had shook her and yelled, "Stop talking about some stupid goddam lake ghost that does NOT exist! You just give everyone around here another damn reason to bitch at me." And then Victoria got mad about his language with the kids, and things went to shit again. So, as he had learned to do, to keep some sort of peace in the family, he let it go.

Alex's fevered mind came back to the trap he felt himself in now. He had the land he needed on option and had solved the nasty access problem. With the signed agreements he had in hand, the new owners could move back and forth to the otherwise cut-off land package he had created. The required geological testing was done, and he had the formal report. His political pals had helped him get all the necessary approvals, zoning and so on. His friends on township council were used to easing the way for Alex's plans as long as there were some crumbs for them to pick up, and Alex always made sure there were. Besides, they didn't know about all the big players in this latest thing. They were good at things like helping him get New Eden set up, and they thought this latest venture was just another one of Alex's land development schemes. No big worries there.

Alex's thoughts shifted, again, back to this damn "New Eden" fiasco that just wouldn't let him go. What a joke that name turned out to be. Township council, urged on by his pals there, had been eager to approve his latest and biggest development proposal. Jobs, increased tax base, growth. He didn't even have to offer any financial incentives. They bought in lock, stock, and barrel. Council put the new access road in, and then his construction guys started on the actual building. He made sure his council pals got lots of the various sub-contracts.

It proved to be much more challenging a project than Alex had expected. He kicked himself for not being more careful with the initial planning and land assessments, but then he had always saved money by cutting corners. Not this time. They had to bulldoze most of the land he had bought, leaving only the trees between the twelve lots to establish New Eden's "exclusive privacy." Drainage problems. Problems setting strong footings. The usual construction delays, even though he made sure there were no unions involved. And then the problems getting the electrical and plumbing and HVAC approved – his non-union guys were hit and miss as far as having any damn idea of what they were doing! A few greased palms made it happen. But the costs just kept going up, and Alex had not been careful enough to protect himself from some very unpleasant financial surprises.

It poured rain the day of New Eden's grand opening. There was no media coverage, and though these damned local yokels had seemed interested as New Eden was being built, they now seemed unable to understand and appreciate what New Eden offered: "Exclusive executive estates! Beautiful natural setting! A perfect place to safely raise your family! Far from urban noise and congestion! A wise investment now and for the future!"

The reaction from the locals seemed to be: "Who'd want one of those over-sized monstrosities? And I'm not an executive. Beautiful - if you like swamps and scrub brush and mosquitoes and a weed-filled lake! Safe? Out in the middle of nowhere? What city and what noise and congestion? Investment? More like a huge bloody mortgage, and for what? Future bankruptcy?"

Alex had tried advertising in the nearest (though still distant) cities, places where the cost of living was sky-high. Their basic response to this chance to experience "quality country living"? It seemed to be variations of: "Exclusive? And these are executive estates? It's the bloody wilderness. Imagine being stuck out there in the winter. My family would rebel if we went there, wherever 'there' actually is. And since when is the wilderness safe? Far? Right, far from shopping, restaurants, entertainment – from everything. That's living? I can find better ways to blow my money. What future would there be out there?"

So, he had to move out here himself. Victoria went nuts. "Living by the lake? Living by a lake is living in a resort – restaurants and beaches and lots going on. With some amenities, damn it! This is a joke!" The kids were sullen for weeks. He managed to pressure some extended family members to buy in. Some business associates realized they had to move out there if they wanted to keep doing business with him, and at that stage they did. He snagged a few newcomers to the area who couldn't find what they really wanted and who were able to overlook New Eden's many drawbacks in their relief at finding anything at all. And all of the sales – all of them, damn it! – at deep discounts, and with him having to guarantee most of the mortgages.

Then the foundations started to get small cracks, and there were some flooded basements. Some of the shingles started to curl. The vinyl siding was already fading and coming loose. Even Mike Holmes wouldn't be able to save this place. Some wise ass altered the large New Eden sign at the front gates to read "Who k**NEW EDEN** was this shitty?" The small disasters kept coming, and the money – too much of it *his* money – kept gushing out. Damn it! The window for him escaping this mess in one piece was rapidly shrinking.

"The big business mogul," Victoria would throw out at him as their fights increased. "You inherit a shitload of money from Daddy and just turn it in to actual shit, like this shithole you make me live in!"

Victoria. Where was the sweet little Vicki he had married? There he was, working in his dad's office, the heir apparent even if no-one there really took him seriously enough. He was in an increasingly bad marriage to his first wife, his high school sweetheart, the bouncy head cheerleader who now was slipping into the sort of fat, shrewish nag this bloody town seemed full of. But then Vicki had been hired on for the summer. He managed to make that permanent, because she was always around, and damn it, she made him feel respected, feel good. And she was young and pretty, just like Mary once was.

Did he pursue her, or did she pursue him? It didn't matter, because before long they were passionately tied up in each other. She didn't push for him to get divorced; it was just clear that had to happen. After too much time, and lawyers, and too much money, and sniggering rumours and all the small-town crap that goes along with this sort of thing, she became the new Mrs. Alexander McKay.

She revelled in her status of small-town aristocracy, especially after his dad joined his mother in the family mausoleum and he became president of McKay Enterprises. It was "Victoria" now, because "Vicki" was no longer good enough. She had arrived!

But somehow McKay Enterprises started to have reverses, didn't really adapt to his leadership. Or was it the economy, or the limited vision of people in this damn backwater, or just plain bad luck? It didn't matter, because after years of slippage he was now clearly in big trouble. To most people he still was one of the town's business leaders, a successful developer, but various insiders were starting to show their doubts. He didn't like the hesitations the last time he talked to Quinlan at the local bank. Various local politicians, like their idiot MPP, took longer to get back to him. His investors were restless, despite his constant financial transfers and manoeuvres to keep them satisfied. He was finding it hard to keep ahead. He had rolled the dice on New Eden, and now here he was.

But if he could pull off this latest deal, this golden opportunity that had seemingly come from out of nowhere, it would all be all right again. Better than all right. He could move out of his mistake by the lake, unload his New Eden obligations on to some speculator as blind as he had been, get Victoria off his case, and become the powerful and respected man his father never seemed to think he could be.

Alone in this dark house with his troubled thoughts, Alex thought he saw some movement out by the kids' play area. The "ghost" that his kids believed in? A prowler? But there was no goddam ghost, and who would come out here to prowl around? He went out and scanned the dark back lawn, but it was empty.

Returning inside, he thought back to his fateful meeting with Member of Provincial Parliament Sterling Fox (*What kind of idiot name is Sterling Fox!*). After seemingly wanting little to do with Alex lately, Fox had suddenly invited him one day to an "important meeting" in his office. He was received like a respected and valued friend and colleague, and introduced to one Elliot Davis, a "key man in the premier's office."

After shaking hands, Davis said to him, "Alex, we think you are the right guy to help us bring an important project to this area. But first, we can only continue if I have your absolute promise of total confidentiality. And I do mean total. This project can bring huge benefits to this riding, and you will be handsomely recompensed if you agree to take on an important role in it. Now think carefully about this. Do we have that commitment from you?"

Alex didn't have to think for long. He was used to making such promises and then making sure that deals always worked out to his benefit. He had always thought Fox was really just a stuffed shirt con man, and he was used to working with con men. This guy Davis was another matter. If he really was a heavy hitter in the provincial government, that upped the ante considerably. However, Alex had grown up knowing he was always just that much more clever than the next guy, and the simple truth was he desperately had to find some way to make some big money, and soon. This could be it! Putting on his most serious and confidence-inspiring look, he said, "Sterling, Mr. Davis, you know you can count on me. You have my solemn promise of total confidentially." Handshakes with the two politicians, and then they sat down to talk particulars. Davis took the lead.

"Alex – okay if I call you Alex? – our government is working with a private concern to support a large project with significant financial benefits coming to this area. Our government has long pledged to our supporters that government needs to get out of the way of the private sector, and so we will play only a supporting role. Of course, we have to make sure that Ontario's infrastructure needs are well taken care of, and the private sector, properly supported by a sensible government, can do it best. They know how to make business work the way it should.

"Our government knows the perfect answer is public-private partnerships. To quote from our website, 'For some of the province's larger projects, Infrastructure Ontario uses a public-private partnerships delivery model. This modern approach is employed on public sector projects with a capital cost over a hundred million dollars or projects that involve significant risk and complexity.'

"So, you'll understand that I can't give you chapter and verse on a project of this scope, but we do need a local man, a proven developer like you, to quietly make sure the right package of land needed for this project is secured. If word about this leaks out prematurely, speculators will jump in, our political opponents and their paid protesters will go crazy, the whole project and its financial benefits to this area – and to you personally, I might add, Alex – will go up in smoke. Are you with me so far?"

"You've come to the right guy, Mr. Davis. Tell me more."

"Please, call me Elliott. I think we've come to the right guy, too. You will have to provide landowners with some information when you look around for the right land package, but you're a developer. People around here know you. Let them think it's another big housing development like the one you've just completed."

Inwardly, Alex blanched at this. They clearly didn't know the full story about New Eden, and the last thing he was going to do was tell them.

"If it gets out that maybe there's more involved, that the government might be involved, let rumours start that you are helping us scout out possibilities for a new provincial park. Be vague. Don't get pinned down.

"Now, once this project is done, the benefits to this region will be clear. The province is also going to benefit, in ways that don't really concern you. We can and will help with any necessary provincial approvals and will carry the ball politically once the project is operational, but your job will be done by then. The private concern we are partnering with will make sure you are very well paid, and you will have the gratitude of our government. Is that totally clear?"

Alex again gave his sincere nod yes, and said, "Perfectly, uh, Elliott," though he really had a million questions.

"Good, good. Now, though our government wants this project to come to a successful conclusion, the first part, procuring the necessary land package, does not directly involve us. That part will be the responsibility of the private concern we wish to partner with. Our government will be hands-off until our future private partners are ready to do business with us. Let me introduce you to your contact with them. He has been waiting in the adjoining room."

With that, a slim, very fit-looking, prematurely grey-haired man dressed in a dark business suit slipped into the room. He was not large, yet he subtly projected power, with even a hint of menace. The man glanced at the politicians who nodded to him, quickly looking away in a seemingly subtle deference to him. He was clearly the man in charge here. He shook hands with Alex, and in a firm, quiet voice said, "Alex, good to meet you. You can call me William. Please join me so I can share more details with you." William nodded to the two politicians, led Alex into the adjoining office, and closed the door.

"I will be your main contact in this matter, and that contact will be on a very regular basis. You will contact me via this number and email if necessary," he said, handing Alex a business card.

"I am now going to explain to you all you need to know to find the right land package for us. I will answer any questions you have and will make sure you have the support you need. You have to appreciate that my employers have very serious interest in this project, and they have engaged my services because I am good at making sure projects like this work out successfully. I am a very serious man and require that you act in a very serious manner. Is that understood, Alex?"

Alex found it more difficult to project his usual glib, confident sincerity, given the sudden tightness in his throat. His realized that his usual feeling of being the top dog had vanished. Part of him was inwardly urging him to get out now while he still could, except he wasn't really sure he could still get out, and he desperately needed the money.

"My employers identified you as the right man to assist us in this matter because you are by far the most active developer in this region, and this is the region they have identified as being ideal for their purposes. I have here the specifications for the land package you need to find for us."

Handing Alex a folder, he continued, "Read this carefully, and keep it absolutely confidential. And I mean absolutely. The package must be at least two hundred and fifty hectares, or six hundred acres if metric measurements haven't made their way here yet. There must be clear access to it from a paved and well-maintained road. It should not be in a town or village. There are various other routine criteria spelled out in the folder.

"Your task is to identify the land package and obtain a firm option to purchase it. The company I represent will ensure the package is appropriate and then authorize you to buy it. I assume you can work out the financing through your normal banking channels, but if absolutely necessary we can provide assistance. Once you have legal possession of the land you will immediately sell it to us. You don't have to know until then the name of the company I represent. You will make an immediate profit on the land flip, and once my employers have developed the land and reached their agreement with the provincial government, you will receive a further bonus payment of two hundred and fifty thousand dollars.

"The only special requirement is that there are some geological assessments that will have to be done on the land. You will need suitable documented test results available at the time of the land transfer, and indeed these will be included in the actual transaction. I will provide you with the contacts you need to get this testing done, but it must be done entirely under your name."

William had walked McKay through the geological testing requirements. He refused to give any reasons why the required information was so detailed. If necessary, Alex could explain there was a need for comprehensive testing to make sure firm footings could be established for the buildings (something Alex had ignored with New Eden, to his later regret). Also, there had to be wells drilled, utilities brought in, sewage disposal or septic systems created.

Alex asked why there was a need to get guarantees that the rock far below the surface was solid and uncompromised. Wasn't this supposed to look like just another residential subdivision?

William just gave him a cold stare, and after a pause, said, "Alex, I need you to be clear that your job is twofold: set up the necessary options to get us the land we need, and maintain total, absolute confidentiality. My employers have specific needs which are not your concern. I repeat, *not* your concern. As I said, I will provide you the contact necessary to get the geological profiles we need. You just need to be the developer of record requesting these surveys and testing. You don't need to know anything else about it. If questions arise, we have given you the secondary cover story to answer them. For a potential provincial park development, the province needs detailed geological information. If anyone pursues that further – and they won't – our friends in government will bury them in bureaucratic red tape and spin.

"However, Alex, my big worry now – and I don't like to be worried – is that you are asking questions that a man who understands his role in this matter would not ask. We contacted you because you seemed to be the only significant developer in this sleepy little backwater. When we looked into your background, it seemed to reveal a man able to be, let's say, flexible. You seemed to understand the need to make rules and regulations work for you. We were confident you were the best man to discreetly arrange for our land purchase and to understand what you have to do to make sure this works out safely for everyone. We were also confident that you would understand the necessity for confidentiality, and that you would be able to understand the unfortunate consequences that can happen if confidentiality is breached.

"My primary responsibility is the protection of my employers, and as I have already said, I take my responsibilities very seriously. I hope you are equally sure about what you need to do to ensure your own personal wellbeing as we work through this project. You are concerned about your personal wellbeing, aren't you, Alex?"

Alex felt frozen to the spot. Gathering himself, he vigorously nodded his head and said, "Yes. Yes, I am. Sorry – didn't mean to ask so much. I just want to make sure I can do my part right. You know you can count on me."

Alex didn't know the exact nature of the subtle threat he had just heard, but he knew it was in fact a threat. God, and he used to think he knew what "serious" meant. He was afraid of William, but he felt he was already in too deep to get out of this. He also dreaded what would happen to him if he didn't make this opportunity work.

Alex left the meeting first. William explained it would not be good for the two of them to be seen together, so Alex went out to the back parking lot and sat there in his car thinking things over. He had been feeling desperate for some time now, but this was a new sort of desperation. Previously, he had been desperate about bankruptcy, lawsuits, a dissolving marriage, and a dissolving life. The threat now included all that but was also more personal.

For the hundredth time he thought back to the death of his older brother. Gary had been groomed by their father to take over the family business. He was his dad's chosen heir. It was always just assumed that Alex would carry on in the business, but in some sort of non-critical role. But Gary had started into some sort of downward spiral after graduating from high school. He was still being groomed to take over the business, but he seemed to have lost the confident, driving energy that made him the logical heir. After Gary's sudden death, his dad had turned to Alex, determined to keep the business in the family.

However, Alex sensed his dad had also lost some of his essential energy after Gary's death. Alex struggled to be ready to take over, but after his father's health faltered and he turned control over to Alex, it hadn't gone well. His father soon died and then Alex had no choice. He was the president of McKay Enterprises. If only Gary had lived, and the company had continued to be successful, Alex no doubt would have had some sort of secondary job there, but with good money, real security, and none of his current desperation. If only ....

Alex was jolted from this reverie when he saw William emerge from the building. The local tow-truck guy, a miserable little prick causing too much grief to the town, was preparing to tow a white SUV. Alex remembered that his name was Harold Scrivener, and that for years he had been mixed up in various questionable activities. William strode over to Scrivener and, through his open window, Alex heard him say, "Let's handle this quietly. Will a hundred take care of it? It's all I've got in cash."

Scrivener said, "It'll take more than a hundred, bud. See you at the yard with the full amount."

With that, William glanced around the lot, and seeing only Alex there, grabbed Scrivener by the throat and effortlessly bounced his head off the SUV. Scrivener lay there moaning. William got into the tow truck, the engine still running, and expertly backed it into a vacant parking slot. He returned to his vehicle, roughly dragged Scrivener away and tossed some bills at him.

Alex heard him say, "It seems we did handle it right here, though maybe not as quietly as it could have been. Fifty bucks off for the insult, and you get the other fifty. But you made the mistake of disrespecting me. If this goes any further, if I ever see you again, the price to you goes way up. Do you think even a dumb fuck like you can understand that?"

Scrivener vigorously nodded his head, snivelling and gasping. He appeared to have wet his pants.

William gave Alex a curt little gesture to leave, which Alex promptly did. He couldn't get out of his mind how casually William had assaulted Scrivener. His eyes had been cold, dead, like he just as well could have killed the guy, but simply chose not to because it wasn't convenient.

The threat Alex felt now was even more intensely personal. For the first time ever, he feared for his life.

The next day a newly determined Alex started on the project. He worked harder than he ever had before. He soon found what seemed to be the right land package. There were four different landowners involved, but Alex was able to make them substantial offers on what to them was useless scrub land. There was a tricky access problem, but he had solved that. Using William's contact information, he authorized the geological testing.

His first real snag had occurred when he approached Mike Quinlan at the bank to get the financial guarantees he needed to secure his options on the land. "Alex, we have been doing business for a long time, and our bank worked with your father for a long time before that. It's worked out well for McKay Enterprises and for our bank, but frankly, I'm concerned, very concerned, about your current financial profile. Your debts from your New Eden project are substantial and there is the matter of your guarantees on the mortgages out there.

"Now, I like to keep local business local, but if it were just up to me, I don't see how we could advance you more credit on another speculative project. To make it worse, head office routinely audits our major transactions, and they aren't happy with me, not happy at all. The brutal truth is that if we called in your loans and various financial obligations now, there is no way you could meet them. The mortgages at New Eden are significantly higher than what head office thinks is their current real market value. We do hear about the various complaints from out there. We've even had some of your neighbours come in to see how they could sell and get out. They think, correctly, that they if they sold now, they would lose hundreds of thousands of dollars. That would trigger your mortgage guarantees. We're holding them off by telling them it's more complicated than just moving out and that they need to be patient until the real value of their investment comes through.

"But Alex, banks don't like being in a situation like this. I'm under pressure from above to call in your loans, take whatever losses we will incur, and get out of an untenable situation. You know what this would mean for you, and frankly, it's not great for me. The only way for you to hold off this pressure, and then maybe get the new financial guarantees you want, is to come up with some sort of rock-solid new financial backing, and where would you get that?"

Alex got Quinlan to give him a few days to work things out and then went to the one place where he hoped he could get the help he needed. William was clearly angry when Alex presented the matter to him. His anger was quiet and intense, and so all the more threatening. "Alex, we obviously didn't look closely enough into your business and financial dealings. Shame on us. Except, good news for you. First, you're still the best qualified person to do our local work for us, and once this matter is finished, we will never have to deal with you again. That is, as long as you keep your damned mouth shut. Second, your debts might seem large to you, but not to us. And third, we are able to satisfy the concerns of your local little bank."

And so it was that in two days Alex met again with Mike Quinlan, this time accompanied by a taciturn man identified only as Mr. Piggot, sent to him by William. As ordered by William, Alex exactly followed the script Mr. Piggot laid out to him and sat quietly as Piggot explained their offer to Quinlan.

After giving his explanation, Piggott said, "This offer reflects the great confidence we have in Mr. McKay's current project. It does, though, require absolute confidentiality from you and your bank. My experience is that banks are more than willing to provide that confidentiality as long as their interests are protected. I believe you will hear soon from your superiors that they do have that confidence, and that you and Mr. McKay can proceed, in confidence, with this current project."

In a remarkably short period of time Alex was able to secure the options on the land he had worked so hard to set up for eventual ownership by his mystery employers. He had negotiated firm, signed agreements for road access to the land package. That had presented difficulties, but Winston had actually proved quite helpful with the negotiations with the owners of the only land over which the access could be provided. Alex had followed up on the contacts William had provided to get the geological testing done. The company had been primed to do this immediately, needing only Alex's signature on the contract. Alex had been able to promptly provide William with all the details of the deal for approval by his employer. For a brief time, the pressure seemed to have been brought down to a manageable level. All he needed was the okay to proceed from William and confirmation from Quinlan that the funds necessary to purchase the land were available.

Except. What a damn word "except" was! William had called him early that Monday morning. "Alex, you are going to have to be even more careful, for two very important reasons. First, the financial support you forced us to provide for you has raised some red flags with some troublesome people. We are still able to proceed with the project, but you may be approached about how you secured the financial guarantees from those particular people.

We are constructing answers for you, but until you hear from me, stay incommunicado.

"The second concerns the geological survey results, which I know they forwarded to you. We have a copy also. They are not acceptable, so we are working on getting the reports we need. But you must destroy that first report. It is going to not exist. Destroy it now, and so thoroughly that there is no trace of it. Got it?

"Yes. Right on it."

Except. That damned word again. Except he had thought it safer to have Harry keep that damn report tucked securely away for him. Weren't chartered accountants the masters of confidentiality, offering the same sort of formal confidentiality that you have with your lawyer? Was this another in his recent string of bad decisions?

"Alex, one last but very important thing. My employers do have possibilities elsewhere for this project, though your region remains our preferred one. Except" – that word again! – "we are concerned about the issues that have been cropping up. We all must work to make sure there are no more such issues if this is to remain a viable project. Let's make sure we do that, Alex."

This led to his current predicament. Harry had become critically important because of his financial knowledge, his help with the access agreement, and now because of that damn report. Alex's concerns about Winston had been intensified by what he had heard about whatever that business had been at Friendlies Saturday night. He had planned to meet Harry and the others there, but earlier in the week Victoria had found the printout of his latest Friendlies bill, for "drinks and services." She went even more ballistic than usual. "A god-damned strip joint! A tits and ass bar! You keep saying we have no money, and you spray it around like this? Mr. Big Shot. Mr. Community Leader? What are these damned 'services'? You just stay away from me."

He couldn't tell her that Larry just created these bills to remind him of what he got in return for Alex helping him out – more a reminder than an actual invoice. Places like Friendlies sometimes had problems and needed well-placed community friends to help make problems go away. However, recently even Larry had started to look at him in a funny way.

Now that Alex thought about it, it had turned out to be lucky he hadn't been at Friendlies on Saturday. However, with these latest developments it was crucial that he meet with Harry. The guy sometimes seemed to care too much about acting the big tough guy, but he was talented, discreet, and knew Alex owned his balls. Alex trusted him as much as he trusted anyone, but now they had some things to sort out, and fast.

When he had called Harry to get his ass out there that night, he got a bullshit story about how he was so injured at that crap dust-up at Friendlies last Saturday that he was still recuperating. Also, the police had been involved. The last thing Alex needed was the police. Was it a coincidence that they were interested in his accountant, a guy who probably knew too much about Alex's business dealings? Lots of guys like him had been torpedoed by blindly overlooking so-called coincidences. At this critical stage Alex needed certainty. Most important, he needed to get back those test results he had given Harry for safe-keeping, or at least make absolutely sure they had been destroyed. He was worried about mentioning the report on the phone now that it seemed the police were nosing about. He made Harry promise to come out as soon as he could on Tuesday morning.

The other piece of good news he had received that day was that William's company had approved purchase of his optioned land package in record time. William had given him the news at 2:30 that afternoon. Alex had immediately contacted Quinlan and had been assured that the necessary financial backing had been approved. Alex had an appointment early Tuesday afternoon with the real estate lawyer he used in Lakeside. William said he would not be present but a representative from Gladstone Holdings, the company he represented, would be. The land options would be activated, giving Alex full ownership of the land. The replacement geological test results would be forwarded by courier to the lawyer's office and the land transfer to Gladstone would be completed. This would, according to William's initial description of the process, end Alex's involvement in the project. In conjunction with the financial arrangements Piggot had established with the bank, the profit Alex would receive would almost put him in the black. The promised $250,000 bonus would see him free and clear. He still had to escape from his New Eden burdens, but Alex had some ideas there. He just might survive all this.

There were only two clear problems he could see. First, getting Harry straightened out and making sure that damned initial report was destroyed. That had to be sorted out tomorrow before his meeting in Lakeside to finish the deal. Alex felt that once he sorted things out with Harry, he would have a tenuous control of things and would be able to survive.

Except for the more serious problem: whether or not he had managed to keep William satisfied, or at least satisfied enough, because William was certainly unhappy with him. Alex was still afraid of him and could only hope William would honour the assurances he had given him. Alex felt anxiety about coming to the end of this project, but when it came to William, the feeling he had was closer to dread.

Alex knew he just had to make sure this project, his last chance for redemption, worked out.

He went back to pacing in his darkened house.

CHAPTER 10
Jasper Slipsliding Away

LATE MONDAY NIGHT JASPER MCKNIGHT LAY AWAKE, STARING AT the ceiling in this unfamiliar room. Just what had gotten him here? Certainly some bad decisions. What would the Jasper McKnight of twenty-five years ago think of the current version?

Where was Jasper McKnight, churchgoer, upright member of the community, devoted family man, a man directed by a strong moral compass? He had made some questionable decisions, starting before the death of his devoted wife, Gladys. He had gradually let himself get too connected with the wrong sort of person. What would she think of him if she saw the place these decisions had now brought him to? He had always convinced himself he was trying to make things better, so why did he now find himself in situations that seemed to do the opposite? She had always been a loyal and loving partner. Why had the quietly upright life she had offered him proved to not be enough?

And now, after the fallout from the Friendlies disaster, and the whole thing with Alex McKay, an intensified moral turmoil had washed over him. He just had to get away. He had to somehow re-find himself and return to being his earlier, better self.

Just what had happened to Jasper McKnight, dedicated police officer? A cop who had made an absolute hash of this McKay investigation. His instructions from HQ had been clear enough: gather as much detail as possible about McKay's local business dealings, his close associates, and whatever he was up to in Harmony. Bring in extra help if necessary. He had looked at the transfer request list and had chosen Kirsten Petersen. On the one hand it had made sense: she had grown up in Harmony, maybe still had local connections and likely could blend in better than some urban cop who didn't understand how small towns work. However, when she had arrived, it turned out she had never maintained any local connections and was bemused by coming back to her hometown. She had become totally urbanized.

To be honest, had he really chosen her because she was a young woman he thought he could more easily control? He did have to control things concerning McKay, because he had his own connections with him. He had to find some way to satisfy HQ and still maintain equilibrium in his town.

Alex McKay was a fellow lodge member, though he always seemed to treat the lodge mostly as a place to make business connections. Was that also part of the reason why he, Jasper, had joined the lodge, to make connections? He was convinced the best way to police a small town was to be part of it, to know people, and to have connections that could help keep him on top of things. McKay had chatted him up and started to come to him for advice. This had soon become gentle lobbying for Jasper to help him get approvals and support for his various development plans. He had congratulated Jasper on being so insightful about what Harmony needed to prosper, which was smart, local men like them who could make sure the right things happened.

When Petersen had reported to him, he realized he didn't have a clear plan of how to proceed. He was used to just finding ways to keep things moving along without causing any big fuss or bother. Some might call this being too casual, but he had always realized Harmony needed consistent management and informed oversight, not intrusive interventions and unnecessary change. Petersen said she was really unknown in town. He had kept her in the office for a few days, doing whatever computer-based research she could into Alex's business dealings and keeping her out of sight. Meanwhile, he had come up with the Friendlies undercover plan.

It was brilliant, he initially thought. It would be a real investigation, wisely using his new department resource. McKay was invariably at Friendlies every weekend with his pals, and guys did talk too much in settings like that. Or so he thought, because he would never visit a place like Friendlies. If she did come up with information, she would report it directly to him and he could decide what to do with it. He had carefully told her, and the rest of his department, as little as possible about HQ's instructions to him. He could make this work.

He had met quietly with Larry Buchannan, the Friendlies owner and manager. Larry was relieved that this had nothing to do with any issues with his club. Again, this was where connections had proven to be important. Jasper initially had been appalled when township council had met to consider the Friendlies application. Buchannan wanted to transform it from an ordinary tavern to an "adult entertainment venue," as his application so quaintly called it. Alex had initially appeared to agree with Jasper about the possible effects on public morals of a place like that. But Alex had then gone to work to persuade him to withhold his objections.

"Jasper, look, this is the way of the world, and we may not like it, but we can't block this sort of thing forever. On the QT, I know some of our neighbouring towns are considering the same thing. That means Harmony would miss out on all the business and all of the economic activity. Just as important, all of the control would then be out of our hands. But if we do it here, Larry is a known quantity. I've worked with him on a few things, and I got him to share some details of his plans with me. He wants it to be a classy place. He would make sure the terms of the application would be totally honoured. To be precise, there would be a visual element, but no physical contact, no prostitution. We know that a little of that stuff goes on already in this town, so this really would just bring things more under control. The place is on the outskirts, would be self-contained, and wouldn't affect the rest of town, other than to actually make things better here.

"It would be a win-win. You could use me as the contact with Larry so you would know what's going on. You wouldn't have to have any direct contact, and it would be self-policing."

Jasper had thought carefully about this but couldn't find any fault with Alex's reasoning. He had quietly let his contacts on township council know he wasn't really happy with this application but would not object as long as council made sure it was properly set up. Alex McKay could help with that. The application was approved, and the new Friendlies was soon in operation.

He had been less than pleased when reports soon got to him that there was more than a "visual element" at Friendlies. His officers started to be called out there far too often for his liking. It also seemed Alex had become a regular customer. When he would approach Alex about all of this, the usual response would be that things would be far worse if Friendlies weren't there, and that he, Alex, had to be around to keep an eye on things and keep channels of information open. There were his not-so-subtle reminders that it was known by important people that Jasper had quietly supported the original application. Jasper realized he had become quite connected with McKay, and that McKay had an uncomfortable amount of control over him.

Buchannan had agreed to support the undercover plan but wondered what the target was. Not the club, Jasper assured him – in fact, he and the police would look kindly on this sort of cooperation.

He told Larry he couldn't say more except that they were trying to get some information. Alex McKay was never mentioned. Larry had supplied the cocktail waitress outfit and agreed to introduce Petersen to her duties, starting on a Wednesday, when things were quiet. It would establish her as part of the scene for the weekend, when it was more likely they could get the information they were after.

When Jasper had gathered his three detectives together to lay out the plan, it was met with shocked surprise. Jane had said, "Captain, there's no guarantee McKay and his pals will say anything useful. And there's no way we could record anything there. Is this really what we should be doing? And Kirsten does have history here, even if it's been a while."

"Sergeant Walden, I can't share all my instruction with you, but this is exactly the sort of thing I've been instructed to do. It won't be our only avenue of investigation. I've already had Detective Petersen start to look into things from here, with online searches and such things. I'll admit I'm not really up to speed on that sort of stuff, but I'm assured she is. You people are the ones who keep pushing me to use more up-to-date approaches, so here it is. I've brought in the perfect person to do this undercover assignment, so let's just get on with it."

Kirsten had been squirming uncomfortably in her chair. "Uh, Captain. I've never done undercover work, and I've never been a waitress, much less in a strip joint. I'm sorry, but I'm not clear on what information I'm after, or how I'm to get it. I have been away for more than ten years, but there still might be people who would recognize me. What would I say if they did?"

"Fair enough, Detective. First, I've ensured the support of the Friendlies owner and manager. He will make sure you're well set up and prepared. I understand there's a lot of staff turnover there, so a new, untrained person won't cause any suspicion. Second, I've told you in confidence the person of interest is Alexander McKay, who as you know is a prominent citizen here. I'm sure any information we get will help convince my superiors they are on the wrong track. Just listen to whatever he and his friends say and report back directly to me. Maybe ask some of the other girls what they may have heard. It's really very simple. It may lead to nothing, but we've got to try.

"As for being recognized, you were only eighteen when you left, and you look different now. A lot of people in Harmony have moved on. If you are recognized, they won't know you're a police officer. Just say you decided to come home and got the job at Friendlies. Surely an experienced police officer can make this work.

"Now, here is your outfit, and Larry Buchannan, the owner and manager, will be expecting you."

Petersen had visibly blanched when she saw the waitress outfit. "Captain, all due respect, but I'm a police officer. I can't appear in public dressed like that."

"Detective Petersen, you applied for a transfer and here you are. You were sent here to do a job, and this is it. I'm sure you want this opportunity to be a positive part of your record. You won't be 'Detective Petersen' in that outfit, and it won't be out in public. The person wearing it is a new hire at Friendlies – that's what undercover means. And you will be dressed just fine for the surroundings. Am I being clear enough?"

Petersen had sat quietly for a moment, and then, with a neutral but determined look on her face, had said, "Perfectly, Captain. Anything else?'

Jane had quietly said, "I did some minor undercover work a few years ago, Captain. I'll be able to help Detective Petersen."

And so his plan had swung into operation. Except it had turned into a fiasco, and if anything had drawn more attention to McKay. It had not gone down well with his superiors. He had invented a pretext to be out of the office on Monday. He would spend the night here and return to his duties Tuesday. He likely had some damage control to do and wasn't sure how to proceed. He had become too enmeshed in McKay's schemes, and he desperately needed some way out. He hoped Tuesday would bring some clarity to the convoluted and compromised mess his life had become.

Jasper McKnight continued to toss and turn, and eventually fell into a restless sleep.

CHAPTER 11
The Trouble with Harry

MONDAY EVENING HARRY WINSTON HAD BEEN HOME, SITTING alone, drinking and watching some crap TV show, when he got a call from a clearly upset Alex McKay. "Harry, I got to see you, right now. Can you get right out here?"

"Alex, I'm still banged up from the cops assaulting me last Saturday. It's getting late. I've had a few. Gonna have to wait till tomorrow."

After futile efforts to change Harry's mind, Alex said, "Damn it, Harry. okay, but first thing. Right? It's important."

Harry was getting more than a little tired being at the beck and call of fucking Alex McKay. He could have made it out there Monday night, but maybe he needed to start to set some boundaries. He worked with McKay, but he wasn't owned by him. Tuesday morning would be soon enough.

Harry was still smarting from the thumping he had taken at Friendlies two nights before. Smarting physically from where his shoulder had hit the wall after that crazy bitch got lucky and he had stumbled over the table. He was much bigger than her, and even though she suckered him he knew he would have won, except that other bitch cop showed up and it turned out bitch number one was also a cop. So there he was, standing, looking like an idiot, shoulder hurting like it had been dislocated even though it turned out it was just a deep bruise.

What he was really smarting from was the insult. The loss of status. He had been used to being the guy in charge ever since he had beefed up in high school and became the football team's star fullback and a guy you didn't mess with. There'd been a few snickers after graduation when he started his training to be an accountant, stereotypically a job for wimps and weaklings. Though he'd never admit it, he liked numbers even better than playing football. He was good at mathematics and business stuff. Who said accountants had to be wimpy little guys? He'd soon silenced the snickers and found that his size and reputation had even helped him get established in Harmony with his own accounting business.

Most important, he was not going to stop being the lead dog in any pack he found himself in. McKay was the official boss, but in person it was Harry people deferred to. He looked like the guy who could easily lay a beating on you, and Harry knew this was true. So, what did it do to his reputation to have this woman handle him? If he was being honest, he hadn't stumbled over the table, he had been thrown over it. His aching shoulder attested to that. Why had he flinched when she feinted that punch to his face? Had it been too long since he actually had beaten on anyone? Maybe he had to reassert himself, physically and otherwise, starting with Alex. Mr. Big Business Tycoon could wait until Tuesday morning, when it was convenient for Harry.

However, early Tuesday morning found Harry Winston on County Road 1, driving fast, significantly over the limit, hurrying to respond to Alex's frantic call. Harry had been planning to head out there after he fully woke up and had fought off his damn hangover. However, Alex called him early, reminding him to get out there immediately. Harry, struggling to wake up, had tried to cool McKay down. "Alex, come on, relax. I've had a rough coupla days. I need time to properly wake up."

"Well, let this 'properly wake you up'! The cops are nosing round. It may even have something to do with that bullshit you got into at Friendlies. I can't say any more over the phone, but I need you here right now, so move it!"

Harry Winston, self-described tough guy, had felt some twinges of real fear. Forgetting about setting any new boundaries with McKay, he instead had hurriedly dressed, gulped a coffee and some pain pills, and was soon on the road, driving fast. As he drove, he thought back over his dealings with McKay and about his current situation.

His big pal Alex! He had worked with Alex for a while now, initially only as an accountant, making sure McKay's various financial records reflected a safe legal reality. Gradually he had become more of a business advisor, and then actually began helping McKay plan out his various projects. Initially he had always urged Alex to just make it all legal. Wasn't McKay Enterprises the big development company in this hick town? Where was the competition? But Alex had won him over – small stuff at first, but eventually the type of stuff that got chartered accountants unchartered.

At some point Harry had crossed over that line between 'prudent but legal risk-taking' and actual illegality. It was minor stuff, or so Harry told himself. Making sure the taxes worked to Alex's advantage. Cleverly hiding certain payments needed to grease the wheels of business and keeping off the books certain incomes that didn't really have to be reported. Alex was persuasive and had seemed like a sharp operator.

"Harry, look. You think everybody always plays by what is advertised as 'the rules?' Whose rules? How do you think big companies got to where they are? Think the very rich don't have their own rules? Think corporations work for anything other than their financial bottom line? And government, think it's an accident that tax legislation and government programs and bullshit always seem to favour corporations and the uber-rich? Those guys own the politicians. So, we *are* playing by the rules, the real ones, where you succeed and make some real money. We're small time compared to the big boys but being small time doesn't mean we don't take care of ourselves. We're the guys out there taking risks to make sure the wheels keep turning, even in a hick town like Harmony. Why shouldn't we get our fair share?"

Harry didn't believe everything Alex said, but he didn't really argue against it either. The perks were so damned good – he was driving his latest, a new red Camaro that told the world just how important and successful old Harry Winston was. It had all been fairly easy up to now, even though he didn't ever know the full story on McKay's various schemes and enterprises. Like, he had given some financial advice to Alex about the New Eden project, advice McKay had mostly ignored. There had certainly been some problems, but the place somehow got built, and despite all the problems, McKay was still operating.

Now he had moved on to this mysterious big new scheme. It seemed different from the rest, more complicated, with more people to satisfy or keep in line. Harry didn't like it. Sure, flashy new car, nice new suits – that was great – but he really was just a small-town accountant, and he was getting more than a little apprehensive. To be more accurate, he was getting scared, especially now that the cops were nosing around, including directly and personally with him. Also, Mr. Sharp Operator Alex McKay was clearly freaking out.

Being scared made Harry's thoughts all the more jumbled and uncontrolled. It *had* been a rough couple of days. That crap at Friendlies! The place had always been pretty relaxed, and now this bitch new waitress got all upset and did her Amazon warrior routine on him. Then it turns out she was a goddam cop! Bitch! Fucking bitch! When he tried to get fucking Jasper to do something about her, to help out like he had a few times before, he suddenly got all huffy and said it was lucky Harry wasn't being charged. He said his bitch cop was just doing her job. He even threatened to have him arrested for interfering with a police investigation.

What police investigation? Friendlies had always played fast and loose with the rules but had always been left alone. Even after the Saturday fiasco it was still business as usual, so he was told, though it'd be a good long time before he went back there personally to see. Why had the cops been there? Was it somehow connected to this new scheme of McKay's? If so, this could be real trouble.

Equally important to him, he'd had enough ribbing about being beat up by a woman. So, she got lucky. Next time … though there'd probably be no next time. Fucking cop bitch! He was really just a numbers guy, not some sort of real tough guy.

Okay, okay– just try to relax. Let it blow over. But damn it, would that happen, or would it just get worse?

Another thing, he'd never seen Alex lose his cool this way. Sure, he'd been more nervous recently, more sharp with everyone, more demanding. What was the big deal about those documents Alex insisted he keep for him? "You're a chartered accountant. They can't go after things from you like they can from me. It's privileged stuff, like with a lawyer. Just put this stuff somewhere safe and secure until I figure some things out." The guy really knew how to overreact. Harry had no more power to keep documents secure from seizure than Alex did. However, it would be best to calm him down, keep him happy. Though Alex sure wouldn't be happy if he knew his precious documents were right now sitting in a blue vinyl case in the trunk of Harry's car.

As he turned on to New Eden Road, Harry saw a jogger coming toward him. He knew he should slow down given the dust and flying stones this damned gravel road churned up. Alex couldn't even get his damned road paved! But Harry hated joggers. Self-righteous health nuts who thought they were so damned special! Instead, Harry sped up and made sure he passed close to the jogger.

Soon Harry pulled into the drive at Alex's pretentious digs at New Eden (*What a damn stupid name! But Alex claimed he knew all about branding and promotion. Sure didn't seem to be working for him now*!). It was as quiet as it usually was out there. Some old guy out fishing on the lake and a few kids playing in their yards. A woman working on a large garden. Some official-looking van at the third house, and a white SUV parked off to the side further down.

Alex pulled him into the house. No-one else was home.

"I can't give you a lot of detail, Harry, but a few things have popped up. Nothing we can't handle, but like I said, the local cops are nosing around. I'm not really worried about that. Jasper McKnight and I understand each other, and he's always been sensible about things, but we do have to be careful and keep our mouths shut."

Harry thought, *Best not to tell Alex about Jasper's new change in attitude. I need to calm Alex down, not wind him up.*

Alex carried on. "This deal is just about completed. I recently heard from Mike Quinlan at the bank that the money is in order, so we're close to closing the deal. But, the big thing, the reason I had to talk to you directly … have you got those documents I gave you to keep in a safe place? Because you're going to get rid of them. I may be under surveillance, so this one is up to you, and it has to happen right now. I've got the replacement documents we need. The ones I gave you have got to go."

Alex often talked too fast, but he was almost ranting now. Exactly what were these mysterious replacement documents, Harry wondered. Replacement for what, exactly? And who was the "we?" Him and Alex? Alex and this unidentified company he was working with? Harry's professional training had taught him to be careful, to always be careful, to be the most careful guy around. However, there was nothing careful about Alex's new shit show. He had to quiet Alex down and get things taken care of.

"Don't worry, I've got them. You know I always take care of things. But frankly, Alex, you're looking pretty shook. Is there anything else I should be worried about?"

Alex glared at him. "If you want to keep being an accountant and want to stay a free man, you have lots to worry about. But destroy the documents, we're okay. You go get them right now. Burn them, flush them, no trace. Got me? Now! Go right now! Watch for the cops. Call me when the job's done."

Harry hurried out to his car and started back down toward the main road. Alex's anxiety was contagious. *How much shit can a guy take?* Harry thought. *I'll get rid of these damn documents and then get Mr. Alex McKay and his big schemes out of my life. I'll miss the extra dough, but I've got my business and got my health, aside from this damn shoulder. If I just get out, I'll be okay. If I stay with Mr. Idiot Big Shot, who the hell knows?*

Harry's anxiety jumped up several notches when he saw an unmarked police car coming toward him on New Eden Road. Was that the bitch behind the wheel, and the other bitch beside her? He started to hyperventilate, panic flooding through his body. Damn it damn it damn it! Had they seen him? Were they turning around to come after him? He couldn't tell in all this damn dust. And what if they searched his damn car and found Alex's damn documents? Alex might think he was some sort of big-time operator, but Harry doubted that and knew he, Harry, was just a small-town accountant. He couldn't cope with the shit show his shitty life had become. What a fucking nightmare! He had to dump the documents somewhere right now! He could come back later and dispose of them properly!

He wheeled on to the main road, barely slowing down. He skidded to a stop on the bridge over Silent Lake Creek, leapt out, and grabbed the blue case out of the trunk. He tossed it into the stream where it would sink out of sight and stay hidden until he could get back to retrieve it. He couldn't see the police car yet. Luckily there was no-one around this godforsaken place. This could work. It had to. He jumped back into the Camaro (*Why did I have to buy such a conspicuous car?* he thought) and drove away, at a safer speed now. There were no cars in his rear-view mirror. *Calm down,* he said to himself over and over. *It's fine. It's going to be fine.*

But Harry Winston didn't see the jogger back in the dust running toward him, waving his arms, futilely shouting. And he didn't see the blue case, surprisingly buoyant, floating gently toward the swampy area between the road and Silent Lake.

Harry drove back to town and called Alex to tell him everything was okay. Alex still sounded shook. "Great. That's great. Just keep your mouth shut and we'll be okay." As usual, no thanks, no regard for Harry. Did the prick have any idea of how much Harry Winston had done for him? He waited a short while and then headed back out in his dusty red Camaro to get the blue case and properly dispose of it.

Harry didn't know he wouldn't be returning.

CHAPTER 12
Percy Runs into Trouble

PERCY LEWIS WAS CRUISING ALONG JUST NICELY. HE CHECKED HIS runner's watch and saw that both his pace and heart rate were right where they should be. He thought again of what the old Perce Lewis, the fat Perce Lewis of two years ago, would be doing right now, five kilometres in to a fifteen-kilometre training run. He likely would be hooked up to electrodes in the ER, or worse. Percy was proud of his sleek, tough new runner's body. Now, when he was on the morning TV in-school news program at his school he always managed to turn a little sideways. Let people check out the new bod! One hundred and fifty pounds. Size thirty-two pants. Why hide it? He usually managed to sneak in some mention of his own progress when he wrote up the announcements for the cross country and long-distance track teams. It was always the truth, wasn't it?

Now, here at the beginning of summer 2017, his training was still on the upsurge. 2014: overweight couch potato struggling to run a kilometre. Once he got to two kilometres, it started to get easier. Buy the right shoes. Subscribe to *Runner's World*. Start a runner's log. Spring 2015, his first 10 K road race. Forty-six minutes. Not great, but the time of a real runner. A few more 10 Ks. Time down to forty-two minutes. Start a marathon training program. Too soon? Real runners ran marathons, damn it! So, train with the school runners, now that he was one of the coaches. Intervals. Hill training. Fartlek runs. How the wiseacres in the staff room chortled when he told them he had been doing fartleks – not that he spent much time in the staff lounge anymore. He was a jock now, and mostly hung out at the Phys Ed office.

Fall of 2016: overcame gut cramps and soreness to become the first guy in his family to do a marathon. His time of 3:54 would have been a lot better without those painful cramps, but he finished the damn thing. Once he got over some minor tendonitis, he might try another one, but for now, easier training for a while. Serious stretching, regular massage therapy. Recover fully, and after he turned forty next year, could he make the Boston qualifying time? He was not a born athlete, but he had found the right sport, one requiring his kind of hard work and dedication more than actual athletic prowess.

He saw a red Camaro coming fast from town. Barely slowing down, it slid around the corner and headed toward him. Most drivers slowed down when they passed him on New Eden Road, but not this jerk. He even seemed to purposely pass him as closely as he could. Idiot! Covering his nose and mouth with his t-shirt, Percy turned on to County Road 1, leading toward Harmony.

Settling back to a comfortable pace, his thoughts returned to the new life he was creating for himself. Some issues remained. Like keeping his wife happy! Real problem there. However, finding their new place out here had been a masterstroke. Wendy was a gardener and had always wanted more room to plant stuff, especially vegetables and berries. When Alex McKay, his second cousin on his mother's side, found they were thinking of a new place, he wouldn't let up about New Eden. Big new development. Exclusive. Could give Percy and Wendy his special family rate, which kept coming down. His teacher's salary was pretty good, especially compared to most salaries around Harmony. Wendy pulled in some income with her various little enterprises. He had a benefit plan, a good pension for the future, and real job security. The finances started to look possible. Alex found lots of ways to persuade them: "Great place to raise a family." "Safe, private." "No traffic." And then, "What a great place to do your running. Most runners would kill to be able to train out here."

However, Alex had discovered the winning argument when he found out about Wendy's gardening and her attempts to market her produce, jam, pickles, and such. "Why, I can promise you the place in the middle of the development, where there's lots of sunlight. It has a gentle slope to the lake. I could make sure you got a little extra topsoil." He promised to share his marketing expertise with Wendy and help her make a real success of her little hobby. "What do you think McKay Enterprises is all about? Let me help *you* be enterprising."

It was Percy who found the clincher for Wendy. After all, he was a business teacher, and he knew something about making a business venture work. He had the graphics guys at school mock up the label for Wendy's new business: bright and colourful, images of pickles and jams, vegetables and produce, and in the middle, his masterstroke: "From the Garden of (new) Eden."

They had sold the old place and got a mortgage to buy the new one, though it was a bit strange that the bank insisted it had to be guaranteed by McKay Enterprises. He knew some financial stuff, and that wasn't how it usually worked. Alex explained it was a special deal he had set up with the bank to guarantee a good mortgage rate. At any rate, they were in. The extra topsoil was delivered, though his neighbours seemed a bit unhappy about that. They had moved just in time for the new growing season, and Wendy was as happy as he had ever seen her. He had to buy her that expensive new rototiller, but he had to admit her new garden was pretty impressive. He sort of resented it when he had to help out – he was a runner, not a gardener! He needed to keep his training up! However, he was smart enough to keep that thought to himself. He had years of practice doing that. Also, Wendy did most of the work. All in all, everything was going as planned.

Except. Except for the problems with the house, with all the houses. Alex always had an answer.

"Cracks in the walls and basement? Show me new houses that don't have a few. Just part of the normal settling process."

"Basement leaks? It's been an abnormally wet spring. I'll have my guys check your drainage."

"Curling shingles and fading vinyl siding? Got my legal guys going after the manufacturers. It may take a while, but we'll get them to fix it."

On and on it went. Alex was managing to avoid an open revolt at the development, but really, what options did they have? They'd all bought these places with open eyes – well, maybe not open enough. The neighbourhood meetings were getting rancorous, with grumbling about getting the township building inspectors under the gun or going for a class-action lawsuit. Now their homes were to be tested for some type of gas! The last two places had just been sold, but there were already two houses with new "For Sale" signs on them.

Damn! And he'd been really careful, had just used his business experience to seize a good deal when he saw one. Wendy wasn't too happy about the house, so he kept reminding her about her great garden and how her sales were going to get them some real money. He managed to imply that it was her garden that was the real reason they'd moved here. Darn it but married life could get complicated!

Enough of obsessing about all that. Here he was, on a really nice day, out in the country, working hard to get himself to Boston. By this time, he had reached his midpoint goal and had turned back home. As he approached New Eden Road he moved to the side when he was passed by what seemed to be an unmarked police vehicle, driven by that new female detective who had recently joined the local provincial force. Man, she sure made a splashy debut with that stuff at Friendlies last week.

Friendlies! Percy remembered how uneasy he felt when his new jock pals at school had insisted he join them there one night a few months ago. He liked to think he was a pretty flexible guy, but man, was that intimidating. All those pretty women, and all that pressure to join one of them back in the private area. "What's wrong, Perce? Wife own your balls?" But no way could he ever explain this to Wendy if word got out. And they were teachers, darn it. What if they were recognized? He'd managed to get through that night and ducked their follow-up invitations until they stopped asking.

The police car turned up toward New Eden. To let all the dust now hanging over the road settle, Percy continued on down the main road. Alex had promised that getting the access road paved was a top priority with the township, but it was still seven kilometres of dusty gravel. He soon turned back, in time to see that same red sports car come tearing down the New Eden Road and swerve onto the county road about two hundred metres in front of him, a large new dust cloud now swirling up behind it. The guy gunned past the road to the reserve and then skidded to a stop on the bridge over Silent Lake Creek. Percy could just make out through the dust cloud that the guy had leapt out of his car and was getting something out of his trunk.

Was this guy going to be the latest idiot to throw garbage into the creek? That was something he and Wendy firmly agreed on – you don't litter, you don't just dump your darn garbage anywhere! Percy tried to sprint, to stop this idiot or at least get a license plate number. He waved his arms and shouted at him, but had to be careful not to aggravate his tendonitis. The guy drove off, fast, and Percy had to slow down until he reached the bridge. He looked over the edge and saw a small blue case of some sort floating toward the swamp, too far away for him to reach.

This guy was going to pay! Percy decided to file a police report. How many red sports cars were there around here? He couldn't give much of a description of the guy, other than he was a big, blonde guy wearing a suit. Percy turned back toward home, getting the details straight in his head.

He had to rest up before today's bike training. Boston was still the goal, but he could swim pretty well, and there were some shorter iron man triathlons coming up soon in the area. The bike training and swimming would let him keep up the intensity while giving his tendonitis a rest. The swimming had been tough. The lake had some weeds, which made it tough to get into a good stroke rhythm. He remembered when he had swum past the old guy out fishing in his boat. Weeds could be good for fishing, he had recalled. He noted that though the fisherman kept his head turned down, he wasn't all that old – he just looked that way slouched down in the boat.

Back to current realities. Maybe he would bike into town to make his report.

Percy Lewis jogged back to his home, thinking how important it was to be a good citizen. He had no idea just how important today's events would prove to be.

CHAPTER 13
Harry's Last Stand

KIRSTEN WAS STILL A LITTLE BLURRY EYED WHEN SHE ARRIVED AT the office Tuesday morning. She had enjoyed the previous evening's sharing session with Jane, both for the opportunity to put some long-ignored thoughts and memories together and for the obvious interest Jane had shown. Since leaving Harmony over ten years ago, she did sometimes think back to her formative years there, but her post-Harmony life had really centred on what she thought of as a personal rebirth. University, the decision to enter policing, her early training, her two postings down south, some new friendships, some romantic involvements, especially with Tim, the exciting early stages of her career – all this, not memories of her often-painful past, had been the core focus of the new Kirsten. She realized she had almost deliberately avoided thinking back to the often confused, often unhappy girl she had been growing up in Harmony (*actually, in DIS-Harmony*, she ruefully thought). She had found the life of the new Kirsten much more interesting and satisfying.

When she had received this out-of-the-blue posting back to her old hometown, she had originally been bemused. She saw it as nothing more than a temporary new placement, a waystation in the life of Kirsten Petersen, career woman. However, being back here had stirred up many memories, bringing them back with a surprising vividness and clarity. She was starting to realize that key aspects of the so-called new Kirsten were firmly rooted in the old Harmony-Kirsten. She had originally surprised herself when she had committed to a policing career, but now was discovering that the roots to that decision went way back.

She was also surprised at how quickly she and Jane were becoming good friends. Jane had been good to her from the moment she had arrived here. She was an integral part of what was a pretty sleepy little police department, but she also was sensitive to what Kirsten was experiencing as a newcomer to it.

Kirsten had almost panicked when McKnight had laid out the strange undercover assignment he had dreamed up for her. McKnight seemed to be working under close instructions from his superiors, so there really was no way she, the new transferee, could refuse the assignment. She was still relatively new in her police career and had some strong ambitions for it. She couldn't just outright refuse to do it, and even a lacklustre commitment to this plan would look bad in her personnel file and could create the very real risk of permanently stalling her career.

Jane had taken her under her wing, had run interference with McKnight, and had made sure the operation was as well-planned as possible. She made sure to be there personally at Friendlies to see Kirsten through it. Kirsten knew that even a determined and independently minded woman like her needed allies and friends, but she had never experienced the acute reality of this need more dramatically than she was now.

There was also something else at work here. Jane was a generation older than her but had also experienced what it was like growing up as a woman in this area. She had chosen not to leave it. She was comfortable living here, had a stable personal relationship, and was very much a part of this community. Jane was certainly aware of the limitations of working under Jasper McKnight, but also had adjusted to it. She was a bright and accomplished woman but had not felt personally challenged and hurt by growing up in this area in the ways that Kirsten had. This made Kirsten wonder whether her early frustrations, confusion, and pain were primarily the fault of what Harmony was, or rather also partly because of who Kirsten was. Would growing up elsewhere have been all that much different for her?

Surprisingly, Kirsten was finding being able to talk to a friend like Jane, a smart woman, a patient and non-judgmental listener, someone whose life was rooted in this area, was opening some important insights for her.

Since Jane was in the meeting about the parking lot business, Kirsten settled in and caught up on some of her paperwork. Before long Jane joined her. They each had a coffee while Jane updated Kirsten on that case. "We have Scrivener dead to rights, and your weasley little pal is going to pay for at least part of what he did, but not really enough. The interesting thing is the criminal involvement of some of the township councillors and a few others. We really have been asleep at the switch there. McKay is far from the only shady operator in our little Peyton Place. Speaking of McKay, shall we go scope him out in his home setting?"

They set out for New Eden in an unmarked cruiser, Kirsten driving, as she was the one marginally more awake. They further discussed how the investigation might intensify now that McKay had been granted his necessary financial approvals.

Not far from Harmony, Jane pointed out that they were now passing the Wyandot First Nations Reserve on their left. Kirsten remembered that there had been some Wyandot Reserve kids at her school, but that they generally kept a low profile. With a twinge of guilt, she realized she had so often been wrapped up in her own issues that she had not really paid much attention to her fellow students. The fact that she had prided herself on being a good student journalist made this oversight even worse.

"I never got to know much about them while I was growing up here. I wish I had," she said to Jane. "How about you?

Jane said, "At first, no. But I did get to know some of them after a while and made some good friends. It's helped me now, being a cop. Too many people around here cling to their outdated views of Indigenous people. I still hear the odd 'damned Indians!' being said around town. Jasper doesn't help. He tries to be fair to them, in his stunted little way, but he mostly seems to think of them as outsiders of some sort. If he had any sense of irony, he would realize how idiotic that is. But that's our Jasper. Reality is, they cause little trouble, though when one of them does, the town rednecks seize on it. Truth is, I like them and try to make sure they get a fair shake. I just wish that happened all by itself."

They passed the road leading into the reserve and almost immediately came to the New Eden Road. They saw a jogger up ahead, first starting to turn on to the access road, and then veering back to stay on the county road, likely because of the dust cloud quickly approaching the intersection. Shortly after they turned on to the road, they saw the oncoming vehicle was a speeding red sports car.

As it sped by them, Kirsten said, "Isn't that my good pal from Friendlies driving? If we weren't on more important business, I wouldn't mind giving that jerk some more grief in the form of a speeding ticket."

Jane replied, "That's him, all right. I forgot to fill you in. I knew I recognized him from somewhere, and that somewhere is a couple of visits to our esteemed captain a while back. One of the uniforms told me he was even in talking with Jasper Monday morning. The conversation seemed to centre on doing something about the Friendlies dust-up.

"I decided to do a little digging while I was sitting around on Sid's balcony during a break in my big parking lot investigation. It seems he's one Harry Winston – chartered accountant, believe it or not – and, interestingly enough, a known business associate of one Alexander McKay. I wonder if that's where he's coming from.

"No record, but the uniforms told me he's a real jerk. He likes to think of himself as a big operator. There have been a few complaints, mostly from women, but nothing that went anywhere. He sounds like McKay's kind of guy. I think we, or rather you, have made a dangerous enemy. He really scoped you out when he passed us. We need to keep an eye on him."

Jane paused for a moment. "Look, you've told me about the deep background to this whole McKay affair. Nothing like this has ever come to Harmony. I've never seen McKnight acting like he has been recently. I mean, he always has been a challenge, but he supports his officers."

Jane's words came tumbling out of her. "I know we talked about this a bit, but I've been thinking about it some more. He actually withheld key information from us before the Friendlies undercover. He put us at risk. And that strange little phone picture thing. And his absence yesterday, when he lied about being away at meetings. I mean, he's always around, often getting in the way, but he's almost never away from the office. And he hasn't shown up yet this morning. Why is he meeting with a guy like Winston? And when you get down to it, why are he and McKay on such good terms? What about that business around Handstrom's drowning? Was that ridiculous undercover thing at Friendlies some sort of way to protect McKay from a real investigation?" She paused to take a deep breath. "Sorry, I'm feeling pretty unsettled about this whole thing."

Kirsten replied, "So both the new kid on the block and the old pro – sorry, experienced pro – have some big questions. You know this whole assignment has me pretty upset. There's too much that just doesn't seem to fit together. We're almost at New Eden. Let's nose around and see what we find out and compare notes later. There might be more from my financial crimes friend, Tim. Also, I've been wondering if we should bring Jeff into this. Jasper seems to ignore Jeff, but he is our colleague, and he's been helpful. He must have some questions about all this stuff going on, and frankly I like the idea of having as many allies as possible."

Jane said, "Yes, we may have to talk to Jeff. He's been here for a while. He's a quiet guy but seems to be fully on to Jasper. I do tend to trust him. He was good about that picture stuff. Let me think about it. And you're right – we've got some work to do here at New Eden. How should we handle this?"

Since they left the county road, they had been driving through a landscape dominated by evergreen trees, some smaller deciduous trees, and scrubby brush-land. At times they descended into small hollows where to their right they could see fingers of the marshland surrounding Silent Creek. They caught the odd glimpse of the creek itself. When they entered the cleared area that held New Eden, they saw a row of twelve houses, separated from each other by rows of evergreens and small bushes. The houses all fronted on Silent Lake, with garages and rear entrances visible from the road. The houses were surrounded by patchy lawns leading down to the waterfront. They were quite large, of similar design, and mostly vinyl-covered with some brick and stonework sections.

Kirsten had not been to this area since her encounter some fifteen years before with what the locals still insisted on calling the "phantom flasher." He had not reappeared since then but had become part of the local folklore. She thought she could see the area where the infamous berry bushes had been, but it was hard to tell in such an altered landscape. The lake itself appeared larger than she remembered, likely because it was now much more visible. It was about eight hundred acres in size. On the other side, she could see the small house and outbuildings that she remembered being there. They were seemingly unchanged in appearance.

Jane said, "McKay's house is the second one in, so let's start at the far end to see what we can find out before we tackle him. Let's stick with cover story but see if anyone will open up about McKay."

They drove slowly past the houses, taking in as much detail as possible. They noted what appeared to be a service van at the third house in. A bit further along they saw a white SUV parked off the side of the road under some trees. After they passed it, the SUV pulled out and headed back toward the county road.

Jane said, "Not to stoke your paranoia, but that is the same SUV, same license number, as the one involved in the parking lot business with your pal Scrivener."

Kirsten replied, "I'm not sure it's paranoia when there does seem to be some serious outside interest in whatever McKay's up to. With the tinted glass I couldn't make out the driver, but it must be our mysterious stranger who handled Scrivener so easily. So why was he lurking there, in view of McKay's house? Maybe they're actually not working together. We need to see if we can find out more about this guy."

"Agreed, though I've got nothing but dead ends so far. Our little visit here is paying off already."

They carried on down the road. The end house had a "For Sale" sign on it and appeared to be empty. At the second-last house they were met by an older woman sitting reading on a deck chair at the front of the house. She introduced herself as Betty Collins.

"I can't really help you about this so-called rash of small thefts. Our children are grown and gone, so no kids' toys to steal – if that's what actually happened."

"You sound like you have some doubts."

"Well, kids lose things all the time. If someone were going to steal stuff, wouldn't it be something more valuable? Visitors here stick out like a sore thumb. There's only the one road in. What thief would be stupid enough to take the risk? I think it's more likely that McKay is stirring up people about all that, and about this mysterious ghost some kids have reported seeing, to deflect attention from the real concerns out here."

"What concerns would they be?"

"Don't get me started. I do like the quiet setting out here. My husband, Jack, and I bought it as our retirement home, though I really wanted something more modest and easier to take care of. But my husband knows McKay. He worked for years for Mr. McKay senior, and also for Alex until Jack got too upset about the way he was running things and so retired. Alex gave him a big song and dance about appreciating Jack's long years of good service with McKay enterprises, about how he could let him in early at a reduced price for company loyalty.

"We came out here for a look-around shortly after the land was cleared, and I did love the setting. Alex promised we would have a range of choices for the house design, and he described all the features they would be providing for the development. But Jack had to grab the offer immediately! So, my poor loyal old husband hectored me in to signing on. It turned out the house choices were all pretty similar. 'The only way I can give you a great house at a reasonable price,' Alex said. The amenities: the paved access road and driveways, the covered picnic area, the fibre cable for internet access, the new tower for cell-phone access – we're still waiting! And now we get word that our basements have to be tested for something. That's why the van is down at the Murchison's place."

"What about this mysterious ghost"?

"No adults have seen anything like that. The kids' accounts vary. Kids make stuff up. I can see why McKay welcomes having someone else to blame for things, even if the someone else doesn't really exist."

Thanking Mrs. Collins, Jane and Kirsten moved on to the next two houses, where they encountered two mothers supervising a number of children out playing. Both reported much the same litany of complaints about New Eden and the way McKay had dealt with them. Added to the complaints were various new issues with the houses, and with topsoil that didn't seem capable of supporting good lawns. "I think the bugger secretly sold the original topsoil and replaced it with crap," said one of them.

At the middle house they met a woman out tending a large garden. Identifying herself as Wendy Lewis, she explained her small business, making and selling various jams, pickles, and preserves. She proudly showed them a jar bearing her "From the Garden of (New) Eden" label. She could provide no real information about the thefts, other than being quite sure things actually were being taken, maybe by other kids.

Kirsten said, "You've really established a going concern here. Some of your neighbours don't seem too happy about living in New Eden."

Wendy replied, "There are some problems with the house, I must admit, but I love my garden. It's on a south slope, so the sunlight's pretty good. Alex did provide the extra topsoil he promised for my garden." *And I know where he got it*, Kirsten thought. She too had seen no "ghost," and also discounted the stories as being the result of kids' overactive imaginations.

"Alex helped me with the marketing of my products, and so did my husband, Percy. He's a business teacher at Wyandot Secondary School. He did most of the negotiations with Alex that got us out here. Oh, and here's my husband now."

Jane and Kirsten saw a thin, rather nondescript man dressed in running shoes, shorts, and a singlet emerge from the house. After they introduced themselves to him, he said, "My god, how did you get here so fast? I just phoned in the report."

Jane said, "I'm not sure what report you mean, Mr. Lewis. We're following up on the thefts out here."

Lewis said, "Oh. Well, I hope there will be follow-up on my report. Littering is as important as small thefts. We didn't spend all this money to move out to the country just to have the landscape despoiled by thoughtless idiots. Let me explain. I was out running, just getting back, when I saw a guy in a red sports car driving down the road like a maniac. He stopped and threw stuff off the bridge into Silent Creek. I wasn't able to catch up to him. By the time I got to the bridge the only garbage I could see was a blue bag floating off in the swamp, too far away to reach. When I got back here, I phoned in to report it, though the person I was talking to didn't seem too interested."

Kirsten said, "A red sports car, you said, and just a short time ago? Have you seen this car before?"

"He almost forced me off the road when I was starting out on my run. I saw a car like it at Alex McKay's once. I don't know much about cars. That's all I can tell you. I've got to go out on my bike-training run. I'm training for a triathlon, you know, my first one, but I'm expecting to do really well. Great area for serious training out here."

Jane and Kirsten thanked the Lewises for their time, wished Percy good luck in his big race, and promised to see about some follow-up to the littering complaint.

As they moved toward the next house, where the service van was now parked, they briefly discussed Lewis's littering complaint. Jane said, "If the McKay enquiry goes nowhere, at least we might be able to get a littering conviction. It'll help Jasper's monthly arrest report."

Kirsten said, "Strange all the same that this guy is hightailing it down the road at one point, and then stopping to pitch garbage into the creek. Why now, and why out here? There's too much hard-to-explain stuff going on."

They knocked on the door and were met by a clearly very upset woman, who identified herself as Helen Murchison. "I talked to the other cops about this theft crap. I've got nothing more to say about that, but I want to file a complaint against that miserable prick McKay for this latest disaster. He can't get away with this."

Jane said, "Mrs. Murchison, I can see you're really upset, but you need to calm down and tell us what's going on here."

Mrs. Murchison took several deep breaths and invited them into her house. "While I'm trying to calm down, you go talk with the guys in the basement. They can tell you what's happening."

Jane and Kirsten went down to the basement where two technicians were doing some form of testing. After they had identified themselves, one of the technicians, George Toomby by name, said, "We don't really need the police out here, though the homeowner seems ready to kill us. Shoot the messenger! We were sent out here by the Department of Health to follow-up on complaints by some of the people living out here about strange odours and various physical symptoms. We're just about done testing and will send in our report after we've tested all the houses. That's all I can tell you."

Kirsten replied, "I appreciate your need for confidentiality, but we are out here on a serious investigation, which may be affected by what you're doing. We'll try not to take any direct action until your report becomes official, but it would really help if you gave us some idea of what's going on."

Toomby said, "As long as you keep it to yourself, though I think there's going to be quick follow-up to what we are finding. And I do sympathize with these homeowners and the mess they're in. We are finding serious levels of various marsh gases and radon. The radon is naturally occurring but can build up in enclosed spaces like basements and cause some real problems, like long-term cancer risks. The marsh gases can be pretty toxic, especially at the levels we're finding out here. It's pretty serious. Someone didn't do the proper testing before building out here."

Jane said, "Surely there's some remedy? Wouldn't their house insurance help?"

"The remedies are expensive and need to be permanent and on-going. This is a chronic situation. With these levels it may not be possible to make these houses habitable. This is really confidential, but last time we found levels anything like this, the health department had to condemn the house. As for insurance help, likely not. Sometimes the only remedy is a lawsuit against the builder, or whoever gave the approvals, but that's way outside of what I do; I just do the testing. I've got to say, I really feel sorry for the lady upstairs. I'd be spitting mad too."

Jane and Kirsten rejoined Mrs. Murchison in her kitchen. She said, "These guys wouldn't give me much information, just that it's serious and I may have to make arrangements for alternate accommodation while things are being dealt with." She held her face in her hands, took several deep breaths, and continued on in a tight, shaky voice. "We had to stretch our finances to move out here. We trusted that damn snake McKay, mostly because my husband has a small transportation company that does business with McKay, if you can call waiting months to be paid doing business. He pressured us, and we were stupid enough to give in. If we have to move out, for how long? Who's going to pay? Will we ever be able to move back? Does McKay's damn insurance policy for New Eden cover us? It would ruin us if we lose this place, and I just don't know what to do. Can't you charge the bastard?"

Jane quietly said, "Mrs. Murchison, we're deeply sorry for your problems, but at this stage it's not a police matter. You would do well to seek legal advice, perhaps together with some of your neighbours. You're understandably very upset. Is there someone I can call to come be with you?"

"I've got a good friend coming out. I'm sorry to be like this, and thanks for your kindness. I didn't mean to take it out on you and those poor guys downstairs. But please, please do see if there's any way you can help us."

Kirsten and Jane left, moving past the seemingly deserted third house and pulling into the driveway of Alexander McKay's house.

After a delay of several seconds, McKay answered the door and grudgingly let them in to his otherwise empty house. "So, officers, to what do I owe the pleasure of this little visit?"

Jane explained about their follow-up to the theft reports and asked if he could provide any further information.

"So, two detectives have come out here after the uniformed cops already investigated some possible very minor thefts. It might help if you told me what really brings you out here."

Kirsten replied, "In fact, Captain McKnight *did* send us out here to investigate the thefts. Your neighbours talked to us about that, but frankly wanted to talk about a lot of other matters too, whether or not they are connected to the thefts."

"Let me guess. Unhappy with the houses, with the unpaved road, with a ton of other shit. Well, they got a great deal on good houses. They should be grateful to me. All houses have problems. They got more than what they paid for, at reduced prices, I might add."

Jane said, "We just talked to the guys doing the testing for the health department. It looks like it might be pretty serious."

"If those guys are spreading rumours, I'll get my lawyer on them. There's no report been issued by the health department, or anyone else. Period! Anything else?"

Kirsten said, "I'm interested in some of the visitors you get out here, in such a remote place, like the guy in the white SUV who drove off when we arrived."

McKay looked startled by Kirsten's question. "I don't know anything about a white SUV. People come out here. It's a nice place. Anything else?"

Kirsten said, "Coming in here we passed a red sports car driving in a dangerous manner. We're concerned about dangerous driving. Can you shed any light on that?"

"Let's stop the games. You know it was Harry Winston, and, yes, he was visiting me. He is my accountant, and we had some routine business matters to discuss. In the interest of full disclosure, I also know you're the cop who chose to assault him last Saturday. If you're out here trying to dig up stuff about Harry, you're out of luck."

"No, we have no further interest in Mr. Winston, though it seems he is also a litterbug."

"Now you are being just plain stupid. What the hell are you talking about?"

"We got a citizen's complaint that your Mr. Winston threw something into Silent Creek after he left here. He takes care of your garbage, does he, Mr. McKay?"

McKay suddenly looked quite startled and stood quietly for a moment. Then, shaking his head, he said, "I have nothing more to say about anything. Any more harassment like this and I talk to my lawyer, or maybe your boss, who is clearly ten times more sensible than you two b …, uh, officers. I've got an important meeting in Lakeside I need to prepare for, so you're going to have to leave."

Jane said, "Thank you for your time, Mr. McKay. I'm sure we will be talking again, and in the meantime, good luck with your little problems out here."

As the two women were about to get into their cruiser, Percy Lewis brought his bicycle to a screeching halt behind them. "I'm glad you're still here. I can save you some time. I was just finishing my training ride and coming back here when I saw that same red car stopped beside the bridge over Silent Creek. No sign of the driver, though. No response when I sounded my air horn."

Kirsten said, "Air horn?"

"It's something I just installed on my bike, a battery-powered version that sounds just like a real air horn. I got tired of cars passing too close, or people not getting out of my way, or animals wandering out on the road. Sound this little baby and they think a sixteen-wheeler is bearing down on them. It sort of evens the odds."

Jane said, "You need to be careful with that, Mr. Lewis, but thanks for the tip. We'll check it out."

The two officers left and drove back down the access road.

Kirsten said, "McKay sure leads a complicated and messy life. Maybe our visit will spur him in to making some mistakes. He looked shook when we mentioned the white SUV, and also when we mentioned Winston's little littering problem. It truly is turning out to be a useful morning. Let's hope we can get more out of Winston. Like, why did he come back out here? Sudden guilt about tossing his garbage? He doesn't seem the type to suddenly become Mr. Concerned Citizen."

By this time, they had reached the county road. As Jane turned on to it, she said, "There's his car, just like Lewis said." She parked behind the red Camaro, and they got out and approached the bridge. It had concrete walls which blocked the view of the creek from the road. When they looked over the edge, they saw what Percy Lewis could not see as he biked past. Sprawled out on the edge of the creek was the body of a large man, face down, arms widespread, with a large bloodstain still growing around his blond head.

CHAPTER 14
The Scene of the Crime

FOR A BRIEF MOMENT THE TWO WOMEN STARED DOWN AT THE BODY, and then they quickly moved into action.

Jane said, "He looks obviously dead, but I'll go down and check."

"While I call in the cavalry."

Indicating with a look toward the nearby Wyandot Reserve, Jane said, "Better if you drop that little phrase."

Reddening slightly, Kirsten said, "Right. I'll radio in and get some uniforms out here."

Jane said, "Jeff is our best-trained scene-of-crime officer, so see if he's in. And the captain, I suppose. Tell them to bring lots of crime scene tape and get them to close this road five hundred metres from here, both directions. And no damned media. Oh, and see if you can alert our new coroner. She works out of the county offices in Lakeside."

Kirsten ran back to the cruiser and made the calls. Jane walked around the edge of the bridge wall and scrambled down the slope. She quickly ascertained that he indeed was dead, and carefully moved away from the body. Kirsten soon joined her.

"I brought the camera. It's best we take some pictures. I haven't been at many of these. I'm trying to remember the official checklist."

Jane said, "Right. Snap away, carefully. We don't get many crime scenes like this around here, so we're preserving the crime scene. No bystanders to keep back. No obvious suspects in sight. No obvious clues. You stay here and take the pictures; I'll wait up by the road."

Shortly after Jane got back up to the bridge an older pickup truck slowly approached and stopped, just as the first cruiser, driven by Keith Sanderson, arrived, lights flashing. The truck's occupant, an older man dressed in overalls, plaid shirt, and straw hat, rolled down his window. "Saw the lights, officer. What's going on here?"

"None of your concern, sir. Please move along."

"Of course it's of my concern, young lady. I live near here. I served on township council for years. Citizens have a right to know what's happening."

By now Sanderson had reached them. Covertly winking at him, Jane said, "Officer Sanderson, please escort this gentleman away from our scene. If he refuses to go, charge him with obstructing a police investigation."

Sanderson gave her a little nod and, with a grim look on his face, said, "Sir, you have to move, right now. I'd hate to have to run you in."

The driver put up his hands defensively. "Of course, officer. Just trying to be a good citizen." He rolled up his window, crunched his truck into gear, and started to shoot backwards. He jammed on his brakes, looked over at the officers, nodded as Sanderson made calming gestures with his hands, and jerkily drove away, this time in the right direction.

Sanderson said, "We may have to polish this little routine, Jane, but it seems to have worked. May get a citizen's complaint."

"... and a seat-cleaning bill," Jane added. She quickly filled Sanderson in about what they had found. Sanderson enlisted the other uniformed officers who had now arrived. They quickly taped off the scene and closed the road in both directions.

Jeff Ripley arrived and was also briefed by Jane, who led him down to the crime scene. "Jeff, this is your area of expertise, so what do you need?"

Ripley replied, "You've already done the most important thing, keeping the scene sanitized. We'll wait for the coroner to check out the body, and meanwhile I'll organize the uniforms into a careful ground search. You two can help with that."

After Ripley gave out careful instructions, they used cord to create a search grid around the crime scene. While the rest were carefully scouring the ground, Ripley checked out the stream from the shore as well as he could. Then, retrieving some rubber boots from his car, he started a careful search of the streambed, starting downstream of the body.

As the officers worked intently on their tasks, a black Crown Victoria approached from the direction of Lakeside and abruptly stopped. Police Captain Jasper McKnight emerged and half scrambled, half slid down to the scene. Ripley put up his hands, "Sir, I have to ask you to move carefully. We haven't checked out the whole area yet."

McKnight turned on him. "I'm in charge here now. And I bet none of you professional investigators have checked out the body yet."

Jane approached and said, "Captain, we're waiting for the coroner. She's on her way."

"And meanwhile we don't know who this guy is, and we aren't out trying to apprehend whoever did this."

"Sir, we already are quite sure we know who it is, and we haven't yet confirmed exactly what happened or who might be a suspect."

"Time is of the essence in a crime investigation, Sergeant. Is speed no longer a part of modern crime investigation?" This was said while looking over at Ripley.

McKnight strode over to the body, turned it over, and removed the wallet. The rest looked on, with a mixture of shock and frustration. McKnight quickly riffled through the wallet. "I recognize this man.

Harry Winston. And his wallet confirms it. So, what do we know about what he was doing here?"

Kirsten said, "We were investigating the thefts at New Eden. We observed Winston driving toward us from New Eden at a high rate of speed. Say, at 11:00 a.m. or so. Percy Lewis, a resident of New Eden, reported seeing him pass us, turn toward town, and make a sudden stop here. He reportedly threw a blue bag of some sort into the creek and drove off, again at a high rate of speed.

"The same Mr. Lewis then reported seeing the same car here again about three hours later when he was out on his bike but didn't notice anything else. Presumably he didn't see the body, since it was close to the bridge and shielded by the bridge wall. About five or ten minutes later he encountered us at New Eden and urged us to stop here to apprehend Mr. Winston for the littering. We got here quickly, maybe another five minutes later. We found the body still oozing blood, so it must have happened not too many minutes before we arrived. We ascertained he was dead, called it in, and started our investigation. I should note that while at New Eden we interviewed Alex McKay, who confirmed Winston, who is his accountant, was at his house earlier this morning meeting over routine business matters."

McKnight was vigorously nodding his head. "So, we already have alibis for two people connected to Winston." Seeing the quizzical looks on his officers' faces, he continued. "First, McKay. The guy we are already investigating. And you, Detective Petersen, who certainly had negative interactions with our victim. Don't look so flummoxed. We have to be thorough, detective. Of course, you're in the clear.

"We have a perpetrator, or perpetrators, who leave no obvious clues and seemingly vanish into thin air. Ah, our esteemed coroner has arrived."

A dark-haired woman, about thirty-five years of age, had made her way down to the group. She was dressed in slacks and a dark-blue blouse. She was wearing stylishly large glasses and was carrying a small medical bag. She had a neutral, no-nonsense air about her.

McKnight addressed her. "Good of you to join us, Dr. Hepburn. You know most of my investigators, except maybe for Detective Kirsten Petersen, our new transfer. Detective, this is Dr. Moira Hepburn, our local coroner."

Hepburn said, "I'm glad to see you took my directive to heart about leaving a body as undisturbed as possible. I can see he has been turned over. Who should I thank for that little complication?"

McKnight drew himself up. "I am responsible for starting our investigation, given you had not yet arrived. Investigators have to be free to investigate."

"Responsible or irresponsible? Nothing like contaminating the *investigation* before it's properly begun."

In a tight voice, McKnight said, "Dr. Hepburn, we are both professionals. I require you to act that way."

Hepburn said, "Since I don't answer to you, you can *require* all you want. So, if you will all move back, I'll begin my *professional* investigation."

Some minutes later Hepburn rejoined the police officers.

"As usual, I can't give a full report until after the autopsy. You already know he has been dead for not much more than an hour or so. Judging from the body's original position" – she gave a stern glance at McKnight – "he could not have fallen from the bridge, and I really don't think he even could have been pushed or jumped. The body's too far from the bridge. Cause of death is a deep wound on the top of his head, but there are puzzling aspects to it. I'll be able to tell more later, but the blow appears to have been straight down, as if he were on his knees when it was delivered. The weapon appears to be something with a fairly narrow blade, maybe five centimetres long – that's a little more than two inches for you traditionalists." Again, he glanced at McKnight.

Jane said, "Like a really broad chisel, something like that?"

McKnight broke in, glancing over toward the Wyandot reserve, and said, "Or a tomahawk?"

There was a brief silence, broken by Jane's tight voice. "Sir, with all due respect, we don't need to start rumours. We have no firm evidence yet, and I believe it has been many decades since anyone over there used a tomahawk."

McKnight said, "I'm just trying to identify possibilities, Sergeant Walden. I'm sure there are still ceremonial tomahawks around, but of course we'll wait for the good doctor's full report. However, we have to start somewhere. Walden, Petersen, I want you to visit Wyandot and see if you can turn anything up, any connection to our victim." Seeing the questioning looks on their faces, he continued. "Nothing to do with tomahawks, but they are just about the nearest people to our crime scene, and our perpetrator had to have gone somewhere close by. It could be he's hiding there in the community. Just see what you can find out.

"I'm personally going to interview this guy Lewis. I'll try to get a more complete version of events from him. I mean, you said this guy was really angry about the littering, and he was on this scene very close to the time of death. I'm not saying he killed Winston because of littering, but he's an important witness. Who knows what might have happened here?

"Detective Ripley, carry on with your ground search. Keep an eye peeled for whatever the fatal weapon might have been. Thank you, doctor. My people will be glad to help you in any way they can. I'm off to New Eden. I may see what Alex McKay has to say while I'm out there."

After he left, Hepburn briefly conferred with Jane and Kirsten. "Sorry about being so snappy with your boss, but I can't get used to working with our own Inspector Clousseau. I'm going to try to forget about that tomahawk idiocy." Seeing them holding back smiles, she said, "What? I know you have to be loyal to your boss, but we also have important work to do."

Kirsten said, "It's just that he's collected so many interesting names. And to be fair, we should ask around at Wyandot, and Lewis really does have to be considered a suspect. You know, like 'mild-mannered high school teacher is secretly a crazed environmentalist tomahawk murderer.'"

The intently searching uniformed officers were surprised by a burst of laughter from the three conferring women. One of them muttered, "I'm okay with more and more women being in charge, but the struggle to get there must really bend their sense of humour. Real laugh riot out here." The officers returned to their meticulous search.

Hepburn said, "I have arranged for the body to be taken to Lakeside. I was recently appointed as regional coroner, but I was transferred to this area as chief pathologist, where my professional training is. That joint responsibility is a little unorthodox, but I guess the people in charge thought it made sense, given how few suspicious deaths there are around here. I will schedule the autopsy for tomorrow morning. You may want to have someone there. Detective Petersen, how about you? I like to get to know the people I work with."

Kirsten, surprised, replied, "Sure. Always up for new experiences. I'll be glad to be there, as long as the good inspector approves."

With a few last smiles, the women carried on with their tasks. Kirsten and Jane clambered back up the slope and got into their car.

CHAPTER 15
On the Reserve

THE TWO WOMEN SAT QUIETLY IN THE CAR FOR A FEW MINUTES. Then Kirsten turned toward Jane and said, "Ok, I'll go first. So now we have even more questions. McKnight suddenly appears out of nowhere, but obviously somewhere close to the bridge. He comes from the direction of Lakeside, not from Harmony. So where has he been? And he grossly disturbs an uninvestigated crime scene. What experienced cop would do that?"

"Jasper McKnight, to answer your question. He almost never gets actively involved in investigations. He just sits behind his desk reading the long reports he makes us write. He asks a few obvious questions, makes a few unhelpful comments, and puts on his 'smart, strong leader firmly in control' expression. But otherwise he stays out of the way so we can do our jobs. He spends a lot of time on the phone, or around town talking with his various pals and contacts, as he calls them. So, okay, did he deliberately contaminate the scene? I don't think so, but truthfully, I don't really know."

"He obviously tried to focus our attention on various unlikely suspects, like Percy fucking Lewis – sorry, still upset. okay, Lewis did have to be further questioned, and we need to keep all possibilities in play. But seriously? Like, okay, he had the opportunity. He may have had the means, and he even had a motive, but a really weak one. Could they have gotten into some sort of confrontation? But he's a skinny little guy, way smaller than Winston. How could he, or anyone else, for that matter, get Winston quietly kneeling in front of him and politely allowing himself to be killed? Could Lewis so convincingly act the outraged innocent for us moments later, having just killed someone in cold blood? And then direct us to the crime scene? It just doesn't add up, at all."

"Agreed, and now our beloved leader is the one getting whatever information Lewis can provide. Get it or hide it? And he is going to talk to McKay? To investigate or cover up? Damn, I hate all this uncertainty."

"And what can we do? Talk to our superiors? With no hard evidence, just that we think a career senior police officer is involved in some sort of murky conspiracy, leavened by a brutal homicide?"

"Ok, we're cops. We're investigators. So, we keep investigating. We read Jasper's report on his New Eden investigation. We try to get some hard, real concrete evidence. We keep all options open. The thing with Jasper is he often has done strange stuff. So, is he just acting like his usual unusual self, or is he some sort of rogue cop? You know, like in that old Italian movie *Investigation of a Citizen Above Suspicion*."

"More movie stuff, huh. Wait a sec." Kirsten looked up the movie on her phone, and then read out the brief plot summary. "'A highly regarded Italian police inspector murders his mistress, only to become part of the homicide investigation that follows. The inspector proceeds to plant clues at the crime scene as his fellow officers either ignore or fail to recognize his obvious tampering.' So, Jasper is planting clues? And we have to avoid being dupe cops?"

"More like we just have to keep our eyes open. No-one is above suspicion. We have to be careful who we trust. Speaking of which,

I'm not sure about involving Jeff. Not yet, anyway. I know he has real questions about Jasper, but it's not like we have real answers. Again, yet."

"Okay, in terms of keeping our options open, I suppose it could be some random crime, though it wasn't a robbery, and it wouldn't explain some of the strange stuff about the crime scene. There is one other possibility, though: our mysterious stranger in the untraceable white SUV. What was he doing out there at New Eden? Was he keeping an eye on McKay, or keeping an eye out for McKay? I mean, McKay had time after we left him to call this guy and send him after Winston."

"And the guy proved that he's a dangerous customer with Scrivener in the parking lot."

Kirsten said, "Right, but why the need to get rid of Winston so suddenly? Something tied into his last visit with McKay? I can't help thinking that this throwing whatever it was into the stream was way more than just littering. But why try to get rid of something incriminating in such an unreliable way? Was Winston spooked when he saw us heading out to New Eden? I'm going to ask Jeff to see if he and his team can take a really close look for whatever that was." Kirsten took out her phone and relayed the request on to Jeff, while Jane started the car and drove the short distance to the road leading to the Wyandot Reserve.

Jane said, "Maybe there was someone else there who had it in for Winston. After we finish up out here, we have to dig into this guy's life. But here we are. Hang on. The road in is more like a gravel pit."

Jane drove slowly along the gravel road, trying her best to avoid the many bumps and potholes. They passed the reservation boundary and started to see modest, generally well-kept houses set back in the bush and scrubland. There were few meadows or farmed fields. While they drove along, Jane filled Kirsten in with as much information as possible about the reserve and reminded her that they had no real jurisdiction here, unless called in by the local band council. Eventually they came to a small clearing containing a two-storey building, neatly kept up but still sagging a little at the corners. The roof was in need of re-shingling. The front door opened, and a medium-sized, middle-aged woman came out.

Kirsten had been thinking over what Jane had told her about the reservation's elected chief. Chief Wanda Cornelius was a self-contained, quiet-looking woman who people often took for granted. In a rare moment of openness, she once confided to Jane that this was a necessary skill. "There's too many people and organizations that might be my enemies, if I let that happen, so I don't. I save being tough for when I have to be. That's too often, but not as often as it might be. I don't pick fights that I'm going to lose. Some people here think I'm not strong enough, but I have to survive if I'm going to be a good leader for my people, and we need good leaders."

She didn't trust many people in authority. They too often misused that authority, seemingly as a matter of routine. They might sometimes be good people who meant well, but they were frequently wrong about what that entailed. Wanda was patient with them, engaged with them, and did her best to make sure she and her people sometimes won, even if it was only small victories.

In the past her people had rarely won, and often lost catastrophically. However, the balance was shifting. They had more to work with. There were times when she had room to negotiate, and she did it well, at her own pace. There were also times now when they could dig in their heels, become more aggressive, and actually achieve real progress. There was a need for both strength and patience, but never the sort of patience that actually meant giving up. And never the strength that brought only brief flashes of victory. Had her American cousins really won the Battle of Little Bighorn all those decades ago? She was a careful woman, respected by most, opposed by a few, and determined to win, even if it usually took a long time.

She didn't like many people in authority, but she did like Jane Walden, and Jane liked her.

Jane and Kirsten stepped out of the car onto the dusty parking lot. Kirsten looked around at an area new to her, despite having lived only a few kilometers away for eighteen years. Wanda looked them over, a neutral expression on her face. She turned to Jane and said, "So, Nancy Drew. You've finally come out to visit."

Jane replied, "More like Miss Marple by now. But then neither she nor old Nancy were actually cops."

"Yeah, where are all those famous women cops? Off doing most of the work when they're not bringing coffee for the boss man. Speaking of which, how is old Pickle?"

"Pretty much the same. Bursting with ideas and energy. Really hard to hold him back."

"Right. Sorry to hear it. If he went any slower, he'd be backing up. Who's the new sidekick?"

"Kirsten Petersen. She used to live around here. McKnight brought her back from down south because he was finally faced with having to do a real investigation. It shook him right up, and so close to retirement. Kirsten laid a few good jabs on him, so I think she's eligible to join the sisterhood. You can trust her."

Kirsten shook the proffered hand and said, "Pickle. Like permanently up his ass? I overheard Jane calling him that. It does seem to work."

"You catch on fast. Say, was it you at that little dust-up at Friendlies couple nights ago? I heard those creeps had it coming to them. Nice work."

They headed toward the band office. "Survived our obstacle course, did you? It's a bit rough, but it keeps the Jehovah's Witnesses away. They don't want to wreck their cars while they're busy trying to save our souls."

"The township still won't do anything? At least send a road grader along it?"

"Nope. Evidently it would, quote, 'permanently harm federal-municipal relations and void their municipal insurance.' I keep getting promises from our regional rep from Indian Affairs, but he can't seem to find his way out here, unless maybe he got trapped in the bottom of one of those potholes."

"I'll check for him on the way out and try not to run him over. It might be hard to find a worthy replacement."

By this time, they had entered the building. It was small, with modest furniture clearly beyond its best-before date, just like the building's exterior. But the vibrant Indigenous art and the muted earth-tone walls saved it from being the usual drab, soulless municipal office. Wanda led them into her office, also of a moderate size, and with only one window, but it felt like a room actually lived in by someone. Featuring a colourful woven rug, some framed pictures and more Indigenous art, it felt quietly welcoming. They sat down around a low, mosaic-topped table.

Jane picked up the conversation. "The Rug doing any better for you?" She turned to Kirsten. "Local MP. He obviously plans to be prime minister one day, and who was the last bald one? He thinks the rug helps give him the right image. "

Wanda smiled. "And you can sweep things under rugs, avoid them, and keep them hidden. He's a real pro at that. Let's see, last time it was 'Moving forward, we'll get this done.' Before that it was, 'I'm going to come to the table with you. Let's set a meeting.' Before that, 'We've got a plan for that,' and then, 'There's fiscal realities, but we can manage that.' I think the first one ever was, 'There's nothing more important to our government than your issues. We'll set up an enquiry into reserve infrastructure and report back to you, soon.' We're still waiting.

"He and his party never ever really say 'no,' never openly disagree with us. They smile and manage things. They're masters at being bland and safe enough to keep getting re-elected. They know what voters respond to, and mostly that's just not bothering them too much. They're sort of like hosts of an afternoon TV chat show: forgettable, affable, and vacuous but they always keep the viewers happy and the ratings high enough. Sorry, going on and on about my pet hobby horse, but we have to work with these guys to get anything done, and it wears you out."

Kirsten said, "Maybe you need to get more creative. Involve the media?"

"They're not interested. 'We need to focus on what matters to our readers.' That's clearly not our damned road – or water, or sewers, or housing. I did try something new on Rug last meeting. As we were leaving, I asked if there was federal funding to provide some relief from the road issues, subsidies for auto repair or chiropractic services. Maybe a repair facility for our cars, or a clinic to house those injured by the road. He was shaking my hand by then, in both of his. Eyes looking around a bit nervously, but still oh so sincere. He asked his assistant to 'note that and ask the minister about it.' She did a nice little eye roll that he missed, but I didn't. Imagine making your career working for these guys?"

"Actually, working under Jasper, I can. Speaking of which, I've got to ask you about a serious incident that just happened down near the intersection with the main road, where Silent Lake Creek feeds into the swamp." Holding out the picture on her cell phone, she asked, "Have you seen this guy around, name of Harry Winston?"

Wanda glanced at the phone. "I have, not all that long ago. Looking livelier than he does in that picture. What's the story? Tomahawk marks? Attempted scalping? Arrows sticking in the trees, so we're suspects, again? We've actually been cutting way back on all that stuff. It doesn't work so well for us anymore, if it ever did. We're also getting tired of being Pickle's usual, and often only, suspects any time something happens, like the big crime wave over at the lake with those thefts. "

Kirsten started to ask if Wanda knew anything about that. Jane's warning look stopped her.

Jane carried on. "Sorry. I've got to ask. We can't say for sure it was murder, but it sure looks that way. This guy doesn't look like the type to go out exploring nature in his suit and leather oxfords. You say he was out here recently. What about?"

Wanda sighed. "Ok, I know you've got to do your job. As for his visit, it's more than a little bit complicated. Settle in. I'll make us some tea and tell you all about it."

After serving the tea, Wanda started in. "A couple of months ago this big developer guy makes an appointment to see me. You know, the guy who tried his best to ruin Silent Lake with that insane development he somehow got past the township council. New Eden, he called it! Clearly no sense of irony, or history."

Kirsten sat up, "You mean Alexander McKay. We've been looking into him. He came to you about what? Financial stuff?"

"Let me tell you the story and then you can ask all the questions you want.

"There's a parcel of land east of the reservation. About six hundred acres. The original surveys – we're talking about almost two centuries ago – meant it to front on our little road we've been talking about. However, when the great white father in Ottawa was generous enough to cede this prime real estate to us, the six hundred acres wasn't included, and now was cut off. Nothing but swamp and wetlands on the other three sides. So, it wasn't ours, and couldn't really be of use to anybody else. We've tried several times over the decades to get the feds to buy it for us, but that proved even more frustrating than getting our infrastructure looked after.

"We did find out, though, some years back, that the six hundred acres is actually part of some larger tracts of land east of the swamp. The various owners never tried to do much with that area, since it was cut off by the swamp They actually tried at various times to sell the land to us. Township councils were more relaxed back then, so they got as far as severing off the required sections. Separate deeds, ready for sale, all set to go. We dumb natives would never turn down such a good deal, they thought, though the land is even more scrubby than what we've actually got.

"Whether or not our earlier band councils were really serious about buying the land, they weren't allowed to. Any purchase had to be done by the federal government. The owners went to Rug's various predecessor members of Parliament for some action, but like I said, that party has the monopoly on smooth talkers who get re-elected despite rarely doing anything useful. They just trot out clichés about how everyone fits under their big tent, and how only they were the natural government … sorry, sorry. Bad me! Got back on my hobby horse. I promise I'll say no more about them. Probably.

"Back to the history lesson. Despite all the leverage these landowners thought they had, of course things stayed frustratingly the same, right up to the present.

"A while back your friend McKay calls me, all excited, and claims he's got to see me, right now, about something beyond important, a big win-win plan for all of us. He comes out here, all puffed up and excited, and lays it all out. He has signed options to buy the land, all six hundred acres of it. He has a big new development planned, but of course I'd understand why he couldn't give me details just yet. Timing was critical! We all had to be discreet, or we'd all lose this big opportunity! All he needed from us was to have an easement to get access to New Sodom, or whatever he'd end up calling that place.

"I kept asking 'what kind of development?' 'What kind of access?' 'What kind of traffic?' 'How much?' He showed me these professionally drawn plans, how he could use existing roads that skirt around the edge of the reserve so no one would be displaced. It would bring us annual lease payments, and jobs for our people. It would help us get our road in shape, and we could likely partner with the development for better water and sewer infrastructure. It'd change our lives out here! Bring us right in to the future! He'd done his homework. We didn't have to involve the feds, because the local band could grant leases and easement as long as the actual ownership didn't have to change. 'We can do this!' he kept saying.

"I'd seen the future he brought to Silent Lake, and I kept hearing whispers about him. How his dad had been a trustworthy businessman and generally good guy. But junior, now that he was in charge of McKay enterprises? Not so much, especially recently. It just didn't feel right to me, especially when he got pretty aggressive about it. I said unless he could give more details, documented plans and solid guarantees, the answer was no.

"He managed to get a special meeting of the band council, over my objections. He was smooth. Lots of sincerity and glittering promises. 'He had lived around here his whole life. It was his community. He was a proven success.' And on and on. I headed off full approval, but he won a concession to upgrade the designated roads – at his full expense! – to bring in some equipment so he could do exploratory work. It might have been at his expense, but it was township crews that did all the work, even though, as I said, it is illegal for them to work on our land."

Jane interjected, "Yeah, too many on township council have been way too friendly with this guy."

Wanda continued. "They did some kind of test drilling, and some sort of geological surveys, but still no detail about the actual development. This all happened not too long ago. He kept working on the band council members. They're mostly okay people, but more trusting than I am, and more eager to grab the glitter while they can. They didn't want to listen to me about getting real answers.

"Still with me, are you? Makes my head spin. Want some more tea? I could use something stronger, but we have strict controls about that out here." Jane was listening intently, and Kirsten was madly scribbling notes, so Wanda continued.

"That brings us up to your dead friend here. McKay introduced him as his accountant, the guy who could lay out all the financial details, all the specifics we needed so we wouldn't miss this golden opportunity. Mr. Numbers showed me and the band council loads of charts and projections and spread sheets. He predicted how the annual lease fees would add up fast enough so we could soon build our long-hoped-for youth centre. He had details about the jobs it would generate, and how much income that would bring in. He had detailed plans, fully costed out, he said, for how we could partner on infrastructure costs – roads, water, sewage disposal. He left glossy folders about all this with each of us to prepare for the next band council meeting, when we could make our most important decision ever, a 'guaranteed new life for us all!'

"My opposition on band council was all starry-eyed and eager, and I was feeling worn down and not sure what to do. Maybe they were right. Maybe it was best to let McKay have his way. Maybe it would be – what did they call it? – 'the dawning of a bright new world.' It still sounded like bullshit to me, but nicely packaged bullshit."

"Bottom line, he won. Band council agreed to his easement. Your not-too-lively friend came out here a few days ago with the final papers to sign. McKay now has full access to his six hundred acres. We're just waiting now to see what actually happens."

Kirsten said, "That fills in some important gaps for us. We've been investigating McKay about various things, including his proposed big new development. We didn't realize it was directly involved with the reserve. I asked at the bank about the location of the land, but for whatever reason they didn't seem to know, or to care. I'm afraid we were a bit sloppy there. I can't really say much more, except to alert you that it's approved to go ahead quite soon.

"It seems my sad little history lesson has helped. I can't say I feel sorry about Mr. Bigtime Accountant, though. I don't trust McKay, but he's slippery and smooth and knows how to pretend to be a nice guy who's on your side. But his big financial lap dog is – was – an arrogant, rude, racist prick. You could tell he hated being out here. He kept looking down his nose at us, and tried to hide his disapproval and discomfort, but it kept slipping out. I hope this doesn't make me a suspect, but I feel no sorrow at his untimely passing."

Jane said, "You're way down on our suspect list. But one other request. Whoever did it seemed to vanish into thin air. Kirsten and I were on the scene not long after it happened, and no sign of anyone. He could have escaped up your access road and gone into hiding. He – given how Winston died, we are assuming it was a male – should be considered dangerous. Can you have your people take a look around? A careful look?"

"Are you sure Pickle doesn't want to send in a SWAT team to really beat the bushes? Though of course we natives have it in our DNA to be able to melt into the wilderness."

Jane smiled. "I'm afraid Jasper's still working on getting us a SWAT team, so it's just us. As usual I'll run interference with him. Can you help us out?"

"Of course. I'll let you know if we find some blood-covered maniac out here."

After getting more precise detail from Wanda about the band's dealings with McKay and Winston, Jane and Kirsten got up to leave. Jane hugged her friend and said, "We're just starting to look into all of this, but I'll keep you informed of anything that might affect you. Like Kirsten said, we've got an investigation going on with McKay, but please stay quiet about that. We'll soon know more about Winston. Stay strong! We've shown before we know how to take care of business, and I intend to keep it that way."

As they were lurching back down the road, Kirsten turned to face Jane. "It may be none of my business, but there seems to be real history between you two. 'We've shown before we know how to take care of business?' What's that all about?"

Jane sighed and said, "My high school time was nothing like the continuing drama yours seemed to have been, but I do have one dramatic incident from back then. So here goes. You're the second person who's heard the full story.

"You know the Indigenous kids have always been bussed in for high school, but they were even less welcome then than they likely are now. There was lots of tension, but not much ever really happened because the administration kept a pretty tight rein on the school. The white kids were sure it was really their school, and that the Native kids would drop out of their school as soon as they could. Shitty, but that's mostly what happened. The Native kids were pretty quiet. They kept to themselves, and never stuck around much when class was over.

"In grade twelve, Wanda was in one of my classes. I was just one of the crowd, one of the nice quiet kids who never make waves. For group work the teacher always managed to get Wanda in with the inoffensive quiet kids, usually including me. She was pretty reserved, but I could tell she was really bright. We both understood stuff pretty quickly, and soon we were doing all of the group's work, and our loser group was actually getting the best marks and most of the teachers' praise.

"The self-declared school stars didn't like it and started to whisper snide comments and lies about Wanda, and some about me. Wanda and I tried to be patient – there's that patience again – but it was getting to be too much, too hard to take.

"In the cafeteria, the stars always sat at the same table, close to the serving line, so you had to go past them. Their power table. When Wanda would pass, they would do idiot little chants and war whoops, or their lame version of Native drumming. A couple of times I told them to stop, quiet little me, getting to be less patient. But they would say shit like, 'Squaw has white friend?' They were just idiots. The teachers were always over by the door and didn't want to make waves. In retrospect, much like old Rug and his mob. The other kids were too scared, or too indifferent, too something. So, no-one dared interfere, other than me – and that just made things worse.

"This one day in the cafeteria the lead idiot moved his chair back, blocking Wanda's way. 'If squaw wants to pass, she needs secret password.' She made to go around the other side, but I could see they were ready to block her there too. Wanda just quietly stood there, all alone. The cafeteria went quiet, and everyone was watching. I hated what was happening, and no-one was doing anything. I was still in the food line, and the dam just finally broke, wiping out any trace of patience. I plain lost it. I grabbed the large ketchup dispenser at the end of the food line and ripped the end of the spout off the pump. Whoever I had just become stalked over to their table, pointed my weapon, and started pumping.

"There was a ridiculous amount of ketchup. It went everywhere. The stars tried to escape but they stumbled over their chairs and each other. The thing had about half a gallon of ketchup, and they got it all. They were slipping and sliding and couldn't get up off the floor. All over their hair, their faces, their nice crisp chinos, their pretty little cardigans. They were screaming and wailing. The teachers rushed over as soon as they saw what was happening. The cafeteria went crazy, cheering and yelling. I don't think the stars had many friends, and this was amazingly sweet for the whole room. I emptied the damn thing, so it looked like bloody carnage. It was bloody carnage. It was surreal. It was scary and exciting at the same time. It was magnificent. Wanda was looking on, amazed. The whole thing was amazing.

"Of course, down to the office. They brought in my parents and a superintendent. 'The school can't stand for this kind of violence! What got into you! Four years of being an exemplary student, and now this! What do you have to say for yourself?'

"What I had to say was to blurt out about the weeks of hurt these creeps put on Wanda. They brought her in, and she didn't say much other than to quietly confirm what I had said. I caught my parents looking quizzically at me and at each other. This was their quiet little daughter? My dad said, 'It seems to me like she was just standing up for herself and her friend.' I saw Wanda give a little smile when he said 'friend.' My mom just squeezed my hand. They agreed to pay for the damage to the stars' clothes but were adamant there would be no more punishment beyond my one-week suspension. They were pretty great.

"The stars got – nothing. Of course! A little lecture about treating the less privileged better. 'Our school's about being our better selves. Now no more of this sort of thing.' Beyond lame.

"And to Wanda? 'You and your people have been in trouble here too many times. We expect better. We expect you to appreciate the opportunities you've been given. Now you may have suffered some, and they were wrong, but we want to see you being a more positive member of this school community. We're not going to punish you for your part in all this, but shape up, young lady! Hear me?'"

"Wanda just smiled knowingly, especially when the superintendent said, 'your people' and 'member of this school community'. She said very little and just left the room as soon as she could. As she was leaving, I thought I heard the principal mutter, 'ungrateful little wretch,' or something like that, but I may have been mistaken.

"When I got back to school the next week, every lunch time the kitchen staff managed to slip a special treat to me. I later heard how the stars used to treat them, the 'hired help.'

"The stars lost their special status. No-one really deferred to them anymore. They started to be laughed at. Like, in art class one of them was asked what her favourite colour was. Some wise ass piped up, 'You mean other than ketchup red?' Their group just sort of broke up.

"I was still pretty quiet around school, but in a different way. I'd had to do a lot of apologizing, but I felt in no way apologetic. I found I could help get the right thing done! The good guys could win! I started to feel more confident. It sort of started to point me to becoming a cop."

Kirsten shook her head, chuckling. "I used to hear reports about some amazing food fight thing at school years ago, but never got the whole story. Amazing."

Jane sighed. "There's one more chapter to it, not well known, and pretty dark, but equally amazing. The stars, their leaders, at least, didn't like their loss of status. They left Wanda and me alone at school, but they were quietly seething. Soon after, one night I was leaving school late after band practice. I lived near the school, and so always walked home alone, even though part of it was down a dark and deserted alleyway. It was safe – except suddenly it wasn't. When I turned the corner away from the school and into the alley, the lead star and two of his friends stepped out of the darkness. I think they had been drinking.

"Can't get to your little red-skinned friend, but here you are. You're going to learn a little lesson, and you're not going to tell anyone, because people will believe me, not someone like you. I've got witnesses. The story is, if we need it, too bad about how you came on to me wanting me to forgive you. Now, just relax, no screaming or we gag you and tie you up. The result is going to be the same, either way. You're going to enjoy this. I can't imagine anybody's ever wanted to fuck you. Just take off your clothes and lie down.'"

"I was terrified, frozen, new confidence totally gone. I was in a horror show. It's bad enough now for women, when they have to deal with abuse and assault, but it seemed totally hopeless back then. I'd found out what being terror-stricken really meant.

"But then suddenly Wanda was there with four or five others. She stepped up to big star and clipped him on the nose. 'We're going to hurt you, and every time you try to report this or do something about it, my friends and I will hurt you again. We've got witnesses too, and really, what more can they do to us? Ready to be hurt, really hurt, big guy?'

"They moved in closer, raising their arms, jostling and pushing him. He started to whimper and cry, and fell to his knees begging and pleading. Snot was running down his face, and there was a pungent odour and a wet stain spread across his crotch.

"Wanda just stood there. Finally, she said, 'No one really laid a hand on you. Nothing to report, or that you'll want to report. We're going to let you go now. But if you ever try this again, with anyone, we won't be nearly as nice. There won't be any police involved, just us. After we're done, you will never be the same again. Now, I want to hear you say that from now on you're going to be our good little boy. Say it!'

"He looked around wildly, struggling to speak. Finally, he managed to say, 'Ok. All right. Just please, please let me go. I promise.'

"'You promise what!'

"'I promise I won't try to hurt her anymore.'

"Wanda kicked him in the chest, making him fall over on his back. 'I need to hear a little more sincerity.'

"'I'm sorry, I'm sorry. I won't do it again. I'll be good. Please, just let me go.'

"'And who is it that owns you now?'

"'You do. Oh god. You own me. I won't do it again.' By this time, he was crying so hard his whole body was shaking and he was almost incoherent.

"Wanda said, 'Ok, you get to go now, but if you even whisper anything about this to the cops, you go down for attempted rape and we will still make sure we have another little session like this, only a much more serious one. Now scram!'

"He scrambled to his feet but was knocked over by one of Wanda's friends. He struggled to his feet again and then scurried away, still sobbing.

"Turning to the other two, Wanda said, 'You brave guys are going to have to be more careful about who you choose for friends. You were going to help him, so you're just the same kind of stinking cowardly shit he is. But we're going to spare giving you the same treatment, for now. You can go, but on two conditions. If you break either one, we'll be getting together again, however long it takes. The first condition is we need to hear that word of your pal's bravery tonight got out to your crowd. In detail. About how he tried to attack a solitary girl, in the dark, but turned into shit when things suddenly got tough. Don't forget the begging, the crying, or the pissed pants. If we don't hear it's out there, we will look you up, and we won't be nearly as patient or forgiving as we are tonight.

"'"The second condition, we better hear you've learned some new manners, have learned to act like good little boys. Just remember, we're around. We're always around. We know how to keep track.'

"'"They scrambled away, grateful to escape. And, though it'd be hard to ever call them good little boys, there at least was no more serious trouble. Word did get out, making the lives of all three that much worse, especially for the former lead dog.

"Wanda walked me back to my house and hugged me. 'My friends are important to me. You're my friend. Okay? You stood up for me. I knew these so-called tough guys would go after you. It's all they've got. Too afraid to come on to the rez to get me, but different for you around this damn fucked-up place. We've been keeping an eye, staying close. We know how to be patient. These guys are bullies and cowards. I don't think they'll be a problem anymore. You just get word to me if they try anything else.' She gave me another quick hug and then left with her friends.

"I gave my parents a sanitized version of what had happened, that these guys had shouted insults at me but had been scared off by Wanda and her friends. I just wanted all this to be over and didn't want my parents upset and involved. I knew Wanda's way of dealing with this had been pretty brutal, but that in dealing with guys like this, to be effective it had to be. I thought it would only get worse if we involved the cops, a bit ironic given I now am one. But even now it often gets worse for women when they report rape or attempted rape.

"As for me and Wanda, we didn't start to do sleepovers, and didn't always see a lot of each other. Different worlds and all that. But to this day I've never had a better friend than Wanda. I don't know what that attack would have done to me. I can't see how my brave new confidence would have survived it. It wouldn't have killed me, but it would have killed part of me. I wouldn't likely be a cop today. So, Wanda saved me, and she says I saved her from giving up totally on white people, helped prepare her for becoming chief."

Kirsten nodded mutely, overcome by the raw power of Jane's story. "I can see why you don't tell too many people. Thank you."

"Martha, my partner, knows. Jeff knows part of it. He's a good guy. Obviously interested in you, by the way. I won't ever try it out on Jasper. The person he would identify with in the story would likely be the idiot superintendent.

"You can see what Wanda and I mean about taking care of business. You can see why I trust her."

Jane sighed. "The story's not quite over. The darkest part is yet to come. Big star was broken. People who used to jump to do his bidding now just sniggered behind his back. He managed to bully a few guys into hanging around with him, but it was only ever the B squad. He had the rich and prominent father, the glowing future running the family business, all the goodies a small town has to offer, but really, in some important way he was done, and he knew it.

"A few weeks later, not long after graduation, his car went off a curve at high speed, no skid marks, right into a tree. No witnesses, no note, no one knows exactly what happened, but we can make a pretty good guess.

"His name was Gary McKay. He was Alexander McKay's big brother, and the heir to the McKay business empire."

CHAPTER 16
Lydia and Christine

THE TWO WOMEN DROVE BACK TO HARMONY IN CONTEMPLATIVE silence. Kirsten finally broke it.

"God, Jane. My high school dramas might have been like an ongoing soap opera, but I think yours wins the Oscar for most compelling drama. Sorry, not trying to be flippant. That had to be really tough. Thanks for trusting me with it."

Jane glanced over and gave Kirsten a tight smile. "It was tough. But it shook me into understanding that the world is a lot more complicated than people in Harmony would have you believe. If it hadn't happened, I'm not sure where I'd be now. Someone's complacent but unhappy wife and a stay-at-home mom? Probably not the big-time cop I am now."

After a slight pause, she said, "I'm starting to realize I have recently been sliding into some form of complacency. I mean, how much of your life should you spend enabling someone like Jasper? Harmony is a nice quiet little place, but do I want to carry on pretending I'm living in Mayberry? McKay has been a fixture around here for a long time, but have we been wilfully ignoring what he's really been up to?

And now this corruption around the parking lot? Jasper seems to think his job is to keep connected with what he calls the key people in town, 'keep his finger on the pulse,' he once said, but should a cop really do it the way he has? Whatever his connection with McKay and Winston and too many other people around town, it's hard to see it as anything good. I mean, he's familiar with all the good-old-boy networks around here, but he has no idea of what life is like for the people out at Wyandot. So, have I been, I don't know, running interference for them through my connection with Wanda? I'm starting to fear I actually just helped maintain an awful status quo.

"I hope this doesn't sound strange, but this whole business, the McKay stuff, the parking lot, Winston's murder, is giving me a jolt. Being able to talk with you has been a big help."

After another brief pause, Jane gave her head a little shake. "Enough of the heavy duty this-is-my-life stuff. We have a murder to solve. We have to report back in about our talk with Wanda. She's given us some important new information, which we need to follow up on, but we have time to talk to some other people first. Let's stop by Winston's office. I know he's got a part-time assistant, and with any luck she'll be there and be able to give us some background."

After they reached Harmony, Jane parked in front of a small house at the edge of downtown. It had a sign out front, "Winston Accounting Services." There was an obviously retrofitted large window showing a medium-sized office. The rest of the house appeared to be a residence. When they entered the office, a woman sitting behind one of the two desks looked up and said, "Can I help you? Did you have an appointment with Mr. Winston?" She appeared to be in her mid to late thirties, conservatively dressed, several pounds overweight, sporting heavily framed glasses. She was looking at some open files on her desk.

Jane said, "I'm afraid we're not here for accounting services. I'm Sergeant Jane Walden, Provincial Police, and this is Detective Kirsten Petersen. And you are?"

"Lydia Grant. Mr. Winston's executive assistant. Sorry – Kirsten. Don't you remember me? From high school? You know, that Christine business? That was a long time ago, but I'm still really sorry about it. I was a snobby little bitch back then. Is it too late to apologize now?"

Jane had a puzzled look on her face. Kirsten said, "No need, Lydia. Water over the dam. It's good to see you again, but we need to talk to you in confidence on important police business. We hope you can help us out."

Lydia said, "Of course. 'In confidence' is routine in an accounting office. Sorry, Kirsten, I'm just so surprised to see you back here, and you're a police officer." She suddenly stopped with a shocked look, and, raising her hands to her face, said, "Omigod, you're the one. I had no idea. That's amazing."

Kirsten said, "We need to talk, Lydia, but can you first tell us what you mean? I'm *what* one?"

Lydia said, "Well, when Harry came in Monday morning, he had a really sore shoulder and some small bruises on his face. He said he didn't want to talk about it, but he sat at his desk muttering, not doing any real work. Finally, I couldn't take it anymore and insisted he tell me what was going on. He said that I would soon find out, it'd be all over this, quote, 'damned little town,' so he might as well tell me what *really* happened. He told me about the incident at Friendlies Saturday night. According to him, he was sitting quietly with some friends, just relaxing, when some undercover cop decided to hassle him and actually assaulted him, cold-cocked him, he said. He gave the clear impression she was a mixture of a Russian weightlifter and a WWE wrestler. He said he didn't have a chance, that there was some other interfering cop there, and that he should press charges, but what's the use. I mean, Harry is a pretty big guy, and he always comes out on top. He's not your stereotype of an accountant. It'd take someone pretty impressive to handle him that way, cold cock or not. And it turns out it was you. I mean, you don't exactly look like Olga, star of WWE. Omigod!"

Jane said, "Sorry to break in," giving Kirsten an enquiring glance, "but Ms. Grant, we have some bad news for you. Mr. Winston was found dead today, and we're investigating what happened. We are trying to find his next of kin. We won't be releasing anything to the media just yet, so we do need you to treat this as totally confidential."

Lydia said, "Harry's dead? But I was expecting him here any time. I mean, he lives in the back part of this house, so I was pretty sure to see him at some point. But dead? He is – was – such a strong, healthy guy. I can't believe he's dead. Was it a car accident?"

Kirsten said, "It wasn't a car accident, but we can't really tell you any more. You're one of the first people we have talked to and we hope you can fill in some background for us. Okay? Like, do you have contact information for his next of kin?"

Lydia said, "Of course I'll help you all I can. Sorry I'm so flustered. But it's a shock. I mean, personally, but also because I'll have to take care of all the business stuff. Sorry, that's not really important now. I'm just all confused.

"Next of kin? Harry's dad died some years ago, and his mother is an Alzheimer's patient in the local nursing home. It's been a long time since she has even recognized him, and I think he stopped even visiting her. He has one sister who moved out to the west coast years ago, and they don't keep in touch. I can give you contact information for her. I don't know of any extended family around here."

"Close friends?"

"I don't want to speak ill of the dead, but I think you probably want me to be honest with you. Harry wasn't a very nice man. He was a bully and often lost his temper. I'm grateful for the job here, even if it's only two-thirds time, but really, a big part of what I do is run interference and soothe ruffled feathers. I think if there were any real competition, he would have been out of business long ago. He has – or had – lots of buddies, but I wouldn't call them close friends.

He had guys he golfed with, and drank with, and went to that awful Friendlies place with, but drinking buddies aren't friends, as far as I'm concerned. You may want to talk to Alex McKay. You know, the big developer guy in town. Harry has been spending a lot of time with him, doing more and more business with him, and it's not all accounting business."

Lydia paused. "I'm pretty shook about all this, but I do want to help you. I mean, Harry was a bit of a louse, but even louses deserve not to be killed. I mean, I'm not stupid. Two detectives following up on a death that wasn't an accident? I think you want to know all about Harry, and I think I'm likely the best person in town to fill you in. I will keep this to myself, but you've likely figured out I'm a talker, and I think the best way for me to help you is for you to just let me talk, and then ask me about anything I leave out. Ok?"

Jane said, "Let's try it. As long as you understand even talkers have to know when to not talk. So, fill us in."

"Okay. Look, my mind is sort of going all over the place, so this might be a little disconnected. Like I said earlier, I was a snobby little bitch in high school. I somehow thought my privileged little life would carry on after I graduated. So, I married this really great guy, but I continued acting the same way. By the time I realized what I'd done to our marriage, he had bailed out, and who could blame him."

Seeing the restless body language of the detectives, she said, "Be patient. I'm getting to Harry. This is the Coles Notes version of my messy little life, but it ties in. So, there I am, divorced, and I realize I don't have many friends, and I have no marketable skills. My family is around, but even they are getting tired of my act. Sort of like my life peaked in high school. I drift around in some office and retail jobs, and with some relationships I'd rather forget about. Then one day I see Harry is advertising for office help. What qualifications do I have? But he interviews me and offers me the job. I figure out later it's likely that he's driven away all the qualified people, but right then it was like a lifeline. I mean, what else could I do? Get a job at Friendlies, if they'd even take on plus-sized women?

"It turns out I do have some useful skills. I'm organized and efficient. I know how to keep track of things. I was learning how to get along with people, now that I had to, and Harry needed someone like that. So, we formed an unlikely team. Of course, Harry soon makes a pass at me, but I knew he would – guys like him always do, sort of like they feel they have to. I managed to convince him I wasn't interested, and that if he wanted me to stick around, he had to lay off. I think he realized how much his business needed me, so for once he acted smart.

"I've worked here for over five years, I get paid okay, and I've got my life back together. Harry and I have what I found out is called a symbiotic relationship. We're not friends, but we both make sure things around here work. Part of it working properly is that Harry started to mentor me, had me doing real accounting work. Not that he's being Mr. Generous, but it serves his lazy streak if he can leave while I do his work. Maybe a surprise to all my teachers who thought I was a brainless little ditz, but I'm good at it. I don't have the paper qualifications, and without the CA behind my name, there's lots I can't do. I'm taking correspondence courses and night courses. I'm not that far from taking the exam, and I think I'll pass. Harry was supportive with that too.

"Sorry, my mind is hopping around. I hope I'm not being ghoulish, but someone has got to pick up the pieces here, and with some short-term help that maybe could be me.

"But look, I hope you can see why I really do want to help you. I'd never give Harry a character reference, but I do owe him. No disrespect to the dead, but Harry was getting into some bad stuff. You need to know this. I hope I'm not outing myself as some sort of accomplice."

Jane said, "Ms. Grant, you're being very helpful. We have no interest in looking into Mr. Winston's business matters, except to the extent it helps us find his killer. Yes, you're right. He was murdered. Please continue."

"Harry always seemed to want to cut corners. At first, I thought it was just because he was lazy and would rather use the time to go off with whoever his buddies happened to be at the time. But legally he was sometimes cutting it pretty fine. There was some stuff he was keeping from me. Often, I could nudge him toward being more careful, but he was far from the image of the one hundred percent honest accountant. It was getting hard, but we kept making it work.

"Then he hooks up with Alex McKay. You know the guy I mean?"

Jane said, "We do, and we are very interested in what you can tell us about him."

"In for a penny, in for a pound. So, Harry starts off doing accountancy work for McKay Enterprises. When Harry was doing his early training, he actually did some co-op work out there for old Mr. McKay, so he and McKay Jr. knew each other. At first it's just accounting, with Harry's usual shortcuts, but soon they are working more closely with each other. Harry seemed to be becoming some sort of business partner. I was never let in on that, and didn't want to be, but soon I was doing most of the accountancy work, short of what Mr. Chartered Accountant had to do personally, while Harry was off with McKay. A few times they would have meetings here, sometimes with other guys, and I might be asked to step out, or be told I could leave early.

"I don't like McKay. I can't tell you exactly why, but I never thought he was acting on the level. He could do a really good schmooze up with me, but you could tell it was just a routine. I think he's a grifter and a crook, and to be quite frank, I was starting to plan my escape route in case things went south. So, I'm shocked someone killed Harry, I didn't really see that coming, but it's not a total surprise either. I hope you catch the guy, and I think you're doing well to be looking into McKay. Excuse the language, but I don't think he has the balls to kill anyone, especially a big guy like Harry, but I can see him being involved.

"End of my long and winding story."

Kirsten and Jane sat thoughtfully for a moment. Kirsten finally said, "Lydia, you've been more than helpful. It would be great if you could take a good look around the office, especially at anything Mr. Winston was keeping private. See if there's anything connected to McKay, or any of these non-accounting matters you mentioned. Anything at all that seems out of place. Depending on how this goes, if his business dealings seem especially important to the investigation, there may be some forensic accounting investigation later, but we can't wait for that. It would also help if we could take a quick look at his living quarters. I assume you have access. I promise we won't disturb anything."

Lydia smiled. "I plead guilty to watching too many cop shows, not that they're ever set in a place like Harmony, so I'm sort of enjoying the role of 'helpful citizen assisting the police.' I'll search the office. His apartment is through that door. It isn't locked."

Jane and Kirsten did a cursory examination of a small apartment that was surprisingly neat for someone living such a disordered life. There was nothing that looked helpful to their investigation, though they knew Jeff and his people, armed with a proper warrant, might turn up something. They returned to the front office where Lydia was industriously working through a file cabinet.

Lydia said, "Nothing yet. I'll let you know if anything turns up. Kirsten, I am glad you're back here, and I hope this makes up for some of my crappy teenage behaviour."

Smiling, Kirsten said, "It's all good, and if I run into Christine, I'll be sure to say hi."

After Jane and Kirsten left and set off for their next interview, they talked over what Lydia had shared with them. Jane said, "I have no doubt McKay is deeply tangled up in this somehow. Winston was far from a model citizen, and McKay is just the guy to point him toward whatever actually happened to him. I must admit I'm getting more and more interested in our mysterious white SUV stranger. By the way, I have a name for him. I looked back over Scrivener's interview, and he reported that when he was lying on the ground half unconscious, he heard someone, McKay likely, calling the guy William. It may not be his real name, but it gives us something to call him by.

"However, now that we've dealt with all that, what's with this Christine stuff and your fraught history with Lydia Grant?"

Kirsten quietly groaned. "Aren't you tired of hearing about my high school traumas?"

"Not nearly. Endlessly fascinating. Good comic relief from a homicide investigation. Besides, you know that in all those buddy cop movies the two guys are always bantering back and forth. So why not us? I won't give up. So, give."

"Okay, okay. This is really the opening episode, entitled *Kirsten takes on grade nine*. You know the two elementary schools in town? The one at Upper River, where all the cool kids went, and mine in Lower Town, where all the plebes and misfits went?"

Jane said, "You're maligning my old elementary school, you know. I just didn't realize I was a plebe, whatever that is, or a misfit. Carry on."

"Like I told you before, elementary school was okay for me. I don't really remember all that much about it. But going to high school was different. I mean, you leave elementary school at the top of the heap, and then in high school you're suddenly way down at the bottom. Wyandot High had set up a cohort system to try to make everyone feel involved and to spur on school spirit. Sort of like the houses in the Harry Potter books – movies to you, Jane. Everyone was assigned to a cohort in grade nine, and you stayed in it till you graduated. I think the plan was to break down the school into smaller units so no-one disappeared into the crowd.

"The cohorts met first thing every Monday morning and planned stuff like our house-league sports teams. There was competition to see which cohort collected the most food in the Christmas food drive. Each cohort had to plan at least one auditorium every year. There were also community projects, like neighbourhood cleanup days. It was all for points, and what they called 'positive competition.' I suppose maybe it wasn't all bad, but I came to hate it. It seemed to be just another way for the cool kids to build little empires, because there was an elected executive, and the cool kids always were in charge. The cool kids always ended up sticking together anyways, whatever their cohort was.

"But, back to my first cohort meeting. Lydia was on the executive. I think she was Spirit Coordinator, or something like that. She had to make sure everyone was involved. Really, to make sure everyone knew their proper place. So, first off, she calls the roll. Returning kids are asked to say one sentence about their experience in their cohort. The grade nines are asked to name something they thought they might be able to bring to their cohort, like athletic ability, or projects they did in elementary school. Of course, my name comes about two thirds of the way through. Lydia stumbles, or pretends to stumble, over my name. She says something like, 'Kirsten – that's not a Canadian name. That's too hard to say. I'm going to write you in as Christine. It'll be easier for everyone. And I'm going to spell your last name correctly. It's 'son,' not 'sen.' She makes some corrections on her list.

"I pipe up and say, 'Kirsten was originally Swedish, but it is too Canadian. I'm Kirsten, not Christine.' She says, 'We'll see about that,' and continues on through the roll. At the next Monday's meeting the staff advisor for our cohort is there. He announces that the lists have gone in and we'll soon get our t-shirts. He calls through the attendance list. When he calls out "Christine Peterson" I say nothing, even though everyone is now looking at me. At the end he looks at me and says, 'You didn't put up your hand. Are you new here? 'I say, 'No, I'm Kirsten Petersen, and I've been here from the start.' He says, 'So you're not Christine Peterson?' and I say, pointing at Lydia, 'No, Christine is some friend of hers. You'll have to ask her about Christine.' Big gasps in the room. I mean, I'm just some grubby little grade niner, and she's one of the cool kids.

"He takes her aside and is clearly angry. I later found out from someone standing close to them that he said something like, 'You're supposed to be a leader here and make the new kids feel welcome. I want no more of this sort of behaviour.'

"So, life carries on, though it's clear Lydia is no friend of mine, and the rest of the cohort are wondering about who this mouthy new grade niner is. However, this incident is not over. Two weeks later our cohort t-shirts come in, with our first names on the back. There's no 'Kirsten' shirt, but, yes, there is a 'Christine' one. The teacher is as pissed off as teachers let themselves be around students. He says to Lydia, 'I guess we'll keep this one until your friend Christine shows up.' The kids all laugh and Lydia glares at me, like it's somehow my fault. The school has to special-order a t-shirt for me, and of course the colour is slightly off, so I'm already somehow different from the other kids, and I've just started grade nine.

"High school being what it is, Lydia becomes the butt of jokes, like, 'Lydia, you can bring Christine to the party if you want.' Some wiseass gets hold of a teacher's group work roster one time and writes 'Christine' into Lydia's group. It's a supply teacher that day, and so she innocently comes to that group and says, 'But Christine doesn't seem to be here. Does anyone know where she is?' The class breaks up laughing, and someone says, 'Ask Lydia. She's the only one who knows where Christine is.' Soon 'Christine' pops up everywhere in the school. Like once, probably the same wiseass forges an announcement for the end-of-the-day announcements: 'Would Christine Peterson and Lydia Grant please report to the office.' It becomes like there's a phantom Christine Peterson in the school.

"It turns out the Christine t-shirt has been spirited away, and soon there are actual Christine sightings. The administration tries to stop it all, but can't, until finally it all seems to die down. Only good thing, I learned early on how to recede into the background and stay hidden. Kids were interested in Christine Peterson, not Kirsten Petersen, thank God. Lydia was in her graduating year, and she thankfully left me alone. I think she was just trying to keep her status as a cool kid, and not some sort of school joke."

Jane said, "I bet she was a little bit afraid of you."

"Well, maybe, but it turns out Christine hadn't gone away after all. That year the school board had just instituted some sort of new computer data system meant to keep track of attendance and all other student information. They used it to generate whatever student lists were needed. I think those systems are pretty good now, but this one had some real problems. From Lydia's initial attendance list the office had replaced my name with 'Christine Peterson.' They eventually managed to re-enter my name in the school lists, but it had to be as someone enrolling after the start of the school year. Finally, I was officially there, and they were confident 'Christine' no longer was. Comes end of the year, and the school yearbook. They always printed the pictures from those awful annual school pictures for every kid, organized by cohort. And you guessed it – I was there in all my grade nine glory, and right next to me was a blank space with the label 'Christine Peterson. Picture not provided.'

"It seems Christine was still in the system like some sort of computer ghost. The kids loved it! Christine was back! 'She' wrote comments in a lot of yearbooks, even if she only lived somewhere in the computer. Most yearbooks had lots of comments written in Christine's blank space, and some kids actually clipped out pictures to put in there, like Christine now sometimes looked just like Buffy, fearless vampire slayer. But again, even though my picture was right next to Christine's spot, I had faded way back into the background, where I wanted to be. So ends the story. Except I'm tempted to see if someone can help me find out if Christine's still alive somewhere in the school's computer system. Who knows? She may be our elusive mystery killer."

"Is this the final instalment of your high school traumas?"

"Really the first one. You've just heard them out of order. Unfortunately, there is a final installment, and I'm not sure it was comic relief. But here we are for our next interview, and I think we need to set high school aside for a while, or maybe for good."

CHAPTER 17
The Rage of Morgan

THEIR NEXT INTERVIEW WAS AT MORGAN CONSTRUCTION COMPANY, located at the edge of town. There was a brick office building close to the road with various outbuildings out back, most with oversized open doors. They could see various construction vehicles and machines parked in some of them: backhoes, bulldozers, excavators. Others seemed to contain piles of lumber and other building materials. There were weeds growing sporadically out of the gravel-covered lot. Around the back of the outbuildings were parked what appeared to be older, rusty construction machinery, some with rusty tools and pieces of metal on them. Much of the site was covered with dust. A few men could be seen working in some of the buildings, but there was a general air of late-afternoon torpor.

They parked in front of the office building, entered, and asked a bored-looking woman sitting at a battered desk near the door if Gary Morgan was in. Morgan was the owner of the company, the largest construction company in the area. He was also the grey-haired man who had received Kirsten's well-aimed kick at Friendlies three days before.

The woman said, "He's in his office at the back. Just head toward the yelling."

They could hear an angry voice further back in the office. They went down a short hallway and came to an open office door. Inside, Gary Morgan was standing in the middle of a small, messy office yelling at a middle-aged man who was standing, slump-shouldered, in front of him. The man was dressed in a poorly fitting suit, while Morgan was in jeans, a blue work shirt and heavy boots.

"Damn it, Hal, your job is to drum up business, not give me the same old pathetic excuses. We need our equipment out on jobs, not sitting out in our damned yard costing me money. My overhead costs don't stop just because you can't seem to bring in new business. I'm still working my ass off doing the real work around here, while you're doing what, exactly?"

In a quiet, whiny voice, Hal said, "Look, Gary, I'm doing the best I can. The economy's just not great right now. When I approach prospective clients, they keep asking about all those problems out at New Eden, and Alex hasn't had anything for us for a while. Damn it, Gary, I'm doing the best I can."

Morgan snorted and said, "Yeah, that may be the real problem. This is the best you can do. Come on, get out of here, and go bring me some goddamn business. I seem to have some visitors."

Hal left and the women entered his office. Jane started to introduce them. Morgan cut her off. "I know who you are. You're Officer Big Mouth and she's the one with the fancy footwork. Officer Jade, isn't it? Hard to recognize you with your clothes on and your tits not hanging out. Here to finish me off?"

Jane said, "We're here to ask you about a serious police matter. You need to settle down and find a respectful tone, Mr. Morgan."

"You want a fucking respectful tone? Well, maybe Officer Jade can apologize to me and then I'll be more inclined to answer your goddamn questions in a goddamn respectful tone."

In a cold voice, Kirsten said, "Turn around, Mr. Morgan, and extend your wrists behind your back."

"What for! I ain't done nothing, and this is *my* private property. "

Kirsten said, "I'm arresting you for assault from last Saturday, and if you don't cooperate, also for resisting arrest. Turn around! It seems we're going to have to carry on our conversation at police headquarters."

Morgan said, "You better call your back-up, 'cause I ain't going nowhere."

With that, Jane quickly stepped forward, grabbed his arm, and swiftly twisted it behind his back, lifting it up high and forcing a squealing Morgan to bend over. Kirsten snapped cuffs onto his wrists. Jane pulled his shackled wrists higher, frog-marching him out of the office.

As they approached the outer door, Morgan turned to the shocked-looking receptionist and yelled, "Don't just sit there looking gobsmacked. Call my lawyer. Call Jasper McKnight. He'll straighten these two goddamn bitches out."

Jane said, "Call the lawyer if you want, but we'll be seeing Captain McKnight in about five minutes."

They took Morgan outside, where Jane called for a cruiser equipped with a cage to meet them. She said, "I believe you actually asked us to call backup, Mr. Morgan. Too bad that'll mean a lot more people seeing this little episode."

The cruiser soon arrived, and Jane told the officers to take Morgan to HQ. Morgan sullenly went with them. Jane and Kirsten headed back to police headquarters. Jane said, "You know, after all the crap that's been going on, that felt pretty good. Not sure how Jasper will react to us bringing in one of his pals, though."

When they got back to headquarters, Jane quickly informed McKnight what had happened. "You may want to sit in, Captain. Morgan was threatening to lawyer up and seemed sure you were going to help him out with your, quote, 'bitch cops,' excuse the language."

They entered the interview room where the officers had taken Morgan. He was handcuffed to a metal ring on the table and sat seething and obviously still angry. Kirsten was sitting across from him. McKnight and Jane joined her.

McKnight said, "Mr. Morgan, I hear you've been causing my officers some problems. Care to explain?"

"Jasper, look, I was ..."

McKnight smacked his palm on to the desk and said, "It's Captain McKnight, and this is Sergeant Walden and Detective Petersen. So, your explanation."

"Sorry, sorry. Look, I admit I was a bit out of line, but I was just chewing out one of my employees. Business is way down, and I was angry. You know how it is. But about this assault business, I didn't know she was a cop, so that's a bogus charge. Captain, look, I know you can sort this out. You're always sensible about things."

McKnight nodded. "Yes, we do have to be sensible here, Mr. Morgan. I fully agree, and yes, we will sort this out. I also agree the assault charge isn't appropriate here."

Morgan started to relax a little. "Way my balls are still aching, you should charge *her* with assault."

Jane flashed a frustrated, tight-lipped look over at a quiet-looking Kirsten.

McKnight continued, his voice gradually getting louder, "Only thing is, Mr. Morgan, I don't see anything remotely sensible about you disrespecting my officers." Here McKnight suddenly pounded the table, causing everyone to flinch. "And I've been looking over the reports from last Saturday's disgusting business, and it seems your friend Winston actually was attempting a sexual assault. And you assisted him, so the sexual assault charge also applies to you. Actually, let's keep the common assault charge too. *And* it seems today you've added resisting arrest.

"Now, my colleagues are busy here with you, so I'm going to go to my office to start the paperwork. If – *if* – I hear that you are cooperating fully with Sergeant Walden and Detective Petersen, and *if* you are behaving in a respectful manner, I can talk to the Crown Attorney about setting those charges aside. I hope you understand what I'm saying to you, *Mr.* Morgan, because we are dealing with serious matters here, and I am dead serious in what I've just said to you. And as for your aching balls, you better start to understand that I now own them."

In quick succession Morgan looked smug, then shocked, and then scared. "Okay, okay, I understand, Captain. Look, I'm cooled down now. I'm sorry for the way I behaved. So, I answer their questions and then it's over, and I can go?"

"Not quite. I said if you acted like a good citizen I would put the paperwork aside. I didn't say I would discard it. We have more time than you might imagine before we actually have to file charges. The paperwork stays on my desk. And if I hear you have been saying anything else – *anything* else – that disrespects this department, or me, or especially my two officers, the paperwork gets filed and you will be dealing with the courts. Sergeant Walden, Officer Petersen, please continue. Let me know if you are in any way unhappy with Mr. Morgan's behaviour, answers, or anything else, and I'll proceed with the charges.

"Oh, and Mr. Winston's sister has been notified. The official release is going out now, so it's public knowledge."

Smiling at all three of them, he said, "Now, I hope you all have a productive meeting," and then left the room.

Morgan sat looking stunned for a few moments. Then he looked over at the officers and in a subdued voice said, "Next of kin? Harry's dead?"

Jane said, "That's why we came out to talk to you. Now let's set this assault business off to the side, so we can have the conversation we wanted to have with you. We can go back to your office, unless you're willing for the real conversation to happen here."

Morgan said, "No way I want to go back there now; I'm willing to talk with you here, because I have nothing to hide. What's going on?"

Jane said, "His body was found this morning outside the city. He appears to have been murdered. Where were you this morning, Mr. Morgan?"

Morgan swallowed a few times, and then said, "You can't think I'm a suspect. Sure, I knew Harry, we did some business stuff, had the odd drink. But you seriously think I could have murdered him?"

"Your behaviour this morning doesn't help, Mr. Morgan. So again, where were you this morning?"

"Just around the yard, checking on some machinery, some minor repairs and maintenance. In the office for a while. There were others around. You can check."

"We will. We'll get their names and contact information later, but right now, we need to know everything you can tell us about Mr. Winston. Who he associated with. Enemies. The nature of your business dealings with him. Anything you can tell us that will help our investigation.

"Ok, I'll tell you all I can. Look, my life is in a mess right now. That equipment you saw at the yard is leased and it's costing me a mint just sitting there idle. That's why I was so upset. Okay, I do have a temper, but it's really all just talk, unlike with that idiot Harry. Mr. Big Shot Tough Guy. Always pushing his weight around. Always needs to be the top dog. So I'm not going to hide I didn't like the guy, but I did not kill him."

"Why, then, did you hang around with him, like at Friendlies last Saturday night?"

"It's because of Alex McKay, you know, the big developer and real estate guy in town. Usually, Alex would be there too. He was going to be in our golf foursome but bailed at the last minute. He said he would join us at Friendlies if he could, but never showed. We often ended up there. Say, is that why you were out there at Friendlies, trying to spy on Alex and Harry?"

"We'll ask the questions. You need to just give us full and honest answers. Tell us about the third guy with you last Saturday."

"That was Arnold Weirness. You know, the truck haulage guy, the township councillor?"

"This is getting to be like pulling teeth, Mr. Morgan. How about you just tell us all about your dealings, business and otherwise, with Mr. Winston."

"I said my business is in trouble, and it's because I listened to that asshole McKay. That's who you need to talk to. I'm just a construction guy. Built my business from scratch. I used to do some work for McKay Enterprises when the old man was in charge. That carried on with Alex when he took over. Things were pretty good back then, things were expanding, even around here. Lots of people coming to the area to build cottages. A few new businesses were opening up, so I was able to expand, get new equipment, and hire more people.

"But you can tell from the way I'm dressed I'm a construction guy, not a businessman. I started to get more work from McKay, and it seemed to be all good. That's how I met Harry. He did some of the numbers stuff for Alex, but we didn't see each other much except through business. It started to be that Alex made clear that he needed people he trusted around him. He had big plans, lots of profit for all of us, but we had to be a team. His team."

Morgan paused for moment, seemingly deep in thought. Kirsten said, "So you and Mr. Winston were part of Mr. McKay's business team?"

Morgan said, "More like an inner circle of some type. Look, I'm not proud about some of this stuff, but I need to get out of this mess. I used to be just a small-time construction guy. Maybe I've always been a bit rough around the edges, but I wasn't a guy who would go to a strip joint and act like some sort of macho asshole."

Looking at Kirsten, he said, "My daughter's your age. She lived with her mother after we split, but I still see her. I could never explain to her about what happened at Friendlies, or even why I started to go there. You probably think I'm just bullshitting you, Detective, to try to con you, but I am sorry. I apologize."

Kirsten said, "Apology conditionally accepted, but while we're on the subject, why did you go there? You were right out of line Saturday night."

"Like I said, it started with Alex. If we were to be his team, we had to hang out together, be real guys. So, I went along, became part of it. It's hard to explain to women, and I'm not good at explaining, anyway, but when guys get together like that, it's like you're in a tribe. Nothing very subtle about it. Sports and drinking and macho big talk, and especially behaving like a jerk with women. You go along with it. You make the other guys go along with it. Nothing to be proud of."

Kirsten said, "There's got to be more to it. You become a different man just because you're doing business with some guy?"

"Yeah, there's something else, all right." He paused and took a deep breath. "Does this conversation have to get out?"

"No guarantees, Mr. Morgan. You're not the focus of our investigation, but we can't guarantee what might become part of the record. I think you want to tell us more, so it's best you just continue."

Morgan gave a big sigh, sat up a little straighter, and said, "The something else is cutting corners, and worse. That damn McKay is so smooth, he gets you in up to your neck before you know it. We were making a lot of money. Weirness was getting a lot of trucking contracts from McKay, so he was glad to grease the wheels with township council. He sometimes helped Alex get confidential information that gave him the inside track on a lot of stuff. McKay got the contract, Weirness would end up with any trucking part of it, and I would get the construction part of it. Things got bigger and bigger. More and more money. And as things got closer to illegal, and likely already were, you had to be a loyal member of Alex's team.

"And you eventually end up in things like Saturday night, where you're getting hammered in a cheap goddam strip joint, with a crooked township councillor and a bullying accountant, waiting for a sleazy developer to show up. You know the rest."

Jane said, "You seemed to indicate McKay was the leader of the pack, but that Winston was the bully, the big shot. Can you explain?'

"Alex was definitely the leader of the pack, but Harry was the big macho jock, the loudmouth, the guy who didn't hide that he could beat you to a pulp if he ever cared to. Alex would sit back quietly, listening and watching, but Harry would instantly shut up if Alex wanted to talk. We might have opinions, but it was Alex who gave the final orders."

"So, it was essentially the four of you?"

"Oh, there were others. They would come and go, depending on what Alex needed from them. That little jerk Will Handstrom was usually there, until that stupid accident a while back, but, yeah, the top dog, the numbers guy, the township councillor, and the construction guy. That was Alex's inner circle."

"I'm still not totally clear on why you didn't just leave, since you have your own business and don't seem to have liked these guys."

"New Eden. I told you my business was expanding, and a lot of the work came from Alex. But then he came up with his big brainstorm, New Eden. The way he put it, he could get the land cheap, since it was essentially useless. Weirness helped with the approvals, especially getting the access road put in. Township councillors are not necessarily really smart people, and McKay and Weirness knew what to say to them. You know, increased tax base, economic activity, reasons for people to re-elect them. So, Alex somehow got the groundwork laid. I don't know the ins and outs of what they did. I guess Harry and Handstrom helped make sure the numbers and some of the legal stuff happened, but all I really know is it got approved and was ready to move ahead.

"Alex, early on, comes to me and says I'll get the construction contracts, except this is much bigger. We were going to build a whole subdivision, twelve houses, so I needed to do more land preparation, more building construction, needed more people to do the plumbing, electrical work, gas installations, a whole lot of stuff. I would have to expand, big time, and fast.

"Like I said, I'm really just a construction guy. I probably really needed a partner who could run the business stuff and knew how larger companies worked. I mean, I was being asked to go from being a hands-on construction foreman to being in charge of a much bigger operation."

He paused and shook his head. Jane gently encouraged him. "It seems you had some serious doubts, but you carried on anyway."

"Alex always had answers for me. Quoted experts he claimed he had access to. Even had me talk to some advisors who seemed to know what they were talking about. So, I bought in. Built the damn subdivision, such as it is.

"All the while Alex said this was only the start. Like, he's telling me this confidential thing he is working on over near the Wyandot reserve will bring me lots of work, but no details and no real reason to believe him. Meanwhile, I have people laid off, some of them owed wages, and not much for the rest to do. You saw all that equipment I leased. Just sitting there. No way I could afford to buy it, but the leases aren't up for several months. I think I'm fucked, excuse the language. Unless Alex comes through at Wyandot, but maybe not even then."

Another short pause. "Okay, I shouldn't take it out on other people, but damn it, I'm really just a common working guy, who not all that long ago was getting along okay, and now I'm sitting in a police station."

Kirsten said, "Tell us more about why the New Eden project worked out so badly for you. It's got to be more than just a bad business plan."

"Oh yeah. I mentioned cutting corners. For some time, Alex has been pressuring me to find what he first called 'smarter ways of getting things done.' My business used to be a success because I took pride in doing good work, on time, doing it properly. With Alex, there was buying substandard materials. He was always putting the emphasis on doing jobs fast and getting out. Even fudging inspections and approvals, with his encouragement and help. Weirness sometimes helped there. No way I should have gone along, but I was making lots more money. You sort of get caught up in being in the fast lane with operators like Alex. So, I just went along.

"With New Eden, we cut corners big time. I knew there had to be proper inspections when building in a new area, especially out in the boonies. Now I hear there's gas leaking into the basements, the basements I built. And we lied about the quality of the vinyl siding, and the shingles, and the roof sheathing. We did a whole lot of lying, but I was in deep financially by now. It was like Alex was driving the toboggan downhill and my only hope was to hang on and try to get to the bottom."

He ruefully shook his head. "To the bottom, best way to put it. Now the New Eden buyers keep bringing their complaints to me. I have corrected some stuff, but you can't really repair crap. They have lawyers threatening me, not just Alex. Even if I get through all this shit, why would anyone trust me ever again to build anything?

"You want me to tell you about Alex McKay? Okay, I'm the guy who has screwed up his life so bad. But McKay is the weapon. Harry's dead? Too bad. Really. I think he is – was – an asshole jerk, but McKay is the guy who deserves to be dead, not Harry. I suppose if McKay ever gets what he deserves, I just gave you my motive."

He paused. "Right now, I just hope I can get out of this mess. I need to move away and get an honest job, even if it's just doing construction work for someone else. Look, I can't really tell you anything else."

Morgan sat quietly with his head in his hands. Jane looked over to Kirsten, who nodded her head.

Jane said, "I do hope you are able to sort things out, Mr. Morgan. We appreciate your cooperation, even if it took a while to get there. We may want to talk to you again, but you're free to go."

After Morgan left, Kirsten was the first to speak, "Ok, first, who is our new captain and what did he do to McKnight? I mean, he destroyed that guy. And 'I own your balls?' I almost choked. But he was great."

"Agreed. Jasper's strong point always has been supporting his officers, and I still have way too many questions about how he's behaving, but yeah, he was great."

"I think Morgan was levelling with us. He'll never be named citizen of the year, but his sad little story makes sense. Our Mr. McKay is turning out to be really something else. We need to lean on him. He may not have killed Winston himself, but McKay seems to be at the centre of whatever the hell is going on here."

"Again, I agree. But it's almost five o'clock, and the captain wants us to meet in his office, see where we've gotten to. And then I have a social invitation for you. You are invited to dinner with Martha and me, and our other guest is your old pal Sid Ray, who is eager to meet up with you, and not just for old times' sake. He says he has some information we really have to know about."

"You're on. Hope you have lots of wine. Actually, I'll pick some up. Let's go see what our new captain wants."

As the two women picked up their stuff from the table and headed for the captain's office, Kirsten said, "You know one thing I'm happy about from the interview? That Jasper said 'he,' not 'we,' owns Morgan's balls."

Jane said, "If anything, I'm even happier than you about that. You know, after your little rearrangement job last Saturday, they aren't even in mint condition anymore."

Laughing, Kirsten said, "May even be factory seconds."

They were still laughing when they knocked on McKnight's open door. McKnight looked up and said, "Well, glad you two are finding something to amuse you in all this. We have to really stay on the ball to get ahead of this mess."

Kirsten and Jane struggled to stifle a new round of laughter and avoided looking at each other. Jeff joined them and all three sat down in front of McKnight's desk. Jeff looked curiously at Jane and Kirsten as they squirmed slightly in their chairs, rubbing their faces and looking down.

McKnight slumped back in his chair, looking tired and worn out. "We need to stay right on top of this murder investigation. Petersen, find out all you can from Dr. Hepburn after the post-mortem tomorrow. Pathologists are often too cautious in their official reports, and we need all the information we can get.

"Ripley, anything new from the crime scene?"

"Nothing that looks useful. We couldn't find anything remotely like the doctor's mysterious weapon. That area has been used as a garbage dump by people for years, so there's no shortage of stuff there, but nothing that looks recent or out of place. No footprints, other than a couple of partials that are likely Winston's. No tire marks, other than his and all of ours. The blood is all from right around the body, so he must have been hit close to where he ended up.

"We looked as well as we could for the mysterious blue object Lewis claims Winston threw into the creek. I used our small boat to look around in the stream from the bridge down to where it enters the swamp. The stream still flows through the swamp, but there's various obstructions, fallen trees and stuff, that likely would have caught something floating. I don't think anything could have gotten more than a hundred feet or so downstream from the crime scene, and I'm ninety-nine percent sure there's nothing more to be found there."

Jane said, "If Winston wasn't trying to recover whatever Lewis said he threw off the bridge, it's hard to imagine what he would be doing there."

Jeff said, "Maybe it was the best his assailant could do to quickly find a secluded place to kill Winston. Though you'd expect Winston would have put up a struggle, and no sign of that."

Jane added, "It could be some random assailant who encountered Winston at the bridge, but why the attack? It wasn't robbery. There's no physical evidence saying anyone else was there. Winston was a pretty big guy. We need to keep that option open, but I don't buy it."

McKnight said to Jeff, "If you're quite sure nothing could have been overlooked at the crime scene, no use wasting more time out there. I've asked that uniformed officers canvass the neighbourhood tomorrow just in case anyone saw anything. I talked to this guy Lewis. I don't understand these fitness nuts, but that does explain why he was in the area. He had nothing more to add to his story. He's the only person we know was in the immediate area, but it'd be a major stretch to see him as being able to kill a big guy like Winston and then be so cool and controlled afterwards. There's no real motive. We have to keep him on the suspect list, but let's not waste time there."

He paused slightly. "I had a short chat with Alex McKay before he had to rush off to some meeting. He claims Winston was just out there that morning on a routine business matter to do with this latest development project. He says Winston seemed normal when he left. Look, I've known McKay for some time. We're in the same lodge. I know some people don't like the way he does business, and his neighbours out there at New Eden are all riled up, but he's had no history of violence or anything close to it. We need to keep all options on the table, but there's no reason right now to investigate him any further about the murder."

Looking at Jane and Kirsten, he said, "I asked you to go out to Wyandot just because it's so close. Someone there might know something. There's the matter of where the killer disappeared to so quickly, since you two were on the scene almost immediately. Anything there?"

Jane gave a condensed version of their conversation with Wanda. "She will have her people look around. If there's some random killer looking for a place to hide, they'll find him. okay, Captain?"

McKnight nodded. "Agreed. Only other thing is this mysterious new development of McKay's being next to the reserve. It does connect Winston with Wyandot, but I don't see how that bears on his death. And so we're clear, I agree there's no reason to concentrate on anyone at Wyandot. Again, let's just keep our options open."

Kirsten said, "I agree there's nothing definite there yet, but I really hate coincidence. McKay's name keeps popping up. We were directed to look into his finances, and then the Friendlies business last Saturday brings Winston in, and then Winston meets with McKay minutes before his death, and McKay and Winston are both connected with this development near Wyandot. I can't believe this doesn't all tie together somehow, even indirectly."

McKnight said, "I hear you, Detective. I agree it is puzzling, and we need more detail about it. I'll ask my superiors if we are to continue our investigation into McKay's finances, given how tied up we'll be in the murder case.

"Of course, we do need to see who else might have had a separate motive to kill Winston. Where did you get to with our Mr. Morgan?"

Jane gave a brief summary of the information they got from Morgan. "McKay is clearly a pretty shady operator, and Winston was closely linked with all that, but that would make McKay the real target, not Winston. Captain, we'll have a detailed report for you soon, but we also were able to interview Winston's business associate, Lydia Grant. She also was highly critical of McKay's business practices and is adamant that McKay was dragging Winston into highly suspicious activities. I think we need to keep looking into all that, though I have no idea why something from that whole mess would end up with Winston being murdered at the bridge."

McKnight said stiffly, "As I said, we will keep all options on the table. Keep looking into Winston's business activities and personal life. Something's got to show up. And one piece of information for you three: I was informed just before this meeting that the Ministry of Health is ordering the evacuation of New Eden tomorrow as a result of their testing. The results were so alarming they felt they have to act immediately. This shouldn't affect you three, but our uniformed officers are on alert to help out if people refuse to leave. I am told they have tomorrow to take a few personal possessions but must leave by mid-afternoon. Another darned complication we don't need right now."

Jane said, "You're right about that, and it gives a whole lot more people a motive to go after McKay."

McKnight said, "But not Winston, who does remain the focus of our investigation. I think we all have lots to do for tomorrow. I want to meet again tomorrow afternoon, or earlier, if necessary, to stay on top of all this. Anything else?"

Kirsten said, "Just, Captain, I really appreciate your supporting us in there with Morgan. Thanks."

McKnight, looking slightly surprised, said, "Detective, you'll soon learn that I always back my officers. Always. Thanks, everyone. Good work so far, even if we are short on answers. Please close the door after you leave."

With that, the meeting broke up. After the three detectives left, Jasper McKnight sat for a while quietly at his desk, with his head in his hands, before he too left.

CHAPTER 18
A Dinner with Sid

KIRSTEN AND JANE WENT DIRECTLY FROM POLICE HEADQUARTERS to Jane's house. It was one of the newer homes in Harmony, located on the edge of town and bordering on farm fields. They were welcomed by Martha Nicholson, Jane's partner. She was a tall, middle-aged woman with long hair fastened back in a ponytail. She seemed to be wearing no make-up and had reading glasses suspended by a cord around her neck. Jane had previously informed Kirsten that Martha owned and ran the largest daycare centre in Harmony. She also was chair of the county library board and a key member of the county's social services committee.

Sid Ray arrived right on their heels, and they all adjourned to a sunroom at the back of the house. Martha took drink orders and announced dinner would be ready in a few minutes.

Jane said, "Sid, I liked your article about the great parking meter scam. Thanks again for your help with taking down Scrivener, and for going gentle on us for not tumbling on to it sooner."

Sid replied, "My pleasure. I wanted a good story, and you helped with that. Maybe this will be the one to get me enough profile to be hired on as a real journalist somewhere. Nothing against Harmony, but it's not exactly a dream location for a reporter. Except, it seems right now there *is* something pretty big happening here."

Martha had returned with everyone's drinks. "I know you three have some important matters to discuss, but after dinner, please. Let's try to cram a little bit of relaxation in first. Like, Kirsten and Sid, I understand you two have some shared history."

Sid said, "Indeed we do. Intrepid high school journalists for the three years we were together at good old Wyandot High. Kirsten, really good to see you again. I'm sorry we lost touch after high school. I have to admit I was some surprised when I saw you doing your thing at Friendlies last Saturday. It didn't seem the best time to renew acquaintances. I must admit, being a cop was about the last thing I saw you choosing for a career."

"I'm getting a lot of that back here. It actually just seemed to happen. And so here I am, back to the scene of my earlier crimes. Ready to serve and protect."

"Like bringing justice to people like that asshole Vice-Principal Andrews from back in high school?"

Just then Martha announced dinner, which turned out to be a lavish traditional roast beef meal. Conversation continued over dinner about Sid and Kirsten's shared time at high school, including the "Christine" event and Kirsten's suspension-causing cafeteria confrontation.

Sid said, "Yeah, that happened the year after I graduated, but the whole town was buzzing with it. That and your 'just desserts' blow-up the next year."

Jane said, "Another big high school drama, Kirsten? I thought I'd heard about them all. Your high school time was a whole lot more exciting than mine."

"Except," Martha interjected, "for your little cafeteria ketchup assault!"

"Yes, except for that," Jane said. "But come on, Kirsten. I keep hearing references to your last big adventure. Time to finish the story. Give, girl."

With a sigh, Kirsten said, "As long as you find my adolescent traumas worth listening to."

She looked around the table but saw only interested faces.

"Ok. You're bears for punishment. Here goes. I've explained that despite my few flashes of notoriety I was never part of the school's in-crowd, what we called the cool kids, the Upper River aristocracy. So, imagine my surprise in my last year when I was chosen to be the school's 'graduation queen.' That was a really weird tradition around the school."

"Not when I was there," Jane interjected, "so remind me what that was all about."

"Well, as part of the graduation celebrations, a school queen and a school king were chosen. Initially it was by popular vote, but that of course made it a popularity contest, and the teachers and even the school board were concerned about some of the choices. I mean, this was supposed to be the cream of the graduating class, and some years this so-called cream was pretty curdled. So, the teachers took over, and they made the final choice, drawing on nominations from the students and others. They made academic standing and 'overall contribution to the school and community' key criteria."

"Which would wipe out most of those Upper River idiots," Sid interjected.

Kirsten smiled. "Yes, there was that. So, imagine my amazement when the teachers chose me to be school queen. Right out of the blue. There was a lot of unhappiness about that in certain areas of the school population. My first instinct was to say 'NO!' as emphatically as possible. It didn't exactly fit with my plan to exit high school as surreptitiously and quietly as possible. Except my parents were thrilled. They had put up with a lot from me during my adolescence, and this was like a dream come true. Kirsten, daughter of immigrant parents, becomes school queen! I just couldn't give them one more big disappointment. I owed it to them. So, I gritted my teeth and accepted.

"It involved a lot more than just being crowned at the grad prom. High school stuff then was a big deal in quiet old Harmony, so the graduation had become a week-long community celebration. The school brass loved the attention it brought to the school, and the rest of the town joined in the festivities. For the week leading up to the grad prom, the king and queen were special guests at service club meetings, visited the elementary schools, officiated at various community events, did appearances at local stores and businesses. It was ridiculous. And there was always a royal court chosen to support the royal couple, three boys and three girls. I think the school did this as a sop to the Upper River aristocracy, because the royal court was almost always their kids. So, we usually had a retinue at these various royal events around town.

"All this would be bad enough, but there was also the issue of how the royal couple got along. In the early days of this little fiasco, it was often a dating couple chosen, or they would at least be from the same school crowd. Not so this year, with Ms. Strange Outsider Girl being chosen. The 'king' that year was Bradley Misener, a guy I hardly knew, and a core member of the school aristocracy. The pressure was on for us to get along."

Kirsten paused for a moment. "The expectation had grown with the students over the years that the royal couple really should be a couple. This was easier in the early days of this idiocy when they often were actually dating. High school being high school, everyone knew who was boinking who, and it became part of the twisted little school mythology that during grad week, the queen and king would be sure to consummate their royal relationship. That would always be weird, but it was easier when they were both from the cool kids' crowd. Good old Bradley was faced with being paired up with someone widely regarded as being some sort of weird virgin outsider. Didn't matter if the middle part wasn't actually true."

Kirsten stopped and pointed at Jane, who was sitting with an expectant look on her face. "And Ms. Has To Know Everything, don't even ask because I ain't telling!"

Jane said, "We'll see, but back to the story."

"Bradley had a real problem. Pressure was on for him to get me into the sack. Maybe a tough situation for an adolescent boy back then, but I wasn't sympathetic then and I'm sure not sympathetic now. I didn't like Bradley but was determined to get through the week, get through graduation, and finally escape high school. Bradley kept cozying up to me, saying things like, 'When do the king and queen get to know each other better?' and 'You do realize being royalty has certain important obligations.' Really sophisticated stuff.

"On the Wednesday of grad week there was the official royal dinner. There were few restaurants in town then, and the most up-scale was Giuseppe's Italian restaurant. The royal court and various school and community bigwigs would also be there. There really was a Giuseppe, you might recall, Giuseppe Moreno. Nice guy. Italian immigrant, though I'm not sure how he ended up in Harmony. He liked the high school kids and sort of took a shine to me, maybe because my parents were also immigrants. He was always glad to see me, always chatted with me and made sure I got special treatment.

"There we were, at a table for eight, the royal couple and their court. Brad was in a tux, and I was wearing the too-expensive strapless gown my parents had bought for me, their graduating royal daughter. We were on a special bench made up to look like a double royal throne. Too cheesy to be true, except it was. The meal dragged on: school chatter I wasn't interested in; insider talk by the cool kids; various people stopping at our table to congratulate us; having to smile and look happy. Absolutely ghastly. What made it worse was that Bradley appeared to have been drinking. He even left the table a couple of times, probably for another drink. He kept edging closer to me, and I had to keep pushing his hand away under the table. He even whispered in my ear, 'So is tonight our big night?' I wanted to just get out of there but was trapped.

"Giuseppe – Mr. Moreno – must have figured out what was going on, and bless him, he rescued me. I think he heard some of what Bradley had been saying, and he seemed to pick up on how distressed I was. He was an old-style European gentleman, and though he had to play the genial host, I don't think he had much use for the cool kid crowd. At the end of the meal, he brought the special royal desserts to the table, lavish, gloppy sundaes covered with sauce and whipped cream. Bradley had his arm around my shoulder, and I was wedged up against the side of our throne. Giuseppe seemed to stumble and fell forward, dumping the whole mess in Bradley's lap. A bit of it got on me, but Bradley took the brunt. Giuseppe apologized profusely, called staff over to help clean up, promised to pay for the dry cleaning, fussed over things, and also found the chance to give me a sly wink.

"In all the confusion, I was able to make my exit. Bradley obviously couldn't carry on, and the evening was clearly over. Except, my parents had given me a small new camera, the latest thing, as a graduation present. I snapped a few shots of the whole scene, especially of Bradley in all his mucked-up glory. When I got home, I got more and more angry about the whole thing. Facebook was still in its early stages, but I had an account. So, I posted a picture of Bradley, covered in goo, with the comment, 'Here's his Royal Majesty getting his just desserts.' Little Miss Smart Ass.

"I don't know what I expected the reaction to be. I had just lost it. Sort of like at Friendlies last Saturday. Well, enough other people in town had Facebook accounts, so it was soon really widespread. General reaction: 'Poor, poor Bradley had his big night ruined, while ungracious selfish weird girl proves she never should have been chosen queen. Who does she think she is?' The Upper River crowd was really up in arms. Big pressure on the school. At the end of school next day, I was called in to a special meeting where it was decided I would withdraw from being school queen because of a sudden illness. I really had no choice. I was going to be out one way or another. Of course, this also meant I couldn't attend the grad prom, despite my beautiful prom dress and my parents' wishes. So, instead of a quiet exit from high school, I instead created probably my most notorious and most public disaster."

Jane said, "That was it? Seems like there's more."

Kirsten said, "Unfortunately, yes. I called Giuseppe – Mr. Moreno – and apologized for all the trouble this would bring him. He was great, concerned only for me. He said honour always had to be protected, and Bradley didn't deserve me. He apologized far and wide, gave Bradley and his family a complimentary dinner, and pledged to make future royal dinners his treat, his gift to the school. The blame all went to me, not to him. I know he passed about five years later, and happy though I was to have escaped Harmony, I wish I could have at least been at his funeral. He was a brave, kind, really class guy.

"My parents were, as always, great. This whole thing broke their hearts, even though I kept from them what Bradley had been doing. I mean, others knew he had been coming on to me, but most of them thought he had every right to. More reason to get out of here. My parents were supportive and focussed instead on my transition to university. The plan had been for me to work in Harmony for the summer. I had a job in place at one of the stores, but instead I went right to London, where I was enrolled for the fall. I was set to live in a residence, and the university managed to move up my move-in date.

"Things weren't great for my parents. Most people thought I had been out of line, and many were keen to express this to my parents. After all, I had personally demeaned poor Bradley and this great high school and community celebration. Some people in town had always treated them like outsiders, immigrants who needed to remember that. Some of the people at her work started to shun my mother. My dad started to lose some of his customers. They were both on the verge of retirement, and so they moved that up. They moved to London to be closer to me, and they still live there now.

"You can see why I felt I had to leave here. Whatever Harmony was, it sure was no place for me."

Martha said, "Small towns can be very close-minded places. Cruel, even. How do you feel being back here now?"

Kirsten said, "It was strange at first. I mean, career-wise I really had to accept the transfer here, and I was curious. I would be here on my own terms and wouldn't have to stay long. But I have to admit, it does feel like a different place."

Sid said, "The world is breaking in on our quiet little backward town. A lot of new people have moved in over the last ten years. It really has become a different place. But talking about the world breaking in, I do need to talk to you about some really important stuff. Martha, great meal, thank you so much. But can I borrow these two?"

Martha smiled. "Of course. You three go back to the sunroom while I put things away. I'll join you later, if it's not too private a conversation."

When they got settled in the sunroom, Sid leaned forward and said, "I need to talk to you about Alex McKay."

He paused and then carried on. "I've been nosing around here for a real story for some time. I mean, being a stringer for some of the media outlets down south is fine, but it doesn't pay the bills. The odd bit of supply teaching helps, and the odd bit of consulting and writing tutorials and other stuff is fine, but I'm in my mid-thirties and I don't want to spend the rest of my life like this. Maybe I've been too comfortable trying to stick around my hometown, but part of me is that I'm a rooted person. I don't want to be constantly moving around, always being a transient. But another part of me wants a career as a serious journalist, which I can't really do just playing out the string around here. So, like I say, I've been trying to find the big story that opens doors for me.

"That business with Scrivener at the parking lot just kind of fell into my lap. My first actual investigative journalism. My stories about that did get picked up some because it's got some interesting angles, but it's too early to tell if it'll help much."

Jane said, "I hope it will. You showed some class there. You could have twisted it into some sort of 'How could the cops be so dumb?' story, something cheap like that, but you played fair."

"One of my journalism profs always stressed that you let the story tell itself. Given some of the extreme journalism stuff you see now – tabloid crap, TV ranting, so-called reporters who really just promote themselves and say anything that will get idiots with a ten-second attention span to pay attention to them – my prof's advice seems almost quaint now. But that's the sort of journalist I want to be: honour the story, try to find what's really happening.

"So, the Scrivener thing was great, but like I say, it just sort of fell into my lap. What I've been nosing into for a while is McKay. I've got a story ready to go about all the problems at New Eden. You know, people think they are buying their dream home out in God's country and end up in some kind of hell. Even has a mythic dimension: another loss of innocence in New Eden, if that's not too literary to be journalism."

Kirsten smiled. "Maybe could be the focus of a longer piece in the *Walrus* or *Maclean's*."

"As if! And that story is still developing. Hot off the press from one of my many sources, New Eden is being evacuated tomorrow."

Seeing the smiles on their faces, he ruefully said, "But it appears you already know that. I was looking into the New Eden fiasco and how McKay is being bled dry financially because of it. But then it turns out he's actually working on a new development. A little digging, and it turns out he's looking for land around here, and he ends up putting together a package near the Wyandot reserve. He was trying to be discreet, but with all the approvals he had to get, and that access road being put in, and the negotiations with the Wyandot tribal council, it wasn't hard to nose out.

"I know this isn't news to you, but bear with me. Strange details start to emerge. He doesn't say exactly what the development is going to be for. He lets people assume it's just another housing development. But this land is even more remote than New Eden, and no lake. How could it ever be a success? What is really going on there? One of the prospective sellers he talked to pressed him on it, asking how he could be sure that McKay would pay him. He couldn't see how his scrub land out near the swamp and the woods would be suitable for a subdivision of some sort. So ol' Alex hems and haws, swears the guy to secrecy, and drops a hint that the provincial government has engaged his services to find potential land for a new provincial park."

Jane sat up a little straighter. "This business about McKay and our mysterious stranger meeting with MPP Fox a while back maybe starts to make a little more sense."

"Agreed, though it's all still just speculation, and McKay lies almost as a matter of routine. But, on top of the mystery about what the land is to be used for, McKay seems to be on the verge of bankruptcy, and then he comes up with substantial financial backing seemingly out of thin air. My source at the bank tells me the manager, Quinlan, who's always managed financial matters for McKay Enterprises, was worried, like *really* worried that the bank would take a real bath when McKay defaulted on his loans. And, it seems the bank's head office was leaning on Quinlan to get things sorted out pronto. But then yet another mystery guy shows up with McKay, they meet with Quinlan, and before you know it McKay has some magical big-time financial backing from somewhere. And what could that somewhere be?"

Sid paused "Look, I know you two know a lot of this, but I'm not sure how much, so I'll continue my gratis sharing so we can see where it gets us. Feel free to add any details I don't know about.

"It soon becomes evident to me that the police have some interest in all this. You transfer up here, Kirsten, and some digging yesterday tells me you worked for a while in the provincial financial crimes unit. I didn't know that Saturday when lo and behold my old star reporter from high school reappears on the scene. And with the police. And obviously very interested in McKay's pals and business associates. And you visit Quinlan at the bank Monday."

Jane said, "You clearly have some good sources. Yet when we were chatting Monday waiting for the parking lot business to happen, you said nothing about any of this."

"We had lots going on with Scrivener, and we ended up talking about a lot of old high school history, but most of all I was still trying to put all this together. When Winston turns up dead today, I've got even more to try to sort out and put together."

Kirsten said, "You're right, we already know a lot of this. And you're right, things have certainly gotten even more complicated. If you can throw some light on this tangled mess, our ears are open. So, what do you want from us?"

Jane added, "You gained a lot of brownie points with us with the Scrivener stuff, but they disappear if you write this up while we're in the middle of serious investigations. Into McKay, and now the murder. So, yes, what do you want?"

"I want to work with you to get to the bottom of all this. I don't want to interfere with your investigation, but I think I have some possible answers about what's behind McKay's mysterious new development scheme. A lot of it is speculation, but if it's accurate, it explains some things and really turns up the heat. Look, I think you need help, and so do I. I think if we pool our resources, we can make some real progress and find out what's really going on here. That's why I thought it was time for us to talk.

"I also want to be the person breaking the story when we figure it out. When the time's right, I want your help getting me interviews with key players. I want to be the first journalist to hear details when you're ready to release them. I want this to be a larger version of what we did with the Scrivener story."

Jane said, "Sid, I do appreciate your help with Scrivener, but the police don't work hand in hand with journalists. We have different responsibilities, and they often don't coincide."

"Agreed, but a couple of points. Note I'm talking with you, not your captain. I'm far from the only person in town who doesn't see Jasper McKnight as a serious police officer. You two, on the contrary, are.

"Second point, I think there's more at work here. I believe there is outside pressure being put on McKnight. This is about much more than bringing down a small-town scam artist. Who are these mysterious strangers in town? Who are McKay's powerful new financial backers? Just what the hell is going on out near Wyandot? Whoever these people are, do you think they care about Harmony? Do you really trust McKnight? I think our friends at the Wyandot Reserve are at real risk here. Do you think their interests will be better served than they have been in the past if McKay's mysterious plan goes through?"

By now Martha had quietly returned to the room. "The one thing I'm going to say is that the larger interests in the world – governments, big business, big media, the rich and powerful – are really good at looking after themselves while not giving a damn when bad things happen to us local people. I don't trust them. I do know Sid, and I think he has shown he can be trusted. I suggest we take a pause while you two go off and talk things over and decide how you want to proceed."

Kirsten and Jane went to a small den off the kitchen and closed the door. Jane said, "I do have some trust in Sid, but we simply can't just give him any control over our investigation."

"Agreed. But our chain of command is through McKnight, and I just can't trust him, despite his support for us with Morgan. Let's be honest, there are even reasons to think he might be somehow involved with the Winston murder. I agree with Martha about what she called the 'larger interests.' I agree with Sid that there likely is more at work here. To bring it right down to basics, we're investigating a murder in very difficult circumstances. It's on our plate, it's our responsibility, like it or not. We have no real suspects and no clear investigative direction with Winston's murder. There's a lot going on here, mostly connected with McKay, and it's hard to see how it all fits together. We need help, and Sid does seem to be able to ferret out useful information."

"So, let's try this. We can promise Sid we'll do the best we can to protect him and his sources and will try to make sure he has first shot to break the story. I think he is eager to proceed. Let's go back and talk with him."

They returned to the sunroom and found Martha was not there. Sid said, "Martha wanted me to extend her apologies, but she was called out to some sort of special meeting about the New Eden situation. She said not to wait up for her. So, where are we with all this?"

Jane said, "Sid, here's the deal. We can't give you firm promises. I mean, if you were to share information about specific criminal activity, we couldn't just sit on it. We can promise we'll do our best to respect your interests, just like with the Scrivener thing. Of course we want this situation, whatever the hell it really is, to be cleared up. I agree we're not getting far with our investigation and could use some help. But as you say, you need some help too.

"So, as a gesture of good faith, yes, we are involved in an investigation into McKay's financial and business dealings, on orders from on high. Yes, the Friendlies thing was McKnight's laughable attempt at an undercover investigation, and yes, he's never going to win any cop-of-the-year award. And we think Winston's murder is somehow tied into McKay's tangled business matters, but we don't know how. And there's good reason to believe all this somehow reaches far beyond Harmony. Why don't you tell us what you know, or suspect, and we'll see where it gets us. That's about the best we can do."

Sid nodded. "Okay, let me continue my little story and, yes, we'll see where it gets us." He took a deep breath and said, "We've talked about all the mystery in McKay's Wyandot thing. But the strangest thing is the geological surveys he had done on the land. I mean, since when does a housing development or a park need that kind of highly specialized testing?"

Jane said, "We know McKay usually cut corners on testing for even the basic stuff, like drainage, off-gassing, solid ground for footings. It is strange."

"You no doubt have figured out I'm an information junkie. I want to know what's going on, so I spend a lot of time on the internet and have identified websites that delve into things like that. I've found other information junkies who like to share stuff."

Kirsten smiled. "Like conspiracy theories, the latest on where Jimmy Hoffa is buried, on Elvis and Princess Di living together in a secret hideaway in the Himalayas."

"Ok, there's a lot of silly shit out there. It's like panning for gold. A whole lot of useless sand and gravel, but the odd nugget emerges. And some of these 'larger interests' we talked about *are* really good at hiding things. I searched for sources who knew something about deep geological surveys, like where and when they are required. One major area is where toxic stuff of whatever sort is being buried, where there has to be solid rock, no fissures, no breaks, and a totally stable underground structure. I accessed information about the geology around here. It turns out there are places in this general area where there is such solid rock near the surface. One of them is where the Wyandot Reserve is located."

Jane said, "Which helps explain why the government so generously gave them land covered with rocky outcrops, gravel, and pretty useless soil."

"No doubt. That's a whole other area of stories that don't get told enough. But back to my research. So, the package could be for a garbage dump. Scoop out the surface soil, maybe sell it for aggregates, and make some nice open pits resting on solid bedrock, which could then be safely filled with garbage. But there's not enough large urban areas around here to generate enough garbage to make that pay off.

"It could be toxic waste from manufacturing or mining, but there's no such thing around here. However, one possibility is that it's exactly what is needed if you need to bury nuclear waste. It has to be solid bedrock where the waste can be sealed in underground vaults by layers of concrete. It must be totally stable with no fissures or cracks, however small. It really helps if it's in a remote area, because though its proponents claim it's totally safe, people are really unhappy with it being anywhere close to them. Not in my neighbourhood, please! There are organized groups out there who are adamant there's no such thing as totally safe nuclear waste storage. Chernobyl, Three Mile Island – there's lots of concern about how devastating leakage of radioactive material can be. So, Alex's land package fits the bill."

Jane said, "Except it is right next to an Indigenous reserve."

"Who are usually overlooked, who don't have a lot of power, financially or politically, who our 'larger interests' truly don't give a damn about."

Kirsten said, "And as Wanda said, McKay – and Winston – bribed the band council with promises of infrastructure improvements, modest investments in things like a youth centre, if they could get access to the six hundred acres via reserve roads. He set it up so it looks like the band is eager for the money and okay with the development. But Wanda knows nothing about any nuclear waste disposal plan. McKay is just the guy to get them to agree in writing to grant access to the site without filling in that toxic little detail. This is starting to make some really horrible sense."

Sid continued. "The other requirement with creating a nuclear waste disposal site is transportation. Let me tell you the next major piece – possible piece, to be fair – I discovered. There is usually community opposition about an actual disposal site, but there is also major opposition to dangerous nuclear waste being transported through your area. Remember the recent opposition to plans for transporting nuclear waste through the Great Lakes and the Seaway? It's far better if the proposed site is close to where the waste currently is located.

"Next thing, what is close to Harmony? Do you two know much about the Gull Lake Nuclear Power plant?"

Jane and Kirsten shrugged their shoulders. Jane said, "Not a lot."

"Nothing like an informed citizenry. So, here it is. It was closed down about a year ago for refurbishment and updating. That process is finished, but the previous government put in place some stringent environmental safety protocols about nuclear waste disposal. The current government is much more concerned with the economy than they are with environmental matters, but they haven't tinkered with those protocols – too politically sensitive. The Gull Lake waste has been accumulating on the site itself, in what they call safe containment, but that stuff is dangerous for centuries. Not years, or decades – centuries. They can't just keep putting it in temporary storage. So, per the current environmental protocols, that waste has to be moved to, quote, 'safe, secure permanent storage' before Gull Lake can be put back into service."

Kirsten said, "And Gull Lake is not far from here."

"There is almost a direct route, on paved county roads, low-traffic-volume roads, to Harmony. There's a few small towns and villages on the way, but no major urban centres. You can see why the Wyandot site would be pretty damn attractive."

Jane said, "You're saying it's the government behind McKay? Wouldn't they just do all this directly?"

"Here's where it gets even more interesting. Our current government was elected on a platform of providing smaller government. Ironic, I know. Remember many years ago when Ronald Reagan memorably said, 'The nine most terrifying words in the English language are "I'm from the government and I'm here to help"'?"

Kirsten said, "You're dealing with two small-town cops here, Sid, even if one is a recent transplant. Give us the Coles Notes version."

"Coles Notes? You're dating yourself. Lazy students and cheaters have moved on to the internet. But okay, I'll try to keep it simple and unbiased, though I really don't like these guys. Since they were elected a few years ago they have been busily selling off government resources, like highways and provincial power infrastructure. They favour what are called 'Three P' approaches: public-private partnerships. Essentially, their belief is that private business is more efficient than government in building and running municipal, provincial, and federal infrastructure: roads, hospitals, electric power; even education and environmental oversight. There're strong rumours that these idiots even want to sell off the liquor stores, which is a cash cow for the government.

"The usual process is that the government puts in some money and support, but essentially the private concern puts up the immediate costs and leases or sells the service back to the province. Its proponents say it reduces our taxes and brings business efficiency to providing infrastructure and services. Its critics say in the short term it makes the immediate government fiscal bottom line look terrific. It allows them to cut taxes and appear to be fiscally prudent. But the government is on the hook for long-term costs. The public has to pay significant user fees, and usually for any hidden costs, upgrades or penalties. Bottom line: folks like you and me have to pay more and get less. Profits trump accountability and quality public services.

"Look, it's a truly complicated issue, so let's bring it back to Gull Lake. The government wants to sell the plant to private enterprise, getting them a big immediate profit. We're not far from the next election, so the infusion of this money will help them balance the books. They affirm that government agencies will still do the monitoring and oversight so that public safety is guaranteed. In return, the company has a long-term contract with the government to provide electrical power, at what they say is a fair market price. This means the government can claim they are guaranteeing sufficient electrical power for Ontario. They neglect to say there is no guarantee that individual hydro cost won't go up. They already have and will continue to. But the government can now say it's not their fault, it's just the cost of doing business."

Kirsten said, "Nice work pretending to keep the editorializing out, Sid. It's pretty clear where you stand on the issue. If I understand what you're saying, there's big money involved here, and the provincial government has some involvement. But tell us more about the push to create the disposal site beside Wyandot."

"One of the terms of the proposed government sale of Gull Lake is that the successful bidder must take immediate responsibility for safe disposal of the nuclear waste currently at Gull Lake. So, whichever company can first provide iron-clad proof of their ability to do so, and which can also meet the government's asking price, gets the deal. It would be this private company that would be backing McKay, but the government would do all they can to make sure it works because then the sale goes through and they can claim another great win for Ontario."

Jane said, "So, it's a competitive process. I know little about big business, but it strikes me there's not many companies that could give the government all they want. Who's the frontrunner?"

"There's a company called Gladstone Holdings that my sources say is really cozy with the government. They've been involved with a lot of the government P3's and sell-offs. They have formally registered their bid on the project."

Kirsten said, "Then, they are experts in providing nuclear-generated electricity?"

"Not at all. Their business model is this: they buy a company, providing the financial resources and taking care of logistics, like approvals and legal requirements. But then they hire a management team to actually run it. It might be the current management or new people, or a combination. As long as the management team respects Gladstone's interests, provides steady profit, and causes no problems, they're happy. They are like an umbrella company. Think of a corporation that owns a sports team. They hire presidents and general managers to run the business side of things and make sure the team operates profitably. The team doesn't necessarily have to win, just safely generate profit. Look, do you think the ownership of the Toronto Maple Leafs really cares about winning as long as their building is filled with the world's most loyal fans, and the TV contracts are secure?

"If Gladstone is behind McKay and the Wyandot land package, they just want the deal teed up and completed. I did some digging into Gladstone. Believe me, there are lots of organizations and individuals out there highly critical of how they operate and about the effect they have on communities and public services. Really interesting is that typically they engage local people to lay the groundwork, to set up the deal, and then transfer the completed package to Gladstone. I'm still really oversimplifying here, but it would be right in line with their business model to get McKay to put the Wyandot package together, get the approvals and so on, and immediately sell it to them. This approach keeps their potential business rivals unaware and prevents other speculators from driving up their costs. It also gives them the chance to bail if problems crop up."

Kirsten said, "This unfortunately is actually making horrible sense. So, if for example McKay, their local guy, ran into financial barriers, they would want to quietly remove those barriers. Sid, something you likely don't know is that in terms of the finances – Jane, are we okay to share this?"

When Jane nodded yes, she continued, "The bank has been empowered to approve all the credit access and immediate funds McKay needs to finish the purchase. It's likely already completed. If there's pressure on to get this whole thing finished, Gladstone might be making an announcement any day now. Sid, how sure are you about all this? You're doing a lot of speculating."

"I have no firm proof. These guys are really good at keeping things secret. It just makes total sense and ties in with what you two already know."

Jane said, "There's no way we can report any of this to McKnight or his superiors. There's not a shred of actual proof. And what would we report if we did have proof? That a complicated business deal, with government backing and approval, just happened? Our McKay investigation was set up to find out what McKay was up to. If this deal is completed, and if it was Gladstone that provided the money, he's seemingly no longer involved. I suppose it's possible that McKay independently contacted these mysterious offshore financial institutions, but really? He's as small time as it gets."

Kirsten said, "What is squarely on our plate is Winston's murder, where McKay clearly does seem involved one way or another. Under this Gladstone scenario it appears there is big money and Martha's 'larger interests' at work in Harmony. Exactly how all that might link to McKay and Winston, I don't know."

Jane had been sitting with a thoughtful look on her face. "We need to focus on where we go from here. But look, my big concern is with the Wyandot Reserve. If your speculation is at all accurate, Sid, and you've got me pretty convinced, those people could be at big-time risk. I can't see Wanda and her people welcoming a potential mini-Chernobyl being established right next door. They could be totally blindsided. Sid, you said you wanted our help connecting you to key people in all this. I know you and Wanda are acquainted with each other, but she really trusts me. I'm going to honour that trust by filling her in. I could do it directly but given the complexity, I'd rather just urge her to listen carefully to you. This might remove some of your control over the story, but this has to happen. If you disagree, our little co-operative investigation is likely over for me."

Sid held up his hands. "All right. It happens I agree with you. I like Wanda. Set it up and I'll tell her what I've told you. It's important she understand it's all speculation, but solid speculation, and that the potential risks for them are substantial."

Jane called Wanda and briefly filled her in on the situation. She gave her phone to Sid so he could talk with Wanda and gestured for Kirsten to join her back in the den.

When they got there, Jane said, "Obviously we have to wait for whatever announcement Gladstone, or whoever, might make. The McKay financial stuff is already on the back burner. I think we have to look for possible links to McKnight with all this, and *that* we don't share with Sid. You'll have the post-mortem results tomorrow, and I can interview Councillor Weirness, and maybe other Winston business associates, friends and so on. I'd like to know more about the provincial government's connection to all this. Remember that meeting McKay and William, the mystery man, might have had with MPP Fox?"

Kirsten said, "Agreed, and it's William I really want to know more about. We're spinning our tires so far with Winston. It's like there's a random something, a wild card we don't know about mixed up in the case somehow. We know William can be violent and is tied in somehow to things happening in Harmony. Let's ask Sid about that." They discussed their options and plans a bit more and then returned to the sunroom.

Sid had just wound up his conversation with Wanda. "That was a tough conversation, but it went pretty well. Wanda is pissed off, and not surprised at them yet again being victimized. She promised to be careful with the information. So, what next?"

Jane said, "We have to wait for whatever announcement comes, but it seems like it will be sooner rather than later. God, I wish things would slow down a bit. I'd welcome with open arms a few weeks or months of nice old boredom. Kirsten and I will continue our investigations, we tell McKnight as little as possible, and we all need to stay in touch. There's so much stuff, so many things intersecting right now – we have to be careful and clear headed. We have to make sure we get actual proof."

Sid said, "Sounds good. That New Eden evacuation happens tomorrow, and I'll be following it. I'll probably file my 'sorrows of New Eden' story, but none of that will likely affect you two. Though who really knows?"

Kirsten said, "Sid, we are interested in the government's possible involvement in all this, but don't see how it could relate to Winston. We are very, very interested in this guy William. Anything else you know about him?"

Sid said, "Well, yes, as a matter of fact. It's even more speculative than the stuff I've already told you, so I left it out. After that assault on Scrivener, I started nosing around, particularly into any connection to Gladstone. I consulted with a few of my internet sources familiar with Gladstone. They all agree that Gladstone usually engages some sort of liaison person to work with the local people setting up their various deals. It's never an actual company representative. Again, no firm proof at all. I described William to them. I even had a shaky picture I took of him on my phone, at a distance."

Kirsten interjected, "Which you didn't share with us. We have resources who can clean up pictures and do facial recognition checks. It might have helped."

"Guilty as charged. But I have access to resources like that too, and they said the picture is pretty useless. I'll send it over to you. It gives just sort of an impression. A couple of my sources said they had encountered someone vaguely like that in some of the Gladstone dealings they have investigated. So thinner than thin, but it makes sense he's connected with Gladstone. They have to quietly monitor McKay, far from the most trustworthy of people. They maybe also need to stay connected with someone from government, who, under this scenario, also would have a keen interest in all this, and who also would want to be invisible. I couldn't find anything at all about William, though I didn't have much to go on. But you have his license plate number."

Kirsten said, "The vehicle was leased by some numbered company that seems to have no traceable connection with anything. I asked my contact with the financial crimes unit, which does have significant resources at their disposal, but so far nothing. So, we all keep an eye out for the mysterious William. Jane, we could check with the motels, hotels, B&Bs anywhere close to here, but I think our William is too slippery for that."

They talked more about next steps and keeping in touch. After thanking Jane for her hospitality, Sid and Kirsten left. As they approached their cars, Kirsten suddenly said, "Sid, I likely would have said yes. About your grad prom. You should have asked me."

Sid gave a rueful smile. "So, something else to add to my far-too-long list of regrets. And fifteen years too late. Thanks, Kirsten. I really am glad we've reconnected, even if it's in the middle of this damn circus."

Kirsten smiled, gave Sid a quick hug, and got in her car. Sid watched it until it turned the corner, and then he also left.

CHAPTER 19
The Quiet Before the Storm

ELSEWHERE IN THE AREA THAT TUESDAY EVENING OTHERS WERE also preparing for the next day.

Eliot Davis, special assistant to the Ontario premier's office, was sitting at the desk in the "executive business suite" his office had rented for him in Lakeside, the seat of county government. He would prefer to be closer to Harmony, but it featured only motels, B&Bs, and a hotel chain inn badly in need of refurbishment. Actually, it was probably better to be in Lakeside, which was only about a forty-minute drive from Harmony and featured at least some amenities, including one three-star hotel with a reasonably acceptable restaurant. Lakeside at least tried to be part of the twenty-first century, unlike Harmony, which almost aggressively insisted on remaining a charming little backwater.

He was in the process of informing several key associates that at 10:00 o'clock the next morning Gladstone Holdings would be making their formal announcement concerning their purchase of the land package near the small town of Harmony. The announcement would detail how Gladstone had received all necessary approvals for the construction of a secure underground storage vault for nuclear waste from the Gull Lake Nuclear Plant at that site. This meant Gladstone had fulfilled all requirements for their proposed purchase of the plant from the Ontario government and were pleased to announce the purchase was now complete.

Gladstone would immediately begin construction of the underground storage vault, drawing on the most up-to-date design protocols and engineering techniques. The construction would be monitored by safety experts from the provincial Ministry of the Environment and from Ontario Power Generation. Once final approvals were received, projected to be mid-September, Gladstone would begin safe transport of the waste materials from Gull Lake for permanent storage.

Gladstone's management team would simultaneously be taking over the Gull Lake plant and preparing for its reopening, projected to be early in October. The electrical power generated at the plant would be sold to the Ontario Government based on a ten-year contract, with renewal options.

The announcement would conclude with a statement by Gladstone CEO Marvin Gronsky:

Gladstone Holdings is pleased to play its role in ensuring that the citizens of Ontario will have safe, reliable electrical power now and into the future. This project reflects how positively private industry and a government devoted to sound business principles can work together to ensure the needs of Ontario can be met in a safe, reliable, and fiscally responsible way.

Davis informed his colleagues they could release the government's prepared announcement of the deal, also at 10:00 a.m. the following day. The announcement would be similar in tone and content to the Gladstone announcement, with a strong emphasis on the government's delivery of a key election pledge: the government was continuing its strong initiatives to move government out of roles served far more efficiently by private enterprise, while ensuring

Ontario citizens received all necessary services, including safe, affordable electrical power.

Neither the Gladstone nor the government announcements would mention the Wyandot Reserve.

Davis informed his colleagues he would remain in the area to ensure there were no problems or delays with the commencement of the project. He reminded them of the joint release he and Gladstone representatives had drafted detailing the proposed benefits of the project to the people of the Wyandot Reserve. This would be kept in reserve in case there were concerns raised by the Wyandot leadership, but he was confident that the local agent used by Gladstone had taken care of that matter.

In another suite in the same hotel, Gladstone executive Malcolm Priestner was pacing the room, trying to anticipate possible snags with the Gull Lake purchase. His official title was "Vice president in Charge of Asset Development." This position brought him a substantial salary and associated perks and benefits, more than he ever would have dreamed of earning back in his lean student years some thirty years before. It also gave him substantial power and discretion over the projects to which he was assigned.

Priestner was a great fan of naval fiction, especially from the so-called "age of fighting sail." He often likened himself to his fictional heroes, such as Horatio Hornblower and Jack Aubrey, and the historical figure he idolized, Horatio Nelson. These bold, brave, and talented leaders worked under the direction of the British Admiralty, but once free of shore they had near total autonomy. So, in a sense, did he.

Gladstone Holdings was an umbrella company, comparable in a sense to the British Admiralty. It engaged in a series of separate and discrete business opportunities, much like the missions given by the admiralty to its captains and admirals. He, or sometimes a more junior colleague, would be assigned by Gladstone to successfully oversee the completion of a chosen project. Gladstone would give firm, comprehensive instructions, like the initial directions given by the Admiralty. He loved a common preface to instructions from the British Admiralty: "The Admiralty requests and requires that ...." So it was with Gladstone. There would be very specific requirements he had to meet; essentially that he would ensure the project was successfully completed.

There were definite advantages to this model. It meant Gladstone would not become a bureaucratic quagmire, but rather could move nimbly and decisively when a business opportunity arose. This was an absolute necessity for a company that by its very nature was opportunistic and aggressive. Gladstone rewarded executives, like Priestner, who were decisive, bold, careful, and effective. It avoided bogging Gladstone down with corporate deadwood that worked mostly to protect and defend their position in the organization.

It also had a further key benefit. If a project manager screwed up, the blame would be solely on him or, occasionally, her. If any liabilities were incurred by the project, the Gladstone mothership would be largely protected, and the offending manager would be the corporate fall-guy. It would be similar to the British Admiralty court-martialling an admiral who failed a mission, who perhaps lost valuable ships, or brought England into jeopardy of some sort. Gladstone/the Admiralty were clear in their verdicts: it was always you, the on-site leader, who independently screwed up.

Priestner and his fellow "project managers" were clear about the unspoken ground rules. If they had to bribe, intimidate, bend the law, or harm anyone standing in the way of their project's success, they would do so, but very carefully. Further, they would keep the details to themselves, ensuring any necessary deniability for senior Gladstone management should that be necessary. There was no acceptable excuse for failure; achieving success was mandatory. They were richly rewarded for their successes. The punishments for any failures would be firm and immediate.

Priestner welcomed this type of professional tightrope walking. From the outside, he appeared to be a non-descript, middle-aged, balding, overweight businessman. He looked like a bureaucrat who would happily work for years in a safe and non-challenging corporate environment until he qualified for a comfortable retirement. A drone. But inside, he was Horatio Nelson, willing to take on any assignment, a bold, innovative, brave and, if necessary, ruthless leader: a warrior to the core. It was the only way someone like him could conduct his personal and professional lives.

On the Gull Lake/Harmony project it had been Priestner who selected Alex McKay to be the local agent for the land purchase and associated business dealings. He knew of McKay's often questionable tactics but welcomed that sort of aggressiveness and flexibility. He was sure McKay would find a suitable land package, if there was one in the area. McKay had the experience and local contacts to finalize the deal. His research had not revealed McKay's hidden financial challenges, a significant oversight on Priestner's part. He was confident he had managed to solve that problem, but it remained a red flag. When he had first engaged McKay in this project, New Eden had appeared to be the sort of successful development that underlined McKay's suitability. The issues that soon emerged there raised a second red flag.

However, the land package McKay had secured seemed ideal. Likely no-one else in the area could have pulled this off, so on balance it looked like a success. Priestner was used to dealing with challenges, with less-than-ideal partners, with the risks inherent in such a project. On this Tuesday evening he did not feel totally content, because he almost never did, but he was sure this would be yet another success for him and for Gladstone.

Priestner had never met Alex McKay. He practiced the same sort of safety protocols that Gladstone did. That meant distancing himself, using someone like the man the Harmony police called William. Priestner also did not know "William's" real name, only how to contact and communicate with him. If extreme measures needed to be taken, William was the man to do so. If McKay were to be brought to the attention of the authorities, the only contact he could identify in this matter would be William, who was an expert at being invisible and disappearing at will. William was also the right man to keep someone like McKay in line. No-one challenged William. And if McKay needed careful pressure applied to bring the deal to completion, William again was the right man. William also had a more extreme skill set if more serious measures proved necessary, as it had been when Will Handstrom threatened the project.

The greatest risk to the project was at this stage. Gladstone would soon take over the land package from McKay, and so would become visible for the first time. Once the deal was complete, McKay would no longer be necessary. Neither would William, and neither would Priestner. Gladstone would put their Gull Lake and Harmony management teams in place and the project would continue on to a successful completion. It was just necessary to make sure the transfer of the land to Gladstone, and the commencement of next steps, came about smoothly.

That was the subject of Priestner's most recent secure phone conversation with William earlier that evening.

"I think matters are in place for tomorrow's announcements. I have been in touch with Elliot Davis, and he seems confident in our arrangements. I presume you have not met with him since we brought McKay into the project?"

"You know I am very careful, Mr. Priestner. Dealing with him is your job, not mine."

"Of course. I too am just being careful. Your main job is keeping McKay in line. You know I am far from happy with him, though it does appear he has delivered the land we need. Do you have any concerns, any concerns at all, with him?"

"I do. His New Eden fiasco has blown up in his face. The houses are being evacuated tomorrow because of serious health concerns, and a lot of people are very unhappy with him."

"Which is not our concern. Why are you so bothered about it?"

"Because right now he is very unstable. I have been keeping him under surveillance, keeping tabs on him, and I don't like the fact the local police have been meeting with him."

"Presumably over the New Eden stuff, and the murder of his accountant. That has gotten my attention. Were you involved in that in any way?"

"No. If I were, it would have been a much more discreet accident, not the amateur mess it seems to have been. There are some benefits to all that, though. Any attention on McKay is about all those matters, not on his latest real estate transaction."

"So you think we are okay there?"

"No, I don't. I think the guy is unravelling, and that can be risky. I may have to remove him from the scene, but if so, it will tie into New Eden, or Winston, not us."

"No details, please. I'm sure you will sort that out. Any other concerns about tomorrow?"

"I have already shared my concerns about how the Wyandot Reserve people will react. I have helped bring a few influential people on their band council on board with the site access agreements. Full access is clearly established in the lease contracts McKay signed with the band council. All legal and airtight. But their chief is opposed, and also a few others. They have not been told what the land will be used for. Finding that out might heat things up."

"We have media releases ready to go if necessary. They clearly gave blanket access to our land in exchange for generous lease payments. If need be, the province and Gladstone will give them infrastructure improvements and money for things like this proposed youth centre you mentioned. Frankly, they will look like greedy malcontents who are just trying to squeeze out more for themselves. And what political clout do they have?"

"That's more your area than mine. But I think that at Oka, Ipperwash, and a lot of other areas they got a lot of attention, the sort we don't want. You mentioned being careful. McKay swears he's got them all sorted out and in line, but should we be willing to trust McKay on that?"

"This may be another reason for you to take firm steps with McKay. Could that be done so the Wyandot people are implicated? That could keep them occupied, maybe shut them down. I've been in touch with our contacts in the RCMP; you know, they have federal jurisdiction over Native matters. They're ready to assist with Wyandot if necessary."

"Again, your area. I will do whatever has to be done with McKay. Anything else?

"No. Just be sure you're available tomorrow. Once we get past the next few days it should be clear sailing."

With that, the call ended.

Priestner continued pacing in his hotel room. He was used to these intense feelings of anticipation and anxiety just before the final stages of a project. He thought of Horatio Nelson hosting a dinner party for his captains and officers on the eve of the Battle of Trafalgar. That had certainly turned out well, one of history's great successes! Except for the fact that Horatio Nelson had died in that battle.

Back at New Eden, Alex McKay sat alone in his quiet house, drinking in the dark. So, he and his neighbours had to evacuate the area tomorrow. They'd want to tear him limb from limb. His phone had been ringing constantly, and there had been loud knocking on his door. He had ignored both.

How would William feel about all this? He'd seen William's white SUV in the area, and knew he was under surveillance. And the damned police! He knew nothing about Winston's death, but they kept circling around. The one person he knew who was fully capable of killing Winston was William, though he had no idea why he would do so. Unless Winston had been doing some sort of double cross, maybe allied with William, but why the hell would they do that? Yet he knew what William was, and that made him very afraid. Also, he had no desire to be around tomorrow to face the music with his idiot neighbours. Best to pack some necessities and get out tonight.

———

Also at New Eden, angry and scared homeowners hurriedly met together, or sat in their homes trying to figure out how they would cope with this latest and most devastating development. How exactly could they cope with being evicted, suddenly and without any real warning? Where would they stay? What of their belongings? Would they lose all they had invested in moving out to this cursed place? Several tried to reach Alex McKay, but he was not responding to phone calls or to them knocking on his door. Who would help them, stuck out here in what had now become a new sort of threatening and hostile wilderness?

The answer to who would help them would come from a surprising source: police captain Jasper McKnight.

———

While his officers had been busy working on the murder investigation, Jasper McKnight had hurriedly arranged for a special meeting that Tuesday evening in his second-floor conference room. When he called the meeting to order at 7:30, he looked around the table at what he hoped would be Harmony's ad hoc disaster response team. Present were retired town police officer Adam Westfield; township mayor Calvin Stewart; police Sergeant Keith Sanderson; and lawyer Eleanor Trygister. Martha Nicholson, a key member of the county's social services committee, arrived just as the meeting began.

"First, thanks to all of you for coming on such short notice. I'm sure you are aware the residents of New Eden are being forced to evacuate their homes tomorrow on strict orders from the County Department of Health. I am under similarly strict orders to make sure they all leave. There can be no exceptions. The county will be turning off New Eden's electricity tomorrow, and the propane will be cut off at the central New Eden propane storage tank. Of course, I will make sure this eviction is carried out and have assigned Sergeant Sanderson to oversee the process. But these people at New Eden are innocent victims, and that is how we are going to treat them. Harmony has long prided itself on being a supportive community, and with your assistance we will make sure that it is. I am asking all of you to be part of what we can call the Harmony Disaster Response Team.

"Those folks are scared, angry, frustrated, and worn out. Who can blame them? The main culprit is Alex McKay, the creator of the fiasco that is New Eden. I have been trying to reach him, to have him at this meeting to maybe help undo some of the harm he has caused. So far, he can't be reached. It's maybe best he's not here, though, because our sole task is to move quickly and decisively to help our neighbours. Helping people is not anything McKay's ever done, so this committee can forget him. My department has some other issues with Mr. McKay and will deal with him accordingly.

"I have asked Adam to co-ordinate this team. He knows this town inside out, he is respected by everyone and has the organizational knowledge and skills we need. Adam, I can't thank you enough for agreeing to take this on. A confession. I've always thought I was running a tight ship here in Harmony, but I think I've been relying on the wrong people. Adam, you were very helpful and professional when the Provincial Police took over from your town police. I'm not sure I ever thanked you enough for that. I guess I'm thanking you now by dumping a tough job in your lap."

Westfield said, "Not necessary, Jasper. Tough for sure, but more than just a job. I've actually been getting bored in my retirement, so let's do this. And thank you for calling us together. There is no clear responsibility for helping these people, our neighbours as you so rightly call them, so we *should* be doing this. I think we are all glad to be of assistance."

He looked around the table to see everyone nodding yes.

McKnight continued, "I will give all the support I can to your efforts. After this meeting I will call everyone at New Eden to let them know what we can offer them. However, my department has some serious matters on our plate, especially a tough murder investigation. There are other matters connected to McKay that I can't say much about. Frankly, I think you people, under Adam's direction, will do this far better than I ever could. My department is directly involved in this, so Sergeant Sanderson will represent us on this team. To be clear, we must have everyone out of New Eden by tomorrow mid-afternoon, but we are not going to just dump them on the roadside.

"Let me identify what I see as some of the key tasks we have. I'm sure you'll identify more. I think this will help you see why I've asked you all to be here. You may find you'll need to bring more people on board. I'll be leaving this meeting soon to let you get on with it, but you know where to reach me if need be. Here's my preliminary list:

"They need housing, immediately. Some of them will have friends or relatives to stay with, here or elsewhere, but some won't, and they would need temporary accommodation. Many of them have children and won't want to have to send them away somewhere. Martha, you're our expert on taking care of kids, and also knowing what support the county might be able to provide. There's precious little commercial space in Harmony, but there are lots of large houses with empty space."

Martha said, "I've got some ideas already. It'll be really tough for them, especially in the first few days. I'm in."

McKnight continued, "They might have to deal with legal matters. I know they have been talking about class-action suits against McKay, but they may need guidance right now about their rights and legal protections. What protection does their insurance provide? How do they get their insurance company to deliver? Eleanor, I think a lot of them may find your immediate advice and guidance invaluable."

Trygister nodded. "I've been quite happy being a small-town lawyer, but dealing with wills, real estate and such can get a little too routine. I'm more than glad to help, and I think I can get some other assistance if necessary. Thanks, Jasper."

McKnight said, "They may have to navigate the system, get access to what Harmony and the township council can offer them. Calvin, you can help with knowledge, support, and cutting through any red tape. Maybe gently leaning on people if necessary."

Stewart said, "Jasper, let me add my apology to yours. Township council was elected to serve people. We haven't been doing the job. I'm ashamed we've let McKay get away with so much. I too have been listening to the wrong people for too long. This will be helping me make amends. There are some good people on council. I'll make sure they pitch in. The whole council needs to face some tough realities, but that's for later. You've got my full support."

McKnight said, "Keith, Sergeant Sanderson, you're clear on your instructions and responsibilities?"

"Yes. I am. We're going to do some important work here. This is way more than just a routine police assignment. I'm proud to work with all of you on this."

Looking around the table, McKnight said, "There'll be other problems that arise. Some of those people are going to want to move out and stay out. We're a bit of a backwater here, but maybe we can point some of them to where they can get help with that. Maybe we can help them get access to their houses to move everything out.

"They may need temporary financial assistance, lines of credit and such. Maybe Mike Quinlan can help there. Simple things like where do they store their frozen food? Maybe the town butcher shop can temporarily help. This is going to be really complicated, but I think you're the people who can make this happen.

"I have some important phone calls to make. I'm going to leave you to your planning. Feel free to use this conference room as your headquarters, unless you can find a better place. Maybe the library, Martha. Right now, this team has as close to carte blanche as I can provide."

McKnight went to his office to make his calls. An outside observer would have seen the lights in the second-floor conference room stay on far into the night.

At the Wyandot Reserve, Wanda Cornelius had finished an emergency meeting of the band council. She had invited several community leaders and elders. Without revealing her source, she told them about the likely imminent announcement that they would soon have a nuclear waste disposal site right next door. Several present refused to believe this could be true, but Wanda kept hammering the key arguments: the site to which they had agreed to give access through reserve roads was entirely suitable for a waste storage dump, and little else. The geological testing pointed to something involving deep storage of dangerous materials. The imminent sale of the Gull Lake Nuclear Plant, not that far down the road, required a so-called safe storage site for their nuclear waste. It all fit together, and it was dangerous.

When some present said they could not believe Alex McKay would betray them like that, she lost her temper and gave a brief but heated summary of how governments had disrespected their rights continually and fundamentally during the entirety of Canada's history. She reminded them of the New Eden disaster, of how McKay had certainly betrayed those people.

By the end of the meeting Wanda had convinced them that this could, and likely would, happen, and that if it did, they would be under severe jeopardy. They decided they would go on high alert, ready to move quickly if need be. If necessary, they would blockade the reserve and allow no one to enter without their approval. They would look for allies and ways to publicize their concerns. They would not ever allow this betrayal, this atrocity, to occur. They would also, for now, keep this matter to themselves, until it was clear what was happening. They could not alert their enemies but did need to be ready to stand up for themselves.

Wanda felt deep concern, deep personal anguish, that this might be happening. She trusted Jane but knew how careful she had to be with her trust. She was confident she and her people were fully committed to immediate and effective action when the time came, and she shared Jane's belief that the time was very close. She felt ready, but also deeply apprehensive.

CHAPTER 20
Meeting Lynne and the Good Doctor

WHEN KIRSTEN ARRIVED AT POLICE HEADQUARTERS THE FOLLOWING morning, intent on catching up on her paperwork before heading off to the post-mortem, she was surprised when the front desk officer informed her she had a visitor, a vaguely familiar-looking young woman sitting hunched in one of the waiting room chairs.

Kirsten approached her and said, "Yes? Can I help you?"

The woman looked up, her eyes flickering back and forth, looking slightly ill-at-ease, something quite common in this room. She said, "Yes, Miss, uh, officer. I'm not sure what I should call you. It's Lynne, um, Cherie, you know, from Friendlies."

Kirsten, surprised, said, "Yes, Lynne. Of course. You can call me Detective Petersen. Certainly not 'Jade.' Sorry, I didn't recognize you at first."

"The old joke, you didn't recognize me with my clothes on. I get that sometimes."

Kirsten smiled. "Yeah, I got that the other day too, even though my state of undress wasn't quite as extreme as yours. So, how can I help you?"

"It's not really important, but do you have a few minutes? Could we talk somewhere?"

"Of course." Kirsten led her up the stairs to the Detective Unit and into an empty interview room.

Lynne looked around apprehensively. "It's the first time I've been in a police station because I wanted to be. Feels kind of strange."

"Well, you're here as a member of the public today. Can I get you anything? Coffee? Water?"

"I'd better not. I live out of town, in Lakeside. I got off work pretty late, so I waited in the Tim Horton's till I thought you might be here. I'm sort of caffeined out. Look, first-off I want to thank you. Larry said that after you left Friendlies on Saturday you asked him to say goodbye to us for you."

"Of course. Everyone was good to me, especially you. It was a tough gig for me, and you made it much easier. I really appreciate that. Of course I wanted to thank you."

"Thing is, ordinary people usually treat us like some form of pond scum, women in particular. And you're a cop. It was just nice. You're being nice to me now."

"Cops can be nice, you know, though I can understand why it might often not seem that way. We have to have our guard up, like I'm sure you do too."

"Keeping your guard up is sort of the other thing I want to talk to you about. Can I just talk away about a couple of things? Do you have a few minutes?"

"I've been meeting quite a few 'talk away' people around here. I have to leave soon; I have a meeting in your town in a little while, but I've got a bit of time."

"Gee, if you're heading to Lakeside, could I hitch a ride with you? My car's gone tits up, and my roommate was going to come over to pick me up. It'd make her day a lot easier. We could talk in your car."

"Sure. Just let me touch base with a couple of people, and off we go."

Kirsten went over to talk with Jane and was brought up to date on the disaster response team. Martha had updated Jane when she returned home early that morning. "Jasper just continues to amaze me," Jane said. "Here he is actually apologizing, reaching out for help, and stepping up in an important way. I have to admit, I'm so wound up in all this other stuff I didn't really think through what it'd be like for the New Eden people, much less about what could be done for them. This team Jasper put together is exactly the right thing to do, and he was right to bring your old pal Adam Westfield out of retirement to head it up. Adam was a pretty impressive cop, a guy I really respect."

Kirsten said, "Agreed about the captain. In the short time I've been here I've seen him be several different people. Do you still have him as a suspect for Winston?"

"He always was a long shot as a suspect. I mean, a police captain being a murderer? But something has shook him up recently. Is he trying to make up for things with all this sudden good behaviour? Especially after our update from Sid last night, there's just too much strange stuff going on around here. This small-town cop is just trying to keep her head above water."

"Me too. I never thought returning to sleepy, uptight old Harmony would be anything like this. With this response team set up, we don't have to think about New Eden. We're waiting for whatever might happen over by Wyandot, though it'd be nice if that held off for a bit. The McKay financial stuff is done, or at least is on the back burner. So, it's full bore on the Winston case. I'm just heading off for the post-mortem. One of the women I met at Friendlies dropped in to see me. I'm giving her a ride to Lakeside, so I can use the trip to see what she wants. Nothing serious, I'm sure – and hope! I've got my friend Tim seeing what he can turn up about William. Anything new on McKay?"

"Just that he's dropped right out of sight. Might be so the New Eden people don't kill him. But we do need to talk to him more seriously about Winston, if we can ever find him. I couldn't turn up any trace of either him or William at any hotel, motel, B&B, campground, or whatever anywhere close to here. No surprise. I think Jeff has nothing new from the crime scene. The captain wants us all to meet after you're back from the post-mortem to see where we are, though I think it'll still be nowhere. One thing I'm going to miss, though."

"Namely?"

"If the new Jasper is for real, we're going to have to retire 'The Pickle' and 'Captain Crunch.' Not that I'll miss those guys."

Twenty minutes later Kirsten and Lynne were headed down County Road 1 on their way to Lakeside. Sensing Lynne was still a little uptight, Kirsten said, "So, tell me about your roommate, and commuting from Lakeside."

"I think I told you I have a son, three years old, best thing in my life. His father is a real jerk and took off long ago, so it's just me and Tommy, and of course Deb and her daughter, who's four. We're sort of like a weird kind of family. She works in Lakeside. Gee, I'm not sure I can talk to you about that."

"Because I'm a cop? Feel free, Lynne. We're just two former co-workers having a little chat."

"Ok, so Deb works in a spa in Lakeside, you know, massages and stuff. It's legal. Well, mostly, but she's in the same situation I'm in. She came from a shitty family, dropped out of high school, and made lots of bad choices. We could work retail or sling hamburgers but wouldn't make the kind of money we do now. Look, maybe it's not exactly elegant, but the world doesn't offer much to chicks like us. We have to take care of our kids. We're okay with what we do. It is what it is."

"I'm not judging, Lynne. Tell me how your untraditional family works."

"Deb starts work around noon and works into the early evening. That's about when I leave for Friendlies. There's often some overlap, but we've got people to babysit for a few hours if necessary. Big thing, one of us is around most of the time for our kids. We're good parents. I know most people wouldn't approve of us, but we love our kids. They're going to have a better start than we did."

"I don't have kids, but I've always thought the big thing kids need is security and unconditional love."

"Yeah, and ours get that. I'm a bit uptight about when they get older. It may be easier for me than for Deb because I don't work where I live, but neither of us will be able to do 'take your kids to work' day or anything like that. I'm not sure what they'll tell their friends about what their mom does. Moms, actually. That's another thing that a lot of people won't accept, but we have some good friends who are good with it. I don't think we're really lezzies. Like, we comfort each other, you know what I mean, but we both grew up liking guys, only it just always caused us more grief than good. I guess that's a downside of our work, we don't exactly see the best kind of guy. Though Larry is actually a really nice guy, believe it or not. And the two bouncers are okay. They take care of us, sort of like really tough and untamed big brothers.

"I guess part of why I want to ask a favour is that I know I have to move on to something else eventually. For Tommy, but also for me. Like, I don't want to be a forty-year-old stripper with sagging tits getting by on sympathy from drunks and losers.

"I'm not sure about Deb. I mean, she can always do her special massages, but guys want younger women for that. Maybe I shouldn't tell you this, but she also has a few special regulars. She has to be careful, cause it's strictly off limits at her spa to see the customers away from work. But she says there are a few nice guys who just want some companionship, and she provides it. I mean, some of these guys are pretty prominent in the community. You, in particular, wouldn't believe who some of them are. But I'm talking too much. I mean, I like you, and you're easy to talk to, but I shouldn't forget you're a cop. Sorry if I'm blabbing too much."

"Not to worry. Even cops can respect that people need to live their own lives, as long as they're not hurting anyone else. So, back to your plans?"

"I want to start doing courses, maybe online or even in the daytime when I'm not working."

"Good for you. Doing what?"

"Maybe childcare, or a receptionist, or a, what did they call it, 'personal services worker.' Something Tommy can be proud of, and that I'll feel better about. But I'm just dreaming big time unless I can stop feeling like a loser. It was beyond amazing when you wiped out those two guys the other night. Like, our bouncers do that stuff, but they're big tough guys. But to see a woman do that, throw that big guy over the table, put the other on the floor whimpering? I was blown away. Did you learn to do that in your police training?"

"Mostly. It's not really that big a thing. okay, I'm five nine, and weigh a hundred and forty pounds. The late Mr. Winston outweighed me by eighty pounds, easy. But I didn't throw him over the table. We're trained to use an assailant's strength against him, so when he rushed me, he was drunk and out of control. I just sidestepped him and gave him a boost over the table. My instructor at Police College taught us techniques like that, and also that if you're in a fight, do what it takes to win. The other guy? He also was drunk and had no idea of how to fight. Maybe not elegant to kick him in the balls, but it sure does work. If those guys had known what they were doing I would have been in trouble. You have to be realistic. But stay alert, know where the help is, stay reasonably fit, you're usually okay. And you're right. Confidence is a big part of it. So, what's the favour you have been building up to ask?"

"I want to learn some self defense. I don't want to always have to rely on some guy bailing me out. I want to have more confidence in myself. I talked to Larry about it. Like I said, he's a nice guy. He helped me find out that you can rent facilities at the high school, like a phys ed activity room, where you could have classes like that. The woman at the school board said they try to help community groups, but something like that would have to be open to the whole community, held in the evening, and there's a small cost. Larry said he would pay for the first four week's classes. We'd have to advertise it, but the school board woman said she could help with that. She said other women have occasionally asked if there were something like that available, you know, physical fitness and self defense. She was sure if we organized it properly, and advertised, that it would work. The only other thing, we would need an acceptable teacher."

"Oh. I see where you're going with this. Look, the only teaching I've ever done is seminars, some teaching assistant stuff at university. I wouldn't know where to start."

"Maybe just do the stuff you learned at Police College?"

"Well, I suppose. I've just never thought about doing anything like that. And I've just been transferred here, and we're beyond busy right now …"

Lynne sighed. "Ok, Deb told me I was just fantasizing big time. I guess I was out of line asking. I just, you know, after last Saturday … well, thanks anyway. The women in Harmony wouldn't want to come to class with someone like me anyway. What would I say when they asked where I worked? Thanks for the ride. You can let me off at the traffic lights up ahead. I know I talk too much, but it was great talking to you."

Kirsten pulled over to the curb and stopped. "Just let me think for a moment."

After a few moments she continued. "The police department does encourage us to get involved in our community, and I really do think it's good for women to have more self-confidence. I think doing some fitness stuff once a week, brushing up on my self-defence training, would be okay. If I say being more self-confident is good, I guess I should be confident about becoming a teacher. Here's the deal. We may have to delay a little bit until things quiet down around here, but I hope that will be soon. I'll agree to do the first few weeks, maybe a couple of months, to see how it goes. Maybe a real teacher would show up by then.

"As for the good women of Harmony, there's a lot of newer people moving in, people maybe a little more open. I could drive you all so hard there'd be no time for chit chat. I'm not sure what type of teacher I'd be, but I think I could handle being hard ass. As for your work, maybe just say, with a little bit of mystery, that you used to work with me, but you really can't talk about it. Sound ok?'

Lynne stifled a giggle and said, "Sounds amazing. I don't know how to thank you. I want to give you a hug, but I guess that'd be too much. I have to learn how to behave properly."

"And it's hard to hug someone in a little car like this. How about a nice friendly, professional handshake?"

They shook hands, and Kirsten gave Lynne one of her cards. "I'll need to talk to the woman at the school board, and maybe Larry. Email me all the information you've got, and we'll try to start soon. That is, after we solve this murder and sort a few other things out. Bye, Lynne, and thank you, too."

Lynne scampered off down the street, and Kirsten pulled out to head to her meeting with Moira Hepburn and the late Harry Winston. She couldn't stop wondering about Lynne's statement about how she, in particular, wouldn't believe who Lynne's partner Deb might be giving special attention to.

———

The regional forensic pathology unit was located in a new medical and administrative building on the outskirts of town. Kirsten went to the reception desk, and soon was following Dr. Moira Hepburn down to the basement.

"I often wonder why places like this always have to be in the basement. Is that your experience, Dr. Hepburn?"

"Afraid so. And call me Moira, please. May I call you Kirsten? I don't like excessive formality, except perhaps with your boss."

"Sure. I sometimes wonder why men like him even have first names."

"Except to use with their good-old-boy friends. I suspect you've had the same sort of experiences I've had banging your head against the system. But here we are."

They entered a brightly lit room where the dominant colours were white and stainless steel. It was about twenty feet square with a high ceiling. There was a counter along one wall, with sinks, and shelves holding a variety of instruments. The floor was white tile, sloping slightly to a central drain. Over it stood an autopsy table holding a sheet-covered body. There were three video cameras pointing toward the table and a microphone at the end of a swivel mount.

Moira said, "When I do a post-mortem, I do the usual recorded commentary to keep a running record of what I find, but I get pretty concentrated and don't like interruptions, unless it's absolutely essential. So, I don't want to be rude, but I hope you're okay with keeping track of any questions for discussion afterwards. I promise that I'm always thorough, especially with homicides. I'll pay particular attention to the head wound, and anything else that even remotely could be linked to his death. Okay?"

"Sure. Where do you want me to stand so I don't get in your way?"

"You're welcome to just stay here, back a few feet. But we pathologists often wonder why police officers need to be right here rather than up there in the viewing gallery, where it's a little more pleasant. If there's anything I think you should see I can call you down, and feel free to ask any pressing questions. A lot of this is pretty technical. I take lots of pictures and our discussion afterwards is the most important thing. Your choice."

Kirsten smiled. "The viewing gallery is fine. About cops needing to be right there, I think it's some sort of test, proof they're real cops. Luckily, I don't feel that particular need."

Moira smiled. "My kind of woman. Look, I'll be finishing up around 12:30 or so. There's a pretty good cafeteria in this building. Can I treat you to lunch, where we can run over what I find? Maybe chat about what it's like to be a professional woman in small-town Ontario?"

Kirsten smiled. "I rarely turn down free lunches. Sure."

Kirsten watched from the gallery, a glass-fronted space about six feet above the floor level of the main room. Dr. Hepburn did a thorough examination of the body. As advertised, she was very intent, and spent considerable time examining the head wound. Throughout, she dictated observations into the mic, which also played over a speaker in the gallery. After she had finished and had changed out of her scrubs, Moira led Kirsten to a surprisingly attractive main-floor cafeteria, where they selected their lunches and found a quiet table off to the side.

Kirsten said, "For an institutional cafeteria, this place is pretty nice. It seems civilization is a little more advanced here than in Harmony. So, what can you tell me?"

"Other than the head wound, of course, it was pretty routine. Generally healthy thirty-something male, overweight, strongly muscled but clearly didn't exercise regularly. If he had lived another ten years, I think his body would have been in significant decline, but he would have been a challenge for any assailant to handle. No sign he was struggling when he died. No defensive wounds or abrasions other than what's consistent with falling onto rocky ground. I think he was still alive when he hit the ground, but likely not for long.

"The detailed tox screen will come back later, but no indication of drug use or significant health concerns. A moderate smoker. Some alcohol in his bloodstream, likely a hold-over from the night before. Your Mr. Winston was in full use of his faculties when he died. But as I mentioned at the scene, his head wound is pretty baffling. As I thought, the weapon was metal, shaped like a thick, wide chisel, or, God forgive, something like a tomahawk or slender axe with a short blade. However, it doesn't really look exactly like either. There was considerable rust in the wound. I don't know if it was specifically steel or iron, but it is like it had been left outside and not kept in good condition. Some sort of garden instrument? A tool I'm not familiar with? I have good contacts with colleagues with more experience and resources than I have, so I'm going to consult with them and see what they may be able to tell me.

"There were other strange aspects. It looked like whatever it was had been violently moved around in the wound, like his assailant was forcefully shaking it back and forth, more than what would be necessary to just pull it out."

"Like maybe he was trying to inflict pain, or make sure there was maximum damage?"

"Something like that. Like it was done with, I don't know, rage. But usually when the attack is done by an enraged assailant, there's multiple wounds. This was one blow given with considerable force, enough to easily penetrate the skull, and definitely the cause of death. As I mentioned at the scene, the blow was completely vertical, straight on to the top of his head. He had to have been kneeling, staying nice and still so a pretty powerful person could administer such a devastating blow. Even if he was kneeling, it would be hard even for a tall person to make the wound go in absolutely vertical. I suppose he may have been leaning his head back, almost as if to help his assailant, but why would he do that? Things for *you* to solve, but I'm pretty baffled.

"Of course, the weapon was pulled out of the wound and not found at the scene. It would have taken significant strength just to pull it out, it went in so deep. Maybe that's why our enraged assailant made only one blow. I think Winston may have crawled on his knees a short distance before he fell over, but not far, because the blood was all right around his head. That's about all I can tell you, unhelpful though I fear it was."

"It does raise a lot of questions. Moira, you've been very thorough. Thank you. I presume you'll email us your full report as soon as possible."

"Yes, of course. Here's my card if you have questions. No thanks are necessary. It's a pleasure dealing with you, and not your boss. By the way, is it true he's called 'The Pickle?'"

"Tales out of school! But, yes, he has at least two not very positive nicknames."

"The other being?"

"The guys downstairs call him Captain Crunch."

"As in the ridiculous cartoon character?"

"Yes, but cone of silence, please. I'm trying to stay on his good side. To be fair, the last couple of days he's been really good. He's even surprised Jane."

"So, there's hope. Fair enough. But I think I'd still like to keep dealing with Jane and you. A lot easier than wasting energy working around the McKnights of the world. You know, it occurred to me we should compare notes sometime, two transplanted city women fighting for survival in Ontario's Ozarks."

"Actually, I grew up in Harmony. This is sort of like a belated return home for me."

"Oops. Not a good way to start a new relationship. Sorry."

Kirsten smiled. "I must admit parts of growing up in Harmony were a bit like being in the Ozarks, and I have spent over a decade remaking myself into a city woman. So, yes, I'm sure we've butted our heads against a lot of the same barriers and bullshit. How did you end up here?"

"If you are an ambitious, fully qualified woman, which I am, you may find getting the promotion you want, and frankly deserve, means coming to a place like Lakeside. There aren't many openings for forensic pathologists, and I leapt at the chance to take over here. I also lobbied to be named regional coroner to avoid having to cope with less-than-competent colleagues. I hope that doesn't sound too arrogant. I'm not sure how long I'll stay here, but at least for a few years. I can build up a resume so I can someday move back to civilization. In the meantime, I'm always looking for kindred spirits around here. That's why I hope we can be friends."

Kirsten said, "I'm not sure how long I'll be here either. The standard minimum for a transfer within the service is usually two years, and I'm surprising myself by finding it actually good to be back in the place I fled from after high school. I'm still trying to get my feet on the ground, though. The Harmony I left was too quiet. The current version is anything but."

"No relationships or connections to draw you back south?"

"My parents still live in London. But, never married. No boyfriends. I guess I came here as a free agent, so, Harmony it is, whatever that brings."

Moira reached her hand over and gently placed it on Kirsten's. "I hope I might be part of the whatever. Harmony is not that far from here. I find you a refreshingly smart and independently minded woman. I hope maybe we can get together sometimes when you're not off seeking crazed killers."

Kirsten sat quietly for a moment, looking at Moira with a slight smile on her face. "I'm not sure when we'll find our crazed killer. I'm sort of a hard-to-get to know person, and pretty traditional, I'm afraid."

Moira removed her hand. "And I've just overstepped the bounds. I won't say I'm sorry. You're certainly an attractive woman, and I've learned you never get anywhere by being passive. I meant no offense, and I do look forward to working with you."

Kirsten said, "No offense taken. Believe me."

"Just don't say some of your best friends are gay."

Kirsten chuckled. "Even though that's actually true? I promise. I've only been back here a short time, but I think it'd be nice to have lunch the odd time. It would have to be here, though. Harmony is okay, but the restaurants could use a major leap forward. Jane and I often have a drink after work. *That* you can do safely in Harmony. You're welcome to join us, if you're ever caught slumming in the heart of the Ozarks north."

Moira smiled. "You're on. If McKnight really is becoming a real person, I may have to stop avoiding Harmony."

Moira looked at her watch and started to get up. "I've got to get back to work, and you certainly have lots to do. I will get that report to you no later than tomorrow. And, you know, it really would have been a little awkward if our first date was over Winston's dead body. Sorry, a little pathological humour."

Kirsten laughed. "Right now, no humour seems pathological. Thanks Moira, for the quick post-mortem, and for the lunch. It was nice."

"It was a pleasant break. I enjoyed it too."

The two women smiled at each other and shook hands. Kirsten then surprised them both by giving Moira a quick hug before she left to return to Harmony.

CHAPTER 21
Critical Meetings

JUST AS SHE REACHED HER CAR, KIRSTEN GOT A CALL FROM JANE. "Are you almost done there? It turns out your pal Sid was right on the money about Gladstone. They put out a release this morning announcing their purchase of the Wyandot land and the completion of their bid to buy the Gull Lake power plant. Construction on the storage site is supposed to start any time now. The Ontario Government put out a simultaneous announcement about how pleased they are to be able to privatize Gull Lake and Ontario's electrical supply is assured, good news all around, blah blah blah. Jasper's been on the phone with what looks like heavy conversations of some type. He wants to meet with the three of us ASAP."

"Just setting out, there in less than an hour. How's Wanda taking it?"

"I haven't had a chance to talk to her, but she knows about it. They're setting up barricades across the reserve access road, right at County Road 1. One of the calls Jasper got was an order from on high to close the county road to keep people distanced from them. He managed to talk them into a compromise, given the traffic on that road. There's no good detour route, and there's also all the stuff happening at Silent Lake today. He told them it would cause such chaos they'd be deluged by complaints.

"The compromise is we have uniforms there closing the lane closest to the reserve, stopping traffic to urge people to stay away, and alternating one-lane each way. It still may get pretty congested. If you get a chance to touch base with Wanda, that would be great, but discreetly. Another instruction to Jasper was that we were to only handle the traffic, no contact of any kind with what they call 'the Natives.'"

"Well, life was getting a little bit boring – NOT. Anything else new, I hesitate to ask?"

"Just that media enquiries *are* flooding in, and we expect the cameras and portable transmission towers here any time. One more thing we'll have to take care of."

"Ok. See you soon."

Kirsten drove on, trying to sort out in her mind how to properly investigate the murder while so much else was going on. She remembered watching a rerun of the old *Ed Sullivan Show* where a performer had a number of plates twirling simultaneously on long rods. He had to dash around madly to keep them all spinning. *We could use that guy here*, she thought.

Soon she came to Silent Lake Road, which had two vehicles waiting to turn onto the county road. The dust hanging over the road made clear how much activity was going on there. Ahead was the notorious bridge with the yellow tape marking off the crime scene. Before that she ended up behind five cars waiting for their turn to proceed past the Wyandot Reserve Road. When she reached the front of the line, she was stopped by Keith Sanderson.

"I take it you've been informed about our latest little challenge," he said.

"Just talked with Jane. Look, she wants me to touch base with Wanda Cornelius, if at all possible. You okay with that?"

Sanderson said, "I take it you've been told we locals are to hold back any contact until the pros get here. Just past the access road there's a wide shoulder. If you were to stop to check some strange noise coming from the front of your car, we're so busy here we'd hardly notice. It takes a bit of time to check out that sort of thing."

Kirsten smiled. "Thanks. Owe you one. I'll be careful. We're having an update and strategy meeting as soon as I get back. Anything I should tell them?"

"Just that with Silent Lake and taking care of this and keeping an eye on the crime scene and all the routine stuff that never goes away, we're getting stretched real thin here. Some reinforcements would be nice."

"Got it."

Kirsten drove on the open lane past the police roadblock, pulled over, and parked on the shoulder. She raised the hood of her car and pretended to check things out. When it was clear no one was watching her, she walked quickly over to where Wanda was supervising the construction of a barricade with a central gate and some shelters and tents nearby.

"Chief, Jane asked me to touch base with you. I was going to ask if everything's okay, but it's obviously not."

"Tell Jane that I'm very grateful for the heads up. Those bastards didn't even mention us in their 'isn't this just too wonderful' press releases. We are used to that kind of shit, but I still get really angry about it. You can tell Jane, and whomever else, that literally those bastards get access to our land over our dead bodies. May be a minor thing to them if a few Natives start to glow in the dark, but we don't quite see it that way. I guess we're just waiting for the government heavy weights to get here to sweettalk us back to our proper place. You know, be ready to put on the Native headdresses we've never actually worn in eastern Canada to provide a nice backdrop at some government photo-op."

"We'll try to stay in touch. For what it's worth, I think this whole thing stinks to high heaven. I know Jane introduced you to our information source, Sid Ray. We both think he's one media guy who can be trusted, but you'll have to make up your own mind about that. I'm not supposed to be here, so I'm off to our meeting. Good luck, Wanda."

Kirsten returned to her car, put down the hood, and drove quickly back to police headquarters. When she reached the second floor, Jeff ushered her in to McKnight's office where the captain and Jane were waiting for them.

McKnight said, "I hardly know where to start, but it'd better be with our investigation. Let's see where we are with that, and then I've got a lot to tell you about this Wyandot thing. But let's be concise. Kirsten, the post-mortem?"

Kirsten gave a quick summary. "The big thing is whatever this mystery weapon is. If we ever locate it, we're a long way toward a solution."

Next Jeff gave an update on the crime scene and his online search for relevant information. "I don't think we'll find whatever Winston threw into that creek. All Lewis saw was something blue, at a distance, disappearing into the swamp. The creek itself runs pretty fast, but once into the swamp, there's a thousand backwaters and blind turns. It likely sank but could have been swept deep into the swamp where you'd need a hundred searchers to look thoroughly. There's nothing else at the crime scene, no sign of anything remotely looking like the missing weapon. I searched the creek bed pretty thoroughly and saw nothing. You'd need our hundred searchers to do any better."

Next was Jane's turn. "I interviewed Winston's other pal from Friendlies, Councillor Arnold Weirness. Like everyone else we've talked to, he didn't seem to have really liked Winston. It's really McKay and his business dealings that drew them all together.

For what it's worth, he has no real alibi for Tuesday morning, just like Morgan.

"One interesting thing, he got pretty upset when I asked for detail about McKay's business stuff. He insisted council treats McKay like anyone else, and how dare I imply he used council leverage to favour McKay's projects so he would get trucking contracts.

"Let me throw a possibility on the table. Suppose they were all involved with illegal activity of some sort. Winston was a careless loudmouth. Suppose someone thought he needed to be shut up before he got them all in trouble. Suppose Winston was blackmailing them or threatening them some way. That, hypothetically, could provide a motive. We know Winston left after dumping whatever it was in the creek. Presumably he came back here to retrieve it. Did someone in town get even more worried because of the dumping thing? Did that someone grab a weapon at hand, follow Winston to the bridge, and still angry, scared, whatever, kill him and flee? There's the means and opportunity.

"That's a lot of supposition, but it does fit the questionable business dealings stuff, the friends who weren't really friends, and a sudden murder leaving no physical evidence. For what it's worth."

McKnight thanked them all and said they needed to work out a plan to keep things going on the murder case, but first he had to talk about the Wyandot Reserve situation.

McKnight paused, took a deep breath, and then started. "Before we get into details about this Wyandot matter, I've got to say a few things to you. I've been doing a lot of thinking about all these things that have been happening, and how I've been dealing with it. Really, how I've been dealing with things for a long time. I've always thought it was important to keep contact with people in town, especially the movers and shakers. You know, talk to them and make sure they kept me informed. McKay was one of them, and so were Winston, Weirness, and Morgan. I agree McKay is slippery, if not outright corrupt and not to be trusted, yet I sort of did trust him. I stood by while he wheeled and dealed. I thought it was good for the town to have business things happening, for these guys to be carrying out their plans and projects. I was wrong. It just meant I was sitting on the sidelines letting too much questionable stuff happen. Maybe I was even enabling it.

"Kirsten, I apologize for putting you into that difficult Friendlies situation. I'm not sure that I wasn't just avoiding really investigating McKay. It was a failure, but because of me, not you, or you, Jane. Maybe my worst fault was not involving you three more. I should have been listening to you rather than just giving orders and sitting in my office reading reports. Now here we are with all this complicated stuff landing in our laps, and I just plain and simple need your help. I can't manage all this on my own, and I'm sorry that it's at this late date I'm asking if we can act like a real team. That should have been the way we always operated.

"We don't have time to talk through all this right now. Not exactly my strongest suit anyway. But I hope you three can trust me enough to bear with me so we can avoid being buried by all this."

There was silence in the room for a moment. Then Jane said, "So, Captain, what's our game plan for tomorrow?" Kirsten and Jeff nodded and looked expectantly at McKnight.

"Thanks, everyone. But there's a new development, maybe the last straw that finally convinced me we needed a new approach around here. I've been on the phone with various of my superiors. This blockade at Wyandot has caught the attention, the major attention, of a lot of people. They've said that for now I stay in charge of things here because they want to keep things low key as long as possible. But they also said don't be surprised if some of the brass move in and take over. They've reminded me of how serious some of these other Indigenous protests have been around the province, and they want this one to end, quietly, and as soon as possible."

McKnight paused. "For the record, I think those people out at Wyandot have every darned right to protest. I pointed out to my superiors that they're only blocking their road, not the county road. However, I've been ordered that we need to keep tight control of the situation, though they have allowed us to keep the roads open.

"I've also been forcefully reminded that there are important people who need this matter cleaned up, fast and effectively. This Gladstone Company, and, it seems, the premier's office, insist this land acquisition has to happen. They say the Wyandot Band Council signed a legally binding agreement to provide unimpeded access to the land Gladstone purchased, and that they cannot break the law by now stopping access. Where it gets really tricky is we, as Provincial Police, have very questionable legal authority in the reserve, so, we might see the RCMP involved, since they are the federal force that maybe does have legal authority there.

"It's all gone political. They really want to talk to McKay because he negotiated the access agreement, but he can't be reached. They are leaning hard on me to find him. I have been ordered to convene a meeting here, in my office, in about an hour's time. A man named Elliot Davis from the Ontario premier's office will be in charge of the meeting. A Gladstone vice president, Malcolm Priestner, will be present. Likely our MP, Wallace Madison, will be there, representing the federal government. They had hoped to get someone more senior, but there isn't enough time. There may be someone from the RCMP.

"This is to be a totally confidential meeting. I am to tell no-one. Leaks, especially to the media, will be regarded with the utmost seriousness, as in, I think, costing me my job if word gets out. That means this meeting we're having right now has to be similarly confidential. Please. I'm telling you all this partially because, as I said earlier, I can't manage all this alone. The other thing is, one commitment I've had during my whole career is that I have a major obligation and responsibility to look after the interests of this town and this region, including, by the way, the Wyandot Reserve. I don't think all these big shots give two flying figs about all of us here. I'm not going to be a tool they use to do significant harm to this area.

So, to heck with their confidentiality. I need your help to make sure we do our best to have all this turn out as positively as possible for all of us here.

"Now, I could brief you after the meeting, but I'd much rather you hear it first-hand. I propose to leave my intercom open. If you three were to gather in the conference room you could listen in, but that could mean putting you in some jeopardy. If you want to opt out, I totally understand. I'm almost at retirement, but I don't want you three to suffer. I guess I'm asking if you're in or out. You can take a few minutes to decide, but they'll be here pretty soon."

Kirsten, Jeff, and Jane looked around at each other and nodded. Jane said, "Jeff may be the best guy to make sure the technology works. Kirsten and I can take notes, since it might be pushing things to record it. Should we be in the conference room when they get here or slip away to it after your door closes?"

McKnight said, "How about one of you being here to greet them and then adjourn to the conference room where the rest of you will be? You'd better lock the door and put a note on it saying the room is closed. And thanks, everyone. We will meet again after they've all safely gone and finalize our plans for tomorrow."

About half an hour later Elliot Davis, Malcolm Priestner, township mayor Calvin Stuart, and MP Wallace Madison were seated in McKnight's office with the door firmly closed. Davis said, "I was asked by the premier's office to call this meeting. Now, the provincial government is not directly involved in this situation, but we need it to be ended, promptly and quietly. We have had too many incidents in Ontario of this sort that have dragged on far too long, and that have gotten far too complicated and damaging. That can't be the case here. We can't have the sale of Gull Lake compromised. Given that the Wyandot people are under the direction of the Federal Ministry of Indian Affairs, there may have to be federal involvement, maybe with the RCMP. I didn't ask them to be represented here today, because we need to contain this situation, not broaden it.

"I have asked Mr. Madison to be here so we can keep the federal side informed. I have also asked Mayor Stewart to be present for two reasons. There may be the need to involve the municipal government to resolve this. Also, as I explained to Mayor Stewart this morning, if this deal goes through, my government will be investing considerable funds in this area for infrastructure development and economic incentives. And I do mean considerable.

"Before we go any further, I demand absolute confidentiality. No leaks, no media, other than what we give them. With that in mind, all media inquiries will be referred to me, and all media releases will be done by me or my people. Captain McKnight, you are the senior Provincial Police officer here, but you need to be very clear that we are in constant contact with your superiors. If, God forbid, this thing snowballs, you can expect a more senior officer to take over. Your job is to keep things under control, with traffic, the local citizens and so on, and to help me. You will share nothing with any members of your detachment other than to convey your orders to them. Understood?'

"Completely. My detectives are all out working on a murder enquiry. Our uniformed officers are mostly keeping things under control at the blockade, though we are also dealing with an evacuation situation at a nearby housing development. Quite frankly, I could use some more people."

"Your superiors agree with me that we will only move more police officers here if absolutely necessary. We want to defuse this, not inflame the situation. I asked you to bring in the local developer who negotiated the actual land-access agreement. Have you tracked this McKay down yet?"

"No, and we also want to talk to him about our murder investigation and the situation at the Silent Lake housing development. You probably know we were also asked some weeks ago to look into recent suspicious financial activities of his."

"Wyandot takes precedence over all your local matters. I'm surprised and disappointed you haven't located him for us. Keep looking, harder. And don't complain about not enough officers. Just deploy your forces in a sensible manner. I have asked Malcolm Priestner, Vice President of Asset Development at Gladstone, to join us. He will be the lead negotiator for Gladstone. Keep this quiet and contained, follow your orders exactly, and get those protesters to remove their barricade. Malcolm?"

Priestner stood up and turned to face the rest. "Elliot has been admirably to the point, so I won't add anything about the current situation. You need to know why the timing is so important to us, and also to this community. I trust that you are aware Gladstone has just completed its purchase of the Gull Lake Nuclear Plant. We are starting final preparations to restart the plant, but first we must remove the spent fuel rods and other radioactive material from the site.

"The government has been very helpful. They will soon need the electrical power from Gull Lake, so we have no time for delays. We had your Mr. McKay negotiate the options to buy the land beside the Wyandot Reserve, which included absolute guarantees of access through the reserve to our site. Frankly, we are very disappointed with McKay because he assured us that everything was in order. Now it appears it's not. Or the Natives had second thoughts or want more money – we need to find out what they want and get the damned Natives the hell away from that damn barricade. Captain McKnight, do you have any idea what's going on with them?"

"It seems they had no idea what the land was to be used for. McKay alluded to it being just another housing development, or maybe part of the creation of a new provincial park. Frankly, I can quite understand why they're upset. It's very close to Harmony, so I think you can expect a lot more people around here to be upset. And if I may, they are not 'damned Natives.' They are part of our community."

Stewart said, "Yes, we didn't know anything about this. It came out of the blue. But I've been getting a lot of calls. Frankly, it's more than just being upset. They are angry and I–"

Priestner was glowering at McKnight and Stewart. He angrily cut Stewart off. "Look, all that the people around here have to know is that this will be perfectly safe. The government has ensured that all safety protocols will be followed. The site is geologically perfect. The only difference around here will be that the damned reserve will have more money and improved infrastructure. There will be significant economic benefits to Harmony. Frankly, you people should be thanking your lucky stars that it's you getting this opportunity and not some other municipality. McKnight, sorry to abuse your delicate sensibilities, but it's the Natives who are reneging on a legal contract and stirring up trouble when they should be thanking us. Now, Elliot, perhaps you have some more reality to share with these people."

"I do. Simply that the number-one factor is what Malcolm has so emphatically stated. *THIS ... IS ... SAFE!* There have been no, I repeat *NO* problems in Ontario with similar disposal arrangements. *NONE!*

Priestner continued. "You need to know we have two other potential sites which are geologically sound and for which we have purchase options in place. The problem is that both would involve much more complex and expensive transportation arrangements. Both would involve delaying the Gull Lake reopening.

"I've shared this with you, in total confidence, so you will understand what I am now going to tell you. If the Wyandot situation is resolved promptly, no more than a few days from now, the deal goes ahead and all the economic benefits Elliot has alluded to will be delivered. If it seems it cannot be resolved in the next few days, then we will go with one of the other sites. They will get all the resources which would have come here."

Davis said, "And you, Mayor Stewart and Captain McKnight, and also our valued Indigenous inhabitants of the Wyandot Reserve, can then try to explain to local people why you all so needlessly and tragically betrayed their best economic interests. This is not a negotiating tactic, but rather a cold hard reality. Also, if you go against the will of our government in this matter, it would not help this region in developing a positive and mutually beneficial relationship with our government.

"Here is how we are going to proceed. There needs to be a quiet approach to the Wyandot leadership to ascertain exactly what they want. We can then meet formally with them to finalize details to resolve all this. Captain McKnight, I presume you have a good relationship with the Wyandot Band Council and can arrange a discreet meeting with them. Is there anyone else you have who could help?"

"Sergeant Jane Walden has an excellent relationship with them, especially with Chief Cornelius. I'm sure she will be glad to help us."

"Excellent. Now, it will cost Gladstone and my government a considerable amount of money if we have to abandon our agreement with them. Don't mention any amounts, but do make sure they know that Gladstone is willing to significantly sweeten their deal with them. My government would also be open to specific help for them as long as we can work successfully with the federal government in doing so. There are things like road improvements around the reserve, maybe some job openings for local Natives. Mr. Madison, do you think your government would be on board with that?"

Madison said, "All I can do is try to facilitate connection with more senior members of our government. However, as long as it did not compromise our responsibilities and initiatives with Native matters, I'm sure they would at least talk to you about it."

Davis said, "Captain McKnight, we need to reconvene this meeting for your updates as quickly as possible after you meet with them. I trust this will be tomorrow, even tonight, if at all possible. I believe all parties will benefit significantly if we can act quickly and with firmness and good sense here."

McKnight said, "And, of course, with respect, honesty and good will."

Davis replied, "Of course, Captain. That goes without saying. So, I think we are done here. It would be best if we leave separately. I look forward to hearing good news at our next meeting."

The men left one at a time, with Stewart hanging back until he and McKnight were alone.

Stewart said, "My God, Jasper, what have we got into here? I'm used to dealing with things like zoning requests and bylaw infractions. I'm not in the same league as those guys. This will turn our town upside down. A nuclear waste storage facility? I know nothing about any of that stuff, but it's scary as hell. And all this money they say will flow in if we do as they say? And what will happen if we don't go along? Were those threats they were making?"

Stewart sat down, flushed and breathing heavily. "I should call an emergency meeting of township council, but we were warned to keep quiet about this. It feels like those protesters are calling the shots. I mean, if we can't trust the provincial government about what's safe and what's not, who can we trust? This could blow up in our faces a dozen ways. I guess we need to do what Davis and this Priestner guy say, but I'm scared as hell, Jasper. What do you have to say?"

McKnight sat quietly for a minute. "A couple of things. First, if this stuff is so almighty safe, why not store it in downtown Lakeside? Or London or Toronto, for all that. But they insist on it being out in the country, or up in the north. I believe these guys have exactly zero interest in us, or Wyandot, or anything else other than money and getting their way. You noticed that Davis didn't even bring in our MPP, Sterling Fox? This all comes from Toronto. I don't blame the Wyandot people for being scared, not one little bit. Also, if something goes wrong, that site's really close to us."

"What could go wrong? Now you're getting me really scared."

"I don't know in any detail, except if there's a leakage, its effects could be widespread. Extreme case, this whole area could become uninhabitable. If it leaks underground, into our water table, that could happen years down the road. How ever would you fix something like that? That stuff is dangerous for maybe thousands of years.

"I'm going to meet with the Wyandot leadership tomorrow, just like I'm supposed to. They want me to report back? Fine. But we need to think of people around here we can quietly consult with. It's our town, our region, not theirs. Why don't you get together a few people you can really trust so we can have a private meeting of our own before our next go-around with them? If word leaks out, it maybe is not such a bad thing. This has consequences, one way or another, for everyone who lives here."

"Okay, Jasper, okay. Let's stay in close contact. My God, and I thought being elected mayor was the best thing that happened to me. It doesn't feel that way now."

After Stewart left Kirsten, Jeff, and Jane reconvened in McKnight's office.

McKnight led off. "You can see why I want as much help as I can get. Did you hear everything okay? Thoughts?"

Jane said, "I think you are exactly right that they don't really care about this region and anybody who lives here. We, and particularly the Wyandot band, are just something that got in their way. I don't trust them or anything they said. Right now, and as long as we do stay quiet, we're on our own. There are people out there who could help. Opposition political parties, environmental and nuclear safety groups. You know, Greenpeace, people like that. But we and Stewart, and presumably everyone else around here, are just supposed to keep our mouths shut."

Kirsten broke in. "That just underlines how political all this is. We're cops, not politicians. The only proper police work involved in all this is protecting public safety. Yet seemingly this guy Davis wants to use the Provincial Police to help him get the political result he wants. Does he think the Provincial Police are the government's own private militia? Captain, I think he was clearly threatening you to do what he says or else. These things should be argued out in the Ontario legislature, or at township council, or a town hall meeting or something. You – we – shouldn't be in this sort of situation."

Jeff was sitting with a thoughtful expression on his face. "Captain, I think you were right to talk to Stewart about involving other people around here. In fact, forcing this out into the public eye is exactly what the people at Wyandot are doing. How do you see this meeting with them going?"

McKnight said, "Jane, I'd really like your advice here."

Jane said, "Davis and Priestner want us, as police officers, to use our authority to bring them into line. That's wrong, it won't work, and I won't try to do that."

McKnight said, "Agreed. So, what do we say?"

"We can tell them these guys have substantial benefits to offer them. In fact, a bribe, though they'll figure that out without us saying it. They won't accept a bribe however it's dressed up – you know, an 'incentive' or a 'renegotiation' or 'just doing business.' These guys used McKay to trick them, lie to them, and lead them to think it'd be just a routine business deal. Wanda was suspicious from the start, but unfortunately it seems a lot of members of her band council are too trusting. So, I think we just give them the information, like we were told to, but with no threats, no persuasion. I think all we promise is to do our best to protect their safety, and to be honest with them."

McKnight said, "That will likely make it a short meeting. I agree, Jane. They have to know we are on the side of what's legal and what's best for our community. We can bring back their response to this next meeting and the big boys will decide what they are going to do. I will consult with Mayor Stewart. If what Davis and Priestner say is truthful, it *would* be in their self-interest to go elsewhere. They may just go on their way and leave us alone, but I doubt they have a truthful bone in their bodies. We have to be careful about what else they may have up their sleeves.

"Here's what I suggest for tomorrow. Jane, you and I go out to Wyandot. We talk with them, decide what to report back, and schedule this next meeting Priestner and Davis want, though a little delay, until at least Friday, might be good. I think it best if one or both of us stay out there to keep an eye on what these guys might try. I may have to come back here and meet with Calvin Stewart.

"Jeff, I'd appreciate it if you would stay here and be in charge while I'm gone. There may be New Eden issues that come up … such a darn mess out there. Davis wants to handle anything about Wyandot with any media that show up. Fine. But the media may also ask about New Eden, or Winston. That's in your hands. Use your own judgment.

"Kirsten, the Winston case is all yours until we get some of this other stuff off our plates. Davis and Priestner be damned, we are not going to stop investigating that murder. Does that sound okay, everyone?"

All three nodded in agreement. Kirsten said, "Can I lay out a few things about the Winston investigation? We have no eyewitnesses, no physical evidence, and a baffling post-mortem result. We have some speculation, like Winston being followed back out there by one of his fellow schemers. I suppose Percy Lewis could be tied into it, but that's such a long shot.

Glancing at Jane, she said, "There may be other really unlikely possibilities, but the one thing I keep coming back to is this blue object Winston disposed of in the creek. I can't help thinking finding whatever it is gives us the best chance to zero in on a suspect. What I'd like to do is a further search tomorrow. I know you looked carefully at the crime scene, Jeff, and I agree about how unlikely it is to find something swept along in the current deep into the swamp, but I think I've got to at least try."

McKnight said, "I'd rather there was someone with you, per standard procedure, but we just don't have the people available. How do you propose going about it?"

"Jeff, can I borrow your boat? I could use it to follow the current along into the swamp."

Jeff said, "Sure. It's still out there, locked to a tree back out of sight. I can give you the key, and a paddle and a pole. You'd likely need both."

"Thanks. Sounds perfect."

Jane said, "If you get way deep into the swamp, how do you get back to your car?"

"I thought of that. If I happen to find it quickly, not a problem, I just fight my way back to the bridge. If I end up going right into Silent Lake, there's no-one there, but I can call to be picked up. I know cell service there is a little spotty, especially in the swamp, but I'm sure I can eventually find a signal. If worst comes to worst, at nightfall come pick me up. Look, I can see you're all doubtful about this, but I've been out there in the swamp before, though quite a few years ago, I'll admit. I'll be armed. I'll be okay. It certainly is a long shot, but our investigation is stalled. I have to at least try."

McKnight said, "Okay. Let's go with what we've laid out here. We all have to stay in regular contact. And all of us, not just Kirsten, have to be careful. Thanks all. Really, thank you."

After everyone left, McKnight sat quietly at his desk for some time, deep in thought. Eventually he too left for what he feared would be a sleepless night.

CHAPTER 22
Deep in the Swamp

KIRSTEN DIDN'T GET QUITE THE EARLY START SHE HAD HOPED FOR. She had to complete some paperwork and then get the padlock key and boat equipment from Jeff. At 10:30 she parked near the bridge and carried her gear down to the edge of the water. She unlocked the boat and dragged it down to the edge of the stream. It was like a hybrid between a punt and a canoe, wide enough to be stable, but narrow enough that it could be paddled. Both the bow and stern were squared off, with the bow being narrower and slightly raised. Jeff had explained the most efficient way to use it on running water. It could be paddled while on open water, but the pole worked best when entering a swampy area. There was a regular anchor in case she needed to hold it in place, and a drag anchor that could be trailed behind the craft to slow it down. It had ropes at both the stern and bow.

Jeff had insisted she wear a lifejacket, which she grudgingly put on. It was already getting warm despite the heavy rainfall the night before and the still partially overcast sky. The lifejacket would restrict her movements, but Jeff had made her give a solemn promise to wear it. She had brought a lunch, two bottles of water, binoculars, sunglasses, sunscreen, and insect repellent. She wore a long-sleeved t-shirt, a baseball cap, and shorts with many pockets to hold as much of her gear as possible. Her gun was in a holster fixed to the back of her belt. Her wallet, phone, and portable charger were in a waterproof plastic sleeve zipped in to one of her front pockets.

She took a few minutes to get familiar with the boat and quickly realized why Jeff found it so useful for searches like the one she was undertaking. It was stable and easy to propel and steer. The anchors worked well to control her speed or hold the boat steady if she wanted to stop and closely inspect the shoreline. She took only a cursory look near the bridge since Jeff had already carefully searched that area.

Soon she was gliding along into the swampy area. The stream was always quite distinct, but at times was closely hemmed in by bushes and the surrounding swamp. Occasionally it broadened out into quiet pools, some with a small beach area. Twice she had to navigate under or around trees that had fallen across the stream. She took her time because this might be the one time the area would be carefully searched for the elusive blue bag. She ventured as deeply as possible into the swamp on both sides of the stream in case the blue bag had ended up being snagged or deposited there. She had to go on the premise that the bag had floated, at least for a while, because that would be the only circumstance in which she would be able to find it.

As the fitful sun rose higher in the sky, it got hotter and more humid. It was hard work manoeuvring the boat through the swampy areas and back against the current so she could search both sides. She took breaks, usually anchored in the middle of one of the pools to avoid the insects. The temptation was strong to remove her sweat-soaked clothes for a quick swim, but she knew time was fleeting, and she was determined to either find the bag or to be able to safely say that it was not there, or so hidden it would likely never be found.

As she moved further into the swamp the sounds of birds and the humming of insects gradually increased. Often, she heard the rustling of small animals in the undergrowth and the splashes of muskrats diving into the water. She was enjoying the exercise, the chance to work off some of the tension that had been steadily taking over her body the past several days. Eventually, when she thought she was about halfway to Silent Lake, she stopped for lunch.

She anchored the boat in the middle of one of the larger ponds and sat quietly for a moment, enjoying the break from her exertions. The sky was still partially overcast, hazy clouds occasionally obscuring the sun. She removed her life jacket and t-shirt, enjoying the feel of a fitful breeze on her skin. She felt a pleasant drowsiness, a feeling she could close her eyes and nap if only there was a place to do so in the boat. She realized that this feeling of peaceful solitude, the absence of city noise and the continual presence of other people, was something she had missed from her girlhood growing up in this area.

Once she had left Harmony – really, had *fled* Harmony, she had determinedly tried to blot out memories of her childhood. She had thrown herself into her studies, into the activity and constant pace of living in or close to urban centres. Her career as a police officer had dominated her thoughts, activities, and energies. New friendships and involvements had made it easy for her to avoid, if not actively suppress, memories of her first eighteen years. It was like those years had become a monolithic block in her memory, a time of constant confusion, anxiety, difficulty, and frequent pain that she wished to revisit as little as possible. It was like pretending her real life, the life she was now living, had begun when she had left Harmony behind.

The idea of returning here had seemed at first like one of life's minor ironies. It was not a personal choice, but rather one thrust upon her. Initially she thought it would be an amusing adventure, a temporary deviation from the central course of her life. However, she had found Harmony had changed significantly in the twelve years she had been gone. Perhaps part of this was seeing it now through adult eyes.

Talking to Jane and Sid about some of her earlier memories had brought them back to her in a vividly detailed, almost unsettling way. What was that quote from William Faulkner that she had encountered during the one English course she had taken? "The past isn't dead. It isn't even past." Or that comment she had read in an article about the late American writer, "Faulkner is about the past, and the struggle to both accept it as a part of oneself and continue into the future." She had surprised herself by coming to realize how textured her early years had been, of the many discreet incidents, encounters and inner struggles that had helped make her the woman she now was. There certainly had been significant down times, but also many positive ones.

Her current surroundings made her sleepily think back to her adolescent skinny-dipping adventure in this swamp. With a start, she came out of her reverie and realized this was likely the pool where it had happened. The then-fifteen-year-old Kirsten had reacted as she likely would now. In fact, as she *had* reacted at that Saturday night Friendlies encounter. With a bemused smile, she thought, *So, already starting to be a cop even then, though I never would have believed it.* Sighing, she pulled her t-shirt and life jacket back on, pulled up the anchor, and continued with what she hoped would not be a fool's errand.

While Kirsten was carrying out her search, McKnight and Jane had planned their meeting with Wanda. Jane had called her friend to arrange for a discreet 11:00 a.m. meeting in one of the tents erected near the barricade. They drove out in McKnight's unmarked patrol car to stay as low-profile as possible. They parked at the side of County Road 1 and walked back to the cruiser parked near the barricade where Sergeant Keith Sanderson was sitting behind the wheel.

"Keith. Anything much happening out here today?"

"Pretty quiet, Captain. Traffic's moderate. Some griping about the delays. We're not stopping people anymore because word has got around about what's happening here. As you see, we've set it up so traffic coming out of town has to stop and then yield to any traffic coming toward it. Problem is, we're stretched so thin it's hard to have someone here all the time. If there's an accident we have to cover, or anything comes up in town, we sometimes have no choice than to temporarily leave. There have been a couple of vehicles that seem to drive by fairly regularly. I noted their plate numbers. They never actually do anything, at least not while we're here, but they sure are interested in what's going on at the barricade."

"We'll ask them at the barricade about that. We are going to have a quiet meeting with Chief Cornelius. Off the record, so if anyone asks, we're not here. I can't tell you anything else at the moment, but we're hoping to get this thing settled sooner rather than later."

They continued on to the barricade where they were met by Wanda and ushered in to one of the tents the protesters had erected. Inside, they sat in folding chairs around a small table.

Wanda said, "I have to admit I was surprised you wanted this quiet little meeting. We've been waiting for the heavy artillery to move in."

McKnight said, "I asked Jane to set this up because I know you two trust each other. Chief, if I have my way, the heavy artillery won't show up. I hope we can resolve this thing before it escalates."

"And with us radical Natives literally folding our tents and letting this thing happen?"

"No. Rather with these outsiders figuratively folding *their* tents and letting you, and our community, return to normal. I want to have two conversations with you, one the 'heavy artillery,' as you put it, wants us to have, and another one off the record."

"We've learned to be wary about 'off the record' conversations, Captain. When even signed treaties usually turn out to be lies, it's hard not to think we're just being strung along again."

Jane said, "I hope you'll bear with us, Wanda. There's people putting pressure on us, but you have my word Captain McKnight is trying to help."

"Okay. So, which of these meetings is first?'

McKnight said, "A representative from Gladstone and one from the premier's office met with us yesterday. I am to convey to you that both are eager to come to a mutually satisfactory agreement with you and the Wyandot Band so this situation can be defused. I am to tell you that Gladstone is willing to put significant new inducements on the table, substantial increases in the agreed-on access payments, and other concrete benefits for your reserve."

"What does the government guy have for us?"

"He said it is complicated by the fact you're under federal jurisdiction, but he is willing to, quote, 'sit down with his federal counterpart to look at significant inducements, and to also provide possible jobs and regional infrastructure improvements that will help your people.'"

"These guys sure like to go on about sitting down to talk about stuff. I presume that in return for all these 'inducements' we are to remove our opposition to their little nuclear waste dump project?"

Jane said, "They want us to get you to agree to a meeting with them where they can be specific about what they can offer you. They're sort of using us like fly fisherman, placing an attractive-enough fly in front of you."

"So they can then reel us in. Well, you can tell them we'll be willing to sit down and talk when they shelve this damn project permanently. I realize that a few Natives dying, or our home being destroyed means fuck all to them, but we don't see it quite that way. Once they shelve this damn thing and leave, permanently, there's really nothing left to talk about."

McKnight smiled and said, "Pretty much what I thought you might say. Chief, I will convey your response to them. Which leads us to meeting number two."

Wanda said, "I hope it's more productive than meeting number one."

"I said what they wanted me to say. Here's what I want to say. These guys have come into our community with no interest other than their convenience and profits – big profits, if I read it correctly. I believe they have put this whole area, and the Wyandot reserve in particular, in jeopardy. They want me to misuse my authority as regional police captain to pressure you into compliance. I believe they want to make this thing happen before any effective opposition, any questioning or public enquiry, can happen. I have no jurisdiction over you, your people, or this project. I will not accept some guy from the premier's office trying to turn me and my detachment into some kind of political enforcers. I am going to have to have some difficult discussions with my superiors. I hope they share my repugnance at this attempt to politicize our force."

"I can see why you want this off the record. What happens next?'

Jane said, "Wanda, one question, just to confirm. When Alex McKay was negotiating with the band council, was there any indication of what the site would be used for?"

"No. He hinted it was just some sort of residential development. I heard that he hinted elsewhere it was going to be some sort of park or campground. He insisted the lease only specify something like 'any legal use of the land.' I wanted it to be much more specific. Hell, I didn't want this agreement at all, but my band council had stars in their eyes. What does McKay say about all that?"

"McKay is missing. No-one can find him."

McKnight said, "I think these guys are sure you will leap at their offer. They seem to think that deep down everyone is only motivated by the same things they are, mostly money. They want this decided soon. They will not stand for what they call a 'protracted and damaging stand-off.' I think we both know, and so do they, that this thing will not stay quiet for long. There are too many people and organizations in this province that oppose this sort of thing. The media are always looking for a hot story, and some of them may even want to do some real investigative journalism. I think the good news for you is that if you stand firm, they will likely be gone sooner than you might think."

"Meaning this whole Gull Lake project falls through? I can't see that happening."

Jane said, "Nor can we. It just means that they'll have to switch plans and go to a more expensive and less convenient option, likely storing the stuff up north somewhere."

"So the problem just gets transferred elsewhere."

Jane said, "Unfortunately, yes, but at least then it couldn't be done surreptitiously. Wanda, we're just small-town cops. All we can do is enforce the law and try to protect our own local interests. There are people engaged with these issues on a much larger scale, and more power to them. All we can do is try to make sure we don't end up being victims."

McKnight said, "Chief, I can't predict exactly how this will turn out. My superiors will determine most of what happens to me and my detachment. They are cops too, and I hope they share my concerns about any inappropriate politicizing of the police. I don't move in those circles, so we'll see. But back to the here and now, these guys want a follow-up meeting. Likely tonight or tomorrow. I will tell them exactly what you said, unless you want me to tone it down a bit."

Wanda smiled slightly. "If anything, I might want to dial it up a bit. No, just quote me. I sort of hope I might get the chance to say that to them in person."

"One other thing. Sorry we can't have a cruiser out here all the time. I tried to get more people, but the powers that be say they don't want to escalate things. My officer mentioned some vehicles passing by here fairly often, but he didn't know what they're up to when we're not here. Any problems to report?"

"Only if rocks thrown at us is a problem, or idiots yelling curses and threats about how it's not our road and asking why are we stopping new jobs coming here."

"Let me see about that. We'll be in touch, likely though Jane. Chief, Jane has been the person I've relied on in matters dealing with you and your people. I fear I should have been more positive and involved. Let's first see if we can get this thing sorted out, and then maybe we can do better in the future."

Jane and McKnight walked back to Sanderson's cruiser, leaving Wanda with a bemused look on her face.

When they got there, McKnight said, "Keith, seems your frequent visitors have been misbehaving when we're not around. Let's put together a plan."

The three police officers conferred and then set about putting their plan into operation.

About half an hour later a pickup truck slowly approached from town. The only vehicle in sight was a nondescript mid-sized sedan parked on the side of the road about five hundred metres from the blockade. Ignoring the stop sign, the truck proceeded slowly toward the barricade. When they got even with it, two men who had been hiding under a tarp in the back of the truck stood up and started to heave rocks toward the barricades and surrounding tents. They yelled loud insults and taunts. "Fucking Indians. Think it's your fucking road? Go back to your fucking drinking and whoring! There are people here who want the jobs you're fucking keeping away. Fucking leave or we'll get some friends and really teach you a lesson!"

After they had passed the barricades, the two in the back ducked back down in the truck bed and the driver started to speed up. He stopped when he saw a police cruiser pull out from a lane leading to a small stand of trees about six hundred metres past the barricade. The driver backed around so he could turn to go the other way, but the shoulder was narrow, and the back wheels slipped into some wet ground. The cruiser quickly approached and stopped sideways across the road. Meanwhile, the sedan had come up and parked across the road in the other direction. Desperate to escape, the driver stepped on the gas and tried to get back onto the road, but this only caused the truck to slip deeper into the ditch.

The three police officers approached and ordered the driver to get out of the truck. He answered by again stepping on the accelerator.

McKnight loudly said, "Sergeant Sanderson, this vehicle is trying to escape arrest and is endangering our lives. You shoot out the rear tire on your side, and I'll take care of this one."

The officers put their hands on their guns, but the driver quickly opened the door and leaped out. "Don't, don't. Those tires are like a grand each. Look, I didn't know who you were. Sorry. It's a misunderstanding."

Sanderson said, "You boys hiding in the back also having a misunderstanding? All of you, out on the road, spread your legs, lean against the truck."

After the three men had been searched and cuffed, Sanderson took out their wallets. "Captain, we seem to have the Montrose brothers here, Mickey, Marvin, and Melvin, believe it or not. Someone's parents sure like the letter 'M.' Do you want me to run these three idiots in and file the charges?"

In a strangled voice, Mickey said, "Charges? Look, we didn't do nothing. Just having a little fun. Like I said, I didn't realize who you were at first."

Jane said, "I guess we need to get bigger lights on our cruisers."

Marvin said, "Please just let us go. We promise we won't come by here no more. No need for charges."

McKnight said, "Sergeant Sanderson, it seems we need to make sure we keep a cruiser out here at all times, so you'd better stay here. Let's handcuff them together and put them in the back of my car so I can run them in. It's been a while since I arrested anyone. About time I got back into practice. As for charges, I've got failing to obey a stop sign, property damage, and failing to stop for the police. That about it?"

Sanderson said, "Well, when he was spinning his wheels, they kicked up a rock that bounced off that tree and hit me. Assaulting a police officer?"

Jane said, "And we heard the threats against the people at the barricades. So, maybe threatening bodily harm? And the threats were directly specifically against the Wyandot people. Is that a hate crime?"

McKnight said, "More charges might occur while I drive these fine citizens in. If they further resist arrest, or attack me or damage my car, we might be able to set some sort of record here. Sergeant Walden, please stay out here with Sergeant Sanderson. I'll process these guys, get our new tow truck operator to come out and impound the truck, and then rejoin you. It seems we have to make it abundantly clear that the police are out here."

Mickey said, "Impound my truck? Look. I know it has to be towed out of that ditch, and we'll pay for that, but I need it for work."

Jane said, "You know, Captain, I have to brush up on a few things about little crime sprees like this one. But can't we seize a vehicle that's been used in a crime, especially when the police are directly involved?"

McKnight said, "I'll make a note of asking about that when I speak to the Crown attorney."

Melvin said, "Do you mean you're throwing us in jail? Taking the truck? I've got a family. I need to get home."

McKnight said, "Well, we may release you on your own recognizance, or the judge may let you out on bail. We'll sort that out in town. You'll have to talk to our tow truck guy about getting your truck back, *if* it's not impounded. But boys, the big thing, I just need you to stop being so darned stupid. I can't really see that happening with idiots like you, so you need to just know that we won't accept this kind of behaviour, ever. You need to tell that to all your redneck friends, all the yahoos, whazzoos, and general idiots you hang out with."

With that, they crammed the three men into the back of McKnight's unmarked cruiser. McKnight drove off toward town, raising his hand in a short wave as he passed the barricade. Sanderson said to Jane, "Think he'll file any of those charges?"

"Not really. I suspect maybe just something like disturbing the peace, or some other minor charge. They'll likely end up with probation and a fine or community service. I think he mostly just wants word to get out that he's serious about stopping this stuff. One thing, though, I don't know if I've ever seen him enjoying himself more."

As the afternoon advanced, Kirsten carried on with her search. She was getting tired now, eager to end the search, and disappointed in its lack of success. By late afternoon she saw by the thinning out of the trees that she was almost out to Silent Lake. Once again, she anchored the boat and carefully looked around the swamp with her binoculars. When she saw a small patch of blue deep in the swamp, she at first thought she was imagining things. She raised the anchor and paddled, then poled, toward it. As she got closer it became clear she was indeed looking at a blue object, but she feared it was just some blue garbage that had been caught in the branches of a fallen tree. Earlier, she had fished out a blue plastic bag and a piece of blue Styrofoam, but this was definitely a blue case of some sort.

She poled the boat as close as she could and tied it to the fallen tree. The blue case was maddeningly out of reach and lodged where she could not get to it with the boat. She sat and pondered her options. It wasn't really safe to try to clamber over the fallen tree, or to try to reach it by slogging through the water. She could mark the spot and come back with reinforcements, but then she saw the case start to bob around in the sluggish current and fitful breeze. Would it drift further into the swamp, or finally sink?

Saying *in for a penny, in for a pound* to herself, Kirsten took a deep breath and removed her shoes and shorts, keeping on the life jacket. She eased into the water off the stern of the boat and tried to move towards the case. Her feet occasionally touched a muddy bottom or the slippery submerged limbs of the tree. She had to work though the branches above the surface of the water and the lifejacket kept getting caught up in them. Frustrated, she struggled back to the boat, braced herself on part of the submerged tree trunk and removed the life jacket and her t-shirt. She rested for a moment, dressed in her bra and panties. *Got to stop taking my clothes off out here*, she ruefully thought.

Gathering her strength, she again struggled through the tree branches, holding on to them to pull herself nearer to the case. She finally reached it and saw that one of its handles had slipped over the stump of a broken tree limb. Holding on to a tree branch with one hand, she grabbed the case and pulled it free. The current was sluggish but still pulled against her body and the surprisingly buoyant case. She slowly worked back toward the boat, but with one hand firmly holding onto the case, she had to first let go of one handhold and then frantically reach for the next one. By the time she came even with the boat she had drifted downstream far enough that the boat was now beyond her reach.

She knew her strength was fading, and she had no life jacket to buoy her up. She knew there was no way she could fight through the branches at the top of the tree to get to the boat. She remembered part of her Red Cross water-safety training twenty years before. *If you find yourself in a situation like this, try to find something buoyant to hold on to – a piece of wood, anything.* She was holding on to the 'anything': a buoyant blue case. Flipping over on to her back, Kirsten hugged the case to her chest. She kicked until she had propelled herself past the tree and out to the central current. Turning against the flow, she continued to kick and paddle herself backwards with one hand.

Once she had finally moved past the boat, she angled herself toward it and half floated, half propelled herself over until she bumped into the side of the boat. She heaved the case into the boat and moved back to the stern. She found a submerged branch to brace her foot against and lifted herself up and over the stern of the boat. She tumbled on to the bottom of the boat against the central seat and lay there for several moments, breathing deeply until she was able to sit up. She slowly pulled her clothes back on and ruefully put on the life jacket.

She had various scrapes and minor cuts, was exhausted and sore, but felt gloriously alive and triumphant. A refrain kept running through her mind, *I found the damn thing! I found it!* She ate the last of her lunch and finished off the last of her water. She was eager to confirm that this was indeed Winston's mysterious blue case, and to see what was in it, but she knew she had to first get safely out to Silent Lake, since propelling the boat back against the current to the bridge was clearly impossible. *Okay*, she said to herself, *no capsizing the boat. Tie the case to one of the ropes. The current will take me out to the lake, and then a short paddle to the shore.*

She was tempted to try to call Jane but knew that her shaky hands were more liable to drop her phone than to manage to get it out of its waterproof sleeve and successfully make a call, if there was even service here. She sat on the boat's centre seat, gently padding, mostly just trying to keep the boat on course. Soon the stream widened, and she was past the swamp and into Silent Lake. *Silent is the right word*, she thought. There was still a fitful breeze, but there was no sign of life, almost no sounds at all. She paddled toward the shore, beaching the boat opposite the second house: Alex McKay's.

The houses were all dark, silent, and obviously deserted. She had hoped that maybe there were stragglers still here, but it was well past the deadline to evacuate the houses and she knew all services had been turned off. *I almost wish you were here, Alex, scumbag though you are*, she thought. *God, talking to yourself. Get yourself squared away, Petersen!*

She was tempted to first call Jane, but her hands were still shaking and her curiosity about the blue bag was overwhelming. *Just get it open, take a quick look, and then call Jane.* She moved over to a picnic table under a small gazebo and put the case on the table. With still-shaking hands she struggled with the zipper, which had proven to be wonderfully waterproof, and finally pulled out what appeared to be a bound report. The cover had a logo for "Geo-Tech Testing and Assessment Services." The document's title was "Wyandot Township lot # 13-789 Assessment."

She turned to the "Executive Summary" on the first page. She scanned through the paragraphs, trying to keep her tired mind focussed on its content. Then, totally engrossed, she read it through a second time. She sat up, shook her head, and said, "Oh my God." The words had just escaped her lips when an arm firmly encircled her neck and a sweet-smelling cloth was held over her face. Just as she lost consciousness, she heard a voice say, "I was wondering if we would meet, Detective Petersen. And look at what you've brought me."

CHAPTER 23
Death Comes to New Eden

KIRSTEN WOKE UP GRADUALLY, STRUGGLING TO CLEAR HER MIND. She was tied to a chair inside what appeared to be the room in which Alex McKay had talked with her and Jane just two days before. It seemed more like an eternity ago. She looked around the room and saw Alex McKay's still body sprawled in an armchair. Hearing the door open, she closed her eyes and pretended to be still unconscious.

A voice said, "I know you're awake, Detective. The movement behind your eyelids is a dead giveaway. Or more like a soon-to-be-dead giveaway. We need to talk, and time is short, so let's get to it."

Kirsten opened her eyes and saw before her the slender, taut figure of the man she knew as William. She shook her head and blinked her eyes, trying to get fully awake. Slurring her words slightly, she said, "So you're William. You've been a hard person to track down. Why don't you loosen these ropes, and then we can talk."

"It appears you know the name I've been using around here. Very enterprising, but then I sensed you were a step up from your rather slow fellow officers. So, Kirsten, since we are using first names, here's what's going to happen. This may seem like that silly cliché you find in too many bad movies, where the bad guy talks at great length to the intrepid hero, but if I didn't need some information from you, you'd already be dead. People like me don't waste time in useless conversations, but this situation is a little bit different. I'm going to suggest an information exchange. I presume you have a few questions, and I certainly do. I got some information from Mr. McKay, after using some methods of persuasion. Unfortunately, that, coupled with the sedative you are now trying to recover from proved a little much, so he is no longer with us. No great loss to the world, and anyway, I think he shared what little useful information he had."

"Why would I talk to a murderer like you if I'm going to end up dead anyway?"

"Please realize that by not lying about how this is going to end I'm paying you a compliment. I expect even now you would like to have your curiosity satisfied, and there's that other cliché that the longer we talk, the greater the chance someone will magically appear and rescue you. I presume that you came here by that little boat pulled up on the shore. It seems you not only were searching for that blue case, but you actually found it. As I said, you are an enterprising woman. If you look over to the fireplace, you will see I had a little bonfire for the case and its contents. They are now ashes, and soon will be doubly so. If only McKay had taken that little step, matters would have been very much simpler.

"I am quite sure you've made a plan for someone to pick you up. I checked your phone, but you haven't called anyone. I imagine there is a default time for them to appear, but I think that won't be until closer to this evening. That does make time short, so you need to be precise in your answers. But my curiosity is such that I'm willing to risk taking a few more minutes. So, shall we talk?"

"You first. Why are you still here?"

"It was a great mistake for my employer to use McKay. He did find a suitable land package, except for it being right next to the Wyandot reserve. Unfortunately, my employer accepted McKay's strenuous assertions that he had the Natives fully under control. But with their unfortunate intransigence, it is very doubtful the deal can now be completed, so I have been asked to tie up any loose ends, McKay being the biggest one. I figured McKay was too limited to know how to successfully disappear, so I hid my car in the woods and staked out his house. Sure enough, it turns out he put his car in the garage and waited until everyone else was gone. All the services were turned off, so he was ready to camp out here in his house. As soon as I was sure we would not be interrupted, we had our little talk, and then you showed up, and here we are."

"So, you tie up loose ends by committing another murder. Sounds more like you're just creating a bigger 'loose end.' I already know your mystery employer is Gladstone Holdings."

"You really are enterprising. With this morning's announcement, your colleagues also have knowledge of Gladstone, but no proof they are connected to me. But back to Mr. McKay. He is going to commit suicide. I drafted an email on his laptop, addressed to his wife and copied to a variety of people in your backward little town. It explains how sorry he is for all the trouble he's caused. New Eden was to have been his crowning achievement, but it turned out to harm so many people that he's consumed with guilt, blah blah blah. And now, this ordered evacuation, and likely the need to tear down these houses, was the last straw. With his wife leaving him, he has nowhere to turn, no hope. He is going to attempt some atonement by destroying these houses. That way his poor neighbours will at least get insurance money. The email will be rambling and maudlin but will make clear why he did this desperate final act. It will make no mention of the Wyandot Reserve matter."

"How will this email explain my death?"

"I have had to revise the email. It seems the very last straw for him was the police showing up to further torment him. McKay is a whiny little cypher, and his last words will give a wandering and self-justifying little screed about how the authorities, especially the police, harassed him and stopped him from setting things right. Now, in his darkest hour, you show up to further torment him, and he snaps."

"What's the explanation for me being here at all?"

"Whatever you told your colleagues. They'll presume you stumbled upon McKay, he surprised you with the illegal little revolver he kept in his bedside table, tied you up, and end of story."

"So, he shoots me and then shoots himself? It's hard to successfully stage something like that."

"Which is why I am doing something much more creative. I have turned on the propane gas in all of these houses and disabled their gas regulators. The investigators will find that McKay put a candle on the second floor of this house and then turned on the gas at the main New Eden propane tank. He has been involved in land development and construction projects, so it's believable he would know how to do this sort of thing. I learned the technique from one of my early mentors. Professionals like me need to know things like that. So, McKay hurried back here, where he has you tied up. Propane is heavier than air, so it takes a while for it to reach the second floor. When it does, this place blows sky-high. I will leave an upper-floor window open on each of the houses, so if the flames don't shoot through the main gas line to all of them, they are close enough to each other that the flames should ignite each house in turn. It should be quite spectacular."

"And you'll be long gone."

"No, I'll wait out on the access road until this house blows. Just to make sure it works properly. *Then* I'll be long gone. I may miss some of the fireworks, but I need to be far away before all the firetrucks and so on get here."

"Why not blow up only this place?"

"To create as much chaos as possible. It will underline how desperate and out of control McKay was. And it's just sort of satisfying to wipe this whole place out. A bit of professional pride,

I suppose, to pull off something so … appropriate. And of course, what's left of McKay will be found with his gun and your gun. His body will be pretty much incinerated, so no trace of his abrasions, and no trace of my little sedative. Your body will be tied up and will have all your other things, like your phone and wallet, on it. This will underline how amateurish and desperate McKay was. And, this blue case and its contents will be totally incinerated, obliterated, like they should have been days ago.

"Now, Kirsten, it's your turn. This blue case was the most important loose end. McKay finally told me he had given it to that idiot Winston, who seems to have thrown it into Silent Creek to get rid of it. Amateurs! Luckily it wasn't found initially, and it seemed it was probably lost forever in that damn swamp. Then the enterprising Detective Petersen not only locates it, but actually brings it right here to me. Maybe that's another reason why I feel well-intentioned enough to slightly extend your life. However, I do need answers. Did you know what was in it?"

"No. We just knew it was somehow important to the case. Important enough to get Winston killed and send McKay in to hiding. You did a good job there. We had few leads. I thought our only chance to solve his murder was to find this case that was so important to Winston, and luckily I did."

"Do you now know what is in it?"

"Enough to know what murderous bastards you and the fucks you represent are. I only read the executive summary, but it was enough to make clear that the site is *not* geologically sound enough for dangerous waste materials. It seems there are small fissures and cracks in this seemingly solid rock. I think the key sentence was something like, 'As a result of this testing and assessment, we cannot recommend this site for the storage of nuclear waste of any sort.' For the sake of a damned business deal you were willing to put this whole area, the Wyandot Reserve in particular, into total jeopardy. You're fucking monsters."

"A little melodramatic, Kirsten. The rock is really quite solid. If you read further, you would have seen the risk is small, and any problems would likely only happen years down the road. Who knows what technology and solutions might be available then? And it would be long after any of us had passed on. I'd call it an acceptable risk."

"Acceptable for you and Gladstone to get even more filthy rich. You disgust me. And the name is Detective Petersen. In terms of loose ends, there's the little matter of the company that did the testing. The report I found can't be the only copy. What would keep them quiet?"

"We know that we have to work with the right companies. Discreet companies. We actually thought the site would test out okay. Unfortunately, not so. But, Geo-Tech Testing, Inc. has proven to be admirably flexible in the past. Any investigation there would only find a more positive report, the one used to get the government approvals. In the very unlikely case that it were necessary, the author of the original report would be safely retired, living in comfort in a locale with no extradition treaties with Canada. That would be a dead end."

"Unless the site was retested."

"Why would that ever happen? Everything would be in order, and all the various agencies involved with the approvals would be very protective of their activities. Red tape can be more impenetrable than reinforced concrete."

"Or of seemingly solid granite rock!"

"Touché, Detective. If anyone were able to do all that, Mr. McKay makes an admirable fall guy, or maybe our hypothetically retired and untouchable friend from Geo-Tech would fill the bill. We have done this sort of thing before. Do give us some credit."

"Despite your fuck-up here."

"Yes, despite that. But, important thing, it appears now that the major loose end has been safely eliminated. Thank you, Detective. I have one more question, and then you get your last one. I really do need to get going. How did you people get on to McKay as soon as you did? We really did slip up there."

Kirsten knew she had to delay William as long as possible to give her any chance. Jane wasn't due to show up for hours yet, and she would not be getting the expected phone call. She had to keep William talking.

"The credit guarantees you arranged for him came from an offshore source our financial crimes unit had flagged. I was sent here to help the local detachment investigate McKay while they followed up on their end."

"Therefore that strange little episode at the strip club, and your inept attempts to find out what McKay was doing."

"Our 'inept investigation' helped us get on to this land purchase and keep an eagle eye on McKay. We were able to alert the Wyandot people something might be up. So, 'inept' if you want, but I think we put a crimp in your plans."

"Fair enough. So, my employers need to know in the future to be extra careful about who they engage as local agents, and to double check on the security of any external transactions. This might help them when they leave here and move on, as they surely will have to do. So, fair's fair. Now, I promised you one last question, but it had better be a quick one."

"Why did you have to kill Winston? How did you do it?"

"Easy answer. I have no idea who killed Winston. I only found out when I questioned McKay that Winston was connected to the report. If you need proof, as I keep stressing, I am a professional. If I had killed him, it wouldn't look like murder. I refer you to the 'accidental' death of Will Handstrom. That's a better indication of how I work."

"Jane was right to be suspicious about that. How did you do it?"

"It seems Handstrom was even more stupid than McKay. In short, he threatened to blackmail McKay for a bigger cut when he had tucked away enough information about our plans. McKay arranged his little poker game so he and his pals had an alibi when Handstrom had his unfortunate accident."

"And you had the brainstorm to get McKnight out there to give them an iron-clad alibi."

"Thank you. That was a nice touch. I detained Handstrom and we had a little talk, supposedly to work out details. I supplied his favourite kind of whiskey. At the appointed time, I knocked him unconscious and applied some of the same hard-to-detect sedative I used on you. It was a bit of a struggle to get him out to the boat, but it is private and quiet out here. He had his unfortunate fall into the lake, though he started to come to and I had to give him some assistance. I returned to shore, pushed the boat out after smearing Handstrom's blood on the top rail, and made sure everything was in order, including leaving the burner phone McKay had been calling on the table. The next time, I answered the phone and told McKay to do his part, which was so simple even he couldn't mess it up. I was soon out of there, your wonderful police captain acted like I was sure he would, and Mr. Handstrom's unfortunate little accident became official. So, I repeat, I did not kill your Mr. Winston, though he certainly needed killing.

"Also, if I had taken care of Winston, the blue case would not be lost in some godforsaken swamp. Amateur hour! I am not pleased that his death was connected to this situation, but thanks to your fine and appreciated work, that now is not a problem.

"But enough, really enough, conversation. It's too bad your return to your hometown will have such a negative ending. Yes, we did poke around in your background a bit. I'm sure your colleagues will give you an appropriate send-off to whatever comes next, not that I really think there is any 'next.' In appreciation of your frankness, I will return you to your slumbers. You won't feel a thing."

William moved quickly behind Kirsten and applied the same cloth to her face. She tried to resist, but quickly fell into unconsciousness.

William left her tied to the chair and made sure McKay's body was properly positioned. He left to finish the last of his preparations.

Kirsten drifted into disjointed thoughts and dreams. Her return to Harmony meant she was going to meet her death. She remembered as a very young girl when she had first asked about death. It was at one of the Sunday School classes her parents had brought her to. The seven-year-old Kirsten had asked the teacher what happened when people died. The response was that you are greeted by angels who take you along a pathway leading to healing waters, where you are cleansed of all earthly sins and prepared for your eternal life in Heaven.

As Kirsten dropped more deeply into unconsciousness, she became vaguely aware that, against all logic, an angel *was* greeting her, was untying her and taking her along an uneven path. She slipped in and out of partial consciousness, but then felt she was on the healing waters. She reached down and splashed some of the water onto her face.

The water helped shock Kirsten into semi-consciousness. She dimly realized she was in her boat, floating about a hundred metres offshore. She struggled to pull herself back to full awareness. She leaned over the side and immersed her head in the cool water. She fell back, gasping in the bottom of the boat, aware she had to do something. She had to call Jane, had to warn her. They had to stop William. She fumbled to get her phone out of the front pocket of her shorts, and then out of the waterproof sleeve she had stored it in. After what seemed like several minutes, she got it turned on and dimly saw she had a one bar connection. She pushed the number for Jane.

"So, intrepid explorer, are you ready for your pick-up? I presume you found nothing, like we were all sure you would."

Kirsten struggled to form words. She said something like "Neesh halp."

Jane said, "Kirsten, are you ok? We must have a bad connection."

Kirsten marshalled all her strength, and slurred out, "At New Even. Willyam tried kill me. Gots to schtop em."

Just then Kirsten felt a firm blow push her back against the boat's central seat. There was a monumental explosion as McKay's house seemed to rise up from its foundation and blast out in all directions. Flames and smoke rose high into the air. Bits of burning material showered down on the two neighbouring houses, into the woods across the road and out over the lake. One flaming green glob of plastic hit the back of the boat, stuck there, and continued to burn. Smaller pieces hissed into the water around the boat, with one landing on Kirsten's leg. She managed to splash water on it, the pain bringing her closer to full consciousness.

Just then the houses on either side of McKay's also exploded, followed by a chain of explosions down the row of houses. Burning debris continued to fly upward, a few pieces exploding in the air like a ragged fireworks display. New Eden became a blazing inferno, the heat even reaching out to where Kirsten held on to the sides of her bobbing boat.

Jane shouted, "My God, Kirsten. What's happening? What's all that noise? Omigod, I can see flames all the way from here! I'm at Wyandot with the captain. Kirsten, speak to me, for God's sake."

"Jane, I'm okay. But William killed McKay and tried to kill me. He's on his way back to the main road in his white SUV. He's armed and very dangerous. You've got to stop him. I'm okay, but hurry."

Kirsten slumped back against the boat seat, closing her eyes and trying to escape the fog that still enveloped her senses.

Jane had put Kirsten's call on to speakerphone, so McKnight had heard the whole thing. "Jane, make the calls." He turned on the lights and sirens and floored the accelerator.

Jane called Jeff on the radio. "Jeff, we need all fire equipment out to New Eden, immediately. Send ambulances and backup. The captain and I are trying to head off a dangerous fugitive on the New Eden Road, driving a white SUV. Hurry, Jeff."

By this time, McKnight had turned on to the New Eden Road and was speeding along as fast as the gravel would allow. They saw headlights quickly approaching, so McKnight braked hard and slewed to a stop across the road. They scrambled out of the cruiser, took positions at either end, and drew their guns.

Jane said, "Captain, it's this William guy. He tried to kill Kirsten. We have to stop him."

McKnight said, "And we will. Brace yourself. If he doesn't stop, we'll have to shoot."

William saw the police cruiser's lights ahead and cursed himself for his arrogance and over-confidence. He had wanted those answers, but the greater need was to get safely away. There was no going back, and he couldn't be arrested. He saw the cruiser wasn't quite across the road, that there was a narrow space on one side, if only the damn shoulder was wide enough. He slowed slightly, aimed his vehicle at the narrow gap, and floored it.

When it was clear the SUV was going to try to get around the cruiser, the officers pointed their weapons at the fast-approaching target. Jasper McKnight found his mind was remarkably clear. His sole focus was stopping a murderer who had threatened his community and his officers. He calmly aimed at the SUV and rapidly emptied his gun. Jane emptied her weapon as well.

McKnight's first few bullets shattered the windshield, and two of the last ones hit William squarely in the head. By this time the left front tire had been shot out, so his vehicle veered back toward the cruiser. It hit the front of the cruiser square on, driving it back hard into Jasper McKnight. The captain's body was thrown violently against a roadside tree, cracking his skull and instantly killing him. Jane, at the back of the cruiser, was thrown less violently into the ditch, where she lay quietly for a few moments. She struggled to her feet and saw that the white SUV had cartwheeled down the road until it had hit a large rock and burst into flames.

Some minutes later the first firetruck arrived on the scene and quickly put out the SUV fire. Jeff Ripley had pulled up to the scene and urgently directed the firetrucks to continue on to New Eden. The first paramedics on the scene quickly went to the still body of Jasper McKnight, but he clearly was dead. They moved over to Jane Walden, who was leaning against the wreck of the cruiser.

Jane said, "I'm okay, just some bruises. Just need to catch my breath, but the captain …."

The lead paramedic said, "I'm sorry. He's dead. Look, we need to get you to the hospital."

Jane struggled to her feet and said, "I told you I'm all right. But we have an officer down and who knows what else at New Eden. Go, go!"

Jeff had just come back from a quick examination of the white SUV. Jane said, "Jeff, the captain's dead. That son of a bitch killed him. Did he survive the crash?"

"No. He's in the wreck, burned beyond recognition. But where's Kirsten?"

"At New Eden. We've got to get there, make sure she's okay."

By this time, another cruiser with two uniformed officers had arrived. Leaving them in charge of the scene, Jeff quickly drove to New Eden. There they found a flaming Armageddon. All the houses were fiercely burning, throwing sheets of flame and pillars of smoke high into the air. The fire trucks were working to contain the flames, putting out small fires in the surrounding woods, which mercifully were still wet from the previous night's downpour. They were hosing down the surrounding area as well as they could.

There was no way past the flames until they died down. Jane's only hope was that her friend had made it to the lake. She got one of the firetrucks to hose down a passage through the inferno between the first two houses. She and Jeff, wearing breathing apparatus supplied by the firefighters, struggled through the passage to the shore of the lake. Jeff saw his boat beached a short way down, opposite the second house. He and Jane hurried over to it through the smoke and heat. They found a shivering, ash-covered Kirsten huddled in the bottom of the boat. They helped her out of it. Kirsten hugged them, weeping and taking deep, shuddering breaths.

Kirsten said, "Thank God you're here. Did you get him? Did he get away?"

Jane said, "We got him. But let's get you out of here." Kirsten stumbled a few steps, her arms around the necks of the two detectives, but could go no further. Jeff then picked her up in a firefighter's lift, and they struggled back to their narrow escape route. They made their way back through the protective shield of water the firemen threw up for them. They retreated to Jeff's car. Jane urged Kirsten to rest in the cruiser.

Kirsten said, "What I need is fresh air. I'm okay. The bastard drugged me, that's all. So, you've got him in custody?"

"No, he's dead, burned to a crisp. I think one of the captain's shots might have got him too."

"So where is the captain?"

"Kirsten, Jasper didn't make it. We blocked the road with the cruiser. The guy wasn't going to stop, and the car crashed into our cruiser, and Jasper, and Jasper …." Jane stopped, choking a sob. She and Kirsten hugged each other, with Jeff also putting his arms around them.

Soon the three officers separated, giving tight smiles to each other. Jane insisted Kirsten go to the hospital. She agreed only after she got Jane to agree to a meeting, including Jeff and Wanda, later that evening, either at the hospital or at headquarters after Kirsten was released.

Kirsten said, "Jane, Jeff, this is worse than we thought. I've got to share some really bad stuff with you. These guys are even more guilty than we ever imagined. We've got to stop them. We have to. We have to meet, as soon as possible."

Jane and Jeff supervised the clean-up at New Eden and at the crash site. Tired, they met later that evening back at headquarters, with

Wanda joining them as requested. Kirsten, who had been treated and released from the Lakeside Hospital, shared the new information she had uncovered. All four of them agreed they had to hold the promised follow-up meeting with Davis and Priestner, despite their grief over McKnight's death. If anything, even more so because of that grief. They met into the early morning, formulating their plans and making sure they would be ready.

CHAPTER 24
Three Options, and an Unexpected Ally

THE NEXT MORNING MALCOLM PRIESTNER AND ELLIOT DAVIS arrived at police headquarters, where they were met by Jeff Ripley and led up to the second-floor conference room. They were surprised to see Sid Ray sitting on a chair in the main office. They were further surprised to see Wanda Cornelius sitting at the conference table with Jane and Kirsten. Jane had a bruise and minor cuts on the left side of her face. Kirsten had a bruise on her forehead. Her face was pale and drawn-looking. Jeff, Priestner, and Davis took their seats.

Priestner said, "I want to extend my condolences to you over the shocking death of Captain McKnight. Terrible, terrible business."

With a tight voice, Jane said, "Considering who killed him, I have no interest in your condolences."

Priestner, looking surprised, said, "I have no idea what you're alluding to, Sergeant. I do understand why you all are so upset. I'm just surprised that you wanted to meet with us so soon after yesterday's tragic events."

Jeff put a hand on Jane's wrist and said, "My colleagues are still recovering from yesterday, so I'm going to start. This meeting couldn't wait, because we will be sharing some important and confidential information with you."

Davis said, "And yet you have a reporter sitting outside this room? A strange way to be confidential."

Jeff said, "Mr. Ray knows nothing about the substance of this meeting. We promised him he would be getting an important story as soon as we can confirm a few matters. This meeting will largely determine what story he'll be getting. In the interest of frank disclosure, Captain McKnight had us listen in to your last meeting, so we are fully aware of what was discussed. You also need to know that our superiors have put Jane in charge, on an interim basis and with a promotion to acting-lieutenant."

Davis said, "I'm still concerned about this promised confidentiality, especially given this unauthorized eavesdropping at our last meeting."

Jeff said, "Please note we have unplugged the intercom. I give you my word there is no recording, no-one else listening in. You are free to search the room if you wish. Further, let us all turn our phones off and put them in this box, and I'll lock them in the captain's office."

He placed a cardboard box on the table. The three police officers and Wanda demonstrated they were turning their phones off and placed them in the box.

Priestner said, "I am not in the least comfortable with this. I can't be out of touch for any extended length of time. Elliott, I think we need to leave."

Jeff said, "This new information has content you must hear. I ask you to give us thirty minutes, and then you can decide if you want to continue."

"And if I don't want to give you thirty minutes?"

"Then we will release our information directly to Mr. Ray. Tomorrow you will be able to read it in every newspaper and hear it on every newscast in this province. I suspect you both would also be looking for new jobs."

Priestner said, "Despite your melodramatic threats, Detective Ripley, I must admit I am curious about all this. Elliot, let's give them their thirty minutes. I note you have invited Chief Cornelius to the meeting. I trust that means there is some movement in this access disagreement. I further note that Councillor Weirness and MP Madison are not at this meeting. I think we need more explanation before we proceed. And yes, here is my phone."

Priestner and Davis put their phones in the box. Jeff took the box out of the room and soon returned.

Jeff said, "You have to know the information you will hear is totally confidential at the moment, and so we invited only those immediately affected by it. The politicians may be involved down the road, but your response will have a major effect on what that involvement might be. Captain McKnight did inform Councillor Weirness of what transpired at your last meeting, because it affected this area so directly. However, neither Councillor Weirness nor MP Madison know what we are about to tell you."

Priestner said, "Enough of the damned foreplay. Get on with it."

Jeff said, "Okay. I ask that you save your questions until we finish, unless you need clarification. Chief Cornelius?"

Wanda said, "My turn first. My people's response to your insulting overtures to us yesterday is 'no.' We will not be bribed or bought off. We will invite as many allies as possible to join us at the barricade. We will share our concerns with the media. We will stay at our barricades until either you leave, permanently, or we're dragged off to jail. But we also do need to talk about some other issues."

Kirsten said, "Me next. You know we are working on the murder of Harry Winston. You likely know that a key piece of evidence was a blue case he dumped into Silent Creek. I found that case yesterday. That detail, and other aspects of yesterday's events, are not yet public, and, despite your fidgeting, gentlemen, they do bear directly on you."

Kirsten then gave a shortened version of Thursday's events. She offered no specific detail about how she escaped and made her way to her boat. Priestner and Davis listened intently.

She continued, "So you see, I know that Gladstone was fully aware the land was not suitable and received approval only because of illegal actions. The original report in the blue case made that abundantly clear. Gladstone was fully prepared to complete this project despite the possible severe consequences for this area, and all for miserable profit."

There was a brief silence in the room, and then Priestner said, "So, for *clarification*, you have no proof of any of these serious allegations because this blue bag and its contents were burned by this William, and whatever was left was later consumed in that inferno yesterday. And even if your unsupported allegations were correct, it only serves to underline the chicanery of Alex McKay and his man, this William. If I'm allowed to insert another piece of clarification, Gladstone is already leaning very strongly toward leaving this backwater. Some other part of the province would then be the beneficiary of all we are offering. Therefore, it does not matter to us what the geological makeup around here happens to be. So, is that it?"

Jane said, "My turn. And no, that's not it. Detective Petersen explained that William affirmed he was working for Gladstone. To suggest a third-rate loser like Alex McKay would be able to locate, hire, and then control someone like William is ludicrous. William killed four people in this area, including Captain McKnight. He did it while under the direction of Gladstone. We have no doubt about that. None at all."

Wanda said, "You were willing to treat all of us in this region, my Wyandot brothers and sisters in particular, as pawns in your big money-making scheme. You are beneath contempt."

Davis said, "I'm hearing a lot of speculation and unsubstantiated allegations with not one shred of real evidence. I have no idea why you are involving me and my government in this preposterous charade."

Jeff said, "It's hard to imagine all this happening without the support, however covert, of you and your people, Mr. Davis. Gladstone was after huge profits from this deal, and that could only come with government approvals and subsequent government energy contracts. McKay was the local dupe, William was the direct agent for much of what happened around here, and Gladstone was behind it all. With some level of encouragement and enablement from the provincial government."

Priestner chortled and said, "Being stuck in this ignorant little backwater must do something to your minds. No wonder you wanted this meeting to be so hush-hush. If you went public with this crap, our lawyers would have a field day. If anyone was going to be looking for a job, it'd be you three sorry excuses for police officers. Now, I strongly suggest – no, I *demand* – that this be the end of it. We are going to leave, and you are going to keep quiet about all this."

Jane said, "You're not leaving quite yet. The last thing we are going to present to you is three possible options for whatever comes next. Now sit still and listen. We'll cuff you to your chairs if need be."

Davis and Priestner looked at each other. Priestner said, "Elliott, best we be informed about what the Keystone Cops plan to do next. Let's listen, and then we're gone."

Davis nodded yes, and they both settled back in their chairs with grim expressions on their faces.

This time Jane took the lead. "As senior officer here, even if only temporarily, I have to make sure everything around yesterday's events is properly dealt with. Option one is pretty simple. As you imply, just close the books on all this and move on.

"For our detachment, that would mean detailed reports, especially by Detective Petersen and me. Our reports would conclude the death of Captain McKnight is attributed to William, as would be the murders of Alex McKay and Harry Winston. There's no need to correct the record on the death of Will Handstrom. We have already filed reports on our attempts to identify William, and would leave that matter open, though it seems likely we'll never succeed. His body and vehicle have both been incinerated, so there's likely not much help there. We could close the files on the deaths of McKay, Winston, and Captain McKnight by identifying William as the overwhelmingly probable perpetrator. That would likely tie up the police matters. Chief Cornelius?"

Wanda said, "I have made clear what we will do, namely stand firm in our resistance to your evil little plan and to look far and wide for allies. If you are telling the truth, always a dangerous assumption with people like you, Gladstone will abandon their attempts to store their vile poison here and will move on to another target. Whatever happens there will happen. Once we are sure you're gone, our lives will return, as much as possible, to normal. We would have some nagging apprehension about what will happen to the plot of land you own next to us, but it's unlikely, given our resistance and the land's shortcomings, that anything further would happen there. That would take care of the, what? Indigenous matters?"

Kirsten said, "One personal and professional issue for me is that I know what I saw in that report. The man who tried to kill me is dead. If, as you would have us believe, he was working solely for or with McKay, I can try to close the book on that part of my life and try to get past it. But, as a police officer, I am duty bound to put everything into my report, including what I read in the geo-tech report."

Davis broke in. "Detective, if I may, you were exhausted by your struggles in the swamp, and then were drugged and tied up. You saw McKay's body and were sure you would soon die. You were under extraordinary stress and trauma, and, as you said, were hallucinating. I'm sure your superiors will greatly appreciate the bravery and resilience you showed. Few people would have been able to escape as intrepidly as you did. In the midst of all this stress, you were able to alert your colleagues so they could apprehend a dangerous killer. That, in my humble opinion, is stellar police work. If no one else does, I will recommend you get a formal commendation.

"However, given all that stress, I'm sure your superiors would find it impossible to take at all seriously your allegations about this geo-tech report, especially given the total lack of evidence. You are not an expert. Did you read it correctly? Did you read it all? Did it even exist at all? Could it have been part of the hallucinations brought on by the drugs you were exposed to? Frankly, should you even include mention of it in your report?"

Kirsten said, "I know what I read, read over *twice,* in fact, before I was drugged. But I agree with you about the possible reception that part of my report would receive. I'll bow to your expertise in creating the facts and reality that best suits your purposes. As I think you're implying, it'd likely be better if I didn't include that in my report at all. That expedient omission would certainly make it more possible for all of us to just move on."

Priestner said, "It sounds like we are getting close to a satisfactory conclusion to all this."

Jeff, who had been clearly restraining himself, said, "Jane and Kirsten won't say it, so I will. They have been through a terrible ordeal. Less than twenty-four hours ago, Captain McKnight was still alive. I'm feeling close to being overwhelmed by all this, and my part was relatively small. Chief Cornelius has been fighting for the very survival of her people, in ways you two would never understand, much less appreciate. I can only imagine what these three are going through.

"But you two care only about handling, what? A business challenge? A vexing complication? You don't give a damn about what this has done to them, to all of us, and to this community. 'Satisfactory' to you seems to include just leaving all this damage in your wake."

Davis said, "Very eloquent, Detective. I am more aware than you might think of the possible personal cost in matters like this. Also, you're right in saying we have significant responsibilities. I agree with Malcolm that it sounds like we are close to a solution. Meeting our various responsibilities means we can take care of the practical matters and you four can get on with your professional lives and your personal recovery."

Jane said, "I believe we have come to the end of part one in our little presentation, namely the 'just get on with it' option. Next, we will explain to you why option one is not going to happen. Chief Cornelius, why don't you start?"

Wanda said, "The history of my people includes decades, centuries even, of accommodation and 'just moving on' when it is convenient for you people. You may have noticed that increasingly across this country we aren't willing to 'just move on.' Who will your next victims be? Another First Nation up north somewhere? Will you come back with more negative ways to exploit that land package you so dishonestly bought? You've brought division and pain to my community. No, I'm not willing to just move on."

Kirsten said, "Me next. I am a police officer, and the oaths I swore almost ten years ago still mean something to me. Mr. Davis, it may be that government and provincial affairs require people like you who are flexible, who are experts in expediency and pragmatism, but I won't be complicit in some sort of convenient cover-up. I almost died yesterday, and the responsibility for that lies beyond what William and McKay did. And, for what it's worth, I believed William when he said he didn't kill Winston. We have an open murder case. My colleague, Detective Ripley, is right: none of us, no-one in this community, deserved the damage you brought here. So, option one does not work for me at all."

Jane said, "Jasper McKnight was a flawed man. He was not a great cop, until very recently when in fact he was. His death cannot be regarded as just collateral damage. We won't let that happen."

Jeff said, "I've already stated my opposition. We four had a long and difficult meeting last night. We all stand behind everything you have just heard us say."

Priestner said, "Well, I may be just an overly pragmatic and unfeeling businessman, but I'm not sure what other sensible and workable option you might have. Kindly educate me."

Jane said, "I will explain what option two would entail. I say would, because I am quite sure you wouldn't like it, and we don't either. Then we will end with option three."

Priestner said, in an aggrieved tone, "Which I'm sure you'll get to eventually. Let's get on with it."

Jane said, "Option two is that Detective Petersen writes a full and accurate report. If our superiors don't actively follow up on it, we will go public. That will be the basis for Mr. Ray's first story. Mr. Priestner, all the groups in Ontario that oppose nuclear power, all the environmental groups, all those unhappy with the corrupt power of corporations and big business would be all over this.

"Mr. Davis, the government's political opponents, plus all the groups I just mentioned, would go after your government with ferocious determination. There will be calls for the area to be retested, and enough of these groups have the will and money to make it happen. When Gladstone tries to stonewall and denies access to the land for re-testing, you just look all the more guilty."

Wanda broke in, "And that testing can be done diagonally, from our reserve. Access for that we would gladly provide."

Jane continued. "The spotlight of all this attention will be put on Geo-Tech. Imagine a court order requiring they open their books and records. Perhaps you did seal off any jeopardy there, as William indicated to Detective Petersen, but did you do that as well as you handled everything else? Did you really silence the technicians who did the testing? How would they respond to an offer of immunity in return for their testimony?

"On another front, we will redouble our efforts to identify William. With all the notoriety this matter would bring, there'd be no shortage of professionals and conspiracy theorists who just might manage to identify him. If that happens, could connections between him and Gladstone be found? Some implied connections with your government, Mr. Davis? Could anyone linked to William also be liable to very serious criminal charges?

"Now, all this activity could, in the end, turn up nothing firm and provable, but even then, Gladstone and the provincial government, who both want this whole thing to be handled as discreetly as possible, would be in a major public shit show. The government might still be defending themselves when they should be mounting their re-election campaign. I believe the next election is in just over a year's time. Mr. Davis, would your political bosses forgive you if this torpedoed their re-election campaign?

"Mr. Priestner, Gladstone might survive actual prosecution or formal sanctions, but what would this do to their reputation? Would all of this be brought up every time they bid on a new business project? Also, would you two survive the shitstorm I just described? I believe both William and McKay have been described as useful fall guys. I can see you two as being just that, fall-guys who could be jettisoned from your organizations with any stray blame and liability on your heads.

"In summary, I really doubt you two want option two to occur."

Kirsten said, "We don't really want it either, even though it is certainly better for us than option one. There would be a lot of unpredictable fallout, and it could affect all of us and our community in a dozen different ways. The three of us could very possibly lose our jobs and careers or be transferred to some detachment you can barely find on the map. I'm sure the government would put every pressure on us they could, whether directly or indirectly. I'm sure Gladstone has very expensive lawyers they could aim squarely at us. Mr. Ray would get some wonderfully dramatic stories, but there would be no shortage of consequences for all of us here."

Priestner said, "So why in hell would you even think of going there? You may not really like your option one, but it would at least be survivable."

Jeff said, "As Detective Petersen said, we're cops. Chief Cornelius has real responsibilities to her people. Highfliers like you two may not appreciate this, that while option one would let you and your organizations carry on, we wouldn't be able to live with ourselves. I suggest you listen carefully to option three, which, with some real reservations, we can accept."

Priestner said, "Let's just stop right there. You four so damned righteous and truth-seeking paragons of virtue are going to suggest a compromise, a deal? Of course we'll listen, but I trust you'll abandon the sanctimonious tone. So, what's the deal on offer?"

Jane drew a deep breath and said, "I'll start with the bottom line. Gladstone will donate their land package to the provincial government. They will buy the remains of New Eden, clean it up, and also donate that land to the provincial government. Gladstone will assist in the purchase of other necessary land around Silent Lake. Gladstone will offer a formal apology to the Wyandot First Nation for the difficulty this matter has brought to them. Note that Gladstone can still scapegoat McKay and William, if you want to mention him. So, no admission of blame, but an apology just the same. Gladstone will also indemnify all the New Eden residents for any financial losses they have incurred which are not covered by insurance."

Priestner said, "If you're going to dream, dream big. This would cost us millions."

"Which to your company is minor expense money. But let me continue. Mr. Davis, your government will gratefully accept the land Gladstone has given them and will announce it will be the cornerstone for a new provincial park centring on Silent Lake. You will start the process to obtain any other land around Silent Lake the province doesn't already own. You will negotiate with your federal colleagues for the transfer of any Crown land needed for this project. The government would start the process to buy or annex any necessary privately owned land. This means that the government will be able to announce its firm intention to immediately create the new provincial park that the unfortunate Mr. McKay occasionally alluded to."

Kirsten said, "There is one special circumstance with the land purchase. It involves the only person now residing on the shore of Silent Lake, a semi-recluse named Arthur Padmore. He has caused no harm, and it would cause him great distress to be removed, so he must be allowed to stay. He lives very quietly, and his presence there would cause no problems for the creation of the park. We propose the government could indeed purchase his land, for fair market value, but would allow him to live on it as long as he wished. Once he moved or died, the land would be incorporated into the park."

There was silence in the room as Priestner and Davis digested all this. Davis eventually said, "Well, you have done something I haven't experienced in some time, namely, genuinely surprise me. Acting Lieutenant Walden, kindly walk us through this rather fanciful option, in detail, please, with emphasis on why we ever would accept it."

Jane said, "The main reason you 'ever would accept it' is that it is not option two, which you'll recall means your organizations being significantly damaged and the two of you possibly being fired, in disgrace, and maybe even criminally prosecuted. The main advantage for you and your organizations is the main disadvantage for us, one we struggled with for quite some time last night. It makes them look really good. Gladstone could present a shiny new public image, a company deeply supportive of communities, and one which lives up to its responsibilities. Out of the goodness of its corporate heart, Gladstone would help create a real benefit for this area, a provincial park that will bring jobs and recreational opportunities. Also, you are such wonderful people you went out of your way to voluntarily help the poor victims of Alex McKay. Again, you can still use him as your fall guy, and you still mention William only if you want to.

You show respect and support for the Wyandot First Nation. What a good corporate citizen you are!

"You might see why this nauseating little fiction gives us serious second thoughts. Does Gladstone use this new image to help them to do similar damage elsewhere in Ontario? The only counterbalance is that your critics and opponents won't be taken in. And, doing this would mean that Gladstone would have to yield its most precious resource, money, to make partial reparation for its actions. I believe this would seriously gall your senior management but would still provide enough benefits that they would accept it. Just compare the effects of the worst-case scenario in option two to the benefits of option three for Gladstone.

"I think a good salesman like you will be able to make a very convincing case to your bosses. They likely see you as the person who screwed all this up so badly. The escape option three would give them could just save your job."

Wanda said, "Your apology to us would be as phony as everything else about you, but it would put on the record that First Nations do have to be acknowledged, and that you can't just run roughshod over us. It also would put our minds at rest about the use of that land next to our reserve. We would welcome a provincial park and the presence of people coming here to appreciate the land. If we are lucky, it would also mean not ever seeing you again. We would want some guarantee of jobs, or at least first opportunity for them. We could develop our own economic activities to serve our visitors. If our brothers and sisters elsewhere were to ask our advice about you people, we could still be frank with them without going public.

"There is one other thing. The federal government is not here today because this all requires confidentiality. But Gladstone might have to deal with them, and the Provincial Government certainly would have to. I have perhaps naïve hopes that this undertaking would show that governments and private business can in fact work with our people to benefit us all. Could this be a model of co-operative success that would force the federal government to move past all their usual delays, lies, and excuses? Could it actually help them to truly honour some of their obligations to us? A slim hope maybe, given what we have experienced for over two hundred years, but I am all for hope as long as it has some real foundation."

Davis said, "I can see how this could benefit Gladstone. Please explain why our government would go in such an expensive direction."

Jeff said, "Let me take that one. You worded that very carefully, Mr. Davis. Your government has been going in a specific direction, namely closing parks and removing environmental protections. I might say this would give you the chance to reverse some of that harm, but we're not here to argue political values and ideology. The cost for you is really quite minimal, given Ontario's overall budget. It would bolster your party's environmental credentials and would bring jobs, recreation and opportunities to this region, one I'm sure your party wants to keep on your side. Cynics might say it's an early election bribe, but it would confound your opposition, and blunt some of their attacks on you. I'm not a politician, thank God, but I think you could much better market your party, particularly in this region, with all these positive benefits, rather than with the likely damage option two would bring you."

Kirsten said, "You raised the issue of compromises. If we were in a university seminar room, we might question whether or not option three would bring about real justice, but here we are in the so-called real world. I have been convinced by my friends and colleagues here that option three would not be a cynical compromise. I must admit option two does have a bit of a quixotic nature to it. I could insist on public sharing of what I read in that report, but would that solve anything? Would trying for some sort of perfect justice maybe just create even more harm, an updated way to tilt at windmills?

"Option three, on the other hand, *would* provide some justice, likely as much as we could ever achieve. You and your organizations would pay a price, not as big as might be argued in that university seminar room that it should be, but a price just the same. Much of the harm that has been created by you, and William and McKay, would be reversed. There would be concrete benefits for some of your victims and for this community. You would be gone, forever, I hope. So, with some strong reservations, I am willing to support option three.

"You would have to know that we will keep trying to identify William, but without the enhanced activity that option two would bring. We have searched diligently, with no success so far. I believe that may unfortunately be a dead end. But you have to know that our accepting option three is not us abandoning our responsibilities as police officers. The case of Harry Winston is still open. I actually believe what William said, that he, the consummate professional, did not perpetrate such a messy murder. However, he is overwhelmingly the most likely suspect, so I can't see any change there."

Priestner said, "I admit that this undetailed plan you have sketched out for us does have definite benefits. I believe I can convince my superiors to give it serious consideration, but to put it into operation would be quite complicated. It will take us considerable time to generate a firm response."

Davis said, "I agree totally. We would need substantial time. I must admit it has crossed my mind that this could be a colossal bluff, and that you might actually be planning to pull off some version of your option two. I pride myself on playing political poker very well, and frankly I would need some assurances if I were to try to sell option three to my superiors."

Kirsten said, "Timing is something we four spent a lot of time on last night. Chief Cornelius was quite eloquent on how damaging a seemingly innocent request for more time usually turns out to be. The Canadian government has, on a variety of issues and initiatives concerning our country's First Nations, seemingly been on the verge of concrete action for years, decades or even centuries. Eternally 'almost there,' but little ever really happens. We will not accept your request for a substantial amount of time. We fear, in fact, it would turn out to be just a way to nudge us into a de facto acceptance of option one. So, of course you need some time, and we will give you sufficient time, sufficient if you are acting in good faith. We will give you three days."

There was a shocked silence in the room. Davis finally said, "You cannot be serious. There are just far too many complicated details to create in three days the comprehensive plan this process would require."

Jane said, "Of course you're right. We don't expect a detailed plan. What we require is that no later than Monday morning, Gladstone will make a formal public announcement that it is apologizing to the Wyandot First Nation, is withdrawing from its initial plans for this area, is donating the lands we earlier detailed to the province, and is financially supporting the New Eden people.

"Also, no later than Monday morning, preferably simultaneously, the Ontario Government will announce formal creation of a new provincial park, incorporating the lands we have specified. You no doubt will also confirm your confidence in Gladstone and that the Gull Lake purchase will go forward, and that Ontario's power needs will be met. Etc. etc. etc., but it's only the first part we care about, and require.

"Now, as long as we get regular updates that confirm that things are proceeding, expeditiously and properly, option three will be in effect. Mr. Ray and other news sources would be able to circulate a variety of positive stories. If, on the other hand, we get seriously negative reports, it would indeed trigger some form of option two."

Priestner said, "It would be hard to explain, in that case, why you sat on this information. You'd all be in serious trouble, including possible criminal prosecution."

Jane said, "So would you. Once your organizations make those announcements on Monday, we are confident it would be hard for any of us to go back. Why would we?"

Davis said, "That partially answers my need for assurances. Can you offer any more?"

Kirsten said, "We give you our word we will abide by the conditions of option three, as long as you and your organizations do. I hope it's obvious that if we intended to carry out some version of option two, we'd already be doing it. This meeting would not be happening. Mr. Priestner is correct there would be major new repercussions for us if we later renege. You have our word, and there is the simple matter of pragmatism and self-interest. Let's just do this."

Jane said, "I want you to write down on these cards I'm giving you your understanding of the key requirements for your announcements this Monday. This will give you any reminder you need, in your own handwriting. Then, I'll ask you to read them back just to make sure we are firmly on the same page."

After this process had been satisfactorily finished, Jane said, "I am giving you contact information for each of us. We have your contact information. There may be details needing clarification, but you have our pledge that we will honour option three. The announcements we hope and expect to hear on Monday will provide your organizations' agreement to also honour option three. Unless there's more, I think we're done here, and we'll look forward to those announcements.

"Oh, and we'll give Mr. Ray details about Captain McKnight's death and Detective Petersen's miraculous escape. With that and the destruction of New Eden, he'll have lots to report on. We will tell him nothing else at this time. Thank you, gentlemen."

Priestner and Davis nodded to them and left together, with Jeff retrieving their phones for them. He asked Sid to wait a bit longer, saying there would soon be information for him. After Jeff returned with the other phones there was a short silence in the room, followed by sighs of relief. They talked about how the meeting had gone and about the various matters they had to attend to in the difficult days that lay ahead. They were surprised by a knock on the door and were further surprised when it turned out to be Elliot Davis. They invited him in, and they all sat down.

Jane said, "I didn't expect anything back from you so soon. What do you want, Mr. Davis?"

Davis looked around, and said, "I will try to be as frank and to the point as you people so admirably were. I presume we are still being totally confidential, because I am about to take some risks.

"First, it is clear you don't like Malcolm Priestner, and I don't either. I just told him I had to use the washroom so I could quietly come back up here and talk with you alone."

With a note of incredulity, Kirsten said, "If you dislike Priestner so much, why do you work hand in glove with him?"

"When you do the sort of work I do, you don't often get to choose who you work with. I am employed by the government, not directly by the governing party. The party currently in power cleaned house, more than is usual, when they were first elected, but I survived, not because I necessarily share their particular political beliefs, but because they feel I am effective. When I was assigned to this current task, my job was simply to bring it to a successful conclusion."

Jeff said, "So, you're some kind of hired gun? Just do the job, whatever it is?"

"I wouldn't put it that way. I imagine you three police officers have had to enforce laws that make you uncomfortable. For example, if there were a court order to evict a single mother from her apartment, despite the fact she is struggling just to take care of her children with the meagre resources she has, I doubt you would refuse to enforce the order, unpleasant though it might be. Also, if the owner of the property is a particularly repugnant slum landlord, I doubt you would then try to claim that this makes the court order invalid."

Kirsten said, "We might try to organize support, advocate for her, and try somehow to make things better."

"Which is pretty much what I'm trying to do here. The first I knew about the falsified test results is when you told your story a few minutes ago. Despite the lack of tangible proof, I do believe you, Detective Petersen. Let me walk you through how this thing evolved. I am trusting you four to keep this confidential. If any of my colleagues were here, they would say I'm possibly committing career suicide.

"The government assigned me to provide whatever assistance was necessary for this project to be completed. Dangerous as the stored materials at Gull Lake are, they do in fact have to be stored safely somewhere. The province does need to have sufficient electrical power. The current government has faith in private enterprise to do this sort of thing. I, in fact, don't necessarily share that faith, or at least not to the same degree. Private enterprise is driven by profit, not necessarily by protecting the public good. However, the stated purposes of this project were and are legitimate.

"If I were in that hypothetical university seminar room you referenced, Detective Petersen, the class could debate what exactly is meant by 'the public good.' We could debate which political or philosophical theory might best achieve it. The group might decide that the ideological bent of the current government is an ethical distortion, and that no one should agree to support what could be called their privatization agenda.

"But we are not in that seminar room. The government is going to move ahead with this project despite whatever my personal beliefs might be. Could I use my skills to help make it work as well as possible? To try to make sure public safety is protected, and the province has the electrical power it needs? Would the person assigned in my stead make things worse? These are real questions for someone like me.

"Let me backtrack a little bit. I believe that when I began my career I was as driven by idealism as much as any of you. That younger Elliott Davis believed good government is vital for a democracy like ours. He believed, and still does, in our democratic system. He knows that people like me can make it work better. If this government is not right for our province, then citizens can work to defeat it. If a government the people feel is more progressive and positive were elected, it would have the resources of people like me to help it function."

Kirsten said, "But that did lead you in to supporting Malcolm Priestner, a man you say you dislike, and in to helping a company like Gladstone do so much damage. I'm not convinced."

"Let's return to the current situation. I accepted what I saw as a legitimate task. Whether or not I would choose Gladstone as the private partner, the government in fact did. If that land package had been honestly put together, if no-one's rights had been trampled, if indeed the site was as safe as could reasonably be expected, I would have had no moral qualms. However, I do believe what you said, Detective Petersen. I believe what all of you have been saying. I hope I didn't show it, but I was shocked by what I heard at our earlier meeting."

Jane said, "That didn't lead you to contradict your friend Priestner."

"Again, not my friend. I could have loudly denounced him, and that would have felt good, for a few minutes. I could have used this as the reason to resign from my job, likely just before I was fired, but who would you be dealing with then? And we wouldn't be having this meeting. So, instead, I maintained the pretence with Priestner that we are on the same side.

"I need to explain some realities to you. Your proposed strategy, or solution – your option three – is creative, enterprising, and bold. It also would have limited chances of being successful without some serious help."

Kirsten said, "From you."

"Yes, from me. Let me throw some hypotheticals at you. What if the announcements on Monday had some of the elements you demanded, but far from all of them? Do you then attack Gladstone or the government? Do you reveal what they would call conspiracy or collusion? What if they did convince you a bit more time was necessary? You are dealing with people far more experienced than you in this sort of warfare, because that is exactly what this is. Have you considered what counterattacks they would mount against you, individually or collectively?

"Gladstone is already going to withdraw from this region because there is simply too much risk for them here. They could offer some goodies to this region. They could offer some form of 'if you were offended' non-apology to Wyandot. They could paint themselves as the good guys. They are good at that sort of thing. Would you then still be able to attack them?

"What would the government do? They could underline how negative your actions were, in that they would delay the critically important safe disposal of that nuclear waste. You would now be the people threatening the province's power supply. They could lean on your superiors. Would your bosses act as police officers and protect you, or as politicians who would instead just protect themselves? I don't really know, and neither do you."

Jane said, "So you are going to be our white knight and save us? At possible great cost to you? What would you want from us?"

"I'm no white knight, but yes, I want to help. The younger Elliott Davis would absolutely demand it. The current version feels he – I – really have no choice. I am already involved me in this, so let's do it right. I want nothing else from you. I'm not asking you for your blind trust. Let's just proceed, and you can judge from actual results whether or not I'm really trying to help.

"Let me be more explicit about the forms that help might take. As I said, Gladstone is definitely on its way out of this region. But they need to keep their contracts and agreements with the government, and their actions to date are already enough to trigger various escape clauses in this one. I am confident I can convince our government to stick with Gladstone but to pressure them to act in as positive a way as possible, namely, to honour your option three. Note that if Gladstone were replaced, the new company would have to offer exactly nothing to any of you and to this area."

Jeff said, "So you enable Priestner to go ahead and screw another part of the province."

"If someone wants to start a pool on exactly when Gladstone fires Priestner, the incompetent who brought so much grief to their company, I'll take thirty days. Believe me, he'll be gone, and soon. And they would know they have to play ball with us, or they'll be replaced by another company, at a significant cost to them. Money, with this cancelled contract. More important, with the likelihood they'd never get any more government contracts, or even many private sector ones.

"As for the government, I have colleagues who share my conviction that even if private enterprise offers some benefits, accountability and oversight must come from government. The party currently in power may not agree with that, but I hope my colleagues and I can eventually convince them that if they don't offer transparently accountable guarantees of public safety and proper process, they'll constantly be in the sort of difficulty they are in right now. In fact, the next situations would likely be even worse. For right now, I think we can persuade the government to ensure the chosen site is indeed safe and that no one's rights are trampled in the process. I hope that doesn't sound too naively idealistic."

Kirsten said, "Do you think you and your like-minded colleague can make this government do the right thing?"

"Only in this limited circumstance, and only out of their own self-interest and survival instincts."

Jeff said, "Okay, so you think you can use leverage to keep Gladstone in check and make the next stage in the Gull Lake saga be more positive. But why would the government do the other things we want, namely, to create the provincial park? You said yourself they are more likely to close parks, not create new ones."

"Let me betray some professional secrets about the leverage civil servants can use. Elected politicians rely on us to do much of the detailed work of government and depend heavily on us. I believe the potential benefits to the government you described in your option three are in fact quite solid. I can help make sure they clearly see how your suggested approach will bring them substantial benefits, at little real cost to them, and perfectly timed for their next election campaign. They are pragmatic people and staying in power is really their main priority."

There was silence in the room, and then Kirsten said, "It's sort of like using your assailant's strength to help you, rather than fighting it."

Jane said, "I think we have nothing to lose. You'd just be working to increase our chances of success."

Jeff added, "If you were going to work against us, we wouldn't be talking now. You're not asking us to change our demands. Chief Cornelius, your thoughts?"

In a thoughtful tone, Wanda said, "I've always thought you find your allies wherever you can. Mr. Davis, I'm not willing to give you my whole trust quite yet, but I like what you're saying."

Kirsten said, "I'm all the more glad to be a simple cop rather than be living in your world, Mr. Davis. But I'm impressed. Thanks for coming back."

Davis was silent for a moment, and then said, "In the interests of full disclosure, I know a bit about your William. I was brought into this project only after the initial interests of our government were represented by your MPP, Sterling Fox. Gladstone used him to get McKay on side because McKay knows Fox and, frankly, we were trying to be discreet. Fox was never going to be involved in the detailed work because he is a bit of a dolt, the sort of non-threatening good old boy who goes over well in places like this. No disrespect intended.

"In the early stages of negotiations, there was an important meeting with McKay in Fox's office. I was there to take over from

Fox, now that he had helped get McKay onside. Fox didn't know it, but this meeting was partially intended to keep him as far away as possible from the project. I also was to introduce McKay to his key contact from Gladstone, though Gladstone was still not to be identified as the company behind the intended purchase. I already knew that any contact I had with Gladstone would be through Priestner. My job was simply to set this man up with McKay so they would continue on with the initial land purchase. I explained various background matters to McKay, made sure he was firmly on side, and turned him over to William, even though I knew nothing about him other than his connection with Gladstone.

"I really doubt this will help you identify William, but it is also one of the reasons I believe your story, Detective Petersen. William was Gladstone's man. Quite frankly, what you told us made me do some personal re-examination. How did I end up helping bring into this situation the man who killed Jasper McKnight and three others? Some of my motivation is my hope for some form of atonement. I think I owe it to all of you to do all I can to be of assistance.

"I have to be going. I'll try to keep you updated, but quietly. I'll do my best to honour your wishes. Detective Petersen, I will make sure your Mr. Padmore is protected. I sense that is of particular importance to you, and even have some thoughts about why.

"Let me add I do greatly admire what you're all trying to do here. Your option one is the safest for you, but instead you're taking some real risks. But then, I guess I am too.

"Detective Petersen, I meant what I said about nominating you for a commendation. That was amazing work.

"It's very likely we will not meet again, but I hope that after next Monday you all will have reason to celebrate. If so, I will be with you in spirit, but physically will be in Toronto. Captain McKnight's funeral is the one thing that could bring me back here. If I can't make it back, again, I'll be with you in spirit. One last piece of advice: if the announcement is a positive one, don't wait for the government to take care of the details.

Lobby them for the specifics you want. Form local committees. Present workable plans to them. Get the media on your side. Try to get your not-so-sterling MPP on side. If you make it easier for them, they are quite likely to go along with you. And sincere condolences to you all on your loss."

Davis stood up to leave, but this time the rest all stood up with him, and they all shook his hand as he left the room.

Jane invited Sid into the room, and they patiently answered his questions about the death of Captain McKnight and about the ordeal Kirsten had endured, climaxed by her narrow escape. They gave him as much detail as they could about the New Eden inferno. They gave brief updates on the Winston investigation and the blockade at the Wyandot reserve. They also made him promise not to report on the meetings that had occurred that day at police headquarters, against their promise that there soon would be more detail for him about those matters. After Sid left to work on the mountain of information he had, the four spent some time conferring about how to handle all the matters now on their collective plate.

Afterwards, when she got home, Kirsten called retired town police officer Adam Westfield and asked him to set up a special meeting for tomorrow, and to attend it with her.

CHAPTER 25
Arthur Redux

THE NEXT MORNING KIRSTEN PICKED UP ADAM WESTFIELD AND they set off for their meeting with Arthur Padmore. This involved a slow trip along a poorly kept one-lane road along the side of Silent Lake opposite the stark ruins of New Eden.

Kirsten said, "I appreciate your joining me, Adam. Word has it you are the only person in regular contact with Arthur."

"It began after that little berry-picking adventure you were involved in many years ago. I always thought you might have recognized Arthur, since he was a fellow student at your school."

"Yes, but a few grades ahead of me, and he really kept to himself and always had a ball cap pulled down over his face. But, yes, I thought it might be him."

"Yet you didn't tell me that. May I ask why?"

"He hadn't done any real harm. I think he was more startled and scared than we were. My friend's dad and uncle were yelling threats. They were macho jerks, and I was afraid of what they might do to him. It was really just a funny little adventure. I mean, how often would a fifteen-year-old girl come upon a naked guy in the woods?

And Arthur was a sort of outcast at school. The kids didn't know what to make of him. I felt it would go badly for him, if indeed it was him, so I kept it to myself. But I also wondered why *you* didn't go after him. He was the only young male living anywhere near that area."

"I felt the same way you did. I knew Arthur and his family, a strange little family to be sure, but really gentle people just quietly trying to live their own lives. If I arrested Arthur, it likely would have destroyed them all. That's not why I became a cop."

"I wanted to ask you about that. So, you deliberately let an offender get away. You actually ignored the law, just like you did when I had my run-in with Harold Scrivener. If memory serves, you not only didn't arrest me for assault, but you also offered to teach me how to properly break someone's nose. A stickler for law and order would have some problems with that."

"I thought you were the victim in that case, and you acted in self-defence, or at least with no shortage of justification. I believe in justice, and in both cases you've mentioned I think justice was done. I think the law and our legal system are essential, but they can be blunt instruments. I think that oath doctors have, 'first do no harm,' applies to police officers too."

"Did you always feel that way?"

"Well, I was just a small-town police officer, but I've always enjoyed reading. My favourite book is *To Kill a Mockingbird*. I'm sure you've read it."

"Had to, in school. I loved it. I loved the movie too, but Atticus Finch was a passionate believer in the law. He's your model for some kind of discretionary justice?"

"Atticus was certainly the stalwart hero, especially in the movie. He definitely is an admirable character, but I always had the feeling he was a little too perfect. Maybe even a bit self-righteous. You know, the noble white man standing up for pure justice. I latched on to someone else in that book as my personal hero."

Kirsten thought for a moment. “The only lawman was Heck Tate, a pretty minor character. Do you mean him?”

“Do you remember after the Finch children were saved? Good old straight-arrow Atticus wanted the whole truth to come out. He said he couldn’t have his children growing up knowing he had betrayed the purity of the law. But Heck knew what the publicity would do to the man who saved the kids. I’ve read the book so often I think I can even quote the gist of what he said. ‘It ain’t your decision, Mr. Finch, it’s all mine. It’s my decision and my responsibility. To my way of thinking, Mr. Finch, taking the man who’s saved your children and dragging him and his shy ways into the limelight would be a sin. I may not be much, but I’m still the sheriff of Maycomb County and I won’t have it.’

“I’ve likely hashed that up, but it’s always made sense to me. The law should have a heart, even a soul, if that’s not too high falutin. So, with the Scrivener thing, the one who was punished was the bad guy. The social order, or whatever you want to call it, was protected, maybe even strengthened. And a certain strong-minded and resourceful young woman was able to carry on with her life.”

“Strangely enough ending up being a cop.”

“Even one who graduated from breaking noses to kicking balls.”

Kirsten chuckled. “I’m quite sure Atticus would not have approved of that, but I have no regrets. I guess maybe I’m just another Heck Tate cop. You know, you’re one of the reasons I became a cop, Adam.”

“And you’re not sure whether to thank me or hold me responsible?”

“Jury’s out on that one but leaning toward the former. Back to Arthur, tell me more about your visits with him.”

“After his parents passed, he lived by himself. He’s done well with that job I helped him get with the township, but he really doesn’t have to socialize there. He’s so good at his job they just sort of accept him as he is. Not such a bad thing, really. Arthur has no problem with solitude, unlike most of us. You know, when I read about this autism spectrum stuff, I wonder sometimes if that describes Arthur.

He doesn't relate to people like most of us do. Like, when I visit, it's never really a social thing, no offer of refreshments or invitations to come inside.

"We sometimes just sit and look over the lake. He's got some sort of fundamental connection with the lake and the land out there I don't fully understand. We may share a few words, but not many. I think he enjoys me being there, but we're not pals or anything. We never shake hands or have any physical contact. I bought him a cheap phone and programmed me on the speed dial, in case he ever needs help, but we never talk on it, just the occasional text so I can check up on him or let him know I'm coming out. He's not great with surprises, so I texted to let him know I'm coming out today. I didn't mention you. Important thing, no physical contact. Take things slow, quiet, and gentle. I think he's actually quite smart, so he'll understand what we say, though he might need time to digest it. Pauses and silence while he's doing that are okay."

"Got it. I'll follow your lead."

By this time, they had reached Arthur's house. It was small and plain, but obviously well-maintained. There was a small outbuilding and a rowboat fitted with an electric trolling motor tied up at a small dock. Arthur was sitting on a picnic table in the yard, looking far across the lake at the ash blowing up from the ruined New Eden houses. He got up and turned toward them. He was of medium height, slender and fit-looking. He wore coveralls over a plaid shirt, likely too warm for a summer day. He had a baseball cap pulled down over dirty blond hair.

Adam said, "Hi, Arthur. I hope it's okay that I brought someone with me. This is Kirsten, one of my good friends. I think you went to school together. Can we sit down at the table with you?"

Arthur nodded yes, with a quick, almost spasmodic movement of his head. He kept quickly glancing up at them and then down at the ground. He occasionally looked over at the other side of the lake.

Adam said, "I'm really sorry about what happened over there, Arthur. I know it must be difficult for you. We need to talk to you about one or two things. Would that be okay?"

After a pause, Arthur nodded yes. He glanced up at Kirsten, and in a quiet voice said, "I remember you from a long time ago, over in the woods. When …"

"I remember that too, Arthur. I'm glad it turned out okay."

"Adam came and told me to be careful. I have been. I remember you at school, and another time. In the swamp when that bad boy was after you and your friends. I wanted to help but …."

Kirsten smiled, "But we weren't really dressed for visitors."

Arthur reddened slightly, and a small smile momentarily appeared. "You took care of him, so I stayed in the woods. I stayed in the woods and followed him. He found a big stick and started to go back, so I threw a rock and knocked him down. He ran away then."

Adam said, "And so the cut on the side of Scrivener's head."

Kirsten said, "That was the first time you helped me, Arthur."

She stopped, tears glistening in her eyes. "Arthur, I know it was you who saved me yesterday. You saved my life. I don't know how I'll ever be able to thank you. I want to give you a big hug …"

Arthur looked up with a startled look on his face.

"… but it's a virtual hug, an imaginary one. I hope that's okay."

There was a pause. Arthur said, "I knew he was a really bad man. I've seen him over there. I saw him when he pushed that man out of the boat. He wanted to hurt you, so I, I …."

Kirsten said, "So you untied me and carried me, or dragged me, out of that house and put me in my boat and towed me out to where I'd be safe. Then it all blew up. That must have been terrible for you."

Arthur nodded. "Those people shouldn't have built those houses there. I'm glad the houses are gone. But it's terrible over there now. I didn't like those people being there, but it wasn't the children's fault. I wanted to protect them. I wanted to protect you."

"Even though I'm not a child?"

"I remembered you. That bad guy shouldn't have tried to hurt you."

"You stopped him, Arthur. That was really brave. I know you liked the children over there. I think you wanted to be connected to them, to help them."

"I watched them. I'd visit their houses after dark, to see if everything was okay."

"You collected small things to help you feel connected to them. They were really lucky to have you here, Arthur. You've been a good friend. I want to be a good friend too. I haven't told anybody but Adam how you saved me. Heroes deserve a medal, but I know you just want to keep living here by yourself. For me, your medal is this lake and all the land around it. I promise that we'll keep it our secret."

Arthur had looked up and was staring intensely into her eyes. The small smile again momentarily appeared, and then he looked back down at the ground. He kept nodding his head quickly up and down. The three sat quietly for a few minutes.

Adam said, "We came to tell you more things, Arthur, good news things. Can we tell you about them?"

Arthur glanced up and nodded.

Kirsten said, "We think that very soon what's left of those houses will be gone. It won't be like it was before they built the houses, but it won't be terrible like it is now."

She paused for a moment. "We think the lake and all the land around it will become a park. People will come and visit, but there'll be no more houses. They'll be nice people who'll come because they really like the lake. There will be a lot of children."

She paused again. "You'll be able to stay in your house as long as you want. If you want to leave, the government will buy your land and you'll have enough money to go somewhere else. But that's only if you want. You can stay here forever at your lake if you want."

A pause. Then Adam said, "Kirsten tells me that you can probably help the people make the park, if you want. You can help make sure they do it right, not like with those houses across the lake. You may be able to get a job here, doing the same sort of things that you do at your job now, but you'd be able to always be here."

A pause. Adam said, "Do you have any questions, Arthur?"

When Arthur shook his head no, Adam said, "We're going to leave you now, but I'd like to come out tomorrow to talk with you more. There's a woman called Chief Cornelius who lives over in the Wyandot reserve across the main road. She and her people will be helping with the park too. She thinks you may be able to work for them too – again, if you want. We can go visit her, if that's okay. They really love the land too, Arthur. I think you would like them."

Arthur sat looking at them, gently nodding up and down.

Kirsten said, "I'd like to come out with Adam and visit you sometimes. Do you know what a fist bump is, Arthur? It's a way friends say good-bye. Can we do a fist bump?

When Arthur pursed his lips, looking uncomfortable, she said, "Let's make it a virtual one."

She and Adam held their fists out toward Arthur, who smiled and held his fist out, at a safe distance.

As they drove back toward town Kirsten said, "I lost track of the number of times we said, 'If you want,' but I guess that was important. Do you think this will be okay for Arthur? It's a lot of change for him to process."

Adam smiled and said, "This is the man who survived being caught by you naked out in the woods, who somehow made it through the horrors of high school, who drove Scrivener away …"

"And survived being flashed by three screaming banshees."

Adam grinned, "Yes, that. And his parents leaving him totally alone. A man who has earned his own living for many years now. He's seen his own private Eden become the horror of New Eden. He has become a ghost who saved at least one child's life …"

"… and has saved the life of one grateful police officer and enabled the apprehension of a very dangerous criminal. Pretty impressive, when you add it all up."

"I think he is far more resilient than so-called normal people would ever realize. We too often underestimate people who seem different from us. He'll be okay. He's enamoured of you, by the way, in his own special Arthur way. If you keep joining me in the odd visit, that will be all the thanks you need to give him. "

Kirsten smiled and nodded. After a short pause as they neared town, she said, "So, I have got a shitload of work to do. Look, I told you enough about our meeting with Priestner and Davis so we could prepare Arthur, but we do need to keep this quiet until we hear those announcements. How's the New Eden support group stuff going?"

"This community has really surprised me. It's been tough on those folks, but I think they'll pull through. Especially if this park stuff does get them safely out of that damn hell-hole McKay trapped them in. I'm enjoying working with Martha. Retirement is fine, but it's even better when you can still do something important. You know, Harmony may just be breaking away from that narrow little time bubble it's been trapped in for so long. It may even enter the current century soon. Exciting times!"

"I'm hoping for a little less excitement for a while. I understand you're giving the eulogy at the captain's funeral next Monday?"

"I am. Monday's going to be a big day."

"Yes, one way or another."

CHAPTER 26
Announcements and Moving Ahead

ON MONDAY MORNING A FORMAL ANNOUNCEMENT WAS RELEASED by Gladstone Holdings Inc.

Gladstone Holdings wishes to announce a change in its plans for the creation of a safe disposal site for the spent nuclear fuel rods and other materials currently being stored at the Gull Lake nuclear power plant. Gladstone's purchase of the newly refurbished Gull Lake plant from the Ontario government is contingent on the establishment of a safe, secure and permanent storage facility for these materials.

Gladstone had purchased a land package near the town of Harmony, Ontario, for the creation of this facility, but has since learned that the local developer who made the preliminary plans for this purchase provided false and inaccurate information to Gladstone. The site is located adjacent to the Wyandot First Nations Reserve and required an access agreement across reserve lands to the proposed site. The local developer, Alexander McKay, had in fact misrepresented the purposes of the site in his negotiations with the Wyandot First Nation, betraying his responsibilities to both them and Gladstone.

Gladstone Holdings offers its sincere apologies to the Wyandot First Nation, and to the town of Harmony and its surrounding region, for any harm coming to them as a result of Mr. McKay's reprehensible actions. Mr. McKay was recently killed by an alleged associate, who subsequently brought about the destruction of the suburb of New Eden, which had been created by Mr. McKay. This as-yet unidentified associate was subsequently killed in a violent confrontation with local police officers. This confrontation resulted in the tragic and heroic death of Provincial Police Captain Jasper McKnight.

Gladstone will soon announce alternate plans for the safe disposal site involving another Ontario location. Gladstone's purchase of the Gull Lake Nuclear site is not affected by this change.

Though Gladstone has no formal responsibility for the damage caused by Mr. McKay's actions, we are pleased to announce the following goodwill measures. Gladstone will purchase the New Eden site and clean up the devastation caused by the destruction of the twelve houses there. This will remove significant financial jeopardy from New Eden's displaced residents. Gladstone will also reimburse those residents for any of their losses not covered by insurance.

Gladstone will then donate that land, and the original land package adjacent to the Wyandot reserve, to the Ontario government, which is issuing a simultaneous release concerning its plans for these lands. Gladstone will also donate $500,000 to the Wyandot First Nation's youth centre fund, an amount which will allow the centre's completion.

Gladstone is proud of its reputation as a good corporate citizen and is pleased to play its part in creating new opportunities for the Wyandot First Nation and for Harmony and its surrounding region.

The Ontario government's simultaneous release read:

The Ontario government is pleased to accept the generous donation of lands near Harmony, Ontario, by Gladstone Holdings Inc. The Ontario government is currently involved in finalizing arrangements with Gladstone for the purchase of the Gull Lake Nuclear Plant but played no role in Gladstone's original plans to build near Harmony the required safe permanent storage facility for materials temporarily held at Gull Lake.

In consultation with the local community and with the Wyandot First Nation, the Ontario government has arranged for the construction of a new provincial park using the lands generously donated by Gladstone, and other nearby lands it will acquire, particularly those surrounding Silent Lake. Though exact plans for the new park are still being finalized, it will be mostly a day-use area, providing significant recreational opportunities for local residents and visitors to the area. There will also be a limited number of wilderness campsites available for more adventurous visitors.

A special feature of this as-yet unnamed park will be the creation of a visitor centre on the land adjacent to the Wyandot First Nation reserve. This centre will emphasize educational opportunities, with displays, facilities designed for multi-media presentations, and also classroom areas. The government is working with the local school board to co-sponsor formal curriculum modules, which will be presented to local elementary and high school students at this centre. The modules will feature explorations of the area's unique wetland areas, and of the steps necessary to preserve them. There will also be modules detailing the culture and history of the Wyandot First Nation.

The provincial government is also working with the federal government, which has formal jurisdiction over First Nation matters, to provide training and employment opportunities for the residents of the Wyandot First Nation. The intent is for the park to be staffed primarily by Wyandot residents, especially in the planning and presentation of the educational modules. There will also be joint federal, municipal, and provincial government negotiations, which will establish joint sponsorship to share with the Wyandot First Nation the park's infrastructure facilities for such things as such as roads, water, waste disposal, and communication access.

The Ontario government is proud to sponsor initiatives that promote job creation, environmental protection, recreational opportunities, and enhanced educational programs for Ontario. This is a prime example of how cooperative efforts involving all three levels of government and the private sector can best serve the needs of our province.

Later that day, the memorial service for Captain Jasper McKnight was held in the largest local church. The building was so packed several attendees had to stand. The eulogy by Adam Westfield was well received. Several other speakers extolled McKnight's contributions to the community and praised his bravery and public service.

Afterwards most participants continued chatting outside in the day's bright sunshine. Much of the discussion was about Captain McKnight, but it also centred on the morning's surprise announcements and on the many recent dramatic events in the area. Kirsten saw Lynne, her former co-worker at Friendlies, standing off to the side with another woman, who she surmised was her partner, Deb. She went over to talk with them. Lynne introduced Kirsten to Deb, who initially looked fairly uncomfortable. Kirsten thanked them for coming but couldn't hide her surprise at their presence.

Lynne said, "I suppose not many in our line of work come to a policeman's funeral, but Deb knew him. It's okay, Deb, Detective Petersen is one of the good guys. She's teaching that woman's self-defence class on Friday I'm trying to get you come to. She's the one who kicked that idiot in his Johnnies at Friendlies. That was so cool."

Kirsten said, "Johnnies. Haven't heard that one before. A little more polite than some other things I've heard. Better to be a Johnny buster than a ball breaker, I guess. Good to meet you, Deb. Lynne really helped me. I wasn't used to working in a place like Friendlies, especially wearing so little clothing."

Deb offered a brief smile. "You sort of get used to it, believe or not."

"So Lynne told me. Think I'll stick with my normal wardrobe, though."

Deb said, "So it's okay for a cop to be seen in public with chicks like us? I know Lynne told you what I do."

Kirsten said, "I doubt many of your clients are here."

Deb said, "Clients. Good one. But you'd be surprised. Look, Lynne, we've got to go. I could only get Peg to agree to watch the kids for a coupla hours."

Kirsten said, "Maybe we can talk more on Friday. Please do join us. Do you think your friend can give you an hour or so babysitting Friday?"

Deb said, "Maybe. A few times I could have used some moves like yours on my tougher, uh, clients. Could I use that answer you gave for Lynne, if anyone wanted to chat about jobs?"

Kirsten said, "Whatever works. You have as much right as they do to be there. I think all women share some of the same vulnerabilities. We should help each other out. I'll look for you Friday."

Kirsten held out her hand. Deb, after a brief hesitation, shook it, and so did Lynne. They hurried away, talking excitedly with each other. Kirsten went over to where Jane, Martha, Adam, Wanda, Sid, and Jeff were chatting.

Sid said, "Who were the interesting new friends you were chatting with? That one looked kind of familiar."

"Just people I encountered in my investigations. No-one you would know. What did you all think about the morning's announcements?"

Sid said, "Adam and I have been briefed a little on those mysterious meetings a few days ago – and sworn to secrecy – so I wasn't totally surprised. Actually, I sort of was."

Wanda said, "I think our unlikely new ally came through for us. It seems we are actually getting even more than expected."

Jane said, "The New Eden people aren't getting that extra compensation we mentioned, but Gladstone likely had to withhold something to save face. Frankly, I'm more than a little pleased."

Adam said, "What I'm amazed at is the supreme load of crap in those damned releases. I mean, despite all the various forms of apeshit, horseshit, and bullshit I've met during my many years of public life, I've never encountered such a towering pack of lies, self-congratulation, and just plain nonsense. Those boys are really pros. I mean, Gladstone must be the purest and most socially responsible company that's ever existed. And our wonderful government is clearly creating a people's utopia in this poor battered province of ours. However, I guess there is a price to every good thing you get, and I think you folks really scored, big time."

Martha said, "Agreed, but I'm not sure I've seen many of these local consultations the provincial government mentioned, except I guess that could have been your secret little meeting."

Jane said, "Elliott Davis said one really important thing to us, namely, to pounce on the details to make sure everyone really delivers. I think for the next few days we have to be all over this. I think we're going to be busy. Let's keep in touch."

Adam said, "I'm not sure I trust our good old boy mayor, Calvin, to properly represent Harmony's interests. Martha, our New Eden Relief Committee has done a great job and is mostly done. Think we can add a few people and make it a, what, civic improvement committee or something?"

Martha said, "Let's talk about that. No, let's just do it."

She thought for a moment. "We *are* going to be more than a little busy for a while, but we still have a lot to talk about. This week will no doubt add lots of new challenges. Jane and I have been talking, and we want to invite all of you to our place next Saturday night for some food, drinks, and a whole lot of discussion. Actually, you may know that Jane loves movies, especially old ones …"

There was a chorus of "Oh really," and "You don't say," and "Yeah, we've all been victims."

Martha smiled and said, "Okay, I get it. But she especially loves those old mystery movies, you know the ones where all the key players get together at the end in the parlour and the detective explains what has happened and ties up all the loose ends? I think she secretly wants to do that to us on Saturday – and Jane Walden, don't you dare look at me like that. But really, though we don't have an actual parlour, we really hope you can join us."

They all looked around at each other and indicated their pleased acceptance.

Jane said, "Okay. A few more days of too much to do, and then we'll all celebrate, or commiserate, or something on Saturday. Say six o'clock? Just bring yourselves. I may like old movies, but Martha is the world's greatest hostess. Harmony's, anyway."

The friends finished their discussions and then went off to what they all knew would indeed be a busy few days.

CHAPTER 27
Parlour Games and Final Answers

THE NEXT SATURDAY EVENING MARTHA AND JANE WELCOMED THEIR friends to their house. Some of them brought bottles of wine. Martha insisted they have a pre-dinner drink and then dinner, with no talk about governments or villains or explosions or anything else remotely connected with the events of the past few weeks.

Later they all enjoyed dinner, as delicious as advertised, with the conversation being strictly about safe topics. Adam told them stories of his days as the town's chief police officer, such as interrupting beer blasts in the woods, or coming upon the daughters of some of the town's most prominent Upper River citizens enjoying midnight skinny-dips with some bad boys from Lower Town. Their parents didn't know what to do first: punish their daughters or pressure Adam into keeping it all hush hush. In the aftermath, the parents of some of the bad boys mysteriously seemed to have more money.

Sid told some of the local stories he had dug up that couldn't really be reported. Wanda told of some of her more ridiculous encounters with "the rug," MP Wallace Martin, and other federal officials and bureaucrats. Kirsten and Jane were made to revisit some of their high school adventures that not everyone had heard about. At the beginning Jeff was mostly quiet, but the others noted that as the wine bottles emptied, he became more forthcoming, including sharing a couple of high school dating disasters.

After the meal, they moved to a pleasantly furnished living room with ample comfortable seating and, despite it being summer, a small blaze in the fireplace. They brought their wine glasses with them, with reinforcements being at hand on a side table. They all settled into their chairs, except for Kirsten, who claimed one end of the sofa. Eyebrows gently went up when Jeff ignored other open seats and settled in beside her.

Martha began. "We're so glad you could all join us. It feels like more than half of Harmony's history has happened in the last month, particularly last week, but we've survived, and more.

"I've got to share some thoughts about all this that have occurred to me this week. I've been reading a sociology book as part of the online master's program I'm enrolled in. It's called *Crossings*, and talks about how centuries ago children grew up in a mostly straightforward and unchanging world, but today's kids grow up in one that's incredibly unpredictable and dynamic, and all too often threatening or damaging. The author details the "essential intersections" kids nowadays will likely experience in their lifetimes. Many of these are positive, and he acknowledges that, but his book focusses on the ones that are dangerous, and often deadly, where metaphorically there may be no traffic lights, or ones that malfunction or are ignored. Here's where kids face real dangers, where their lives can be destroyed. He insists it's the job of all adults to make kids aware of these deadly intersections, help them recognize and avoid these dangers so their lives can progress in positive ways."

Adam said, "Afraid it sounds to me like a whole lot of metaphor to explain some simple truths, but then I'm just an old, retired town cop."

Martha smiled and said, "You sure like that country philosopher role, Adam, but I must admit it's too much overly analytical sociology stuff even for me. Those people sure know how to create their own impenetrable language and have some pretty obscure and complicated ways to explain things. However, given recent events, the deadly intersections part resonated with me.

"Let me explain. Jane has just retold the great ketchup war story, where her and Wanda's lives crossed in a very positive way. But that was also the time their lives collided with a really bad guy, Gary McKay. Luckily his misdeeds led to his own destruction, not theirs, like he intended. However, imagine if he had survived. He was the same sort of bad actor as his younger brother, maybe even worse, but their father was grooming him to take over the family business. He surely would have been better at it than Alex was. Imagine Alex ending up not running things, but rather just working in sales, or whatever safe little place within McKay Enterprises. Being the loser he was, he likely still would have lived a messy life, but if he hadn't inherited all that money and influence, would he have caused anything like the same amount of damage?

"I mean, add up the total. Two disastrous marriages. One largely destroyed company, and with it a lot of local jobs. A life cooking up bad projects with business friends who weren't friends at all. Look at his effect on Harry Winston, certainly no shining light, but connected with McKay he becomes an actual criminal and dies a violent death. Will Handstrom was certainly a worthless grifter, but his connection to McKay makes him a *dead* worthless grifter. Think of the slow corruption of people like Councillor Weirness. Look at Morgan, who would have been happy just running a bulldozer for the rest of his life but ends up instead being an aggressive and barely in-control idiot building bad houses.

"And his crowning disaster, New Eden. Just how many lives were damaged by that utter fiasco? Without McKay and New Eden, would any of this recent stuff have even happened? When his twisted little life intersected with Priestner and William, what a recipe for disaster. The captain dead. Kirsten almost dead. The Wyandot reserve under threat and up in arms. Except for strong action from everyone here, especially the initiative of you and your people, Wanda, and except for, let's admit it, some amazingly good luck, McKay's malignant little life could even have caused this area, for hundreds of square miles around, being contaminated for the next ten thousand years. His life has been like a rogue tank crashing through lives, creating nothing but misery, pain, and even death."

Martha sat back and took a deep breath. "Sorry, maybe a little too much wine, but I'm appalled at the destruction a third-rate loser like Alex McKay inflicted on the world."

Kirsten said, "You'd certainly never call him a tragic figure, because he never was anything but a lowlife. But you're right, what a cautionary tale. Imagine his mother looking at her newborn son, with no idea that it'd be best by far if he hadn't ever been born."

Wanda said, "Traditionally for our people, when a life goes so far out of balance, when the community suffers so much harm, there are healing ceremonies to try to re-establish balance." She looked slyly around the room. "But then, you people aren't advanced enough for that."

Jane took a drink of wine and said, "Maybe tonight is sort of our informal healing ceremony. The captain's funeral was a bit like that too. McKay's gone. Gladstone will soon be gone, and there's actually some real good coming out of all this. Maybe we are all healing."

Martha paused and took another deep breath. "And maybe I get far too maudlin after too many days of stress and *clearly* too much wine. Sorry, everyone. We're here for a celebration, so let me start with a special announcement. My wonderful partner, Jane, has just been informed that she is now *permanently* Police Lieutenant Walden. And her clearly not-as-obtuse-as-I-thought bosses have decided that a detachment the size of Harmony's can be perfectly well run by a lieutenant, so she is now officially the top cop in town."

After a toast and congratulations, Jane said, "The really good news is if they had transferred in someone else, one of us would have had to go. So, detectives Petersen and Ripley, meet your new boss."

Jeff said, "But definitely not like the old boss. Great news Jane – I mean Lieutenant Walden."

Jane smiled. "Most times it will still be Jane. Kirsten, in terms of confirming what my detective complement is going to be, you were transferred here primarily for a special investigation. It's now over. You likely could manage to get transferred back south, away from all the reminders of your traumatic past here. What say you?"

Kirsten looked around the room. "I can sense my eighteen-year-old self sitting back there somewhere laughing at me, but coming back has been an eye-opener for me. Harmony is a different place. I'm for sure a different person. I *have* worked at becoming an urbanized person for the last twelve years, but there's still a small-town girl not far beneath the surface. I like being back here where it's quieter – or soon will be again. I like the country, the outdoors."

Jeff said, "Like leisurely boat trips down Silent Creek, drifting around in the bucolic splendours of Silent Lake ...."

Kirsten gave him a punch in the shoulder. "But next time in a proper canoe, and with no blue cases or dangerous criminals anywhere in sight."

Holding his shoulder, Jeff said, "My boat is perfectly proper, except for the scrapes and dings and scorch-marks *someone* recently inflicted on it."

Kirsten said, "If the peanut gallery is quite through ... I'm still sorting things out, but I see no reason not to finish my two-year appointment here."

Jeff startled everyone by smacking the table next to him and shouting, "Yes!"

Looking around, slightly abashed, he said, "Well, it's hard work breaking in someone new. I mean, who knows who we might get?"

Kirsten said, "Maybe a couple of conditions. Like my new boss putting me on no more undercover missions. I do need to find a proper apartment before we get the onrush of people coming here, and … maybe that's it."

Jane said, "Glad that's settled. Besides, it's likely Detective Ripley's turn for the next undercover operation."

Adam said, "Since we're now sharing big announcements, I've got one. Been a long line of good old boys running things in Harmony, but I think we've outgrown that. I've talked with Calvin Stewart, and he told me he feels overwhelmed and unqualified for everything that's going to happen around here soon. He plans not to run for re-election."

Sid said, "So his honour finally sees the light!"

Adam said, "Municipal elections are coming up before too long. Martha and I have been working pretty closely together on the relief committee. She tried to talk me into running, but this old dog is looking forward to resuming his quiet retirement. Besides, I've always been more comfortable hanging back in the wings a bit. However, one little task I think I'd like to take on is working on the election campaign of one Martha Nicholson. Might as well finish this female takeover of Harmony."

Wanda said, "Long overdue, I'd say. Going to say yes, Martha?"

Martha smiled. "I think anyone who has learned how to ride herd on a mob of ankle biters will find it easy to ride herd on a township council. Yes, I'm interested."

Jeff said, "Hey, and that would make this house the town's one-stop power centre."

Jane said, "Detective Petersen, kindly punch Detective Ripley in the shoulder, and a little bit harder this time."

Kirsten smiled, raised her fist, and turned toward Jeff, who put up his arms and pretended to cower in the corner of the sofa. He said, "Please, anything but the fury of the Friendlies enforcer!"

Kirsten said, "How about the battery of the bucolic banshee?"

Jeff said, "Word has it bucolic banshees have a special type of uniform. You're clearly overdressed for the part."

Martha said, "Lieutenant Walden, please get your overly giddy people under control. Though it does feel better to be laughing again. However, I think we have a few more things to discuss."

Jane said, "Jeff, if you're feeling sufficiently unthreatened, you compiled and wrote up our report on the Winston investigation. I presume there's nothing new there."

"I talked with our sterling MPP – sorry – but he either can't, or deliberately can't, remember any detail about that meeting Elliott Davis alerted us to. There's nothing in his office's records or appointment book, just like it never happened. I'll keep scouting around, but I'd say William is proving to be a genuine phantom.

"I tried to find some way to tie people like Weirness and Morgan into the picture, but there's no evidence, and no reason to think those guys could have pulled off a violent murder and total disappearing act. And, well, the captain was behaving pretty strangely the day of the murder, but there's surely no connection there. I mean, that just can't be.

"Now, McKay and my esteemed colleague here both had motive …"

He winced at another punch to his shoulder. "… but managed to alibi each other. Unless there was a random murderer loose on the county road that day, or Percy Lewis really is secretly a deranged environmental avenger, it has to be William. I just wish we had some direct proof."

Kirsten added, "For what it's worth, William's disavowal of any responsibility there still rings true to me. I mean, he thought I was soon going to be dead. Why lie to me?"

Kirsten drew a deep breath. "However, I can shed some light on the captain's erratic behaviour that day. We need to keep this among us, because he died a hero, and let's keep it that way, but I had my first self-defense class last evening and had a chance to talk more with the two women you saw me with at the funeral. Lynne is a dancer at Friendlies, and she really helped me there, so, long story short, responding to a request from her, I ended up with my new career as a self-defence instructor."

Jane said, "Before you go any further, how did your debut as a teacher go?"

"Pretty well. Only eight people there – I didn't see anyone in this room there – but okay. We just talked about what they were looking for and what we'd be doing. Frankly, some of them had to convince themselves it's okay for women to be doing this kind of physical stuff. Some had concerns about their physical limitations. We talked some about self-confidence and the need to exercise and look after your body. We did a couple of simple moves. I was mostly just trying to make them feel comfortable.

"The woman at the school who does all the community bookings dropped by. She assured me the numbers would grow. She brought along one of the school's phys ed teachers. She's really interested in adapting this to become a formal curriculum module for the girls, likely in grade eleven. She has a male colleague who would in the meantime take the boys. Their module would focus on what he calls positive male gender roles, like how to relate properly to the various women in their lives. You know, counterbalance some of the toxic masculinity stuff boys pick up. Ironically, that might even make the girls' self-defence class a little less necessary. So, to my new commanding officer, do you think I could occasionally get some time off for some community resource work?"

Jane said, "I'm just starting on sorting out how I'm going to approach my job, but I think that'd be quite wonderful. Anything else you would need?"

"One thing last night, we didn't have someone to be our sample assailant. Jeff, you interested in doing a little community resource work?"

"Like playing the sort of dangerous assailant they have to be on the lookout for? Nothing like stereotyping the black guy."

Kirsten smiled. "I'm sure they would soon come to learn what a sensitive new-age guy you are. Jane, think you could spare another of your detachment the odd time?"

"Let's talk about it, but the Friday evenings are strictly up to you two. I'm sure Jeff would find it a real burden to give up his Friday evenings."

Jeff said, "Hey, the whole thing sounds pretty good. I mean, Fridays are pretty quiet around here, and ..."

He looked around at all the quietly smiling faces. "... yeah, let's talk about it. But, Kirsten, you were talking about these two women."

"Right. So, Lynne brought her roommate, Deb, her partner, really, to the class. Deb works in a massage parlour in Lakeside. You know, one of those under-the-radar places where the patrons enter by the back door and leave the same way, only a little bit happier? When Lynne and I first talked she let slip that Deb breaks the rules at work by seeing some of her clients privately, away from the massage place. Lynne said a curious thing – that I in particular would be surprised about who Deb's clients were. We went for coffee after the class. Deb has convinced herself I'm a cop it's safe to talk to, so, after a little bit of prodding and persuasion ..."

She paused and took a breath. "Captain McKnight was one of those private clients. He started to come for massages, well before the passing of his wife. She said he often wanted to talk, would say that he felt restrained by his job, and was glad that she was one person he could talk to. Deb says that happens a lot, that many of her clients are just lonely ordinary guys who only want some intimate companionship, or at least the illusion of it. She said she ended up liking him, that he was really a gentle and hurting guy. When he said he'd like to see more of her, she eventually agreed.

"They'd meet in a motel room in Lakeside. She would have to rent the room, and he would join her there. Of course, she eventually found out who he was. She said that recently he seemed really upset, at odds with himself. He would talk about what a phony he was, how hypocritical his life had become. But then, the Monday before Winston's murder, when he lied about being at a headquarters meeting, he spent the whole day in Lakeside, this time in a better hotel. She spent as much time as she could with him, and for the first time spent the night with him. He wanted to take her to dinner and out for breakfast the next morning. He said he was tired of skulking around.

"She talked him into ordering in instead. She said that during that whole time he now seemed somehow more at peace with himself. He talked about how he was going to start living a proper life and be a better cop. He even alluded to that picture he took of me, and of how sorry and ashamed he was. He didn't specifically say it was of me. Deb said he was calm, but she was still worried about him.

"So that's where he was that Monday, and that's why he showed up at the crime scene Tuesday coming from the direction of Lakeside. I think this all helps explain his strange behaviour that day and the changes we saw afterward.

"One other thing – this is a bit harder to talk about. She said that physically he could be a pretty passionate man. It wasn't all just talking with her. They also had a lot of sex. She said it was like the release of something he had always kept under tight control. I mean, this is the man who prided himself on being a churchgoer, an upholder of family values, whatever that really means. A pillar of the community. A so-called model of propriety and rectitude. But Deb described a whole hidden side to him."

Jane said, "I likely knew him better than anyone else here. Let me speculate a bit. He did always seem like he was sort of acting the way he thought a cop should behave. His marriage always seemed, I don't know, stilted. He was somehow too much the churchgoing model of social propriety. He always seemed a bit like an actor trying to stay in role."

Adam said, "Let me chime in a bit here. I talked with him a lot during the transition to provincial policing in Harmony. We agreed that it was of the utmost importance to know your community and the people in it, but for him it seemed more like blending into the local power structure, trying to influence things from within. But a cop can't do that. You sometimes have to take on that power structure and hold them to account. For what it's worth, it may have shook him to the core when he finally realized just what Alex McKay was, and how slippery people like Weirness and some of the other local bigwigs were. He may have come to think he had been a fraud, an imposter, and not a real cop."

Jane said, "So he could have been trying to make up for that, to try to be the cop he always should have been. He supported Kirsten and me against Morgan, a man he previously might have protected."

Jeff said, "He finally seemed willing to trust me, to respect what I can do."

Wanda said, "When he and Jane came to meet me at the barricade, it was like I was meeting someone for the first time. Someone who respected us and wanted to be on our side. The old McKnight would have given those yahoos in the pick-up truck some kind of meaningless warning. But instead, he stopped them. He made it clear he would stop anyone else threatening us.

"Our traditions talk of the man who has abandoned his spirit, who loses it so it is somewhere outside him, floating around untethered. This man is a shell, not a real person. We had ceremonies for such a man to reunite with his spirit self, to become whole again. I think Captain McKnight was trying to become whole again, or maybe whole for the first time."

Jane said, "Both as a police officer, but also as a man. I think he wasn't comfortable with his own feelings and emotions. He shocked himself by taking that picture of you, Kirsten. I think he questioned why he put you into that situation at Friendlies. He was trying in his own flawed way to make amends. Look, I don't really understand this kind of stuff. You likely put it best, Wanda. It's sort of hard to say this, but maybe his death wasn't all tragic. In his moment of his death maybe he was finally the cop he always wanted to be.

"Thanks, Kirsten. It's better to know all this. I think I'm going to able to remember him in a better way now."

Adam said, "In terms of remembering him, Martha, can we share that thing we're working on?"

When Martha nodded, Adam continued, "It isn't official yet, but our relief committee has already started to work as an unofficial community resource committee. You know that it has long been in the works to build a new municipal building. With all the expansion that's going to happen around here, our committee started to talk about how soon this should be done, and we ended up making a quiet unofficial presentation to county council. They agree we should move ahead immediately. The basic plan has always been that it should house all the municipal departments and a proper police headquarters. We urged them to add a tourist centre and a new town library, to build for the future of the town. If things go as they should the new police wing, or maybe even the whole thing, will be named after Jasper."

There was a brief silence in the room and pleased smiles.

After the pause, Wanda said, "Since we're sharing positive updates, maybe it's my turn. These infrastructure improvements and new job possibilities have all of us feeling more positive than maybe we ever have. Our kids are really excited about the town kids coming out to learn with us, rather than always only the other way around. We've been meeting with some of the teachers at the high school who have wanted something like this for a long time. It's going to be a formal part of the curriculum in many of the courses, like all students will be studying some aboriginal literature. Plans are still incomplete, but it's going to start this fall.

"We have people on the planning committee for the new park and think we can help make it more than just a place for recreation.

Our people have lived apart for too long, sort of imprisoned on our reserve. It's going to be good for the community to be more involved with us, but also for us to be more involved with the community. I've been approached by the Assembly of First Nations. They like how all this is working out and may even come here to study it. This may be held up as an example of real co-operation and joint planning leading to real change. I may be asked to come speak to the organization.

"Adam also brought Arthur Padmore out to meet with us. We're going to look into him doing some of the maintenance and mechanical work for us, maybe a shared position with the province for the park infrastructure. I think he is going to help with the park planning. No one knows the area around here, especially around the lake, better than he does."

Adam said, "I was surprised how comfortable he seemed to feel out there. People really welcomed him."

Wanda said, "We treat people like him as being special, not just different. It was obvious he has a deep connection with the land. You know, you people always talk about owning the land. We feel more that the land owns us. Arthur feels that way too."

Adam said, "I'd like to propose a toast to Arthur Padmore."

With brief glances at Kirsten, they raised their glasses. "To Arthur." No-one felt the need to say anything more.

Kirsten said, "Sid, Mr. Ace Reporter, you've been strangely quiet. Thanks for respecting all the conditions we put on you, but is this all going to be your long sought-for ticket out of here? Are we going to see you on the CBC news, or in the *Toronto Star*?"

Sid said, "Yes and no about my ticket out of here. There's a new media company being formed. It's going to be like an information hub creating material for the traditional print and broadcast media, but also for podcasts, social media, and various online sources. They are going to have regional co-ordinators for information gathering, and they want me for Midwestern Ontario north through the Bruce Peninsula. So, I may be sort of everywhere. They aren't interested in traditional physical offices and such, but I'll need some sort of headquarters. They won't let it be here, but they are okay with Lakeside. I'm afraid I'm still going to be biting at your heels for a while yet.

"Thanks for the help on all the local stories. These people are really impressed by the range, you know, crime stuff, breaking news, but also human-interest stories and different perspectives. You may have created a bit of a monster here. I guess I'll be part of the wider world but will also stay rooted here. Who would have thought?

"As for updates, I can give you a bit more information. Gladstone has settled on a site north of Sudbury, and there's already the start of local backlash. A citizens committee is being formed. Their MPP is from the NDP, and she's already started to ask questions in the legislature. Some good media strategies are emerging. It's likely going to go through, though, because of the timing for the government. They have to put that damned stuff somewhere, but it's more likely now to be done by the book. The issue isn't going to go away, but I think we've done our part to make things better.

"My sources up there tell me the local Gladstone agent is not Malcolm Priestner. We may have to enter that pool Elliott Davis mentioned, about when Priestner gets whatever golden parachute he sure-as-hell doesn't deserve. I'll keep you informed."

Jane shuddered. "I'm not sure I really want to know. I'm mostly just glad to have them gone. Except, I suppose even in a place like Harmony we have to stay informed and involved. Was there ever a time when the world was a sane and simple place?"

Martha said, "I really doubt it, but maybe for a while things will be a little simpler around here. They can't help but be more sane.

"I think we're all caught up. Thanks, everyone. It was great having you all here. Something tells me we're all going to be sleeping better the next few days."

Taking the hint, everyone started to stir and get up, but Jeff interrupted them. "Look, am I the only one who's not happy about our one glaring loose end? Jane, you wanted this to be like some cozy parlour detective-story ending, answering all the key questions, but we still have an unsolved murder. If we really have ruled out all the suspects one way or the other, who in hell did kill Winston?"

Adam chuckled and said, "I can see you reopening this as a cold case every few years. Son, you have to just learn to let things go, or it'll drive you crazy."

Wanda said, "I can try to teach you about how to live with uncertainty and ambiguity, if that will help. We're experts at it."

Sid chimed in with, "You know, in a way, it makes it an even better story."

Jane said, "Sit back down, everyone. Let me tell you all a little story, to see if it will help someone feel a little more comfortable about all this uncertainty. So, there was this movie made in 1945 ...."

There were groans, and someone said, "Please, not another movie!"

Jane smiled and said, "Bear with me. It's a neat story. The great director, Howard Hawks, filmed a version of *The Big Sleep* in 1945. You philistines may not appreciate it, but the novel was written by one of the great detective fiction masters, Raymond Chandler. One of the screenwriters was Pulitzer Prize-winning novelist William Faulkner, who was slumming in Hollywood at the time. Chandler's detective was Philip Marlowe, the classic hard-boiled private eye. In Hawk's movie Marlowe was played by Humphrey Bogart, who was great in the role. Better than the first Marlowe, Dick Powell, or later ones, like Elliott Gould, though actually Robert Mitchum was maybe the absolute best ..."

More groans. "Okay, okay, I'll get on with it! So, Hawks finished the movie, or thought he had, because when he looked at the first cut, he realized to his utter dismay there was a big hole in it. Partway through the story the chauffeur of the wealthy family that hired Marlowe was murdered, very prominently. Hawk's movie doesn't solve the mystery. The other characters in the movie seemed to have forgotten all about it. You can't leave dangling such a big unsolved mystery in a classic film noir detective movie, so Hawks was desperate. Faulkner couldn't help him. No one could.

"In desperation he sent a telegram to the book's author, Raymond Chandler, again, maybe the best mystery writer ever. Surely Chandler could tell him who did it! But Chandler's legendary response? 'Damned if I know.'

"And so, Mr. stickler-for-the-truth Detective Ripley, if people like Hawks and Faulkner and Bogart and Chandler can live with an unsolved murder in a piece of fiction, especially great fiction, you're going to have to do the same living in messy old reality."

Seeing a frustrated look on Jeff's face, Jane continued, more gently. "Sorry, Jeff. I'm afraid unsatisfactory answers are just part of the job. Look, we dug up all we could about Winston's death, and credit to us all for doing so. We may lack the clinching physical evidence, but despite your colleague's doubts, it had to have been William."

Adam stood and said, "This time I really am going to leave. Way past my bedtime, though not sure I should drive after all that wine."

Wanda had been carefully watching how much she drank, since she had to drive back to Wyandot. She offered to drop Sid and Adam off on her way out. Kirsten announced that since she lived nearby and needed the fresh air, she too would leave her car and would walk home. She accepted Jeff's offer to escort her. No-one commented on the fact that Jeff actually lived in the opposite direction.

After everyone left, Martha and Jane surveyed their house and decided the clean-up could wait until the next day. When they were lying in bed, Jane turned to Martha and said, "You know, I tried my best to make Jeff feel satisfied about Winston, but really, I do wish we had some real answers there."

Martha said, "I expect you're going to sleep as soundly as I plan to. Maybe the solution will come in your dreams."

"As if, but I'll try to take my own advice. I guess we truly can't expect to get the final answer to everything."

If Jane's dreams were to take her back a few days earlier to the Silent Creek Bridge, she first would see Harry Winston's red car screeching to a halt and Harry throwing the blue case into the creek before speeding away. She would see a panting Percy Lewis stop at the bridge, shaking his fist at Winston's car and looking over the bridge parapet to see what Winston had thrown in.

A bit later she would see Lewis peddling his bike over the bridge toward town. Later still Winston would return, park his car by the side of the road, and scramble down to the edge of the creek. He would frantically look around in vain for the blue case, constantly scanning the road for cars and trying to figure out how to search further into the swamp.

Winston would see a bicycle approaching from town and would scramble under the bridge for cover. It was a cramped space, so he would have to crouch down. The bridge was crumbling, long overdue for replacement. Chunks of concrete had fallen away from the underside. One particular piece had broken off and hung suspended briefly by a piece of rusted reinforcing steel. It eventually fell off, leaving a seven-inch piece of steel hanging straight down. It was almost rusted through at the top, but the bottom had a sharp edge. It was shaped vaguely like a fat, oversized chisel, or a small hatchet. Winston was crouched directly beneath it.

When Percy Lewis crossed over the bridge, looking for the driver of the red car, he would raise his middle finger over his head and with the other hand would sound the truck's air horn he had arrogantly installed on his bike. The sound was startlingly loud. Harry Winston would be shocked into a reflexive attempt to leap upright. The strength of his athlete's still-strong legs would drive his head straight onto the piece of rusted steel, causing it to penetrate almost three inches into his brain. Racked with agonizing pain, Winston would try to free his trapped head. He would reflexively shake his head back and forth, doing great internal damage, but breaking the steel off from where it was rusted almost through at the top.

Winston would half crawl, half stagger from under the bridge. Blinded by the pain, he would fall to his knees, reach up and grab the four inches of steel sticking up from his head. He would wrench it out, causing the pain to briefly become unbearable. He would tumble over, his arms reaching out to break his fall. Halfway on the downward arc, his hand would let go of the steel so that it would fly out over the stream. After it hit the water it would sink to the bottom, nudged along by the current, and nestle into the debris and rocks littering the streambed.

Harry Winston's body would lay on the rocky shore, blood gushing out of his fatal wound. His body would twitch a few times, and then lay still, waiting to be discovered a short time later.